More praise for
KEEPERS OF THE DAWN

"The book is a rollicking read, and a reminder of how colorful, inspiring, and funny human speech was, back in the days when it was the main form of communication and entertainment. . . . The heroine Molly Brant would seem almost too strong, courageous, generous, and wise if I didn't know [my wife] Dark Rain and other Native American women."
—JAMES ALEXANDER THOM
Author of *The Children of First Man*

"Silver skillfully draws the reader into the mythology, history, family life, religion, politics, warfare, coming of age, childbirth, and whole culture of the tribe and its League. The author's grasp of these matters is truly phenomenal."
—ALLAN W. ECKERT
Author of *The Frontiersman*

"What a monumental work of art and history! It is well written, with lively prose that will captivate readers everywhere."
—CLIFFORD TRAFZER
Professor of Ethnic Studies
UCLA Riverside

"An extraordinary historical and biographical novel . . . It will excite the imagination of all those readers thirsting for accuracy in the details and dramatic events of colonial America during a time of rebellion and civil war."
—ROBERT S. ALLEN
Author of *His Majesty's Indian Allies*

By Alfred Silver
Published by Ballantine Books:

RED RIVER STORY
LORD OF THE PLAINS
WHERE THE GHOST HORSE RUNS
KEEPERS OF THE DAWN

KEEPERS OF THE DAWN

Alfred Silver

BALLANTINE BOOKS • NEW YORK

DEDICATION

This book is for all those delvers and detectives, both professional and amateur, who ruin their eyes and sinuses digging through dusty archives so that people like me can peruse the results of their work at leisure and give the impression we know what we're talking about.

IROQUOIA

LAKE

Grand River

Fort N

LAKE ERIE

ALLEGHEN

W

Legend

— · — · — · — Muskingum and Si-isha's journey
— · · — · · — Modern international boundary
· · · · · · · · Modern state boundary
✕ Battles

Muskingum River

Ohio River

Map by S.T.Palmer

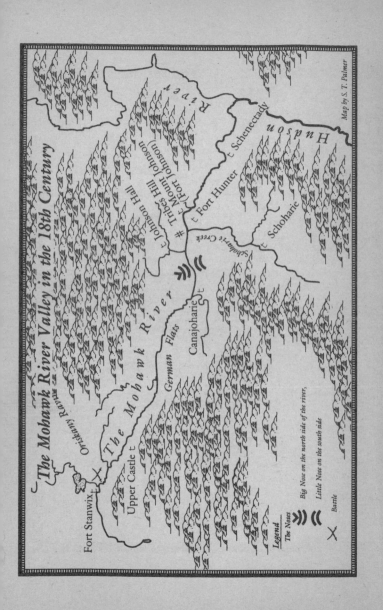

The Mohawk River Valley in the 18th Century

Map by S. T. Palmer

Legend

The Noses

Big Nose on the north side of the river,

Little Nose on the south side

Battle

A NOTE TO THE READER

The purpose of writing a historical novel, it seems to me, is not to invent events and characters, but to try to understand the real ones. I hope this shot comes close.

Since this is meant to be a story, not an exercise in frustration, I've used English names and translations. But there are a few Iroquois terms that can't be translated. In recent years a spelling system has been developed using the English alphabet in combination with punctuation marks for sounds that exist in Iroquois but not in English. But that's only of use to those familiar with the system. So I've used the spellings we ignorant English first came up with to come as close as possible.

Even that isn't entirely reliable—English spelling being what it is. "Hodenosaune" is actually pronounced "Ho-de-no-*shaw*-nee," or thereabouts. This author hereby declares that whichever the way an Iroquoian word wants to pronounce itself to you is the way it should be pronounced.

As Cayuga chief Jake Thomas put it: "English is such a crazy language. It messes you up."

PROLOGUE

"The Woman Who Fell From the Sky," the old man said, "had twin grandsons—the Creator and the Destroyer. . . ."

He moved a little closer to the fire as the wind hurled pellets of sleet against the elm-bark walls of the longhouse. It wasn't much of a longhouse, but the Mingo tribe—an ever-shifting stew of young Delawares, Wyandots, and adventurers from the Six Nations Confederacy—never built to last.

"The white men call them the Good Twin and the Evil Twin, but we know better. We call them the Right-Handed Twin and the Left-Handed Twin—the straight-minded and the crooked-minded."

He was surprised that they all bent in closer to hear him. He was hardly a storyteller or a Keeper of the Faith, just a wanderer who happened to be passing through the Ohio country. But those who chose to become Mingoes for a few years, to hunt the rich country between the Six Nations and the western tribes, didn't get much in the way of stories and ceremonies. And at least he wasn't one of those self-styled Storytellers who always trilled the same phrases in the same order, like a flute player with big lungs and no music.

"The Left-Handed Twin was jealous of his brother's handiwork. When the Creator made a fine, clear-running river, the Destroyer piled rocks in it to make a cataract to break canoes. When the straight-minded twin made fire to warm the longhouse, the crooked-minded made the contrary wind that carries embers onto the roof. When the Creator made the deer, the Destroyer made the wolf. When the Right-Handed Twin made the

1

rabbit, his brother made the weasel. But there will always be more deer and rabbits than wolves and weasels."

There were two pairs of children's eyes that distracted him, they were focused on him so intently. The girl was perhaps ten summers old, sitting with her arms twined around a boy about half her age. Her eyes were slanted and as black as the pond at the bottom of a cave; her brother's round and soft and brown. It didn't seem likely that the eyes of two children could confuse a grown man telling a story he'd heard a thousand times before, but he found he had to keep his eyes from catching theirs or he'd slip off the trail.

"Finally the twins grew too big for the earth to hold both of them. They fought to see which one would destroy the other. For three days they wrestled. The heels of their moccasins, pushing against the earth to get the advantage, pushed up mountains and dug valleys. They pushed against each other so long that they began to push into each other, and to see into each other's minds. They saw so deep that each could see the secret at the back of the other's mind—the secret of the one thing that could destroy him.

"But the secret at the back of the Creator's straight mind was a lie, while the secret hidden behind his twin's crooked mind was the truth. And so the Destroyer was destroyed."

There were murmurs of satisfaction at the end of the story. A hunter proffered his tobacco pouch for the storyteller to refill his pipe. The brown-eyed boy in his black-eyed sister's arms said: "Tell us another story. . . ?"

PART ONE

SI-ISHA AND MUSKINGUM

It would be a strange thing if Six Nations of ignorant savages should be capable of forming a scheme for such a union and able to execute it in such a manner that it has subsisted for ages and appears indissoluble; and yet that a like union should be impracticable for ten or a dozen English colonies . . .

—BENJAMIN FRANKLIN TO THE ALBANY CONGRESS

CHAPTER 1

On a summer evening some three hundred years after the planting of the Tree of Peace, or 1747 years after the birth of the savior the white men nailed to a tree, the little Mingo village on the bank of the Ohio River was settling down to sleep.

At the first hearth inside the doorway of one of the long-houses within the stick-work stockade lived a family from the Canienga Nation of the Hodenosaune. For some reason no one had ever been able to explain, the white men called the Hodenosaune "Iroquois." They called themselves the People of the Longhouse that Grows, because the original Five Nations of the League of Peace were always willing to make their longhouse longer to take in any other nation wishing to dwell under the Tree of Peace—as the Tuscaroras had, to make it the Six Nations Confederacy.

The family at the first hearth consisted only of a woman sewing by the fire, and her black-eyed daughter and brown-eyed son on their sleeping platform on the other side of the hearth. Their father had gone hunting when the moon was full, and tonight's half-moon still found him somewhere in the forest. His gun still rested on the shelf above the sleeping platform his wife would have to warm alone again tonight. Guns were for war, not hunting.

The woman was kneeling close to the fire her family shared with the second family past the doorway, sewing the first pair of moccasins her son would wear without holes in the soles. Not that she had become so Mingo as to allow her family to go about in clothes with holes or patches, but very young children's moccasins had to have holes. They were so recently come from the land of souls that they could still hear the other souls calling. But if the other souls saw that a child's moccasins were in no condition to travel along the long road where the strawberries were always growing, they wouldn't call.

Five springs had passed now since she'd first dipped her red and squawling son into the ice-swirled Muskingum River. Most mothers would have had him in holeless moccasins before now, but she'd seen that, longer than most children, he'd held on to the eerie habit of listening to things no one else could hear.

His sister had been another matter entirely. By the time she'd been old enough for her first pair of moccasins, it was quite clear she had no intentions of leaving this world unless dragged kicking and biting.

It gnawed at the Canienga woman that her children had never known any other life but that of Mingoes. Out of all the people in the Mingo tribe, the Caniegas had the farthest to travel to get back to their own nation. First they would have to cross the eastern range of the wild Ohio country until they came to the western gate of the Hodenosaune and the country of the Senecas—the Keepers of the Sunset—and then travel through the lands of the Cayugas, the Onondagas, and the Oneidas before finally coming home to their own country and the eastern gate in the beautiful valley of the Caniega, the Keepers of the Dawn.

After ten years as a Mingo, she didn't know what might have changed back home. But she suspected there were a great many more white people living there now, because the Caniengas were losing their name. It seemed more than unfair, since the Caniengas were the Oldest Brother of the League of Peace, the first to listen to the words of Hiawatha and the Peacemaker. But the white men had first met the Caniengas through the tribes east of the Dawn Gate, who called them Mohawks—"They Eat Their Enemies." Most Caniengas couldn't even pronounce "Mohawk," since their own language had no lip sounds such as M. But the influence of the whites had grown so strong that even other Hodenosaune were calling their oldest brothers "They Eat Their Enemies," instead of the "People Who Live Where the Flint Comes From."

As the Canienga woman sewed, drawing deer sinew thread through moosehide with a steel needle, she listened to the evening murmur of the longhouse: the roof breeze kindly drawing the smoke straight up the smoke hole instead of into her eyes, the soft voices of several hunters conferring in Mingo patois around a hearth a little farther down the aisle, a mother crooning a Delaware sleep song to her baby, the muted clatter of a Seneca hunter trying to pack together his possessions as stoically as possible. . . .

The Seneca hunter had come home from the forest to find another man sharing his wife's sleeping platform. It wasn't the first time a Hodenosaune man had come home from hunting or the war road to find his wife had a new man, and it wouldn't be the last. Hodenosaune children were their mother's, and it was her business who their father was. If she decided she wanted a new man, all the old one could do was find himself another place to sleep.

The Canienga woman smirked to herself that perhaps someday she might do the same to her own man, then sighed for all the reasons that made that highly unlikely and went on with her sewing and listening. Out of the general murmur of dreamworld-bound voices, she heard the voices of her own children from their willow-lattice bed. The boy said, "I liked the—" then interrupted himself with a yawn.

His sister muttered: "Go to sleep."

"Yes, but," the boy plugged on, "didn't you like the story the old man told?"

"You can't tell stories in the summer. The beings who live on the other side of the turtle will sneak up outside the longhouse to listen to them, instead of helping the corn grow, and so will the deer and beaver, instead of making more of themselves to hunt."

"I'm not telling stories—just talking about the one the wanderer told in the winter."

"He told a lot of stories. Go to sleep."

"I mean the one about Hiawatha and the Peacemaker and the Tree of Peace."

"Hm."

"I liked the most the part about Hiawatha and the monster."

" 'Monster'? . . . What monster?"

"The monster Atotarho."

"Atotarho was no monster, he was just a man. Now go to sleep."

"He was so a monster! He had snakes for hair! The story said Hiawatha combed the snakes out of Atotarho's head."

"That didn't mean he was a monster. It meant Atotarho was all twisted up and mean, like he had snakes in his head, and Hiawatha soothed them away. Now go to sleep."

Their mother just about dropped the moccasin into the fire. Ten-year-old girls weren't supposed to think like that. Maybe someone was trying to give a message that it was past time the family headed back to where her daughter could be introduced to the Clan Mothers of the League of Peace.

Her son grumbled sleepily: "I liked it better when Atotarho was a monster. . . ."

CHAPTER 2

Si-isha didn't think of herself as Si-isha. She would've been hard-pressed to say exactly what she did think of herself as—unless it were "me," or perhaps "the hub of the wheel of the world"—but it definitely wasn't Si-isha.

She was willing to admit there might be other child names as bad or worse than Si-isha: "Are You Laughing?" But it was still only a child's name, which had no real meaning to it. Except an embarrassing reminder that her father could still see her as the baby who'd screwed up her face in a manner he found amusing.

Her little brother's name, Muskingum—pronounced more like "Uskingun" by their Canienga tongues—at least meant the nearest flowing water to the place he'd been born, where their mother had staggered off to dip him as soon as the cord was cut. Si-isha could remember sneaking along behind them and being amazed at how white he was when he was pulled back out again, and that anything so small could make so much noise. Whenever Muskingum grumped at her that it wasn't fair a person had to wait to be grown-up to get a real name, she snapped back that he should be happy he had a name that had something to do with who he was, instead of one that might just as well be a whistle to get a dog to come.

The morning after Muskingum had kept her awake with his nonsense about "the monster Atotarho," Si-isha was out helping her mother and the other women hoeing the arc of cleared fields between the stockade and the forest. The hoers had all left their moccasins and overdresses and leggings back in their longhouses, and the profusion of bouncing and wobbling breasts at Si-isha's eye level—pointy young ones tilted up toward the sun, wrung-out old ones slapping against skirt waistbands—made her wonder what hers were going to be like, if and when they ever sprouted. Her mother's were round and barely sagged at all, despite the fact she wasn't young. Maybe it was because she'd only suckled two children. That seemed like the smart way to go.

Her mother began to sing a song of the second hoeing, the hilling-up when the corn is knee-high. The women and girls fanned out along the rows on either side of her joined in. Si-isha hummed the melody, singing the occasional phrase that came to mind. Mostly she concentrated on trying to imitate her mother's swift, certain hoe strokes, raising the corn hills and chopping the weeds out at the same time. She had yet to find the secret of how her mother knew that this sprig of skunkroot or that choke-weed could be hacked out without chopping through the roots of the corn plants or of the bean and squash vines twined around their stalks.

When the song was done, her mother said: "You should listen more carefully, Si-isha, so you can know the song without a leader's voice to follow."

"I know it as well as the other girls."

"You're not like the other girls."

"How not?"

Her mother stopped and turned to her, taking one hand off her hoe haft to reach out and cup her chin. "Like it or not, little one, so art thou made. You can be as wild as you like in your time—and I suspect you will be—but someday you are going to have to lead the songs."

Before Si-isha could ask why, a male voice called her mother's name from the edge of the fields. Si-isha dropped her hoe and went running through the corn rows, dodging around the other hoers and leaping over squash vines.

At the border of the tobacco patch stood a tall, thin, thick-lipped man with a deer carcass slung across his shoulders. He wasn't wearing a hunting shirt, so anyone could see that the triple line of tattoo dots running down from his right eye continued down across his neck, chest, and stomach. Si-isha knew the lines ran all the way down his right leg to his toes. His head had been plucked bald except for a scalp lock pluming up from the crown, daring any enemy to try and take it. Although his body had the stretched-too-far look that ignorant people might compare to a boy whose bones have grown faster than his muscles, Si-isha knew that those ropy arms and shoulders might well have been carrying that deer for two days.

But for all his warrior attributes, Si-isha could see he felt bashful standing at the edge of the tobacco patch. The planted fields were the domain of the Three Sisters—corn, beans, and squash—and a man felt as out of place there as a woman in the forest.

Si-isha flung her body full-bore against one fringe-buckskinned leg and wrapped her arms around his waist above the thong holding up his breechclout and leggings. He grunted at the impact, settled one hand on the top of her head and said: "I don't think I can carry thee and sister deer as well." She giggled, having no doubt he could carry her and the deer and Muskingum if he had to. For all his gravity of manner, her father always made her feel a spring of laughter bubbling up behind the long bone where her ribs joined in front.

Si-isha's mother's voice came from above and behind her: "So you had some luck, then."

Si-isha's father grunted offhandedly, then added: "And there's a buck hanging in a tree a half day's run south. I'll have to go back for him."

Mother said throatily, "He can wait until tomorrow," and pressed herself against Father. They nuzzled each other, with Mother's breasts belling out against Father's chest and buoying down on the top of Si-isha's head. Mother's smell of sun-licked skin and earth, and Father's smell of woods and sweat and deer blood, filled Si-isha's nostrils.

Father stepped back abruptly and said: "I'd best go get her skinned and cut up so you can go to work on her."

Si-isha followed her mother back to the cornfield, where the other women stood leaning on their hoes at the end of the rows they'd made into lines of earthen breasts with corn plants for nipples, trading jokes about unhoed furrows and women who chose to sleep alone when their men were gone hunting. Mother paced off a number of unhilled rows equal to the ones they'd done, took up her position at the center of the line of hoers and sang them back to work.

By the time they'd hoed their way to the end of the new rows, the sun had moved its width across the sky. Mother announced that that was enough for today, prompting another freshet of titters and sly jokes. Si-isha didn't understand them all, but she laughed anyway. Her mother affected not to hear them, which seemed to be part of the joke.

As the women carried their hoes back inside the stockade, Father was just finishing cutting up the last haunch of sister deer and hanging her up on the rack between the two longhouses that made up the village. Muskingum was standing guard with his toy bow and blunt arrows, in case one of the dogs licking the blood off the ground should jump too high.

Si-isha was dispatched to the edge of the forest to fetch juniper and white cedar. When she got back, with a sheaf of fragrant boughs bulging the willow net slung over her shoulder, Muskingum with his wooden knife was helping Father scrape the hide, and the women of their longhouse were well on their way to turning sister deer into venison. Some of them were boiling the haunch cuts and skimming the fat off. Some were making a paste of cornmeal and crushed chestnuts to coat the loins for roasting.

The first lesson in cookery Si-isha could remember was that the animals of the forest were separated into three kinds: those who had to be boiled twice before roasting, those who only had to be single-boiled, and those who were tender enough to go straight onto the fire. Large animals like deer were confusing, because they were part one kind and part another.

Si-isha's mother was out behind the longhouse, stirring a bed of coals in the village fire pit. Si-isha helped her wrap the doe's quartered rib cage in cedar and juniper, seal the wrappings with a skin of wet clay, then lower the ribs onto the coals and fill the pit with loose earth.

By the time the pit was filled in, Si-isha's mouth was watering over, but there was still a long while to wait. She passed the time by playing with Muskingum and their corn-husk dolls. His was a warrior he called Snowshoes; hers was a woman she just called She or Her. "She" kept trying to kiss "Snowshoes," and he kept running away. When that ceased to be entertaining, Si-isha rummaged out the pin-and-bone game that Father had made for them, but Muskingum was still too young to be much competition. It was all he could do to get one of the strung-together bone segments to jump back onto the pin, much less all of them.

At dusk all of the people from both longhouses gathered into the one that was dripping with the smells of hot venison, cornmeal-squash bread and bean soup, spruce-maple beer and sassafras tea. The hunter who served as Keeper of the Faith for the Hodenosaune in the village crumpled a bit of tobacco into the first hearth past the doorway and said: "May the scent of the tobacco I have given to the fire reach thee and let thee know we are still here. That's all." And then it was finally time Si-isha could discover whether her stomach was big enough to hold several mouthfuls of every different taste.

It wasn't quite, but almost. When there was nothing left of sister deer except her bones, and everyone was leaning back and sighing, politely belching their appreciation for the hunter and the cooks, the Keeper of the Faith began to tap softly on a drum and sing.

It was a song of how the Peacemaker and Hiawatha and the original five nations planted the Tree of Peace. Even some of the Delawares joined in singing. Si-isha had heard the song and others like it many times, but as she listened to it this time, a strange thing happened. As far back as she could remember, she'd known that a tall and mighty tree had been planted in the olden times, with long roots running out in the four directions so that all the nations of the earth could follow the roots to where the Hodenosaune would sit them down in the middle of their longhouse and make them welcome. And she'd known that an eagle had been placed at the top of the tree to scream a warning if any evil was approaching along the roots, so that all the nations of the longhouse would come running to the eagle's cry to stop all evil from entering under the shade of the Great Tree of Peace. But as she heard it sung again, tears began to roll out of her eyes and wouldn't stop.

When the song was done, her mother leaned across to finger-comb her hair out of her eyes and say: "What makes thee to weep, my Si-isha?"

"I don't know ... I can't tell you. ..."

"Since when has there been anything you could not tell me, daughter?"

"Not *now*, not with everyone looking at me. ..."

The woman who shared their hearth got a sudden inspiration to begin another song. As the people around the hearths and perched on the sleeping platforms joined in with their voices and drums and rattles, Mother shifted closer to Si-isha and said: "No one is looking at you now, except me. What made thee sad?"

"Not *sad* ... It seemed ... I thought all the stories—of Hiawatha and the Peacemaker and Atotarho and the Tree and all—I thought they were a bag of pretty-colored beads to take out and look at one by one for a winter night. But they're not, are they? They're strung together to make a picture, like a wampum belt."

"And what is the picture of?"

"Of ... of what the song means with 'the glad tidings of peace and power.' In the olden days, maybe the Onondagas or the Senecas would come to try to kill Father and make slaves of us. But now all the nations under the Tree of Peace live together, and they're too strong together for anyone to hurt them. And the Delawares could be safe, too, if they made it Seven Nations, or the Ojibway, or ..." Her eyes started running again and her nose filled up. It was terrible, like being a baby again that couldn't control its fluids or explain itself.

Mother didn't seem to mind. She cupped Si-isha's chin in one hand, reached out the other to dry her cheeks and smiled.

When the longhouse settled down to sleep, Si-isha was quite sure she'd stuffed more than enough in her belly to hibernate till next spring. But instead she lay there feeling the seams of the longhouse wall against her back and Muskingum's back against her front, watching the embers die in the hearth pit and listening to the sounds the wind made. The creaking of the longhouse's hooped-pole rib cage was joined by the creaking

of the lattice sleeping platform across the hearth from hers and
Muskingum's. The new creaking was accompanied by a low,
husky whimpering that sounded barely like her mother's voice.

Muskingum snuffled in his sleep and squirreled his bottom
farther back into her stuffed stomach. She felt a strange sensation between her legs, not exactly a twitch or an itch or a
tickle. It made her curious, so she slipped her hand down the
drum-taut swelling of Muskingum's belly and fumbled with
her fingers. He mumbled: "What are you doing?"

"Nothing. It's just a game." She found nothing resembling
the pointy hardness she'd felt under her father's loincloth in
the morning.

CHAPTER 3

Muskingum awoke to the smell of cornmeal soup. Si-isha
had somehow managed to climb out of bed without waking him, and was sitting by the fire, not eating. Father was up
and dressed and spooning up soup to fuel him back into the
woods and fetch the buck he'd left hanging in a tree.

It was a warm enough morning, and Muskingum felt no
need to get dressed until he went outside. So he just rolled off
the sleeping platform, picked up his bowl and spoon and presented them to Mother. She ladled out one measure into his
bowl and stuck her big stirring spoon back into the pot. He
said: "That's all?"

"Eat that first and then see if you have any room left after
last night." Then she stood up from the pot and began lifting
off the baskets and other things stacked on the unused sleeping
platform that butted up against the one Muskingum shared
with Si-isha. She went about shifting the things off the bed
onto the crowded storage shelf above, or onto one of the over-

head poles for hanging things. When Muskingum asked her what she was doing, she said: "It's time you had a bed of your own."

"But I'm still small enough to fit in easy with Si-isha—aren't I, Si-isha?"

Si-isha didn't say anything. Mother said: "You can't expect to sleep with your sister forever."

He whined: "But it'll be *cold* in the winter."

Father set his licked-clean bowl and spoon aside and said, "If you're going to grow up to be any kind of a hunter and warrior, you have to learn not to cry against the cold," then unfolded his legs in that remarkable, smooth motion that transformed him in a wink from a cross-legged figure with eyes the same level as Muskingum's to a tower that Muskingum had to crane his neck to see. "I will be back before sunset. Unless another buck allows me to see him."

Si-isha was sent off to the edge of the woods to fetch some sumac bark for tanning the deer hides. Muskingum spent the morning watching some of the older boys playing a practice game of baggataway. One of them even gave him a try at hefting up a playing stick and throwing the ball out of the webbed cup at the head. Muskingum just barely managed to lift the stick off his shoulder, and the ball dribbled out and rolled a foot or two. They laughed at him, but not too cruelly.

He was on his way to the cornfield to tell his mother he'd thrown a baggataway ball, when one of the sentries came running from the forest. Muskingum stopped to watch a number of other men gather around the sentry at the gate of the stockade. After a moment the sentry turned and ran toward the cornfield. Muskingum tagged along behind him. The sentry stopped at the edge of the planted rows and called Muskingum's mother. When she came out from among the Three Sisters and their attendants, the lookout said: "There are three canoes coming down the river, carrying two French traders and maybe ten men who wear dresses. You can speak the Frenchmen's words. . . ."

She replied: "I can—a little. But there is no need for them to know that at the start. I will come along and stand and listen to what they say among themselves."

Muskingum followed his mother and the sentry, eager to get a look at men wearing dresses. All the men of the village, with the women and children falling in behind, were heading down toward the river, which seemed strange—the last batch of white traders had been met at the stockade gate and ushered inside. When they got to the riverbank, Muskingum's mother joined the front rank of the men, some of whom were carrying their guns. Muskingum held onto his mother's skirt. Si-isha appeared beside him with a basket over her arm and whispered: "What's going on?"

He whispered back: "Some Frenchmen are coming with a lot of men wearing dresses."

After a moment's waiting, a big birchbark canoe rounded the bend in the river, then another and another. Muskingum stood on tiptoe to try to see the men in dresses, but there were only two white men in blue coats—one the color of a robin's egg and the other one dark—and a number of Hodenosaune men who weren't dressed any different than the men of the village.

The Hodenosaune paddlers beached the canoes at the landing place, the men in blue coats stepped onto the shore, and the paddlers proceeded to lift out shiny objects and stack them where they would catch the sun: a new gun with a polished barrel, rainbow strings of glass beads, glinting copper kettles, brass-hafted knives. . . .

On a closer look at the paddlers, Muskingum saw that they weren't quite interchangeable with the men of the village after all. Some of them wore cloth shirts or leggings instead of deerskin, and some had wooden crosses hung around their necks. But that was hardly the same as wearing dresses.

One of the men in blue coats had a comfortable-looking brown face, the other a rather painful-looking red one. The red-faced one nodded at one of the paddlers, who stepped forward from the pile of trade goods, smiled a smile that made Muskingum want to wipe his hands, and said in a Canienga dialect Muskingum could just manage to follow: "Where is my old friend Tehowaghwengaraghkwin, A Man Tying on His Snowshoes?"

Muskingum's mother replied in Canienga: "My husband Tying Snowshoes is gone to the woods to bring back a buck he killed."

Muskingum's father's "old friend" turned to the two Frenchmen and said something to them in their own tongue. They didn't seem to be paying much attention to him; mostly they were staring at Muskingum's mother, in her hoeing skirt. The red-faced one said something out of the corner of his mouth that made the other smirk.

The man with the oily smile turned back to face the people of the village and announced: "We have come all the way from the fort at Thundergate to bring the things our Mingo brothers need to live out here so far from their home countries. We have many more guns like the one you see here, and powder and shot and sewing needles and blankets and kegs of the Water That Makes You Sing."

A Delaware Mingo, who was usually the one to speak for the village to strangers when Muskingum's father wasn't there to do it, said: "We have all the powder and shot we need. An English trader came by in the spring."

"You should not be trading with the English. They break the white man's law by coming here. This country belongs to the King of France."

It was the wrong thing to say. The Keeper of the Faith raised his majestic voice with, "This country belongs to the Hodenosaune!" which wasn't much better, judging by the looks he got from some of his fellow Mingoes. He added: "And to our brothers of the Delaware and other nations. We trade with whomever we please. Everyone here is free to trade with *you* if they wish—but I doubt anyone will wish to, if the French still demand twice as much for their goods as the English."

The two men in blue coats looked very angry when that was translated to them. The red-faced one spat out a stream of harsh-sounding words that didn't sound nearly so harsh through the mouth of their translator: "Your French brother says the reason the English ask so little for their goods is because they're no good. The English guns may look shiny, but one of these days the barrel will explode and take your fingers with it. The English put sand in their gunpowder and—"

"That is not what the Frenchman said," Muskingum's mother cut him off. Muskingum was astounded that his mother could be so rude to anyone. The only thing more impolite than starting to speak before someone else finished was to directly contradict people to their faces, and she'd just done both. "What our French brother said was: 'Tell these cannibals that if they don't obey our king's law, the king will send an army to teach them—and those few our army doesn't kill will find themselves chained to the oars of the king's rowing ships or sold in slavery to the Sugar Islands.' " She turned to the two men in blue coats and added something in the French tongue. The one with the red face turned even redder.

There was a pause while the Frenchmen and their translator tried to figure out what to say next. Muskingum took advantage of the lull to tug on his mother's skirt and call up to her: "I want to see the men wearing dresses!"

The people of the village burst into laughter, growing louder as what he'd said was relayed to the back of the crowd. Muskingum couldn't see what was funny about it. In fact, the Frenchmen's translator and his fellow canoe paddlers looked like it was just the opposite of funny. Muskingum tried to crawl inside his mother's skirt.

Some of the villagers drifted forward to have a look at the French traders' goods. Muskingum's mother herded him and Si-isha back toward the longhouse to give them something to eat. Muskingum protested: "But I still want to see the men that wear dresses! And why did everyone laugh when I said that?"

His mother replied: "A long time ago, back in my grandmother's grandmother's time, the French persuaded some Hodenosaune people to go live near them at Montreal, and take up the French religion. We call them the Men Who Wear Dresses. Some say we call them that because the French Keepers of the Faith wear long black robes like dresses; some say it's because a Christian warrior might as well be a woman. Either way, the Men Who Wear Dresses don't much like it."

It was another disappointment. First Atotarho turned out not to have snakes for hair, and now the men who wore dresses didn't really wear dresses. It would've been a much more interesting world if words meant what they said instead of just being a fancy way of saying something else.

A couple of the hunters who'd taken furs down to the riverbank came back with bark buckets of rum. Mother put on a stone face and went on about her business. The noise of laughter and the clatter and shouting of the two sticks hand game at the back of the longhouse grew coarser and louder.

Father came back long before sunset, without the buck he'd gone to fetch. He murmured something to Mother, who called,

"Si-isha, reach down your back basket and mine," then turned to the woman who shared their hearth. "I have in mind to go get something from the edge of the forest. Will you help us?"

The woman grunted up off her sleeping platform and reached down her own deep-bottomed basket with its carrying straps for shoulders and forehead. Muskingum asked his mother: "Where are you going?"

"As I said—to the edge of the woods."

"I'll come, too."

"No."

"Why not?"

Father squatted by the fire, patted the ground beside his knee and said: "I will tell you."

Muskingum went and sat beside his father, looking back over his shoulder at the three females stooping out the long-house door with their baskets bobbing on their backs.

Father said in a low voice: "They are going to bring in the buck I left butchered at the edge of the forest."

"Were you too tired to carry him?"

"Not so much. Although I did not mind putting him down. But if a hunter brings in meat from the forest, it belongs to the whole village—as it was with sister deer yesterday. What meat a woman brings in belongs to her. It is a fine thing to have a feast like we did yesterday. It is also a fine thing to have food stored up for the winter, so when you come in from a day of snowshoe-racing your mother can give you a stick of jerked venison to chew on."

"But other hunters bring in meat and keep it for themselves."

"That is their business. They are not Hodenosaune and do not have our customs. Or they have become all Mingo—who have no customs. It is a fine thing for a boy to be Mingo for a time—even a boy as old as me. But there will come a time when we go home to the valley of the Keepers of the Dawn, and there we will have to live like Caniengas. Do you understand?"

"A little, maybe."

"In this life, that's about as much as can be hoped for." Father turned his head toward the noise at the far end of the longhouse, rubbed his fingertips back and forth across his mouth and said: "I think I will go and play two sticks for a while."

Muskingum started to follow his father along the aisleway of hearths, but there was something in the sound of the voices around the last hearth that made him a bit afraid. So instead he went outside and killed several hundred Frenchmen with his wooden knife for the way they looked at his mother.

His mother and Si-isha and the woman who shared their hearth came back with their basket packs sagging. Muskingum trailed along behind them to the smokehouse, set as far away from the longhouses as possible while still being within the stockade. Blood was dripping down between the ashwood splints at the bottom of Si-isha's basket onto where her over-dress stuck out in back.

He sat and watched his mother get a fire going. Si-isha was sent back to the woods to gather more hickory while Mother and the woman who shared their hearth went to work cutting the meat into strips to hang in the smokehouse overnight. They gave him a bit of raw liver to eat, which only served to remind him that he hadn't eaten a real meal since the middle of the day.

Fortunately, Mother kept a bit of meat aside to boil up with leeks and onions from the forest, and cornmeal dumplings stuffed with cranberries. He and Si-isha and their mother could only manage to eat their way halfway down the pot. Si-isha said: "Shall I go tell Father there's food?"

Mother glanced slit-eyed toward the raucous bonfire at the far end of the aisle and said: "He will come when he is ready."

Si-isha picked up Father's bowl and spoon and moved toward the pot, saying: "But I could bring him a bowl of—" A burst of angry shouting from the far end of the longhouse cut her off and jerked her eyes toward the bonfire. She put Father's bowl and spoon down and sat back down, hugging her knees.

Father still hadn't come back to get something to eat when it came time for Muskingum and Si-isha to crawl into their lonely beds. They laid down head to head, so he could hear her breathing, but it wasn't the same thing.

What with the noise from the hand game and no warm body to curl up against, Muskingum didn't sleep, or didn't think he did. When the hearth fire had burned down to coals, he heard a strange scraping and mumbling sound. He sat up and squinted his eyes to make the most of the weak light from the embers, made even dimmer by comparison to the crackling fire at the other end of the longhouse. By the foot of his bed was a hunched, amber-dusted shadow making hacking motions at the earth. It was his father, digging up the bark-lined pit where the family kept their valuables buried in case the longhouse should catch fire: strings of wampum, their fancy festival clothes, the gold coins that came back from the pelts and deer-skins his father sent across the mountains with the English traders every spring. . . .

Muskingum's father glanced up at him and grunted: "Go back to sleep." It didn't sound like Father's voice at all. Muskingum lay back down and pulled the blanket over his head, clutching his fists around the rope of hemstitched, coarse-woven wool. Something soft brushed against the knuckles of his right hand. It was Si-isha's hand, reaching across the frame poles where her sleeping platform ended and his began. Her fingers wrapped themselves around his fist. He went to sleep.

CHAPTER 4

Once Si-isha had rubbed the sleep out of her eyes, she noticed a number of gray faces and wispy voices in the longhouse this morning. None were grayer or wispier than her father's. When she ladled out a bowl of venison broth for him, he said he didn't feel much like eating. When Mother took it from her hand and thrust it at him, he tried to push it away, mumbling: "I didn't get much sleep last night."

"Neither did any of us," Mother replied, forcing his bowl into his hands, "thanks to you and your rum-swilling friends.

You have to get some food into your belly so you can think a little, because we have to talk now."

"Now?"

"Yes, now. It's past time we started thinking of going home. Ten years out here is too long. My children are growing up thinking that a few women shuffling around in a circle waving cornstalks is a Green Corn Dance, and that a dozen hunters smoking tobacco is a council. Si-isha has an *onikonhra* that should be used for something more than hoeing a Mingo cornfield."

Si-isha felt her face growing warm, and hunched tighter around her bowl and spoon. *Onikonhra* meant mind, heart, spirit, disposition—the Canienga didn't separate them.

Father said: "We decided long ago not to go back until we had enough gold to buy a cow and horses and other things that would let us live well."

"I should think we have enough now, after ten years." Father muttered something into his soup. "What did you say? I couldn't hear you."

"I said: 'We *did*.' I won a lot of times last night, but more times I lost."

"How much?"

"Not so much that I cannot make it up in one good winter's trapping. Next summer, when the snow's gone from the mountains again, we can carry my furs ourselves to Gets Business Done." Si-isha had heard that name bandied about as far back as she could remember. When she'd been about Muskingum's age, she'd formed an impression of a huge being that dwelt on the other side of the mountains and ate furs and shat out gold.

Mother said: "Next *summer*? A whole *year* because of one night's drinking and gambling? The other players can't hold you to what you bet when you were drunk."

"It is a debt of honor."

"What does honor have to do with rum and gambling?"

The woman who shared their hearth said: "A Man Tying on His Snowshoes is right. They all played fair and laid down their wagers in good faith."

Mother snapped at her: "So *your* man won?"

The woman sniffed: "I would say the same thing even if he'd lost."

Mother snorted, "No doubt," and turned back to Father.

"What's done is done. But come next spring, we turn our backs on the Ohio."

Father said somberly: "You have my word that I will not drink from the white man's cup from this day until I have drunk again from the river of the Caniengas."

"The word of Tying Snowshoes has always been enough for me."

It seemed to Si-isha that Father recovered a little of himself with that, but not much. He sat dipping his spoon into his bowl but only taking small sips of broth, looking into the bowl so as not to meet anyone's eyes. She had never thought it possible that her father could do anything that would make him feel ashamed.

He straightened his back, handed her his bowl and spoon and smiled: "Well, Si-isha, I guess I'd best start readying my traps for a long winter. But first, I think I will go drink half the Ohio." She giggled at his joke, although she wasn't quite sure what it was. The important thing was that the pillar of her longhouse was standing up again.

It turned out to be a lean winter. Not that Si-isha or anyone else went hungry. There was plenty of dried corn and beans in the storage pits, and plenty of smoked fish and eels, and deer and partridges abounded in the woods. But her father would be gone to his trap sets for days on end, and come back with only a mangy wolf pelt or a couple of muskrats. His springy walk grew increasingly stiff-legged, with permanently squared shoulders, putting Si-isha in mind of a man carrying a too-heavy pack basket he couldn't unstrap.

She wished she could unknot the straps for him. It was a new and disturbing feeling to think of her father as someone she wished she could help.

At the Midwinter Festival, the Keeper of the Faith began the ritual of putting last year's bad thoughts and deeds in the past by holding up a belt of pure white wampum and confessing: "In the first moon of the summer, when we had all used up all our tobacco and the leaves growing in the field were still too green, I found a corner of an old leaf in my fire bag. I took it out into the woods and smoked it myself. I did not even crumble a few flakes into the fire."

He turned and held the belt out to the person on his right—

Si-isha's father. Father took the wampum in his hands and said
simply: "I got drunk and gambled foolishly with what did not
belong to me, but to my wife and children." But when he
passed the belt on to Mother, it didn't look to Si-isha like he'd
put what he'd done in the past. She could see the pack still
weighing down his shoulders.

Si-isha's mother stood up with the belt draped over both her
hands and said: "I spoke sharply and unfairly to the sister who
shares our fire, when it was my husband I was angry at. And,
much worse than that, I have made my husband feel he is at
fault for a lean winter that no man can change."

And then, instead of handing the wampum to the next adult
Hodenosaune in the circle, she extended it downward toward
Si-isha. Si-isha stared at the broad white belt gleaming like fish
scales and then looked up at her mother, shaking her head.
Mother nodded emphatically and thrust the belt at her again.

Si-isha stood up and held her hands out awkwardly, palms
curled toward the earth. The white belt settled over the backs
of her hands, tickling the thin skin between her bottom knuckles and weighing down her wrists. She licked her lips and
swallowed a few times and then burst out with: "I touched my
brother!"

She waited for the eagle at the top of the Tree of Peace to
come screaming down on her. But instead the man on her right
just held his hands out to take the wampum for his own con-
fession.

When the bad deeds of the old year had all been brought out
to fly up the smoke hole and the dancing began, bringing in
those Mingoes who didn't follow Hodenosaune customs, her
father covered her shoulder with his hand and said: "When I
was a boy, I played those same games once or twice with the
daughters of my mother's sisters. Since we were of the same
clan, it was as bad as if we'd had the same mother.

"All children are curious about the world and so make
mistakes—at least all children with an *onikonhra* that wants to
learn. But now you are becoming more than a child.

"I bet I'll make as many mistakes this year as I did in the
old year—I just hope not the same ones." He laughed and
shook her shoulder. "Listen to this fool talking like he has any
wisdom to impart."

* * *

The second half of the winter didn't bring Si-isha's father any more pelts than the first half, so she ended up spending another summer living the only life she'd ever known: hoeing in the fields, gathering chestnuts and walnuts in the woods, playing the women's ball-and-stick game, trying to grow more adept with a corn-shucking hook, singing along with the songs of the Ripe Corn Festival and the other markers of the seasons when those Mingoes who remained Hodenosaune gathered at the far end of the longhouse.

Some things changed. Her boyish nipples began to itch and bud. In the autumn she began to bleed for the first time. Her mother showed her what to do with spagnum moss and mint leaves and then took her a half day's walk into the forest, along with a Canienga woman recently come to the Ohio. They came to a hollow with a trickling stream and a low, elmbark lean-to so covered over with moss that Si-isha thought at first it was just another hummock on the forest floor.

Si-isha's mother handed her a blanket and pointed at the lean-to, saying: "That is the husk that will cover you. While you are husk covered, this woman is your mother. You will see or speak with no one but her. She will come from the village every day and set you tasks to do, and you will do them."

"Yes, Mother."

Her mother turned and went back the way they'd come. The Canienga woman set down the basket she'd been carrying and took out two ears of corn still in their husks and a fire drill. "This is what you have to eat until I come back in the morning. I will take the fire drill with me, so start a fire fast. There is wood there." She pointed to another patch of mossy elmbark beyond the lean-to.

Si-isha went to look. There was a bark-roofed storage crib as long as she was tall, but there were only a few small sticks of firewood in it. She brought them back to the shallow fire pit in front of the lean-to, reached into the fire bag the woman had shaken the drill out of, and found nothing there. She said to the woman: "There is no tinder."

"You had best find some. And find it soon—I have a long way to walk back before night comes down."

Si-isha flicked her eyes around the rim of the hollow until they found the red blaze of a maple tree. She hurried over to it and picked through fallen leaves. When she had ten brittle, dry ones, she carried them back carefully, crumpled them into a powdery mound in the fire pit and sat down to work the fire drill. It was the kind with a one-handed slat to work the thongs up and down, rather than a quicker, two-handed bow drill. She set the point of the drill in one of the notches in the fire board, locked her left arm around her left shin to hold the drill steady, and began to work the slat up and down to set it spinning.

Just when she thought she'd got it spinning well and a bit of smoke was starting to show, the woman said: "Hurry along now. I don't intend to be lost in the forest at night just because you can't work a fire drill."

Si-isha worked the drill faster. The blackened powder sifting down through the notch in the fire board finally showed a spark. Si-isha lifted the sparked powder with a piece of bark, breathing on it softly as she shifted it toward the fire pit. It didn't help that the Canienga woman snatched up the fire drill and thrust it back in its pouch as soon as Si-isha turned away from it.

Si-isha settled the spark onto the mound of powdered leaves and fanned it with her piece of bark. When the tinder began to burn, she added a few dry twigs. They'd barely caught when the woman said: "I will be back tomorrow. There is plenty of firewood in the crib."

"No, it's empty."

"Is it, now? It should be filled. It *will* be filled by the time I come back. And filled with *firewood*, not green sticks." She took a hatchet out of her basket and dropped it on the ground, then said, "You still have plenty of daylight left to work in," and went away.

Si-isha watched her go. If Mother said the woman was to be her mother while she was husk-covered, she would obey. The woman didn't have to be so rude about it.

Si-isha fed the fire until it was built up enough to leave safely, and then got up to start scouting the forest for fallen trees and dead branches. She found a big, forked oak limb and dragged it back. It was difficult enough without being doubled over from time to time by a twisting pain below her stomach, as though her intestines were trying to strangle each other.

Her first blow with the hatchet told her the blade was so dull she might just as well be using the blunt end. She found a coarse-skinned rock by the stream and scraped the blade across it, but it wasn't much better. By the time she'd hacked the oak limb into pieces, the fire needed feeding again. She put a few lengths from the oak limb into the fire, stacked the rest in the crib, and went looking for more.

Night came down in the forest earlier than in the cleared fields Si-isha was accustomed to. When the only sunlight left was the distant scrap of blue directly above the hollow, she'd only filled half the crib, and the hunger gnawing at her stomach was almost as bad as the pains lower down. She used the hatchet head to push the coals in the fire pit aside and to dig a little trench to lay the corn in, then scraped the coals back over and threw on some more sticks to give enough light to continue chopping up her stack of deadfalls. Her arms and *onikonhra* were growing duller than the hatchet blade. After she'd been hacking by firelight for a while, the blade glanced off and just barely missed her shin, taking a nick out of the side of her calf.

She chewed up some willow leaves to cover the cut, then sat thinking. She hated the thought of not being able to finish what she was supposed to do, but there would be time in the morning while the Canienga woman was making her way from the village. And as much as she'd always hated it when anyone suggested she'd grown too tired to keep on dancing or to carry sap buckets to the boiling kettle, she had to admit that the next dull swing of the hatchet might not just miss her shin.

She burned her fingers peeling the husk off the first roasted corn ear, and burned her mouth before learning to take it more slowly. Before settling down to sleep for the first time in her life without other human beings all around her, she put a thick log on the fire to keep it burning. She needn't have worried. She woke up so many times she could've kept it alive with twigs.

In the morning she ate water from the stream and went back to work. She didn't want the Canienga woman to come before the task was done, but didn't want to have to go much longer without hearing the sound of another human voice.

She heard several human voices approaching the hollow and dove back into her husk-covering lean-to. The Canienga woman came down alone into the hollow, with a pack basket weighing down her back. She stopped, looked around, and called: "Girl?"

Si-isha crawled out of the lean-to. "I'm here."

"You think to sleep all day?"

"I wasn't sleeping! I heard voices, and my mother said—"

"Is the crib filled with wood?"

"Almost."

"*Almost* is not filled."

"I can finish it today."

"No. You have other things to do today." The woman shrugged her pack off and dumped out a pile of unshucked corn, then carried her empty basket out of the hollow and came back with a full one to add to the pile, then two more. "This corn is not for you to eat, but you will shuck the husks off."

"But I have no shucking hook."

"You have fingers. You may eat from this." She shrugged off a shoulder pouch to add to the pile. "But I have counted the ears of corn. And now I will see this 'almost.' " As the woman went to look at the wood crib, Si-isha looked into the pouch. Her own bowl and spoon were there, along with a stick of smoked venison and a bit of cornmeal. The woman came back wearing an odd expression and said: "What kind of corn are you to shuck?"

Si-isha peeled back one of the ears and said: "White flint—not sweet or for popping."

The woman just grunted and walked out of the hollow. Si-isha spooned a bit of cornmeal into her bowl, forcing herself to remember that if she ate too much, it would swell up in her stomach enough to burst, and went down to the creek to mix some water in. When the bowl and spoon were licked clean, she went to work shucking corn. By the time she needed fire-light to see again, her fingers were bleeding and the pile of shucked corn ears wasn't much bigger than the still-husked pile. She ate her stick of jerked venison and crawled back into her blanket, telling herself that if she shucked any more corn tonight, she'd just ruin it with blood.

She ate the rest of her cornmeal in the morning and went back to work, humming to herself for company, not for joy. The Canienga woman came down into the hollow balancing a piece of wood as tall as Si-isha on her shoulder—a peeled log rounded at both ends and a narrow waist carved into it. The woman looked at the remaining pile of unshucked corn and said: " 'Almost' again?"

Si-isha knew better than to reply. She wanted the Destroyer to knock the woman on the head, and she wanted her to stay and talk a little longer.

The woman dumped her burden on the ground and said: "I hope you know what that is."

"A corn pounder."

"And you know which end to use?"

"The end that's been knocked rounder," although no one had ever been able to explain to her why you were always supposed to use the same end when both ends started the same—it was just the way it was done.

"You will pound that shucked corn into meal today. If you can find something to pound it in."

"There is a stump with a hollow burned into it. I wondered why someone had done that here."

"You are lucky indeed that someone did. You may eat all you like of the cornmeal you make—but I will count the shucked cobs and know if you have hidden any away unstripped. Here." She tossed down a deer's jawbone for stripping the kernels off the cobs.

Si-isha picked it up and said: "But there's hardly any teeth left . . ."

"If it comes to that, you have teeth of your own."

The woman turned and walked back up out of the hollow. Si-isha cleaned the mouse droppings and fallen leaves out of the bowl in the stump and then went to work scraping corn kernels into it. When the bottom of the bowl was covered over, she heaved up the pounder with both hands wrapped around its waist. She discovered a surge of power when she pictured that Canienga woman's face in the corn kernels. The pounder crushing it felt so light, she was quite sure she could mash up all the shucked corn, shuck the rest and have it all turned into cornmeal before the evil descended into the hollow again tomorrow.

She was wrong. The Canienga woman raised her eyebrow at the pile of shucked but still-unground ears beside the pile with its husks on, and presented a rusty knife and a soaked deer hide. "Stretch and scrape this."

"But I have no stretching rack."

"Make one."

The next day she came with a cracked kettle to boil the meal into corn bread, and the next a tattered moose hide and a sliver of a needle to make four pairs of moccasins with. As Si-isha stared dully from the needle to the moose hide, the woman said: "Are you still bleeding?"

"Some of my fingers still— Oh, you mean from *there*. That stopped yesterday . . . or maybe it was this morning. . . ."

The next morning, Si-isha was just starting to patch together the last shreds of moose hide into the last required pair of moccasins when she heard moccasins crunching the leaves on the path into the hollow. She started to cry and threw the pieces down and turned to face the inevitable yet again. But the woman who appeared out of the falling leaves was her mother.

Si-isha jumped up and was about to run up the path when her eyes caught on the rubbish heap she'd made out of the hollow: the piles of corn ears, the deer hide flapping slackly in a rickety frame, the tangle of unchopped deadfalls. . . . Her exasperated weeping turned into tearing sobs. Her mother's arms came around her and her mother's voice crooned: "Ssh . . . Si-isha . . . It's all done now."

"It isn't! I couldn't do anything! I *tried*, but I couldn't. . . ."

Her mother stepped back, still resting one hand on her shoulder, and raised the other to finger-comb the damp hair out of her eyes. "What is anyone to do with a daughter like you? Si-isha, the tasks set for a girl when she is husk-covered are not *meant* to be done."

Si-isha snuffled: " 'Not meant' . . . ?"

"No. When a girl begins to change into a woman, it is time for her and the Clan Mothers to learn what can be expected of her: how strong her body is, how hard she can make herself work, whether she can make herself obey her elders even when she'd rather cut their throats. . . . That poor woman has been twisting her *onikonhra* into knots every night trying to think of something you could not do that was not so hard you would hurt yourself trying."

"Then I'm *not* no-good?"

"That remains to be seen. But you are certainly not lazy."

CHAPTER 5

Muskingum felt Si-isha was a little different since she came back from her husk-covering, although she wouldn't tell him what had happened there. When he watched the women tending the Three Sisters, Si-isha hoed her own row now, instead of helping Mother with hers. She spent more time talking with the grown women instead of playing with him. There seemed to be some sort of secret joke she shared with them, which made them smile when she passed by.

But then, everyone had always seemed to think Si-isha was more interesting than other children, which she never seemed to notice. Muskingum didn't mind, most of the time, as long as Mother and Father paid attention to him when he wanted them to.

Whatever had happened to Si-isha when she was husk-covered, it didn't seem to have hurt her much, and was no reason to prevent him from hurling himself into another Ohio winter. He was big enough to have his own baggataway stick now, though not a full-sized one, and his own line of rabbit snares in the woods just north of the village.

He didn't catch many rabbits, but he seemed to have better luck than his father, who was foraging farther and farther from home and had taken to muttering that maybe the country was getting trapped out. Muskingum couldn't quite understand why his father was so unhappy about it. They had plenty to eat, and the longhouse was warm, and the few furs Father did bring in were enough to buy the few things Mother and Father couldn't make with their own hands. He knew that getting more furs had something to do with whether or not they could leave the

Ohio next summer, but if they didn't, it seemed like no sad thing.

Father had been off in the forest for ten days the day a strange man stooped through the longhouse door and sat down by the first hearth past the doorway. He was dressed strangely for a Hodenosaune—in a black coat with brass buttons, and cloth breeches instead of leggings. His high-topped moccasins had a pattern of snowshoe lacings frozen into them.

Mother was out at the smokehouse, so Si-isha played the woman of the hearth, filling a small pot from the big one full of water and saying: "I am making tea."

"Thank you, I have brought my own," and he handed her a pouch of English tea. While she was boiling it up, Muskingum watched the stranger unbutton his coat, showing a cloth shirt and waistcoat underneath, take out a short-stemmed pipe made of some shiny, yellow-white stone and light it without first crumbling a pinch of tobacco into the fire. His pipe smoke smelt like straight tobacco, without a leavening of willow bark. He was shorter than Father, but few men weren't, and Muskingum guessed younger, too, given that there were fewer lines on his face. It wasn't a rugged face like Father's, rather the kind girls called handsome, with a short, square nose and soft eyes.

Mother stooped through the doorway shaking snow off her heavy winter blanket and knelt by the fire, neither remarking on the stranger's presence nor ignoring him. After a moment of warming her fingers, she said, "So, Canadiorha"—A Man Carrying News—"it has been a long time."

"Since Si-isha was too young to remember, and Muskingum not born."

"Was it a hard walk over the mountains?"

"Not so much. It was good snow, and the wind only blew hard one day. I was surprised when they told me I could find you at the first hearth past the doorway. I had thought, with all the families that must have come and gone in the years you've been here, you would have worked your way back to the warm end of the longhouse. And then I realized that so long as your family were at the doorway, any enemy would first have to pass Tying Snowshoes."

They went on to talk about this winter's storms as compared to last year's, how far Tying Snowshoes had to walk on them these days to find any pelts worth curing, and the health of various people whose names meant nothing to Muskingum. Finally Carrying News got around to mentioning: "What has brought me to the Ohio is that my father heard from Tskleleli—the little bird who flits from ear to ear singing stories—that the Miami chiefs mean to burn the fort the French put up in their country. My father sent me with a string of wampum to ask the Miamis whether Tskleleli sings the truth for a change.

"Since I would be passing this way, I was asked to bear another string of wampum, by Someone Lends Her a Flower."

Finally there was a name that meant something to Muskingum. It belonged to his mother's mother. He had never met Someone Lends Her a Flower, since she lived at the Dawn Gate far across the mountains, but he'd heard her talked of many times.

Carrying News reached inside his shirt and came out with a string of white wampum dotted with three of the dark purple beads that people called black. He said: "With this wampum, Someone Lends Her a Flower says to you, her daughter, that her childbearing days are done, and it is time her daughter came home to take the name of Someone Lends Her a Flower and sit upon the empty mat in the circle of Oyanders."

"Oyander" was a word Muskingum only understood vaguely. He knew it was the female version of "Royaner"—the councillors who spoke around the Fire That Never Dies—but he'd never laid eyes on either a Royaner or an Oyander.

Carrying News put the string of wampum in Mother's hand. She sat looking at it for a long while, sipping her English tea and saying nothing. Then she tucked it away and they began to talk again of people and places that meant nothing to Muskingum.

Muskingum went out to check his snares and found a fat gray rabbit dangling from one, with its neck snapped cleanly when the sapling snapped upright. Muskingum bent the sapling and set the snare again, then gutted the rabbit and tossed the offal to the one dog who'd followed him from the village. On his way home he thought of the custom about hunters bringing meat in, but decided it didn't apply to rabbits.

Carrying News took out his knife and helped with the skinning. As the rabbit's coat peeled off like a glove, Muskingum saw that he hadn't quite gutted it cleanly. Carrying News said nothing about it, just finished the job with a surreptitious flick of his knife. They all four had a fine feast of roast rabbit larded with deer fat—the guest and the women praising the hunter between mouthfuls.

When it came time to sleep, Carrying News rolled up in a blanket on the floor between the hearth and Mother and Father's sleeping platform. Muskingum crawled into his own cocoon of wool and woven rabbit skins under his sleeping platform. In winter, everyone slept under their sleeping platforms instead of on top of them, so the warmth of their bodies would be held within low-roofed little boxes.

Muskingum lay awake for a while listening for something, although he wasn't quite sure what. Whatever it was, he fell asleep before he heard it.

In the morning, Carrying News strapped on his snowshoes, saying quirkily, "Here I am, a man tying on his snowshoes," and trotted down the frozen river toward the country of the Miamis. Later in the day Father came home, with two otter skins and one muskrat.

Once Father had been sat down by the fire and his bowl filled with soup, Mother said offhandedly: "Brant was here."

Father looked more than a little surprised. "Old Brant?"

Mother shook her head. "His son, young Nickus."

Muskingum said: "Why do you call him Brant? I thought his name was Carrying News."

Father said: "Brant is his white name. Nickus Brant, the same as his father. His father is one of the four Royaners who traveled across the water to England to meet with the queen in the days when the English had no king."

"He has the same name as his father when his father's still alive?"

"White names are different."

"Must get confusing."

Father shrugged. "The whites are used to being confused," he said, then turned back to Mother. "What brought Brant so far from home?"

Mother told him. When she got to the part about the wampum from Someone Lends Her a Flower, Father put down his bowl, and his face slumped into that worn-down look again. Mother put her hands on his shoulders and said: "Tying Snowshoes, we have enough gold and furs to buy the things we need the most. And you said yourself the country here is getting trapped out."

Father sighed, scratched his chin and said: "Just when I was getting used to spending half my life sleeping in snowbanks . . ."

CHAPTER 6

Come spring, Si-isha's father went to the Delaware village downriver to buy horses, and came back with five. Si-isha could remember being lifted onto the back of a horse when she was little, but she'd never really ridden one. All the traveling she could ever remember doing had been on foot or by canoe.

The horse that she and Muskingum were to ride was white with yellow spots. They tied a blanket across his back to sit on. Her father led the way on a big black horse. Mother followed them on a gray horse, leading the two brown packhorses loaded down with her possessions. In Hodenosaune families, everything except the man's clothing and hunting gear and weapons belonged to the woman.

As they approached the border of the clearing around the Mingo village, and the mouth of the road to the east, Si-isha turned to look back. It was a gray day. The smoke from the two longhouses fingered up to meld with an iron sky. In the black fields, the women were hoeing the seeds of the Three Sisters into the earth, singing behind a new leader. A pack of boys and dogs was roistering toward the creek to rebuild last summer's fish weir.

Muskingum snuffled. He had craned around to see back past her. She tightened her arms around him and said: "You must've known, with all the families we've seen come and go, that the time would come when we'd leave, too."

"I thought I did, but I don't think my *onikonhra* believed it."

"You remember when it came time to leave the old village because the fields had gone stale? It seemed terrible to have to lose our home. But when we got here and saw the men girdling the big trees to kill them, and burning off the brush, and the new longhouses going up, we stopped missing the old village."

"I don't remember."

"I guess you were too young. But it is true. We are going to see many new and wondrous things on the other side of the mountains."

"I know. But it hurts to lose the old ones."

"I know." The forest closed around them and Muskingum turned to look ahead.

The road they followed was a footpath barely wide enough to accommodate one horse at a time. On either hand were endless colonnades of cloud-raking trees rooted in a head-high tangle of underbrush and vines. The spring buds had just barely grown big enough to be called leaves, but already made a canopy so thick that Si-isha rarely caught a glimpse of the sky. Enough sunlight filtered down onto the path, though, to make the forest on either side a place of shadows that Si-isha's eyes couldn't penetrate.

The nights were still cold, but Mother invariably told her to smother the fire as soon as the evening's cooking was done. She and Muskingum slept curled up against their mother for warmth. Father would spread out his blankets alone, with his rifle by his right hand and his hatchet stuck in the ground beside his war club. The last thing Father had done before leaving the village was to dig up his war club and hatchet. The war club was a beautiful and terrible construction carved from a single piece of ironwood. The head was the head of a bear, the emblem of his clan, with its teeth clamped around a ball the size of a baby's head. Si-isha had only seen it a few times before, on those mornings when her father set off on the war road or when he came home to bury his weapons again.

Between camps, Father rode with his rifle propped across his horse's neck and didn't speak. Si-isha knew from the posture of that long, lean back sprouting up from the back of the black horse—as though his spine had been replaced by a pine tree growing straight up through his scalp lock—that those wide-set black eyes were flicking constantly over every leaf or rock or patch of moss along the trail. She strained her ears to hear what he was listening for among the creak and rustle of the boughs overhead, the chirping of chipmunks and birds and the loam-muffled thud of hooves.

She let Muskingum take turns holding their horse's halter. It didn't seem to make much difference to the steady rolling-up-and-down of the white and yellow back plodding patiently in the wake of the black tail—the black plumes of horsetail and scalp lock waving in unison. She and Muskingum whispered and giggled to each other, pointing out soft-colored little birds with songs ten times their size, bright-colored mushrooms and lightning-blasted trees. Sometimes they'd forget themselves and their voices would grow gradually louder until their father shot a black eye flare over his shoulder, and then they'd go back to whispering—until the next time.

The path began to rise and grow rocky. The elms, maples, and sycamores gave way to birch, pine, and mountain ash. The nights grew even colder. They climbed past plunging waterfalls and gorges torn down into the womb of the earth, where the voices of water demons echoed up an invitation to jump down. They spent one night huddled in a rock cleft while the Thunderers did their best to crack open the Stone Giants' home.

The day after the storm, Si-isha got the distinct impression that she and Muskingum had to lean backward against the slant of the spotted back more often than forward. When they stopped for the night, Father announced: "In two or three days, if we're not stormbound again, we pass through the gate of the Keepers of the Sunset. From then on we'll be traveling under the Tree of Peace and can light up the sky with our campfires if we like."

He turned to Muskingum and added, in that dead-serious tone that always made Muskingum squirm and laugh, "It is a sad thing, my son, that you will never have the chance to learn real deer-hunting. By the time you are of an age to hunt deer, you will be living in a country where our grandfathers cut clearings through the woods to chase the deer to where the hunters sit waiting. I would hardly call it hunting at all. I tried to explain this to your mother, but women have no understanding of these things."

Si-isha said: "And men have no understanding of anything else." There were few sensations she enjoyed more than surprising her father into laughter. He laughed even harder when she shook his shoulder and said: "Si-isha?" Are you laughing?

Si-isha woke up in the middle of the night without knowing why. It was a full moon in a sky of drifting cloud, turning the night from bright to dark and back again. At the moment it was so black she had to flicker her eyelids to be sure they were open.

There was a soft scuffing sound that she didn't exactly hear—it was more like she could feel it brushing against the little bones inside her ears. Even though it was warm inside the blankets with her mother and Muskingum, she began to shiver with remembered stories of bodiless heads that scudded through the forest at night with their long hair streaming behind them.

The moon came out and gleamed on a distorted parody of a human face hovering in the air at the foot of the blankets. She screamed, and heard Muskingum scream at the same time. Both screams were drowned out by an explosion, coupled with a tongue of fire as Father's gun went off. The distorted face disappeared, but was replaced by another and another—painted warriors bounding forward out of the darkness.

Father's hatchet whistled through the air into a paint-daubed chest. Mother was on her feet slashing at a shadow with her long skinning knife. From out of nowhere a hand took hold of Si-isha's hair at the top of her head and yanked her upright. She saw a knife coming toward her and flung her hands up to catch the wrist behind it. Above the thick wrist was a thick neck with a wide, purple ribbon around it, and above the ribbon a laughing mouth as the knife arm slowly and easily pushed downward against all the strength in her arms.

The laughing mouth turned into a grimace, and the fist in her hair unfurled. She hurled herself backward and away. As she fell, she saw the man with the knife kicking out his leg to break Muskingum's teeth out of his ankle, then Mother's knife slashing through the purple ribbon.

The night was torn down the middle by the hunting howl of the Destroyer. In a patch of blue light as bright as a bonfire, a ropy-armed, naked figure with three tattoo lines running from his scalp lock to his toes swung his war club against the side of a feathered head with a crack like lake ice splitting in the spring, then leaped onward, whirling the bear's head club over his head and shouting for the night crawlers to please stay and fight with him a little longer. Then the moon went out again and there was no sound except the shrilling and stamping of the horses.

Father hissed: "Move back among the horses, against the big pine tree."

Si-isha pictured the broad-trunked old pine tree they'd tied one end of the picket rope to. She fumbled in the darkness for a blanket to sling over her shoulder, then for Muskingum's hand. The two of them moved up the slope together, stooping to feel their way along the ground. They were almost to where Si-isha thought the tree should be when her hand came down on a large, warm, human foot.

Her father said softly: "We're here before you. Move around behind us and put your backs against the other side of the trunk."

They did as they were told. Muskingum hadn't thought to scoop up a blanket, so she wrapped hers around both of them and they huddled together with their backs against the scaly skin of the tree. From the other side of the trunk came the sound of their father's ramrod snicking in and out to reload.

The horses quietened down again. Father whispered just loud enough for Si-isha and Muskingum to hear: "Don't be frightened if you hear them moving about on this side. We'll let them come back to get their dead and wounded. But if you see or hear anything coming through the woods on your side, lean around and tap us." There was a grim tightness in his voice that made her skin tingle even harder than it was already.

The moonlight continued to come and go until it went out for good. Every creaking bough or shifting shadow seemed to Si-isha to be the painted men coming back, but she forced herself to look or listen twice before raising any alarm. The beating of Muskingum's heart against her ribs gradually slowed to a gallop. From time to time she could just make out her mother's and father's voices whispering on the other side of the tree, but never quite loud enough to hear what they were say-

ing. They stopped just around the time the world started turning from black to shades of gray.

Si-isha waited until the colors seeped back into the rocks
and moss and horses. Then she disentangled herself from
Muskingum, stood up and stepped around the tree. She started
another scream, but her mother stopped it in her throat with a
hissed: "Ssh! Do you want them to know?"

Si-isha's father was lying in her mother's arms with the
shaft of an arrow sticking out of his ribs and his eyes staring
unblinking into the rising sun. Mother's hands and the side of
her body he was leaned against were black with blood, pooled
and still red in her lap. Her face looked like the tears were
stone weights dragging all the corners down.

Mother whispered: "He told me what to do. Go bring your
brother here, and make sure he keeps his hand over his
mouth."

Si-isha stumbled back up the needle-strewn rock face, trying
to find a voice that wasn't a shriek. But before she could open
her mouth to tell Muskingum what Mother had told her to say,
he saw her face and his mouth shot open. She clapped her
hands over it and whimpered: "No! We must be quiet." He
nodded and she took her hands away. "Come around the tree,
but Mother says you are to keep your hand over your mouth."

Mother was sawing at the arrow haft with her knife. Even
with Muskingum's hand obediently holding his mouth shut, Si-
isha heard the muffled scream. Mother said: "Go together and
get your father's ax, if it's still there. And whatever clothing
you can find. Don't run or look scared, but don't stay out there
any longer than you have to."

Si-isha took hold of Muskingum's hand as they stepped out
into the open. The only signs that anyone might have been
killed or wounded there a short while ago were a few dark
stains on the rocks. The raiding party had ransacked the campsite, grabbing whatever their hands touched first and scuttling
away. Most of the blankets were gone, along with the iron pot
and Father's fire bag, and his hatchet had been dragged away
with the body it was planted in. But his ax was still where he'd
set it in a cleft between two rocks, in case he needed to get his
hands on another weapon. There was no sign, though, of the
quill-worked, moose-hide bag with his fur money in it.

She let go of Muskingum's hand and they went about gathering the clothing scattered on the ground. Muskingum was snuffling and sobbing. So was Si-isha, but she found it easier to hold it in to keep him from breaking. She picked up the ax and they walked back up into the stand of pines as calmly as they could manage.

Their mother had lain their father out facedown, with his arms and legs straight. At the foot of the tree where she'd sat with her dead man in her arms gleamed the quill-worked bag of gold coins. She said to her children: "Go and cut me four straight boughs or saplings, at least as big around as your fist and as tall as Si-isha's waist or longer."

They went and did so, hacking awkwardly with the heavy-headed ax. When they got back, their mother had wrestled their father's breechclout and leggings onto him and donned her own overdress and moccasins—her skirt and leggings had gone with the blankets and pot. She cut the blood-soaked blanket into strips, trimmed the boughs and saplings they'd brought back and lashed three of them together into a triangle, tying two of the points to Father's shoulders. Then she took the longest stick and braced it along his spine, twisting his scalp lock around the top of it.

Between the three of them, they just managed to get him up onto the shying black horse. Mother stood holding him in place and said: "Now you two tie his feet under the horse's belly. Tight."

When that was done, she said: "Si-isha, climb up in front of him. You are riding with your father today, just like any daughter might do from time to time on a long journey."

Muskingum gave her a boost up so she could squirm in between her father and the horse's neck, while Mother held him from falling over. Once Si-isha was in place, her mother shifted her father's cold hands up around her waist and said: "If you feel his balance start to slip to one side, tug on his other arm." Then she draped a blanket over Father's shoulders and propped his gun across Si-isha's lap.

"Now, Si-isha—as we ride along, you will *talk* to your father. You will chatter away about the birds you see by the side of the trail or whatever else catches your eye, as carefree as though we were already traveling under the Tree of Peace. Because you have no need to be afraid of anyone, so long as—"

Something seemed to catch in her throat. "So long as you are riding with A Man Tying on His Snowshoes."

Si-isha sat waiting while her mother and little brother packed together what was left of their possessions and climbed onto their own horses. When Mother said, "We go now," Si-isha wrapped the halter around her wrist so she could hold the rifle with both hands and nudged the black horse with her heels, wondering what she was going to do if the horse took it in mind to turn back up the trail instead of down. It didn't. But as they started downward, her father's propped-up torso slumped forward. She leaned back as hard as she could, feeling his cold skin through the shoulders of her overdress, and he didn't quite topple over.

Her mother's voice called lightly: "Si-isha?"

"Yes, Mother?"

"You do not seem very talkative today."

"Oh! I was just ... thinking ... Oh, look, Father! There's a blue jay. Do you remember the time Muskingum caught a blue jay in a net and you spent all day cutting off the little bits of meat so he could say the family had eaten from his hunting, and just when I was getting hungry enough, you told me if I ate brother blue jay my voice would go as shrill as his? Do you remember the time when ..."

They traveled all day without stopping. By sunset they were out of the mountains and Si-isha could barely croak. They came to a stream and Mother called: "It's dark enough to stop now." Si-isha pulled on the halter to stop the black horse. Her mother came forward to help her down, saying: "Go and drink and ease yourself."

Si-isha hobbled into the woods and then down to the stream to cup up handfuls of water into her mouth and over her face. Her legs began to tingle back to life. When she came back from the stream, Muskingum was feeding a fire with the sticks that had propped up his father, and Mother was sewing one of their few remaining blankets into a shroud around Father, singing as she sewed:

"Hai!
A Man Tying on His Snowshoes
Hai hai!
Even dead

Tying Snowshoes
Kept his family safe
Like no man living."

CHAPTER 7

On the second morning after her father died, Si-isha shared the back of the yellow and white horse with Muskingum once again. He had charge of their horse's halter; she held the leads for the two packhorses. Mother rode in front on the gray horse, leading the big, black horse carrying the big, blanket-wrapped bundle draped across its back. She hadn't quite been able to bend it out of the posture of a man sitting on a horse.

Si-isha couldn't bear to look at that jouncing bundle, but could not take her eyes off it. She couldn't imagine a life without that tall warrior to tease and play with and be comforted by. It seemed they'd had such a short time since she'd realized that he was a human being who needed comforting of his own, yet still was able to protect her from all harm.

The family rode mostly in silence, although every now and then, when Si-isha's salt-stung eyes couldn't look at the black horse any longer and she looked away long enough to forget for a moment, there would be a flower or a bird by the side of the trail that she couldn't help but point out to Muskingum, or he to her. But even that was subdued. She wasn't sure what she and Muskingum were supposed to do: whether they should go on being numbed and silent for the rest of their lives, whether it was wrong for them to be aware of anything except that their father was dead.

The forest had grown thick and tall again since they'd left the mountains behind. The trail wound past strange stands of trees: chestnuts, walnuts, and another kind Si-isha had never seen before. It was eerie that the nut trees all grew in groves with no other kinds of trees crowded in between them, and no undergrowth to speak of. There was a far-extending swath of sugar maples that was the same—more like a giant's garden than a forest.

The trail angled up the side of a ridge. At the top the woods came to an abrupt end. Muskingum gasped and pulled the horse to a halt.

They were looking down into a river valley whose bottom flats were miles of black fields speckled with the green sprouts of the Three Sisters and tobacco, with a few old forest giants left standing here and there for shade. A pink-white cloud bank of blossoming apple trees and cherry trees hovered beyond the cornfields. On the riverbank was a palisaded town that the village on the Ohio resembled about as much as a hunter's wigwam did a longhouse. At a guess, Si-isha numbered the roofs of the longhouses as upward of fifty. The stockade around them was actually three stockades ringed within each other.

Muskingum squawked: "Are there *that* many Hodenosaune?"

Si-isha said authoritatively, "Those are only the Senecas, and only one of their towns," although she found it difficult to believe herself.

Mother had got ahead of them while they stopped to gape. Si-isha nudged the horse with her heels to catch up. The women working in the fields had started coming forward when they saw Mother coming down the hill. By the time the yellow-spotted horse and the two packhorses caught up, the black horse and the gray were the apex of a horseshoe of several hundred women. As Si-isha helped Muskingum haul back on the halter to stop their horse from plowing into the crowd, she heard her mother announce: "I am Hemlocks Rustling, daughter of Someone Lends Her a Flower of the Wolf Clan of the Canienga."

One of the Seneca women stepped forward and laid her hand on the halter of Si-isha's mother's horse, saying, "Come, sister," which meant she was of the Wolf Clan as well.

A lane opened up in the crowd to let the Wolf Clan woman lead the way toward the town. Looking from side to side as the spotted horse carried her between the ranks of women, Si-isha saw that the people she'd thought of as old back on the Ohio weren't old at all. It had never occurred to her that human faces could gnarl up like the bark of an oak tree, or that hair could fade to the color of corn silk.

At the entrance to the stockade a group of men in ceremonial robes stood waiting, as though their arrival had been expected. An old man wearing a double-rowed headdress of turkey feathers stepped forward. The Wolf Clan woman addressed him as Royaner and told him who Si-isha's mother was. Mother added: "My man, A Man Tying on His Snowshoes, walked the road where the strawberries always grow two nights ago."

The old man's hands and eyebrows went up and he sighed: "Not Tying Snowshoes?"

A younger man, wearing a neckpiece with a bear's head beaded onto it, stepped around the Royaner. The Bear warrior laid his hand on the blanket cocoon bent over the black horse and said softly, in that strange, R-less Seneca dialect, "Tying Snowshoes—you stood beside me at the Little River when we taught the Ottawas to stay at home." He raised his eyes to Si-isha's mother. "Who was it?"

"I don't know. It was dark. He took three of them with him—maybe four."

"So he would."

The Wolf Clan woman said, "Come, sister," and led Si-isha's mother's horse through the stockade gate. Si-isha clucked the spotted horse to follow the tail of the black horse. Inside the gate there was nothing but the solid wall of the second ring of palisades. The Wolf woman turned to the right and led them along between the two walls until they came to an opening in the second ring. Through there, she turned to the left along another hemmed-in passageway. Beyond the third gate a riot of people burst on all sides: children squealing and laughing and chasing each other in circles, women pounding corn, men shouting bets and encouragement around a wrestling match. . . . There were so many people doing so many different things, Si-isha started to get dizzy from trying to look in so many different directions at once.

Muskingum whispered: "How do they remember each other's names?"

"I guess they get used to it."

The longhouses were arranged in a maze, some offset almost side by side, some with their doorways pointing at the wall of another. The Wolf woman led the horses on a zigzag course until the top of the stockade had disappeared behind humped roofs, then stopped in front of a longhouse's awninged entranceway and beckoned Si-isha's mother to climb down. Muskingum whispered: "How can they tell which longhouse is which?"

"Silly—look at the wooden wolf's head over the door."

"Half the other ones had wolves on them, too."

"Well . . . maybe they count as they go along the rows."

The Wolf woman held the door curtain aside and Si-isha's mother stooped through. The Wolf woman, still holding the curtain open, gestured Si-isha and Muskingum to follow their mother. Si-isha took hold of Muskingum's hand and did so.

Mother hadn't stopped inside the doorway to wait for them, but continued walking along the aisle of hearths between the rows of sleeping platforms. Si-isha hurried Muskingum along to catch up.

It was a long walk. Both Ohio longhouses laid end to end would have fit inside this one. And not only end to end, but side by side: the sleeping platforms on either side of the hearths looked wide enough to fit whole families. Each hearth was compartmented by elm-bark walls, to make a tunnel of open doorways that Si-isha and Muskingum followed their mother along.

Mother wasn't walking very fast. Not that she was plodding. She moved with a stately gait Si-isha had never seen before, and her back appeared to have stretched itself several inches taller.

At the far end of the tunnel a fire was burning, even though the day was warm. Beside the last hearth was a wolf-pelt mat with an old, old woman kneeling on it. She said to Si-isha's mother: "Thou art welcome in my longhouse, daughter."

"I thank thee, Oyander."

The Oyander nodded and continued in her sibilant, snakelike rasp: "I know thy mother, daughter. I remember well the council at Onondaga when she told me thou hadst set thy mind to court a fine young warrior named Tying Snowshoes. Thy grief is ours, daughter."

"I do not wish to bring sorrow into thy house, Oyander."

"Thou bringest *pride*. We mourn with thee that thy husband

has returned to the land of souls, and we rejoice that the children of such a man belong to our clan. He was sure one rabid head-cracker of a wildcat when his blood was up. These are thy children?"

"My daughter Si-isha and my son Muskingum."

"Come to me." The withered eagle claw of a hand beckoned. Muskingum's hand clamped tighter around Si-isha's fingers and he dug his heels into the earth. Si-isha moved forward, pulling him along with her. The Oyander's smoke-filmed eyes drilled into hers. Their piercing gaze suddenly went quizzical, or perhaps confused, and shifted to Muskingum, then back again. The snake voice hissed: "What have you brought into my house?"

Si-isha's mother said: "What, Oyander . . .?"

"Did I speak? Sometimes an old woman forgets herself. Your children must be hungry. Leave them with me. My daughters will help you with Tying Snowshoes."

Mother went back toward the front of the longhouse. The Oyander put her hand on Si-isha's shoulder for a prop as she creaked to her feet. From a storage shelf she reached down a covered basket and a clay jar with a face etched on it. The basket turned out to have corn cakes in it, the clay jar chestnut milk. While Si-isha and Muskingum were eating and drinking, the Oyander asked them questions, apparently fascinated with what life was like as Mingoes in the Ohio country. Soon the three of them were chattering away. Si-isha was surprised to discover that everyone who lived in the Oyander's longhouse were her children—her daughters and granddaughters and their husbands and children. The Oyander seemed surprised that she was surprised.

Si-isha's mother came back wearing her ceremonial dress with the silver broaches all down the front, carrying Si-isha's and Muskingum's beaded and quill-worked festival clothes. When they had changed, she streaked their faces with ashes from the Oyander's hearth, then did the same to her own. Kneeling in front of them, she put one hand on Si-isha's shoulder and the other on Muskingum's and said: "Now it is time to say good-bye to your father forever. If his *onikonhra* comes back into the body of a bird or an animal, he will remember everything, and recognize you when he sees you. If he comes back into a person waiting to be born, he will have to forget all of the life he lived as A Man Tying on His Snowshoes. But

I'm sure that person will still feel something for you if you ever meet, because you were the hearth of his heart."

Mother stood up again, took them each by the hand and led them back down the tunnel to the door of the longhouse. Father was lying just inside the doorway on a kind of bed made out of a blanket stretched across a framework of fresh-cut saplings. He was wearing his dancing clothes. Three eagle feathers had been wound into his scalp lock, and a rainbow painted across his face. His hands were folded across his war club, with the blood and hair of his last enemy still on it. The warrior he'd stood beside at the Little River was standing beside him now, along with three other warriors of the Bear Clan. They picked up the bier and followed Si-isha and Muskingum and their mother out into the bright sunlight.

The Royaner who'd met them at the gate was standing there, holding a belt of black wampum. He began to sing:

"Hai!
A Man Tying on His Snowshoes
Hai hai!"

Si-isha's mother and the four Bear Clan men joined in on the "Hai!" and "Hai hai!" Si-isha managed to loosen the knot in her throat enough to add her voice to theirs as they followed the Royaner down the lanes of longhouses toward the gates of the stockade.

"Hai!
Where shall the Bear Clan find another
Hai Hai!
Like Tying Snowshoes . . .?"

Si-isha heard a constricted version of Muskingum's voice piping up in unison on the other side of their mother, but it grew harder and harder to hear him—because every longhouse they passed by disgorged a stream of people singing "Hai!" and every group of corn-pounders or arrow-makers or hide-scrapers put down their tools to stand up and sing: "Hai hai!"

"Where shall the League of the Hodenosaune
Hai!

Find another Tying Snowshoes?
Hai hai!
He spoke softly in the longhouse
Hai!
And roared like a bear on the war ground
Hai hai . . . !"

They passed through the gates and along the border of the cornfields. But it seemed to Si-isha that the voices of the people they'd passed by on their way through the town weren't dropping behind them. If anything, they seemed louder. Si-isha looked back over her shoulder. Behind the four warriors carrying her father, there was a long line of men and women and children three or four wide, stretching all the way back through the stockade gates and showing no sign of ending. At the sight of all those strangers—or what she'd thought of as strangers—singing her father to his grave, Si-isha's eyes sprouted fountains and her nose plugged up so she couldn't sing anymore.

Up the valley slope, among towers of oak and elm and maple, there were a lot of low, moss-covered hummocks. Some men with ash-streaked faces were standing there beside a pile of rocks. As the Royaner led the singing procession toward them, Si-isha saw that there was a long trough dug in the earth beside the stones, and layered sheets of fresh-cut moss on the other side.

The four Bear Clan warriors set down their burden in the trench. Si-isha's mother let go of her hand and Muskingum's to pick up a stone to set beside Father's head, then gestured Si-isha and Muskingum to do the same. Si-isha hefted up the largest rock she could lift and stooped to settle it down gently. But when she looked down at his swollen face—gray-blue between the rainbow streaks of paint—her hands started to tremble and her body was seized with a shaking fit that sprung the rock out of her fingers. It just missed coming down on his forehead, but it crushed his scalp lock and eagle feathers into the ground.

Mother put her hand on Si-isha's arm to let her know she hadn't done a terrible thing, and they stepped back as the men of the Bear Clan stepped forward to start layering on the stones. The Royaner finished his song with a last crashing "Hai hai!" and presented the belt of black wampum to Si-isha's mother. Mother held the belt over her head to catch the sun, the glistening beads rippling over her hands like a deep purple waterfall. Then she did something that caught Si-isha completely by surprise—and everyone else, judging by the murmurs and gasps. She bent down over her husband and laid the fabulously wealthy belt across his chest. The men of the Bear Clan looked at each other but kept piling on stones. When the body was completely covered, they laid the strips of fresh moss over the stones, to join together and grow again.

When Si-isha and her mother and brother returned to the Wolf Clan longhouse, the Oyander told two of her granddaughters to make sassafras tea and maple cakes, then beckoned Si-isha to sit beside her and said: "Back in the ancient days before the Tree of Peace was planted, we of the Five Nations used to bury our dead in the same way as the Hurons. Do you know how that was, child?"

Si-isha shook her head.

"First the body would be put up on a scaffold for the birds and the sun to pick clean. For six days all the family would lie facedown in the longhouse with no fire in their hearths, even if it was winter. After that, they still had to keep on mourning for a full year. Every twelve years was the Feast of the Dead, when all the bones were taken down from the scaffolds and washed and prayed over in the longhouse and then buried all together in a big pit. Before the pit was covered over, the people would throw in gifts—all the good things they owned— and tear their clothing and furs to pieces. Not gifts from the heart—as your mother did with the black wampum—but to prove that they mourned harder than their neighbors.

"The Peacemaker and Hiawatha put a stop to that among the Hodenosaune. So that now, if your father had gone to the land of souls from your own longhouse, a Keeper of the Faith would bring black wampum and stand by your hearth and speak of the man your father was and what a fine life he'd had. When he was done speaking, he would give the wampum to your mother, and then—as the Founders of the League decreed—*they shall be comforted.*

"Now, why do you think the Founders decided the old ways should stop?"

"I don't know, Oyander."

"I didn't ask you what you *know*, I asked you what you *think*."

"Well ... I think ... I think if my father was to look down from the strawberry road and see that we were making ourselves so miserable because of him, he wouldn't be happy. And ..."

"And what, child?"

"And it must've been hard for people to do their corn-planting and hunting and all the other things you have to do to stay alive, when they were so busy fussing over the dead."

The Oyander nodded. "And what happened to the Hurons?"

"My father told me that. When the Hurons wouldn't stop making war on the League of Peace—because the French kept giving them presents to kill us—our warriors went into Huron country and burned all their towns. And the few Hurons they didn't kill, or that we didn't adopt to replace the Hodenosaune the Hurons had killed, all ran away."

"Just so. And the reason we won that war is because the Hurons had not listened to the words of Hiawatha and the Peacemaker. Our warriors had gone into Huron country in the summer, the season for war, but the Hurons proved too strong for them. But instead of coming home, our warriors stayed camped in the snow in the depths of Huron country all winter. The Hurons were so busy fussing over their dead, in the old, foolish way, they didn't notice that their enemies hadn't gone home. When spring came, our warriors sprang out of the forest and surprised them.

"And so it is, child, that while we in this longhouse grieve with you on this day, we also ... Look down there, at those two there...." Si-isha followed the pointing claw to a hearth farther down the longhouse, where a young man and woman were self-consciously taking articles from a stack of household possessions on the floor and arranging them on a storage shelf. "The youngest daughter of my oldest daughter was married in the spring. But no man may make his home in the longhouse of his wife until he's started a child inside her. Tonight is the first night they live together as a man and woman should."

"But how could they start a child if they couldn't sleep in the same longhouse?"

The Oyander cackled. "Oh, they find ways. Don't worry, child, that's one thing no one's going to have to teach you."

CHAPTER 8

When Muskingum and his mother and sister left the Seneca town, they left the big black horse behind. The Oyander had given them blankets and a cooking pot to replace the ones they'd lost; Mother had given her the black horse.

As they rode on day after day toward the rising sun, the trees of the forest grew full-leafed and filled with nesting birds. The nights were spent either camped by the trail or in a Wolf Clan longhouse. At every longhouse they stayed in, Muskingum and Si-isha were petted and feasted and made much of. Muskingum began to feel a little uncomfortable, that they should be so pampered because their father lay under a pile of stones. His sister didn't appear to think of it that way, but she'd never been one to make herself feel uncomfortable when she didn't have to be.

Parts of the trail passed along the shores of beautiful lakes named after the nations whose home countries they formed the heart of: Seneca Lake, Cayuga Lake, Onondaga Lake. Near Onondaga Lake were three hills with a large, walled town nestled among them. Once the family had been welcomed into one of its longhouses for the night, Muskingum's mother said, "Come with me," and led him and Si-isha out into the evening.

In the center of the town was a longhouse bigger than any of the others, with a painted pole in front of it. Mother said, "This is the Council House of the Six Nations," and ushered them inside. The place seemed empty of everything but ghosts. There were no sleeping platforms or storage shelves, only a line of low benches along both walls. Down the middle of the longhouse were dotted a few small hearths and one large one in the center. A low fire burned in that one and two men were murmuring on mats beside it.

Muskingum's mother walked him and Si-isha toward the two men, then stopped a little ways away. They were both old, old men, and one of them held a cane covered with carvings. When the one without the cane had finished murmuring, and both turned to look at the intruders, Mother said: "Hai, Royaners."

"Hai, daughter of Someone Lends Her a Flower, widow of A Man Tying on His Snowshoes."

"I wanted my children to see the Council House."

The one without the cane said: "It is hardly the same place as when it's filled with councillors and singing. They must be disappointed."

Si-isha said: "No—it's like being inside a drum."

Both old men looked at her as though she'd just sprouted wings. The one toying with the cane said with a crooked smile: "I shall say that in my next speech, and everyone will say 'Yo' at the eloquence of Atotarho."

Muskingum gaped: "Atotarho?"

Si-isha said: "My brother is disappointed that you don't have snakes for hair." Both men laughed. If there'd been a rock handy, and no one looking, Muskingum would happily have brained her.

Atotarho turned to Muskingum. "I am not quite old enough to be *that* Atotarho—although in a way I am he. I am Atotarho as my brother was before me, and his uncle before him, and his uncle's grandfather before him. . . ." As he spoke he moved his fingers up the cane, as though the figures carved there were telling him the story. "So it is with this fire. We Onondagas are the Keepers of the Fire, but we always have one Keeper of the Fire." He nodded at the other old man on the other side of the hearth. "The coals of this fire have never died since it was kindled by the first Atotarho and Hiawatha, and by Dekanawi-dah."

Muskingum had never heard that name before, but didn't want to embarrass himself again. As usual, Si-isha said what he hesitated to say. "Dekanawidah?"

"You would know him, child, as the Peacemaker. His name may not be spoken except around the council fire. His

name alone, out of all the Founders, is not on the roll of Royaners—because how could there be another Dekanawidah?

"It is true that it was the Onondaga Hiawatha who first
spoke of a League of Peace, but Dekanawidah made the
league. Cruel Atotarho hated peace, and drove Hiawatha out to
wander. He wandered toward the dawn until he came to the
valley of the Caniengas, where lived Dekanawidah.
Dekanawidah heard his words, and persuaded all the Canienga
to hear the truth of them.

"Then Dekanawidah sent to his neighbors, the Oneidas, and
they, too, heard the glad tidings of peace and power. The
Caniengas and Oneidas came to the Onondagas, but still cruel
Atotarho would not listen. So Dekanawidah and Hiawatha
went toward the sunset, to the Cayugas and the Senecas. Once
all four nations were in agreement, they came again to
Atotarho, and Hiawatha combed the snakes out of his hair.
And so the Tree of Peace was planted."

On the way back to the longhouse where he and his mother
and sister were to spend the night, Muskingum felt his chest
getting bigger at the notion that the man who'd made the
League of Peace was a Canienga just like he was. He said:
"Someday I'm going to be a Royaner and make speeches in
the Council House."

His mother said: "That you never can. Did you not hear
what Atotarho said? I am neither sister nor daughter to any of
the forty-nine Royaners. When a Royaner walks the strawberry
road, or if the Clan Mothers take the antlers off his head for
disgracing his name, the Clan Mothers can only choose who
will take his place from among the men descended from the
Founder whose name that was."

Si-isha said: "That doesn't seem fair."

Mother laughed. "Not so unfair as it seems. What with the
line slanting between brothers and nephews and sons, and sisters and daughters marrying men from other clans, the roll of
who is or isn't in one of the Great Families changes from one
generation to the next."

Muskingum grumbled: "Guess I just picked the wrong generation to get born."

Mother stopped and crouched down in front of him so she
could hold his eyes with hers. "Listen to me, Muskingum. Thy
father was no Royaner, but thee heard how even the Senecas

mourned him. Some who wear the great names are great men. Some are not near so great as men who wear no names but their own. Thou art thy father's son. You will find that difficult enough to live up to."

"Yes, Mother." But it still didn't seem fair.

The country of the Onondagas blended seamlessly into that of the Oneidas. They camped by a willow-shrouded stream and discovered that the woods around it were filled with just-ripe strawberries. Muskingum had half made himself a vow that he would never eat strawberries again until he ate of the ones along the road his father had traveled, but he didn't keep it. He and Si-isha scampered through the bush, peeking under drooping ferns and low-hanging boughs. They brought a filled basket back to the campfire and sat stuffing themselves while their mother made cakes with strawberries and cornmeal. With red juice dripping down her chin, Si-isha said: "The next town we come to, will they be having their Ripe Strawberry Festival?"

Mother said: "It seems likely. Which is why we won't stop there."

"But, Mother . . .!"

"We are getting very close to home now. The more time we spend dawdling at other people's festivals, the longer it will take us to get there."

At the next few campsites it seemed Muskingum had barely wiped the sleep out of his eyes when Mother was already wrestling the loads back on the packhorses, and that he'd barely unforked his legs from across the spotted horse before she was bustling him and Si-isha off into the woods to fetch firewood so she could get them fed and abed.

The trail grew mountainous again, always slanting either up or down, and always enclosed by the forest that only this narrow path and streambeds threaded through.

There came a day when Mother couldn't seem to stop her horse from breaking into a trot. Muskingum and Si-isha would call out to her in panic as the bundles on the packhorses began to rattle and bounce from the effort to keep up. She would hold her horse back for a while, but invariably would end up forging ahead again.

The trail sloped down yet another wooded hill into yet another mountain valley. But through a break in the trees, Muskingum saw that this valley was much broader than the others, with green meadows and a big, blue river winding through. Mother's horse broke into a gallop. Si-isha helped him haul back on the halter to keep the white-and-yellow horse from doing the same. When they got to the riverbank, they found their mother and her horse both up to their knees in the river. The horse was drinking, and Mother was scooping up double handfuls to sluice over her face and hair.

She turned and called impatiently: "Come down here and drink." Muskingum loosened his hold on the halter, and their horse picked its way down the bank, with the two packhorses following. As soon as the horses were in the water, Mother beckoned: "Get down. Put your feet in the river of the Caniengas." He and Si-isha obediently tried to get off the horse at the same time, getting their legs entangled. He clutched a handful of mane to hold himself on, waited until he heard Si-isha's feet splashing into the river and then slid down.

The water was cold, and the rocks underneath were slimy and slippery. Mother said: "Drink!" Muskingum cupped his hand and stooped forward so he could get it up to his mouth before it all dribbled out. It tasted sweet and cold, but not noticeably different than the Ohio or Muskingum or any of the rivers the trail east had forded across. "You are drinking your home. This is the river your father was dipped in when he was born, and so was I, and so were your grandmother and her grandmothers before her. This is the most beautiful valley in all the world, and it belongs to you—to all the Caniengas—and you to it. The Mohicans tried to take it from us, and the Algonquins, and the Huron, and the French, and other tribes whose names are forgotten because they are no more, but we're still here."

Si-isha put her arm across Muskingum's shoulders and they both stood looking out across the river and valley they belonged to. It *was* a more beautiful valley than he had ever seen, with wider meadows and taller trees and higher, sloping walls. The tugging against his knees of the same currents that had washed his father seemed to be trying to tell him that his father wasn't dead but was still here in the valley of the Peacemaker, with all his grandfathers before him.

Si-isha said huskily to Mother: "Father is here."

"That he is, child. And *will* be for as long as there are Caniengas in this valley."

But when they got back on their horses, Muskingum was surprised to discover that the trail along the River of the Caniengas passed by squared plots of land with white men or black men tending fields of tall green grasses instead of the Three Sisters. And instead of longhouses, there were little square houses made of logs stacked sideways.

Toward evening the trail slanted sharply down into a gorge with saw-toothed cliffs and a stream descending a stone floor of jumbled steps. The splashing of the stream and the clopping of hooves on stone echoed, as did Mother's voice: "We call this the Boiling Kettle, which is where our town of Canajoharie got its name." On the other side of the gorge was the town of Canienga longhouses, with ripening cornfields and orchards spread wide around it. But though it was at least as big as any of the towns of the Senecas or other nations they'd passed through, this one had only a single ring of palisades around it, and some of the point-topped uprights were sagging out of line.

The horses had barely carried them through the gates when people began to call out to Muskingum's mother and come running. She called back to them and clasped their hands or touched their shoulders as she went by, but didn't stop or climb down off her horse. The strangest part was that some of them called her Oyander. Muskingum whispered at his sister: "Why do they call her that?"

"I guess because that's what she is."

Mother stopped her horse at a longhouse with a running wolf painted over its entranceway. A woman stepped forward to hold her horse. Two men Muskingum had never seen before reached up to lift him and Si-isha down. Mother said: "Come along," and brushed past the corn-husk curtain in the doorway. Muskingum took hold of Si-isha's hand and followed her.

Mother was standing with her back to the curtain, gazing straight ahead down the long aisleway of hearths and pillars of red sunset light through the smoke holes. She didn't turn to look at Muskingum and Si-isha or say a word, just angled her arms out beside her with her hands cupped back toward them. Muskingum let go of Si-isha's hand to take hold of his mother's. As they walked forward, the people around the hearths stood up and stepped back without speaking. A baby rolled and gurgled into their path, but its mother scooped it out of the way.

At the far end of the longhouse a woman started to stand up, and kept on standing and standing until she'd become the tallest woman Muskingum had ever seen. She didn't step out of their path, just stood waiting at the end of it. The firelight flickered on a thick silver necklace and the high-boned, long-nosed face above it. Muskingum's mother stopped in front of her, so he did, too. The tall woman said in a sonorous, smoky voice: "The news of thy coming flew before thee, daughter, and of thy husband—he whom I'd hoped would someday show thy sisters' sons what a man is." The long arms spread open. "You are home now."

Muskingum's mother let out a little, choking cry and flung herself at the tall woman, dragging him along with her. He just managed to keep his feet, and found himself with his nose buried in a beaded deer-hide skirt that smelled of smoke and herbs. Above him, his mother was wailing and shrieking like a whipped dog. Whether because of his terror at such sounds coming out of her or because they meant he was finally allowed to let loose, he screamed and howled and made rivers on the skirt with his eyes and nose and mouth. He could hear Si-isha doing the same on the other side, and low groans from somewhere in the vicinity of the longhouse roof.

Mother's voice quietened. The tall woman said, *"There,"* and stepped back, wiping her cheeks. " 'Now they shall *be* comforted.' " Then she crouched down to bring her eyes on a level nearer Muskingum's. "And these are my grandchildren."

Mother said: "Si-isha and Muskingum."

"Muskingum ... I had thought that you were born only eight summers ago ...?"

"Answer your grandmother, Muskingum."

"I was ... or I think so. That's what Mother tells me. I don't remember."

"Well, I'm sure *she* does. Eight years ... You're tall for eight years. Do you mean to keep on growing?"

"I'll try."

"You may yet be as tall as your father. And so much like him, too—thick kissing lips and all. And you, Si-isha ..." The black eyes glittered brighter as they slid away from

Muskingum, and the smoky voice grew softer. "Si-isha . . ."
Everyone was always more interested in his sister than him.

CHAPTER 9

Si-isha woke up in yet another strange longhouse, wondering whether there would be time to eat before climbing on the horses again, and how far her mother was intending to travel today. Then she remembered that they weren't going to be traveling today, or any other day soon. She rubbed the sleep out of her eyes and looked for Muskingum on his sleeping platform, next in line to hers. It seemed odd that she should be thinking of these strange new beds as "mine" and "Muskingum's," but so they were.

Muskingum was nowhere in sight. A lot of other people were: babies hanging in cradleboards, naked children chasing each other around, women mashing beans for pudding or taking down their hoes to go out into the fields, men arguing over whether the morning sky boded a good night for spearing fish by torchlight. . . . Si-isha knew that all these people were her blood relations, but so many new names had been thrown at her last night, she couldn't remember any of them.

She heard her mother's voice coming from toward the back of the longhouse, so she rolled down off her corn-husk sleeping mat and headed in that direction. People called out "Si-isha" and bid her a cheery good morning as she went by. She mumbled back at them, blushing at the sudden intimacy. On her way down the longhouse, she noticed that every second or third hearth looked like it hadn't had a fire laid in it for some time. The sleeping platforms on either side of the dead hearths were piled with baskets and pots and dusty bric-a-brac.

Si-isha's mother was sitting beside Si-isha's grandmother at the last hearth. They both had the happily haggard look of people who've been sitting up talking all night. Her grandmother said: "Well, Si-isha, are you back from the dreamworld yet?"

Mother said: "Si-isha was always a slow waker."

"Come sit." Grandmother patted the bearskin they were sitting on. "And have a cup of tea. That'll wake you up."

Si-isha sat. Grandmother picked up a painted white cup and ladled it full from the pot steaming on the hearth, then handed it to Si-isha. The cup seemed to be made of some sort of white clay, but Si-isha couldn't fathom clay so smooth or shiny. She took a sip. It was English tea, like Carrying News had drunk in the longhouse back on the Ohio. She didn't much care for it.

Grandmother said: "You'll get used to it. Now, tell me—what were you dreaming that you slept so long?"

"I don't remember."

"You will have to learn to do better than that, my girl. At the Midwinter Festival, when the Keeper of the Faith asks me what the people in my longhouse dreamed this year, I can't very well tell him 'they don't remember.' "

Si-isha flustered to come up with something that would please her grandmother. Grandmother patted her hand and smiled: "Don't worry, when you dream something you should remember, you will." Then she glanced down and clucked: "Look at you. You are getting too old to be getting your pretty ankles all scratched up running bare-legged through the thorns. It's past time your mother made you a pair of leggings."

"I can make them myself. I've helped her make hers."

"Good. Then you should soon. You won't set the young men to wondering what's under your skirt if the part they can see looks like peeling birchbark."

Si-isha forced down another sip of tea and said: "Do people go away from Canajoharie all summer to go fishing or hunting, or for something else?"

"When men go on the war road, they are gone all summer."

"I meant whole families."

"No. Some might go away for a few days from time to time, but not all summer. What made you think they might?"

"All those hearths that no one uses, and the sleeping platforms no one sleeps on . . ."

"Ah. You do have eyes, just as your mother told me. Some

of those hearths have not been lit for a good many summers, except at festival times. As I was telling your mother, some of her sisters have decided they would rather plant their own gardens—which is not so strange in itself; a Hodenosaune woman can always ask to have a part of the cornfield set aside for herself, provided she also does her part in the rows we all hoe together. But these ones are not satisfied with that. They have chosen to move off down the valley and live in little houses like the white men and put up fences to show where their farm stops and the next one begins."

"Why would they want to do that?"

"That is a good question. Many reasons, I suppose. For one, the white man's log houses keep the winter out better than a longhouse will, and with much less smoke inside. For another . . . we of the eastern gate have had the white men brushing against us for a long, long time. First the Dutch in the time of my grandmother's grandmother, and then the English—and the English brought over a great many Germans who'd been chased out of their own country because they did not pray the same way as their neighbors."

As Grandmother talked, some of the women of her long-house drifted over, ladled out cups of tea for themselves, and sat around the hearth to listen. "Through all those generations, the white men have been learning things from us, and we from them—some good, some not so good. And our mingling has become even more since your mother went with A Man Tying on His Snowshoes to the Ohio to spend a year or two that turned into thirteen. The summer that you were born, an Irishman named William Johnson came to live on a big piece of our valley that the English king gave to his uncle."

"But how," Si-isha wondered, "could the English king give away a big piece of what is ours?"

"Another good question. Mostly what the king gave was his permission for William Johnson's uncle and some other white men to pay us money for the land. It is difficult to understand all the twistings of the English *onikonhra*, but in the end this Johnson has been a good friend to us."

Si-isha said: "He sounds more like a thief!"

Her grandmother threw back her head and let out a full-throated guffaw. "Many who've traded furs with him have said so. But he *is* an honest man—if you keep in mind that he is also a good trader. He makes a straight road between us and the council of New York Colony, and thus to the king. We have adopted him as a Canienga and given him a voice in our councils and a name—Gets Business Done—and he has given us his son to raise."

One of the younger women giggled and said, "Along with all the others," then leaned across to put her hand on Si-isha's knee and confide: "He has fathered seven hundred children."

"Seven hundred!"

"Be that as it may," Grandmother dismissed the gossip, "the boy he has given us to raise is his *true* son, the child of his second wife, who is a Canienga."

Si-isha said: "What happened to his first wife?"

Grandmother said somberly: "She has been hesitating on the lip of the strawberry road for many years now. She was a German servant girl who ran away from New York Town. Her master offered money to anyone who caught her, and he set the hounds of the English law on her trail. When they found that the trail led to William Johnson, they slunk back to their kennels."

The unchastened gossip put her hand on Si-isha's knee again to say: "And Gets Business Done went to her master and said he would give him either five pounds or a horsewhipping for her. He took the five pounds."

Si-isha considered that maybe this William Johnson might not be entirely bad after all. But she still found it difficult to get her *onikonhra* around the idea that one man could own a piece of land like she owned her spoon or her moccasins—especially land that was part of the Canienga Nation. She was quite sure that if her father had known about that, he would've simply sent this William Johnson's scalp back to the English king.

Grandmother said: "Si-isha—you should pay attention. It is important for you to understand the links in the Covenant Chain that bind the Hodenosaune and the English, so you can help us to keep them strong."

"Me?"

"Yes. Thy mother and I have been speaking of thee. Downriver at Schenectady there is a school where the English and Dutch girls are taught how to become white Oyanders. A small part of the money your mother brought back from the Ohio could pay to send you there—"

"But I don't want to go away! We only just came here!"

Mother said: "Nor do I wish you to go away. But you could learn a great many things at Schenectady. And anyone who speaks before someone else has finished speaking has clearly a great deal yet to learn."

"Forgive me, Grandmother."

"I do. You have too much spark for your own good sometimes, Si-isha. But I do not wish for you to go away from us any more than your mother does. You must try to understand what a useful thing you would be doing for us—for all the Hodenosaune. Every year more and more white people come across the water, and the ones that are already here make children faster than rabbits. They all have a burning thirst for land that is never satisfied. And many of them believe—unlike William Johnson—that any land some other white man hasn't already built a fence around is free for the taking.

"Every day now, somewhere along this river, you will find a white man and a Canienga having strong words with each other, with their hands on the handles of their knives. We have been friends with the Dutch and the English ever since their guns made us strong again after the French almost destroyed us. But there are many things our white friends do that make no sense to us, and it is hard to have peace where there is no understanding. It would be a great help to the Clan Mothers if we could turn to someone who understood how the whites think—because she had been educated like one."

Si-isha waited until she was certain her grandmother had said all she had to say for the moment, then protested: "But I'm only a girl."

"Thou art fast becoming a woman, granddaughter—a woman with an *onikonhra* that can take in many things. The Clan Mothers of Canajoharie have been talking of this for a year and more, but whenever we have found a likely girl, either her mother will not let her go, or the girl is too afraid, or there is not money to pay for the school. Thy mother believes, and I think rightly so, that it would not only be a help to us, but a help to you in your own life. The days are gone when a Canienga could live out her life in our valley without having dealings with white people, and it will be easier for a woman who is not bewildered by them.

"But before you can learn at the English school, you must learn to speak the English language—at least enough to understand what is said to you. Your mother will start teaching you now. Pay attention to her while I make us something to eat."

From the moment that verdict was pronounced, the summer might just as well have not bothered coming at all. Si-isha's summer was a dreamworld assault of strange words and strange symbols: symbols drawn in the ashes of the hearth at first, then later with chalk on a piece of slate, to help her identify those lip-popping sounds so alien to her mouth.

Getting the sense of the written letters and individual words turned out to be the easy part; it was the way the English went about making thoughts longer than one word that made Si-isha's head feel like someone was whacking it with a wet moccasin. In all the varying dialects of Hodenosaune, people expressed themselves by taking a word and blending it with others, so that *karonta*, "tree," and *kowa*, "great," became Karontowanen: "the Great Tree." The English strung their words together like beads on a string, so that they only clicked against each other instead of singing in harmony.

The few times Si-isha was allowed to go roaming to let her *onikonhra* rest, she was less aware of the birds and flowers along the riverbank than that she was constantly tripping over her new leggings. The drawstrings were either tied too tight and were cutting off the blood below her knees, or were tied too loose and slipping down her calves. But she did have to admit she spent fewer evenings rubbing boiled-down sumac bark into nettle-scratched shins and ankles.

On her solitary rambles, she passed groups of girls her own age washing clothes in Canajoharie Creek and trading taunting songs with the boys out fishing in the deeper water. Once, one of the older boys ran up to her and gave her a fish he'd caught, and everybody laughed. But the expression in his eyes looked more like hunger and fear than good humor.

Once, when she wandered into the woods to get away from the heat of the day, she heard an odd thrashing and grunting sound. She moved forward cautiously and peered through the leaves. It was one of the girls from her grandmother's longhouse, with a man on top of her. Si-isha backed away and went back to her mother and her slate and chalk.

The leaves turned while she wasn't looking. The ripe corn was picked and shucked and stacked in its cribs to wait for shelling, or the husks were pulled back and braided together to make long bundles of multicolored corn ears hanging from the roof poles of the longhouse. Everyone else in Canajoharie busied themselves with preparations for the Harvest Thanks Giving, but not Si-isha. Her mother helped her squeeze all her possessions—her clothing, spoon, knife, sewing things, the silver broach her father had given her, her corn dolly—into her pack basket. The next morning, Carrying News appeared at the door of the longhouse. He lived alone on a farm a little ways downriver, and had volunteered to deliver Si-isha to Schenectady.

At the doorway of the longhouse, filled with the smells of baking pumpkins and cranberry dumplings and the sound of popping corn, Si-isha's grandmother said, "I will say good-bye to you here," and put her arms around her. "When next I see you, you will be teaching *me* things."

"I don't think so, Grandmother."

Mother and Muskingum walked Si-isha and Carrying News to the stockade gate. Muskingum was dragging his toes and snuffling: "Why does she have to go away?"

Mother said: "I have told you that ten times ten times. She will be back for the Midwinter Festival. You can't expect that you and your sister will be together every day of your lives."

Waiting outside the gate was a wagon like the white farmers rode in, with its back loaded down with sacks of the white man's tiny-kerneled corn. Carrying News lifted Si-isha's pack in among them and climbed up onto the seat. Mother held out a little deerskin pouch that clinked and weighed down Si-isha's hand when she took it from her. "That is money to pay for the school and buy what you need. Ask one of the other girls to show you how they make their dresses and where to buy cloth and English shoes. And a coat. They will look oddly at you if you go about wearing a blanket."

"Yes, Mother."

"Remember that we thirst for the day when we see you walk back through the door of the longhouse—and that if you use the *onikonhra* you were born with, you will learn as much and as fast as any two other girls, even though it may seem slow to you."

"Yes, Mother."

Her mother hugged her and kissed her forehead, then stepped back, wiping her eyes, and said: "Every day you make me prouder of you." And then Muskingum hurled himself against Si-isha and they were both soaking each other's necks with saltwater and clinging fiercely. Mother pried them apart. She didn't appear to understand, as Si-isha did, that no amount of explanation would stop Muskingum thinking that if his father could go away forever, so could anyone.

Carrying News reached down his hand to help Si-isha climb the wheel spokes to the wagon seat. He said to Muskingum: "Would you like me to bring you back a new knife from Schenectady?"

Muskingum replied, "In trade for Si-isha? Fair deal," and laughed through his tears.

Carrying News clucked to his team—each of them twice the size of any of the horses Si-isha's father had bought from the Delawares—and the wagon lurched into motion. By the time they reached the edge of the cleared fields, Si-isha's neck had cramped up from looking back. The trees closed in around the trail, and she turned to face forward, wiping her cheeks and rubbing the back of her neck. She supposed she should feel proud and privileged, but all she could think of at the moment was a family of lowly Mingoes she once knew.

CHAPTER 10

Si-isha grudgingly began to acknowledge that she didn't mind sitting high up on a wagon seat watching the valley of the Caniengas amble by. She did feel a little odd, though, when the trail came out along the riverbank and a canoe with two lithe-backed young men skimmed past as though the wagon were rooted in the earth.

She had never seen the valley past Canajoharie. The river was studded with wooded islands where a girl could easily build a little hut no one could see, instead of following the river down to the white man's school.

Just when she'd decided that Carrying News spoke to no one but his horses, he said in English: "Your mother tell me to speak only in English to you. She say you have learn it very well."

"She talk not so true."

"For the short time you have had, I think she *spoke* very true."

Si-isha gritted her teeth against that other horror of the English language. They couldn't be satisfied with just one word for "talk," they had to have "speak" and "say" and probably several tens of others. She closed her mouth and devoted her attention to the trail and the blazing reds and golds of the forest mounting into the sky, and the odd way Carrying News held his hands out in front of him with the four long leather reins ribboned through his fingers. His fingers were shorter and wider than her father's—not squat or blunt, just different, with a different kind of strength in them.

They crossed the river on a ferry run by a bearded white man who spoke in a bantering way with Carrying News and called him "Brant." As the trail wound down the eastern shore, they passed by more and more farms where the forest had been hacked away. Carrying News pointed out parts of their valley: "Those two hills that do push in against the river are the Noses. The Big Nose have many rattlesnakes; the Little Nose have many caves we do not tell the white man of. . . . The hill you see ahead there call by the white man 'Tribes Hill,' because there we Canienga all did meet in early days. . . ."

At the foot of a steep mountain the forest opened up around a mountainous stone building on the riverbank. There were pastures, orchards, gardens, barns, towers, and a building with a huge, turning wooden wheel splashing in a creek. The trail passed between the cluster of buildings behind the big stone one and the barns and fields on the other side of the creek, so Si-isha could see there was a town's worth of white people and black people, and Caniengas in white people's clothes, hoeing or scything or scrubbing or sheep-shearing or horse-training or leaning on fences.

Carrying News said: "This is Mount Johnson."

"Where lives Willya Johnson?"

"Willia*mmm* Johnson."

"Why does not you or some other Canienga man chop Willia*ng* Johnson's throat for him?"

Carrying News laughed and laughed.

The rutted trail grew into a wide, tramped-down road with no grass between the wagon tracks. They were still traveling when the sky began to mimic the autumn colors of the trees. Carrying News turned the wagon in among the trees and reined the horses in. "It is another half day travel to Schenectady. We will camp here."

"I no foods bringed for the burning."

"You bringed no food to *cook*. I know. Your mother offered to me to send food with you, but I tell her I got plenty enough."

Carrying News climbed off the wagon and lifted up his hands to clasp Si-isha's waist and lift her down. She gathered firewood while he tended to the horses. Carrying News struck a fire with flint and steel instead of a fire drill. Si-isha rummaged through his bag of food and found a chunk of cow meat and a loaf of the white man's bread. She cut a green stick to hang the cow meat over the fire. When the outside of the meat was brown and sizzling, they cut off slices and worked their way in layer by layer, eating the cooked slices while the fresh pink surface darkened and dropped fat flares into the fire. When their knives came down to the green bark of the spit, Si-isha licked the spit clean while Carrying News lit his short-stemmed pipe and made her talk English a little longer.

When his pipe was smoked out, Carrying News got up and laid some blankets on the ground under the wagon bed. He kicked off his moccasins, crawled between the blankets and said: "Come sleep with me."

She gawked at him across the fire. He folded back the corner of the top blanket invitingly, then shrugged. "If you want to sit and to watch the fire all night, do. But you will regret it in the morning." He rolled over on his side and tugged the blanket up over his ear.

She sat wondering what to do. She reminded herself that her mother had approved of her traveling with him. She reminded herself that the only clothes he'd taken off had been his moccasins, and that she was only a child still, even if she had been husk-covered and the front of her overdress stuck out a little.

But she was still sitting there when the fire died down to coals. She started to shiver. If she threw on fresh wood to flare it up again, she'd have to stay there long enough for the new flames to sink low enough to be left alone safely.

The dimming circle of firelight had shrunk to where Carrying News was just a vague lump under the wagon bed. The lump grunted in Canienga: "It's getting cold in here."

Si-isha stiffened her spine, threw some earth on the few flamelets still alive, and crawled to the wagon. His back was to the unoccupied half of the bed. She raised the edge of the top blanket, scuttled in without even taking off her moccasins and quickly rolled over with her back to his. She lay there like a strung bow, wondering what she should do—or would do—if he rolled over or reached his hand back. She began to regret putting her knife back in her pack. Then he started to snore, and she began to feel insulted.

She remembered hearing stories of men who liked other men instead of women. Maybe that was why he had no family. With that thought, she fell asleep.

That thought was still there when she woke up cold and alone to find Carrying News brewing tea over the morning fire. The thought consumed her while they ate cold corn cakes, hitched up the wagon and rolled back onto the road again. The dawn mists burned off and the day grew surprisingly warm, as though taking heat from the fire in the leaves. She grew more and more curious about why he lived alone and why he'd done what he'd done last night—or hadn't done. But it was very difficult to think of a way to ask him that wouldn't sound ill-mannered—especially in the English he'd relegated her to again. She thought about it for a long time, barely aware of the rumbling lurch of the wagon or the changing countryside, then hit upon: "Canadiorha, why . . . is it be . . ."

"If you say 'why is it,' Si-isha, you do not say 'be.' 'Is' and 'be' are the same thing."

"Well they do not goddamn sound the same."

"Hm. I wonder where your mother learn her English. But 'why' what?"

"Why . . . is it . . . fine gentleman like you . . . got no wife nor no childrens? I do not mean to be . . . oh damn . . . to be . . ."

" 'Rude.' And rude you are not being. Not with a friend, as I hope I am. The reason I have no wife and no children is . . . a bit foolish, I am afraid. But I have become accustom that I am a bit foolish and there ain't a whole hunk I can do about it. Long time ago, when I was almost young as you, I became in love with— Did your mother tell you that word 'love'?"

"Yes. Two *onikonhra* that are the same."

"Well, not always. But, so, when I was a boy I became in love with a girl—a woman—who was some bit older. Not much older, just enough that by the time I became old enough to ask a woman could I be a man to her, she was already wife to another—and a fine gentleman he was, too. It never left me. Oh, I liked other women, but those ones I liked a lot I liked too much to have them live their life with a man that loved somebody else. That is all there is to it. Like I did tell you, it is foolish, but . . . so it is."

"It is not foolish. It is beautiful. But sad."

Carrying News laughed. "Well, in English those three mean about the same thing. Or in any other language."

The dull thud and rumble of the horses' hooves and the wagon's wheels became a clatter and rattle as the earthen road became a lane packed down as hard as stone. Tall houses of wood and stone sprang up shoulder to shoulder, some of them with painted boards outside that Si-isha could read but didn't know: "Tavern." There were wagons and horses and white people everywhere. Some of the white men were standing nose to nose and yelling words at each other that Si-isha didn't need to know to understand. What she couldn't understand was how anyone could allow someone else to be so bad-mannered and not either walk away or draw a knife.

Carrying News turned the wagon onto a narrower trail that skirted a garden with white girls in big straw hats digging with hoes that were more like spoons. He halted the horses in front of a big house made of square orange stones and said: "Here we are."

The doorway wasn't covered by a curtain or a woven mat,

but by a slab of polished wood. Carrying News put his hand up to a brass earring made for a moose and made clicking sounds with it. The slab of wood was swung open by a monumental woman with skin as dark as a roasted chestnut and lips thicker than Muskingum's. She led them along a wood-walled tunnel and tapped her fist against another wooden curtain. A man's voice called from beyond it: "Enter."

There was a dark room made of wood and paper, with a thin man sitting behind a kind of big box made of wonderfully glossed-up walnut wood. Carrying News said: "I am Nickus Brant."

"Ah yes. And this would be your daughter. . . ."

"Not my daughter. The daughter of a friend of mine. This is Si-isha."

"How do you do, Sissy?" The thin lips stretched wide to expose two rows of teeth like a muskelunge's. "Welll . . . commme, Sissy. You . . . willl . . . bee . . . hap-pee . . . here."

Carrying News said: "She brings the money to pay you."

The hairless eyelids fluttered. "*She* does? Our girls don't usually . . . Very well, I'll have my wife attend to it."

Carrying News turned to Si-isha and said in Canienga: "May thee walk on moss until I see thee again, Si-isha. Come the midwinter moon, I will come in my horse sleigh, and you shall see the road home fly away beneath us."

Si-isha wanted to touch his hand or his shoulder, but his manner had become very stiff and distant the moment they crossed the threshold of the white man's house. So she just said in English: "Thank you, Canadiorha."

When Carrying News was gone, the thin man rang a metal bell and a fat, paste-faced woman came in and said something in a squirrellike chatter that Si-isha had to listen to again in her memory's ear to hear: "Come with me, dear."

Si-isha picked up her pack basket and followed the fat woman out the doorway. There was a strange arrangement of wooden boxes piled up in a hill, with wooden bars slanting up beside it. The fat woman climbed the hill. Si-isha took a firm hold of the rail and followed her dubiously. At the top of the hill was another squared-off tunnel with doorways on either side. The fat woman opened one of the doorways—Si-isha taking note of the metal ball that the fat hand turned to make the door move—and said: "This will be your room." Inside were three wooden pens with puffy white things inside them. "This afternoon there are no classes, the girls are working in the garden. Do you garden?"

"Guarding?"

"Garr-denn!" The fat woman made a hoeing motion at the floor. "Farm? Flowers? Corn?"

"Corn! Yes—but I have not no . . ." Si-isha imitated the hoeing motion.

"No fear, dear, we have plenty of garr-denn tools. Come down and join the other girls in the garr-denn."

"Yes! But . . . first I do . . ." She gestured down at her clothing.

"Of course, dear—first you must put on your garr-denn apron. I will be in the garr-denn."

As the door closed behind the fat woman, Si-isha stripped off her moccasins and leggings, pulled her overdress off over her head, tugged the money pouch out of the waistband of her skirt and tucked it into the top of her pack, then made the door work and headed happily down the wooden hill and out into the warm sunlight, relieved that there was at least something about this place she knew something about.

As she bounced out into the open air, the white girls in their broad straw hats looked up at her. Their mouths fell open and one of them squawked and fell backward into her flower bed. A couple of black men spreading sod stood up to gawk and grin. The fat, white woman came running toward Si-isha fluttering her apron and shrieking a stream of English too fast to understand.

Si-isha said, "What is—" but the fat woman didn't seem to hear her, just kept on shrieking and stripped off her apron to hold it up in front of Si-isha's breasts.

The white girls were laughing now. Si-isha's face was burning and she had to squint hard to keep the tears from coming out. The fat woman kept on shrieking while trying to open the door, push Si-isha back inside it and cover her with the apron at the same time. As she was dragged through the doorway, Si-isha yanked the apron up and shouted at the English girls in English: "Tits! No sun no grow!"

Si-isha sat on the edge of the wooden pen that the fat woman had told her was her "bed," with her overdress back on, crying. She didn't understand why white women were ashamed of having breasts, and didn't understand why her mother hadn't warned her.

She could hear the chirping of the white girls in the garden. At least they couldn't see her crying. She got up and went to the window—made of little squares of flattened bottle glass with the color taken out. The rows of pink flowers and bright-dressed, broad-hatted girls rippled as she moved her eyes along the glass. One of the girls looked up and pointed at the window. Si-isha backed away.

She went to the door and turned the brass ball. As she'd suspected, the clicking noises after the fat woman closed the door behind her meant the brass ball didn't work any more. She turned back to her "bed" and pushed down on the fluffy white thing fenced in wood. It felt like a bag of feathers. She sat on the edge of the frame and sidled her buttocks backward, then swiveled around and lay down.

She sank into the bag of feathers. It wasn't entirely unpleasant, but it didn't have the same spring as a willow-pole sleeping platform, and it did make her wonder how many white people suffocated to death in their sleep. It wasn't easy to get out of, either, but she managed, and set about exploring the rest of the cage she was locked in.

At the foot of each bed was a big wooden box. She raised the lid of the one at the foot of "her" bed and found it empty. The one next door was filled with clothing and little pouches and emanated a sweet, flowery smell. She closed the lid quickly, feeling like she was peeking into someone else's privacy, and went back to her own box and her pack basket. All her possessions, including the money bag, left the box less than half full. The last thing she put in was the little silver broach her father had given her when he came back from buying horses from the Delawares. He'd said: "One is hardly enough to ornament a skirt or an overdress, but when the boys back home get through trying to best each other with presents, you'll have so many rows of them you won't be able to stand up, just sit and shine and grow fat."

Two sets of footsteps were approaching the doorway. Si-isha closed the box and stood up. There were those same metallic clicking sounds, and the door was opened by the schoolteacher's fat wife. She said: "Do you know what you did wrong now, Sissy?"

"Yes." Although she still didn't understand why it was wrong.

" 'Yes, *ma'am*.' "

"Ma'am?"

"We call our elders 'ma'am'—or 'sir,' if it's a man."

"Yes, ma'am," although it was a fight to get her lips around two M sounds so close together.

The schoolteacher's wife stepped back into the hall and said: "All right, Juba, you can go in now."

A shrivel-faced little black woman with her arms full of white cloth shuffled in cautiously and said: "You ain't going to scalp me, now?"

"No, ma'am."

"Don't be calling *me* ma'am, missy."

"But she say—"

"That just for white folks, and not for white servants at that. I'ze just Juba. I just do the cooking 'round here—and the bed-making and floor-sweeping and everything everybody else too lazy to do."

Juba set down her layers of cloth and began to shake them out into thin white blankets and put them on the beds. Si-isha helped her, with Juba showing her how. "You tucks in the corners like this, missy. . . . This is how you puts the pillow in the case. . . ."

A twittering and stomping approached. Juba said: "You don't want to be helping me no more, missy."

Two girls came in. One was big and pudgy and had orange hair and orange flecks on her skin. The other one was thin and sharp and had yellow hair and skin like fresh snow. The orange one said: "I'm Hattie and this is Laura. And you're Sissy."

Si-isha wanted to correct her, but it would've been impolite to contradict someone directly, and perhaps white mouths found "Si-isha" as difficult as hers found "ma'am." So she just said: "Hello, Hattie. Hello, Laura."

Laura said: "My my, don't we talk white good," and proceeded with hanging her hat and apron on a peg and washing her hands in a big bowl on a wooden stand.

Hattie plumped down on one of the wooden boxes and said:

"We just have to get washed up and then we'll all go down for dinner."

" 'Dinner' . . . ?"

Yellow-haired Laura tossed over her bony shoulder: "Food. Heap good."

Hattie said: "Dinner is the evening meal. What do you call it in Mohawk? When the family sits down in the evening to eat together . . . ?"

Si-isha's mother had warned her that white people would call her Mohawk, and not to take offense. So Si-isha just answered the question: "Not do. Morning, Mother make a big pot of food and all eat together. Rest of day, any hungry, dip in pot."

"Oh." Hattie left it there and jumped eagerly to: "Do you know William Johnson?"

"No."

Laura tossed in airily: "I thought all the Mohawk girls _knew_ William Johnson."

Hattie said: "Pay no attention to Laura. Her family would be twice as rich if William Johnson hadn't set up shop upriver from Albany and bought all the furs coming down."

Laura said: "The man is a thief and a scoundrel and no better than an Indian himself."

A bell clanged from somewhere below. Hattie said, "That's dinner!" and leaped up to whip off her apron. Si-isha lifted the lid of her bed box and took out her bowl and spoon. Hattie said: "What's that?"

"My bowl and spoon."

Laura giggled: "Which is which?"

Hattie said: "There's plenty of bowls and spoons downstairs. We better get cracking so's we don't keep anyone waiting."

Si-isha allowed herself to be hurried out of the room, although the idea of eating with someone else's bowl and spoon didn't seem very clean.

Down the hill of wooden boxes there was a large room with two rows of one-person benches with backs on them, lined up on either side of a long, cloth-covered platform. Hattie whispered: "Sit by me." Si-isha did so gladly, as the other benches filled up with girls who smirked in her direction without meeting her eyes.

In front of Si-isha, and every other girl, was a blue and

white bowl and several small platters, flanked by several silver miniature fishing spears, dull-looking knives and spoons too small to be of any use. Hattie whispered mystifyingly: "Just start from the outside and work your way in." Si-isha reached for one of the long-handled, tiny-bowled spoons to get a closer look at it, but Hattie hissed: "Not yet!"

The schoolteacher stood up from his bench at the head of the platform. All the other girls lowered their heads and clasped their hands, so Si-isha followed suit. The schoolteacher gave a long speech thanking his father for providing what they were about to eat. Judging from the schoolteacher's gray hair, Si-isha would have thought his father was too old to do all the hunting and fishing and gardening for so many people.

When the speech was finished, two black women and a black man brought in three big, blue and white pots of soup, and each girl filled her own bowl. Si-isha watched which spoon Hattie picked up and how she held it. The soup had a great deal of salt in it, but it wouldn't be polite not to eat it all, even with a spoon that was awkward to hold and hardly held a mouthful.

The soup was brought away and meat and vegetables brought in. The little silver spear and dull knife were even harder to work with than the spoon. Si-isha naturally began to eat all her yellow beans first, then her meat, then the other items on her platter one by one. But she noticed partway through that Hattie was mixing different tastes together, so she did the same.

Juba the cook came in to help the other servants clear things away. Serendipitously, Si-isha had been feeling a big belch building up, so she let it out to show the cook her work was appreciated. All the other girls burst into laughter. The schoolmaster said: "Silence, ladies. Christian charity."

The schoolmaster's fat wife at the other end of the platform said: "Sissy, ladies hold their wind."

"But . . . how cook know food good?"

"A simple thank-you to your hostess will suffice. It ain't necessary to thank servants for doing their duties."

When Si-isha and Laura and Hattie were back in their room, Laura went behind a screen standing in one corner and came out wearing a frilly white garment, like a long overdress. Hattie did the same. Si-isha sat miserably on her bed box, unsure of what to do. Laura said: "Oh lordy, I bet they sleep in their skins."

Hattie said: "You got no nightgown, Sissy?"

Si-isha shook her head. "I must to ask you show me how you make English dresses."

Laura said: "*We* don't make dresses."

"You no sew?"

"Of course we do," Laura replied. "Fine sewing, such as embroidery and needlepoint. We hire a seamstress to make our clothing."

"Where is . . . seangstress?"

"I said we *hire* a 'seangstress,' and she sends the bill to our parents. I doubt any seamstress in Schenectady will trust to receive payment from 'Mohawk Wigwam, Somewhere Upriver.' "

"I have monies to pay."

"*You* have money?"

"Ten guineas, nine shillings and fourpence." They both gawked at her. "You got no monies?"

Laura sniffed: "Of course our *families* have money . . ."

Hattie said: "I'll ask tomorrow if the coachman can take you and me to the seamstress. Meantime, you can borrow one of my nightgowns, if'n you don't mind drowning in flannel."

What with the softness of the bed and the constricting feeling of sleeping in a dress—even one as big as a tent—Si-isha didn't sleep much. But the nightgown did smell wonderfully of an English herb Hattie said was called lavender.

In the morning there was another meal almost immediately. Si-isha found it difficult to eat when her body hadn't had a few hours' work to get it going, but she forced down a few mouthfuls for politeness. After the meal, the girls all trooped into a large room with little benches set in front of wooden ledges in rows. The schoolteacher opened a book and handed it to a girl on one of the front benches. The only book Si-isha had ever seen was Carrying News's Bible, which her mother had borrowed to show her what a book looked like.

The girl stood up and began to read. More than half the words were ones Si-isha had never heard before. It seemed to be a story about a child in England who had some troubles with his bowels, but she couldn't swear to it. The girl was still reading when the schoolmaster interjected, "That's enough.

Next," and the book was passed on. It seemed to Si-isha that people who spoke before someone else had finished speaking didn't have much to teach about good manners.

As the book worked its way down the rows of girls, Si-isha realized with terror that it was going to come to her eventually. When it did, she stood up and squinted at the page crammed with letters so cramped and curlicued she couldn't tell one from the other.

The schoolteacher said gently: "Can't you read, Sissy?"

"Yes. Some. But not so long word."

"Here." The schoolteacher opened a thinner book with bigger pages. "Try this."

The lines of letters were shorter and there were fewer on a page. She licked her lips and began: "Thu-ree—"

"Three," the schoolteacher interrupted.

Si-isha told herself not to be offended at something all white people seemed to do to each other, and just asked: "Like number?"

"Yes, Sissy. Just exactly right. The number three."

She refrained from asking: "Then why they don't goddamn write 3?" and started again. "Three blinn-ed mick-ee, three blinn-ed mick-ee—"

Laura exploded in giggles, and most of the other girls followed her lead. The schoolteacher said: "Ladies! Silence, if you please! I think that's enough for one day, Sissy." Si-isha gave him back the book and sat back down with her cheeks burning and her fingers knotted together.

At midday there was another meal, after doing nothing all morning but sitting. After barely enough time for so much food to even begin to settle, all the girls were herded into another big room—this one with cushioned sitting benches and pictures on the walls—for what Hattie told Si-isha was "Deportment."

The schoolteacher's fat wife picked up a book and said: "You see, Sissy, we not only eddycate ourselves by putting books *in* our heads, but *on* them." All the other girls laughed as though it were their duty. "Laura, would you show us how it's done?"

Laura stood up, and the schoolteacher's wife set the book on top of her head. The schoolteacher's wife stepped back. "Now, walk all the way around the room, Laura, please. . . . Good.

Now sit down on the chair. . . . Good. Pick up the teapot on the side table—Oh!" Laura caught the book as it fell. "I doubts even I coulda done that one. Sissy, would you care to try?"

Si-isha stood dutifully, and the schoolteacher's wife placed the book flat on her head. Si-isha knew there had to be some hidden trick behind the exercise: a person's head always stood straight up on a person's neck, unless the person was lying down, so why shouldn't a flat object on top of a person's head stay there? Dutifully following instructions, Si-isha walked around the room, sat down, stood up, picked up the teapot and put it back down, took down another book from a high shelf, took off her right moccasin and put it on again. . . .

Finally, the schoolteacher's wife said, "That's enough for one day, Sissy. Let's give some of the other girls a chance," and lifted the book off her head. It seemed there wasn't any trick to it after all. Perhaps it was wearing heeled shoes instead of moccasins that made white girls clumsy.

After Deportment, Hattie said: "You saved me from Music, Sissy. Coachman's waiting to take you and me to the seamstress."

The seamstress was a widow in a brick house on the edge of town. Hattie's happy gossiping along the way gave Si-isha an understanding of a new word every sentence. And Si-isha discovered that if she imitated Hattie's voice in her mind, English came off her tongue much more easily.

The seamstress showed them lovely bolts of calico and velvet and rolls of lace, saying: "With your eyes, dearie, you could even carry purple." Then the widow took out a long string with knots spaced along it and said: "Just shuck your dress, dearie, and I'll take your measure."

Si-isha looked confusedly from the seamstress to Hattie, mindful of white women's taboos about their bodies. Hattie said: "Um . . . I think Sissy don't wear underclothes."

"Oh. Then I'll have to make her a couple of shifts as well. That's all right, dearie, just raise your arms and I'll measure you in your clothes. . . . Hm, you keep growing like this, you'll need a corset soon. Enjoy hanging free while you can."

It took a week for Si-isha's new wardrobe to be delivered. During that time, she listened carefully to every voice around her and spoke as little as possible. She didn't mind Hattie laughing at her English, since it seemed that Hattie was laughing less at her than at oddities of words Hattie hadn't noticed before. But the other girls laughed differently, especially when Laura was there to lead them.

It was gardening day when the dresses and shifts and coat arrived. The cobbler still hadn't finished her shoes, but Si-isha was just as glad to have a few more days in moccasins. Once Hattie had buttoned her into her blue calico day dress, Si-isha gasped: "How do you *breathe*?"

Hattie stuck her tongue out in a gagging mask and said: "Wait'll you get corsets!"

Si-isha put on her new gardening apron and she and Hattie went down to join the other girls toying with their spoonlike hoes in the flower garden. Laura began to sing, "Thu-ree blinn-ed mick-ee, thu-ree blinn-ed mick-ee/Suh-hee how-oo thee-high roon . . ." and most of the other girls joined in. Si-isha tightened her lips and the corners of her eyes. She knew that if she took hold of Laura's yellow hair and dragged her skinny body to the manure pile, everyone would say it was just a wild Mohawk acting uncivilized.

Among the border of stones flanking the rose bed Si-isha was weeding, there was a flat, black, palm-sized stone with a gritty surface. Si-isha tucked it in the pocket of her new apron.

After dinner, when Si-isha, Hattie, and Laura were back in their room, Si-isha took the stone out of her pocket and took her knife out of the blanket box filled with her new clothes. She sat down ankles-to-hips on the lid, spat on her stone and began to hone her knife. Hattie said: "Why are you sharpening your knife?"

"Woman must keep knife sharp just like man's. When time to use, no time to stop and sharpen. Maybe tomorrow must cut up venison, or make strip of rabbit fur for weave blanket. Maybe tonight must cut throat of skinny little white pig while it sleep."

CHAPTER 11

The white men called the walled Hodenosaune towns "castles," and many Caniengas had fallen into the habit, along with other white man's habits. The town downriver from Canajoharie was called simply the Lower Castle. Muskingum and his mother went there on snowshoes one day.

It felt good to jog along the frozen river with the forest sleeping in its robes of snow on either hand. It was warm enough that they both pushed back the hoods of their coats to let the wind blow through their hair. Mother had put aside her winter blanket in favor of Father's old winter hunting coat, sashed tightly around the middle to keep it from falling off her. She looked pretty funny and Muskingum told her so. She pretended to be insulted and threw snow at him. But it seemed to Muskingum there was a sadness underneath her pretending. It took him a while to puzzle it out: with every intake of breath she was smelling the coat.

From time to time they slowed down to a walk to catch their breath, which gave Muskingum the chance to try to read the animal tracks in the snow as they went past. The pointy-toed ones with the snake curving through them were a muskrat. The trail of two little feet and two big ones, which came to an abrupt end with nothing but unbroken snow in front of it, showed where a rabbit had met up with an owl. But there was one set of prints that was just a zigzag line of little round holes in the snow, which might have been a fox, or a mink, or maybe something else. He asked his mother.

She said: "I do not know. It's time we found you a Teacher who can tell you such things."

"I'm too young yet to have a Teacher."

"In the normal way of things you would be, but you have no father to teach you the things most boys would learn before they start with a Teacher. Think over whether you know of a man you would like for your Teacher, and I will do the same."

As they got closer to the Lower Castle, a lot of high-pitched, shouting voices came through the trees. Muskingum and his mother rounded the bend above the town and found themselves on the edge of a battle. A lot of boys—maybe a hundred of them—had cleared the snow off a long stretch of Schoharie Creek and were playing baggataway on the ice, skidding and sliding and flailing their racquets like war clubs. On the bank opposite the Lower Castle, some white families were gathered in front of Fort Hunter to watch the Canienga boys play baggataway—which the whites for some reason called "lacrosse"—and the Canienga men gambling over who could skim his snow snake farthest.

Mother said: "After we have had something to eat, perhaps someone will loan you a baggataway stick so you can join in the game while I'm talking to the Oyanders."

"I'm not hungry." He'd been ravenous until he saw the game.

"Well, when you are, go in to one of the Wolf Clan long-houses and someone there will know where to find me."

Muskingum whipped off his snowshoes, stuck them upright in the snow and looked around for someone who might tell him how to get into the game. A group of men were standing halfway between the snow-snake run and the baggataway game, cradling their long, slickened hickory snow snakes, laughing and pointing out to each other whose sons were getting the best of it. Muskingum trotted over to them and asked which team was short of players.

A man with smallpox craters on his face said: "The white team. But you don't have a racquet."

Another man said: "My son has two. Here, take his spare one." He also handed Muskingum a band of white leather. In the summer it was much easier to see at a glance who was on your team, when everyone stripped down to breechclouts and painted their bodies red or white.

Muskingum tied the white band around his forehead, snatched up the borrowed racquet and ran out to join the game. As soon as his feet left the snow for the ice, they shot straight out in front of him, landing him squarely on his bottom. He slid full-tilt into the legs of the red-team boy running with the ball. The runner's legs came to an abrupt halt while the rest of him kept moving forward.

Muskingum disentangled himself, jumped back up and ran after the melee chasing the escaped ball. He got there just as one of the littler players on the red team—almost too little to be playing—scooped it up and made a clumsy attempt at a throw toward the white team's goal. After he'd completed the throw, one of the bigger boys on Muskingum's team—almost too big to still be playing on boys' teams—slid up behind him with his stick held crosswise and deliberately drove it into the smaller boy's back.

Muskingum caught a fleeting glimpse of shocked-wide green eyes as the little boy went down. Green eyes weren't unheard of among the Canienga. After all the generations of adopting captives to replace the endless war losses, no one could say any longer what a true Canienga was supposed to look like.

Muskingum spared a quick glance to make sure the green-eyed boy had hit the ice with his chest instead of his face, then charged after the ball with his moccasin soles slipping crazily underneath him. The ball came arcing back in his direction out of the flailing anthill around his team's goal. He tried to stop to meet it, but his feet kept skating on. He stretched his baggataway stick up as high over his head as he could reach and just managed to catch the ball in the webbing. He bobbled it as the momentum of his forward slide slowed enough that he could turn and run for the red team's goal. By that time they'd caught up with him, whacking their racquets at his arms and legs and angling him toward the snow banked up around the playing field. When there got to be too many of them, he hurled the ball forward at a knot of white headbands headed toward the red goal, then slumped forward with his baggataway stick propped across his knees, hauling in slow breaths to calm his bursting lungs.

The stampede of red and white headbands passed him by. Trailing after them came the little green-eyed boy, huffing and puffing but still waving his racquet gamely. Out of nowhere, the boy who'd knocked him down before appeared, paying no attention to where the ball had gone, and stabbed the butt of his stick into the smaller boy's stomach.

The green-eyed boy doubled over and went down. Muskingum straightened up and said to the big boy: "Don't do that."

"If the little half-breed can't take the game, he shouldn't play it."

Muskingum said: "That wasn't part of the game. That was some coward using the game as an excuse to beat up on people too little to fight back."

"And you think you're big enough?"

"Maybe I am." Muskingum's heart started beating harder. He had his doubts whether it had been the smartest thing to say, but he couldn't think of anything else.

The big boy came at him, swinging his racquet at his head. Muskingum threw his own stick up to block it. The hafts met with a crash that sent a shock back through Muskingum's elbows, but he managed to keep hold of his stick. There was an instant of strained stillness with the two sticks locked against each other. The big boy could either force Muskingum's racquet down by main strength or whip his own back for another swing. Before the boy could make up his mind, Muskingum broke the lock by chopping two-handed as hard as he could at the older boy's face. It hit home with a whack that broke the hoop around the webbing, and also the man-boy's nose. The big boy dropped his racquet, clapped his hands to the fountain of blood in the middle of his face and ran wailing away. Muskingum picked up the dropped racquet, dropped the broken one in its place, and ran toward the whooping mob that showed where the ball was.

But he had barely got back in the game when it began to stop. All the boys in his vicinity were lowering their racquets and stepping back. Muskingum was just starting to look around for an explanation when a heavy hand took hold of the back of his coat and spun him around. The big boy with the bloodied face was standing there, holding a crust of snow to his swollen nose, alongside a very large man with a glowering face, who said: "Is this the boy?" The big boy nodded. The glowering face focused on Muskingum. "Take me to your father."

"I can't."

"You mean you are afraid to."

"I am. He's in the Land of Souls."

"Then take me to your mother."

"I'm not sure where she is. She came to talk to the Oyanders of the Wolf Clan. . . ."

"I know where they are. Come along. But first, give my son back his baggataway stick that you stole."

Muskingum wanted to say: "I didn't steal it!" But it would have been very ill-mannered to directly contradict the man to his face, so he settled for handing over the racquet and mumbling: "I'm not a thief."

The three of them marched up the riverbank and through the gates of the stockade. It seemed that everyone they passed was staring at him. He could feel his ears burning, and not from frostbite.

The bloodied boy's father stopped at the doorway of a long-house and gestured the two boys to go in. About a dozen women, including Muskingum's mother, were sitting on mats around a crackling hearth fire. They broke off their conversation and looked at the doorway as the glowering man stooped through it, pushing the two boys ahead of him. The man said: "Forgive me, Oyanders, but I must show this boy's mother what he has done."

Muskingum's mother stood up. "I am his mother."

"You see my son. He was playing baggataway. Your son set upon him far back behind the teams chasing the ball, and broke my son's nose with a blow of his stick and took my son's racquet, which was a better one than his."

Mother turned her glittering eyes on Muskingum. "You are the one who did this?"

"Yes . . . but . . ." He struggled to find a way to explain what had happened without saying right out that the glowering man hadn't spoken the truth.

A cavernous, effortless voice emanated from somewhere behind Muskingum: "I believe I have a word or two that should be said beside this fire."

Muskingum looked back toward the doorway. The little green-eyed boy was standing there beside a lean, silver-haired man with a gold-edged black blanket draped over his left shoulder and under his right arm. The man had slanted eyes and a wide, puckered scar hooking upward from one corner of his mouth almost to his ear, so that one half of his face looked to be perpetually grinning. Muskingum had never been introduced to him, but certainly knew who he was: the Royaner whom the whites called King Hendrick.

King Hendrick said, "My son, Willy," settling his right hand on the green-eyed boy's shoulder, "tells me he was playing today in his very first baggataway game—a great day in a boy's life." The white-sleeved right arm rose up again to gesture, as Hendrick paced slowly toward the Oyanders while he spoke. "My son Willy was doing his best to keep up with the game, but his legs are still short and awkward, and a baggataway stick itself is taller than he has grown yet. But even though he touched the ball but rarely, he threw his heart into the game as a boy should, and did his best to keep up with the longer legs, and took the blows on his arms as manfully as the other boys.

"But it seemed to him that there was something that was not part of the game as it was meant to be played. There was a bigger boy on the other team, a much bigger boy, who would knock Willy down from behind when the play was long past— even spearing him with the butt end of the stick." The merest hint of a jabbing motion from Hendrick's right hand made Muskingum feel the stick butt in the pit of his stomach. The marvelous, white-sleeved right arm went on gesturing as though it had a life of its own, dancing partner to the impossibly deep voice for such a thin chest. "But none of the other boys said what the big boy did was wrong. So Willy— knowing no better—did not cry out against it, but did his best to rise up again and again and follow the game, though it grew harder each time.

"And then a stranger, a boy Willy had never seen before, a boy playing for the other team, spoke up and said to *your* son," the scar-crossed face and gesturing arm swiveled back toward the glowering man, " 'What you are doing to this smaller boy is not baggataway—it is the way of a coward and a bully.'

"Your son, much bigger and older than the stranger, did not take the just rebuke as any person with honor would, but instead came at the stranger swinging his racquet at his head. The stranger defended himself, as any boy or man would. And that is how your son came to have his nose squashed flat like the frog the tree fell on." The swan-wing right arm fluttered down to roost beside the black-blanketed, thin chest.

The glowering man looked down at his son and said a terrible thing: "You have shamed me." The boy didn't quite shrivel up into a cinder, as Muskingum would have, but he did turtle his head down between his shoulders and twist his arms together. "You will give your baggataway stick to this boy to replace his, which he broke on your lying face."

Muskingum said: "It wasn't my stick. Mine's back in Canajoharie. I had to borrow one here."

"Then my son's will go to the boy you borrowed it from. Royaner—I thank thee and thy son for stopping me from causing further shame. Come, boy."

Muskingum felt bad watching the bully follow his father out the doorway, but he couldn't think of anything to say that might soften things. King Hendrick turned to him and said: "You are the son of A Man Tying on His Snowshoes . . . ?" Muskingum couldn't find his voice, so he just nodded. "It shows. My son and I will remember thee. Oyanders, forgive me for intruding upon thy council."

On the way back home, Muskingum said to his mother: "I thought of someone I'd like for my Teacher."

"Who is that?"

"King Hendrick."

"Um-hm. That is a very wise choice. I'm sure you could not ask for a better Teacher, and he would not take the responsibility lightly. No more lightly than he takes his responsibilities as a Royaner. Some say he should never have taken Willy for a son, because he already has so many people pulling at the hem of his blanket, he can hardly attend to his own children. But he did, because William Johnson asked him. If he asked him to be your Teacher I believe he would say yes, because of your father and because of today. But it would be another stone for him to carry. Shall we ask him?"

"No, I guess not."

"I know it seems impossible that a mere boy could show kindness to a man as great as Hendrick, but you have just done so. I have been thinking on this matter of your Teacher, too."

But she said nothing more about it. A little farther on, when the blue shadows on the snow were deepening to purple, she sheered off toward the riverbank. Muskingum guessed she was just looking for a place in the woods to squat for a moment, so he stopped and waited. She looked back over her shoulder and beckoned him to come along.

There was a clearing with a little log house and many horses in a maze of fencing. Wood smoke and the lowing of cows rose from the snow-wreathed chimney and the white-capped shed behind it. Mother crouched by the door of the cabin to take her snowshoes off. She hesitated in front of the door, raising her fist as though to knock like the white men did, then just pulled the door open and walked in. Muskingum followed her.

Carrying News was sitting at the table, darning a woolen sock by the light of a candle and the hearth. He glanced up, set the sock down with a clunk, and went wordlessly to the hearth. Muskingum's mother pulled Father's hunting shirt off over her head, went to the table and sat in a chair. Muskingum followed suit reluctantly. Chairs were an awkward invention—you couldn't lean or stretch out—but Mother had told him they were something he would have to learn to get along with.

Carrying News came back from the hearth with two tin cups of tea, set them down in front of Mother and Muskingum, then sat back down and picked up his own cup. After they'd all taken a sip, Carrying News said: "You're a long way from home with the sun going down."

Muskingum's mother replied: "We had to go to the Lower Castle. There is enough of a moon to light us home."

They sipped some more, and Mother and Carrying News talked of this and that while Muskingum calculated how close they'd be to Canajoharie and his grandmother's corn-and-pumpkin pudding if they hadn't stopped here. He became interested in the conversation when his mother related the story of the baggataway game and King Hendrick and the boy with the busted nose. When she was done, Carrying News said to him: "And you didn't take his scalp?"

Mother said: "It's time Muskingum had a Teacher. I think you would make a good one."

Muskingum was taken by surprise. Carrying News seemed more capable of teaching a boy to be a white farmer than a Canienga warrior.

Carrying News pushed his shoulders back against the rungs of his chair, clasped his hands together and thrust his arms out forward to make an inside-out cat's cradle of his fingers. Finally he said softly to Muskingum's mother: "It kindles a warm fire in my *onikonhra* that you should think so much of me. But there is another honor, even greater, that would stop me from becoming Muskingum's Teacher. If that other, greater honor is not to be—then, yes, I would be proud to teach as best I can the son of A Man Tying on His Snowshoes."

Mother said: "What honor do you mean?"

Carrying News looked at his fingernails and said: "A boy's father cannot be his Teacher."

Muskingum's mother's eyes grew wider. She stared across the table at Carrying News for what seemed like a very long time. Muskingum kept glancing back and forth between the two of them, waiting for one of them to say something further about the matter at hand, which was him. But when Mother's lips finally parted, it was only to say: "We are a long way from home with the sun going down."

CHAPTER 12

The week that most of the other girls went home for Christmas and New Year's, Si-isha stayed behind, making up in advance for the week she would go back to Canajoharie for the Midwinter Moon. It seemed odd that the whites should have their Midwinter Festival when the winter was just getting started, but Si-isha was beginning to get the impression that all white customs were created for another country with a different climate.

The last class the day before Carrying News was finally due to come and fetch her was Divinity Class. Once a week the minister from the church down the street would come to teach the girls about the Bible and the Hymnal and the Book of Common Prayer. Some of the stories in the Bible were entertaining, if a bit rude, and the message wasn't all that different from that of Hiawatha and the Peacemaker.

Today's Divinity Class was just easy questions so the girls could all feel proud of themselves. The minister asked them about faith, hope, and charity, and who came to the manger and who killed God's son. And then he asked: "How did this world and all things in it come to be?"

Si-isha had never volunteered in Divinity Class before, preferring to keep in the background while her grasp of the English religion and language grew more certain. But now she felt an impulse that she tried to resist. As usual, she didn't succeed. The minister beamed when he saw her hand go up. "Sissy, could you tell us how the world was created? Don't be nervous if you don't get it all perfectly, just tell us as much as you can remember."

Si-isha stood up, clasped her hands in front of her and said: "A long time ago, a woman of the Sky People fell through a hole in the clouds down to the Water World. She would have drownded, but two geese flew under her arms as she was falling and set her down on the back of a turtle."

She was aware of a stunned silence around her, punctuated by a few stifled titters. The minister's face was turning purple, but he appeared to be having some difficulty deciding whether she was making a fool of herself or him. She hurried on before he could make up his mind: "But the Woman Who Fell From the Sky couldn't live on the back of a turtle forever, and there was no land to set her feet on. A beaver offered to dive down to the bottom of the Water World and bring up some land for her. He dove down and down and was gone for a long time until his drownded body bobbed back up.

"The otter said that he would try, but he drownded, too, without ever reaching the bottom. Then the muskrat dove. He was gone far longer than the other two and he came back up drownded, too—but in his paws was clutched a little piece of earth.

"The Sky Woman set the piece of earth on the edge of the turtle's shell and fell asleep on the turtle's back, rocked by the waves. When she woke up, the piece of earth had grown into all the land in the world, and little willow trees—the first trees—were growing along the edge of it.

"To this day, the land still rests on the back of the Great

Turtle. Which is why we call this land that you call North America, Turtle Island. Another time I could tell you of the Sky Woman's twin grandsons, the Creator and the Destroyer, but that's most likely enough for one day."

She sat back down again. The minister unlocked his jaws and bit out through the gap: "That was a very amusing story, Sissy. But we are here to learn about the revealed Word of the One True God and his son, our Lord Jesus Christ—not about superstitious heathen nonsense."

"Well, it makes at least as much sense as some old man in the clouds making people out of mud."

So once again Si-isha spent the bulk of her afternoon in the kitchen helping Juba the cook peel potatoes. Wizened little Juba was more usefully educational than the minister, anyway. She told wonderful stories of her childhood in a steamy forest on the other side of the ocean, which rested on the back of a huge, gray animal with ears like barn doors and a nose like a snake. She also told gruesome stories about chains and auction blocks and masters who'd used her to make lighter-skinned slaves until she grew too old and ugly. Si-isha was beginning to get the distinct impression that the white people's religion didn't have a whole hell of a lot to do with how they lived their lives.

While she and Juba peeled potatoes, Si-isha got to play Teacher for a while, teaching Juba a Canienga corn-husking song that wasn't unsuited to potato-peeling. As fair trade, she coaxed Juba into singing Si-isha's favorite of her songs, which Juba was wary of singing when anyone else might overhear:

De white man got de whip
and de white man got de triggah,
But de Bible and Jesus
made a slave out o' de niggah.

All in all, Si-isha would've been quite happy to get herself "punished" every day by being banished to the kitchen— except that her mother and grandmother had sent her to Schenectady to learn to read the *onikonhras* of white people, not their black slaves.

In the morning, Si-isha packed her pack basket—leaving her constricting, white-style dresses and the horrible heeled shoes in the trunk at the foot of her bed—then went down into the parlor to try to finish the needlepoint sleeve band for Muskingum before Carrying News arrived. She expected that even Carrying News's swift horse sleigh would take at least half the day to reach Schenectady, so she was surprised when he walked through the door before she'd got her needle threaded. She was even more surprised when her mother followed him in.

Si-isha could feel the pitying glances of the other girls seeing that Indian men were so unchivalrous as to precede a woman into the room. She pitied them in return. The Hodenosaune had little notion of women as fragile, helpless creatures. About the only special treatments a Hodenosaune woman received were that her blood price was twice that of a man's, and if she and a man were going through a doorway, the man always went first—in case there was a knife waiting on the other side.

Si-isha's mother, instead of flinging her arms around her, adopted the same stiff formality that Carrying News had when he'd crossed the white man's threshold in the autumn. She stopped a few feet away from Si-isha and said in English: "Well, daughter, are you ready to come home for a few days?"

"You can bet the farm on that, Ma."

Mother went in to talk to the thin schoolteacher and his fat wife. Carrying News stood looking out the frost-laced parlor window. After a few moments the schoolmaster's wife came out of the office to say, "Mister Brant . . .?" and beckon him inside, which seemed strange. What seemed stranger was the simpering look she cast in Si-isha's direction.

When Mother and Carrying News came back out, Mother said, still sticking to English, "You and me, Si-isha, we walk outside in the garden some little time before we go. Canadiorha, he take your bag."

Out among the stubs of winter-clipped rosebushes poking through the snow, Mother said: "So the English has come easier to you?"

"Better'n my Divinity."

"Hm. Already you have words I do not know. Your teachers say you learn fast. They say after this year and one more you will have learn as much as any girl who come here already English. You change so much in so little a time. . . ." Although it seemed to Si-isha her mother wasn't saying that as much as working her way around to saying something else. "And things do change at Canajoharie the same time. I now be Someone Lends Her a Flower."

Si-isha felt a tightening in her throat. "Grandmother is . . . eating strawberries?"

"What? No—Oyander name not the same like Royaner. Not die, just step back. So much of English you have learn while I have teach you so little to be Hodenosaune, not Mingo." She seemed to hesitate, then went on: "And other things themselves do change. . . . Were you surprise to see Carrying News and me here so soon in the day?"

"You coulda knocked me over with a feather."

"Why would I wish to . . . ? Well, to tell what I mean to tell, why we can be here so soon in the day is because we come to Schenectady last night and stay in an inn. Carrying News and I. In the same bed. Because we have been married. Married as Hodenosaune. We will be married in the church soon, because Carrying News is a Christian like his father. I thought to tell you in a letter, but—"

"You're *her*!"

"I am who?"

"The woman Carrying News loved, who married someone else! That's why he never married."

"What kind of story is this?"

"It's true. Carrying News told me, when he was bringing me to school. He said he'd always been plum crazy for this older woman."

" 'Older'?" Mother arched her eyebrows. "Then it could not to be me. But what I was begin to say, before you spoke while I was speaking—"

"I'm sorry, Mother."

"Some things they do not teach you very good here. But what I was to say: when Carrying News and me are married in the church, you and Muskingum will have to be baptize, and you will have for to . . . have to— Oh, goddamn this English," and she switched to Canienga. "You and Muskingum will have to take Christian names, to go along with Brant. I hope you will be happy to have Carrying News for a father. He is not A Man Tying on His Snowshoes, but he is a good man."

"I think so, too."

When they came out of the garden to Carrying News's sleigh, he kissed Si-isha and called her "daughter." They climbed in and settled wraps of fur and blankets over their legs. Carrying News popped the whip over the horse's head.

Si-isha had seen cutters skimming back and forth along the road beside the school, but she'd never ridden in one. The soaring feeling of gliding smoothly instead of bouncing and jouncing, and the rush of air against her cheeks, were as freshening as the morning's first faceful of cold water.

But the flush on her mother's cheeks wasn't just from the nipping of the wind, and the sparkle in her eyes wasn't just a reflection of the sunlight glinting off the snow. She giggled and flirted like a girl. Si-isha found it a little unsettling, but all in all she was grateful to Carrying News for the transformation, and more than a little astounded at his ability to work miracles. But she still couldn't bring herself to call him "Father."

Carrying News had been right when he'd said the two-day trip would take less than a day in the cutter. The journey also wasn't quite as far. The sun was setting when they turned off the road a few miles short of Canajoharie, up the side trail to Carrying News's farm. Muskingum came flying out the cabin door. When the kissing and clasping and weeping had slowed down enough for Si-isha to step back and have a look at him, she saw that he'd grown even taller. That made her weep harder. It was the first time in their lives he'd grown since the last time she saw him.

Carrying News apologized that his house hadn't been built for a family. He would add on new rooms in the summer, but at the moment the only sleeping arrangements were a small side room for him and Mother, a pile of quilts and blankets rolled up in one corner of the main room for Muskingum, and another roll of bedding on the other side of the hearth for Si-isha. Si-isha would've been just as happy to forgo the rooms and walls and lie down to sleep in a longhouse with a dozen other families on either hand. Happier, in fact.

She and Muskingum sat up whispering long after their mother and her husband had gone to bed. Muskingum said: "Is the white school worse than being husk-covered?"

"Not so hard, but longer. It hurts your head instead of all over."

"Do they feed you good?"

"Not like home food. The cook says she could make much better food, but they won't let her use much pepper."

"Pepper?"

"Something like salt, but different."

"At the Ripe Corn Festival we had popcorn pudding and boiled squash-flower sauce and beans in bear grease and . . . I thought we'd had some Thanks Giving feasts on the Ohio, but I was wrong. Tomorrow the False Faces will be out, and the Corn Husk Society. . . . We never saw Corn Husk people on the Ohio. They wear masks and false hair all made from pieces of the tallest of the Three Sisters, and they make sick people better, just like the False Faces. Grandmother says when the Husk Face Society wears their masks, they *are* the people that live under the Turtle, that taught the True People how to grow food out of the earth."

" 'The True People' . . . ?"

"My Teacher says when there weren't white men here, people just called themselves Hodenosaune or Delaware or some other nation. But now, we know that there's white people—no matter if they're Dutch or French or English—and there's us True People of Turtle Island, no matter if we're Hodenosaune or Ojibway."

It did seem odd to have her little brother teaching her things. She said: "Mother told me you had a Teacher, but said it wasn't up to her to tell me who it was."

"King Hendrick's brother, Little Abraham."

Si-isha vaguely recalled a man almost as short and shriveled and dark as Juba. "Does he treat you hard?"

"Sometimes. He has to make me strong before I'm husk-covered. I heard some older boys talking about when they were husk-covered. One of them said he had to take a sharp stone every morning and make his shin bleed. The other ones laughed like that was nothing."

Si-isha built up the fire and sat staring into the flames. She'd never been in Carrying News's house before, but as long as her brother was lying down to sleep in the same room, and her mother nearby, she was home.

In the morning, Carrying News appeared in a black broad-cloth suit of clothes, with knee-high white stockings and buckled shoes instead of moccasins. After eating, they all climbed into the cutter and headed downriver to Queen Anne's Chapel of the Mohawks. The queen's coat of arms was painted over the door. Inside was a reed organ in one corner with wooden tablets above it inscribed with the Lord's Prayer and Ten Commandments in Canienga. On the altar were the immense Bible and silver communion service that the queen had presented to King Hendrick and Carrying News's father and the other two "Indian kings."

Si-isha's mother whispered to her: "We thought Mary and Joseph would make good Christian names for you and Muskingum. Is that all right with you?"

"One's as good as another, I guess." But she wondered when she was ever going to get a name of her own.

There were only the four of them and the minister in the chapel. The minister read out a lot of nonsense about Si-isha's mother obeying Carrying News, and that the husband was to his wife what Christ was to his church. Then he told Carrying News he was now allowed to kiss the bride, which—if the ride in the cutter was anything to go by—he'd been doing nothing but for the last few months without permission.

The minister led Si-isha and Muskingum over to a stone basin and dipped his fingers in. "Mary Brant, I baptize thee in the name of the Father and the Son and the Holy Ghost. Joseph Brant, I baptize thee . . ." Muskingum looked very solemn and serious about it all, but then he hadn't had the advantage of alternating Divinity Class and Juba.

Back at Carrying News's house, Si-isha's new stepfather changed his clothes again. It was the first time Si-isha had seen him dressed entirely like a Canienga, even down to shaking his hair free from the ribbon that bound it at the back of his neck. They all four squeezed themselves back into the cutter between baskets of corn and bags of sassafras and tobacco and a frozen side of beef.

The cutter made music as it went along, of jingling harness bells and drumming hooves and hissing runners. But even before the walls of Canajoharie Castle came into view, Si-isha began to hear another drumming and the sound of several hundred voices singing in unison.

Carrying News hitched the horse to one of the palisade pickets and they left the cutter there. As they passed through the gate, Mother said: "Now, Si-isha, you will see a true festival for the first time. There is no reason for you to feel afraid or awkward. Remember you belong here as much as anyone."

"Yes, Mother."

Inside the stockade the only living things in evidence were the dogs and crows. Si-isha felt an eerie fancy that all the people had been witched away, then scoffed at herself. The mountain of sound rising out of the big ceremonial longhouse was ample proof that everyone was crowded inside. Nonetheless, the webs between her knuckles tingled as she walked with her mother and brother and stepfather toward the longhouse with the painted pole in front of it.

Just as they reached the doorway, two demons jumped out, one two-legged and one four. The two-legged one was a man of the False Face Society, wearing the twisted, goggle-eyed visage of Old Crooked Nose, the Great World-Rim Dweller. The four-legged demon was a dog rigged up with a mask like a wild pig's face.

Old Crooked Nose howled through his contorted, swollen mouth and shook his turtle-shell rattle in Si-isha's face. His dog jumped up at her and snarled through his pig snout, getting into the spirit of things. Carrying Nowa produced a bribe of tobacco and the demons let them pass.

Si-isha stooped through the doorway after her mother, straightened up and stopped moving. The longhouse was filled with brightly dressed singers, crammed happily knee to knee along the benches lining the walls or standing in rows. At the center of the longhouse a dozen men in a circle kept up the rhythm with water drums, rattles, and Jew's harps, and led the singing with their voices. Through the firelit haze around the drummers, cavorted and leaped the men of the False Face Society, and men and women Si-isha guessed must be the Corn Husk Society, from their crinkly yellow hair and corncob noses.

She recognized the song as one of gratitude to the Three Sisters for seeing the Canienga through the past year and into the one to come. But it was a much more complex and enveloping version than she remembered from the Ohio, given so many voices to take different parts and harmonies. And this version wasn't all solemn. There were lines woven through it for the men to sing, comparing their women to Sister Bean, who wraps herself around anything that stands up straight and spreads out fickly in every direction.

She realized that she'd been homesick for the past six months for something she'd only known dimly. What it truly meant to be a Canienga was here around her for the first time, with everyone one in celebration of it.

She felt a sudden stinging sensation against her arm. She looked down and discovered it was only her mother's hand reaching back to touch her elbow—her skin was so tingly, the touch had felt like a bee sting. Her mother's mouth moved, but no voice could penetrate that echoing roar. Si-isha cupped her hand behind her ear and shook her head. Mother gestured toward a bench where Grandmother sat singing her lungs out and stamping her feet in time. They started toward the bench, but before they got to it, there was some signal Si-isha didn't understand and everybody rose up to dance.

Si-isha did her best to imitate her mother and grandmother and the other women. There seemed to be two kinds of steps to the women's dance: a stiff-armed shuffle and a short-hopping stomp. The men danced with leaps and whoops, with the women sidling shyly around them singing soft soprano undertones to the bellows of their men. But it seemed to Si-isha there was something decidedly sly in the shyness and softness.

She would've been far too embarrassed to pick out any man to dance around. But they came to her, young men with painted faces and caps of silver filigree and feathers, vying to show who could jump the highest or whoop the loudest. She did her best to pretend she didn't notice them.

The dancing went on for a long time and then the music stopped. Si-isha collapsed on a bench. Six months of lifting nothing heavier than a book or a crochet hook hadn't done much for her endurance. The Clan Mothers and their male cooking helpers left the longhouse and trooped back in with platters of everything generations of cooks could invent out of corn, beans, squash, pumpkins, venison, maple syrup and apples, fish and bear fat, dried berries and wild herbs.

After six months of English food and an afternoon of dancing, Si-isha had an appetite. She was wolfing down a concoction she'd never tasted before when her grandmother said: "It isn't necessary to eat *all* of festival food to show good manners. What you're eating is made by the women who are

Keepers of the Faith, out of all the gifts of the garden and the forest mingled together. Every night of the festival each family must take some of it home to eat in their own longhouse."

Si-isha's family became part of her grandmother's longhouse again for the five days of the festival. On the first night, Si-isha noticed Carrying News unfurling his blanket on Mother's sleeping platform, and whispered to Grandmother: "I thought that wasn't right."

"What wasn't right?"

"A Seneca Oyander told me a man couldn't sleep in his wife's longhouse until he'd started a child inside her. Is it different for us Caniengas?"

Grandmother's mouth twisted into a strange smirk. "No, Si-isha, it isn't different."

Si-isha would've thought it difficult to fill up five days with one festival. But in between the feasting and dancing and singing there was the Dream Speaking, the public confessions of last year's mistakes, the False Face Society going from longhouse to longhouse to banish the bad ghosts of the old year, the Keepers of the Faith stirring the ashes out in every hearth to kindle new fires for the new year.

And besides the Dream Speaking, there was the Dream Guessing. As everyone gathered in the ceremonial longhouse again, Grandmother explained: "You see, Si-isha, there are some dreams that root so deep the dreamer cannot speak of them. But if the yearning felt in the dreamworld is not satisfied, the dreamer's *onikonhra* will shrivel up and wither like corn deprived of sun. So, all the dreamer can do is act out the dream to the Keepers of the Faith and hope one of them can guess what the dream was and, more important, what it was trying to tell the dreamer."

Si-isha watched the Keepers of the Faith puzzle out that one boy's dream meant he wished his Teacher wouldn't push him quite so hard; that a lame old woman yearned to travel once before she died, to visit her son who'd married a Cayuga woman; and that a young man yearned to spend a night with his brother's wife—which last the Keepers of the Faith determined wouldn't be wrong, since he and she were of different clans. Provided, of course, that the woman was amenable.

Then a woman who was neither young nor old began to crawl about the floor as though looking for something. She stood up and began to make motions with her hands as though pulling on a rope. As the Keepers of the Faith murmured bemusedly, the woman grew more frantic, alternately searching the floor or the longhouse walls and pulling on her rope: sometimes pulling down, sometimes up, sometimes sideways.

The invisible rope Si-isha was watching the woman tug suddenly transformed itself into something else. The rope-pulling could just as easily be hoeing motions, except hoeing at earth that kept disappearing into the air. Out of Si-isha burst: "She wants her own garden!" The Keepers of the Faith turned to Si-isha, offended, but the woman stopped searching and beamed at her.

An Oyander said: "If that is true, I believe my sisters will agree she may have five furrows of her own this year—if attending to her five furrows does not keep her from doing her part in the furrows that belong to us all."

As the next Dream Guessing started, Grandmother settled her hand on Si-isha's shoulder and murmured: "They didn't teach you *that* at Schenectady."

During that day's feast two guests arrived who'd been taking part in the festival at the Lower Castle. One was the Royaner King Hendrick, and the other was a beefy white man even taller than Hendrick: William Johnson, whom the Caniengas had named Gets Business Done. They sat down among the Royaners in the center of the ceremonial longhouse. As Si-isha ate she couldn't help but sneak curious glances at the man whom some named a thief and a scoundrel, some named a good friend to the Caniengas, but all named the richest and most powerful man in the Mohawk River valley, white or Canienga.

Except for a clubbed brown wig, he was dressed entirely in Canienga festival clothes that seemed to sit naturally on him. He looked to be nearer Hendrick's age than Carrying News's, but he still ate robustly and had a laugh like an overgrown child—a *very* overgrown child. Caniengas weren't in the habit of sputtering and flushing like Si-isha had seen white people do in the face of someone they deemed important, but she could see the Royaners vying to be the one to pry that big, booming laugh out of William Johnson.

After the feast, King Hendrick gave a speech of thanksgiving, and then Gets Business Done did. His was naturally not as eloquent as Hendrick's, but his Canienga was only slightly eccentric, and there seemed to be genuine gratitude in his thanks for the feast and all the other good things that had come his way in the past year.

As the two great men were leaving, they passed by the spot where Si-isha's grandmother was showing her the steps for the next Woman's Dance. William Johnson stopped and said: "I greet thee, Oyander."

Grandmother said: "I am no longer Oyander, Gets Business Done. My daughter is now Someone Lends Her a Flower. This is my granddaughter, Si-isha."

"I greet thee, Si-isha."

Si-isha couldn't raise her eyes to meet his and couldn't think of anything else to say, so she just bobbed her head and just barely stopped herself from making a curtsy as they'd taught her in Deportment. Then William Johnson was gone and the drums were beating again.

The five days came to an end. It was horrible to have to climb back into the cutter to drive back to the Brant farm, because that meant she'd be on her way back to school the next day. Muskingum took her around the farmyard and the surrounding woods to show her all the things he'd discovered about their new home. They were leaning on a fence and he was pointing out the names of Carrying News's horses when he suddenly turned away from her and said: "Sometimes when you miss someone it's almost worse when they come back for a while, because you know they'll only go away again and leave you alone."

"You're not alone here. There's Mother here . . ." Even as she said it, she knew it wasn't the same now that Mother had a new man who had started a new child inside her. ". . . and Carrying News, and Grandmother nearby, and your Teacher, and the other boys. . . ."

He didn't turn to face her, just stood there with the shoulders of his blanket coat quivering and the white puffs of breath huffing out. He said: "And you have your teachers and the other girls, so you're not alone."

"I am."

He turned around and she put her arms around his scrawny, too-tall-too-fast torso. He snuffled: "My Teacher says it's all right for a warrior to cry if the pain is in his *onikonhra*, not his body." She just sniffed and patted his back, then let out a grunt as his arms tightened around her. "Just last Midwinter Moon, maybe we Mingoes didn't have much of a festival, but we were all together."

"I know." She leaned her cheek against the top of his head. "But I'll be back here all summer. And then just one more year and I'll never have to go away again." He pushed against her harder and they fell in the snow, fighting to wash each other's faces.

PART TWO

GETS BUSINESS DONE

He always did more than he promised.
—*Documents Relative to the Colonial History of the State of New York*, correspondence regarding William Johnson

CHAPTER 13

Big Billy Johnson of County Meath and points west woke up cold and alone. It only wanted "wet" to make it a clean sweep.

It had been almost three years since pretty Yellow Shoes had died, along with his third son to be born at Mount Johnson, but there were still occasional mornings when he woke up expecting to find her there beside him. Not that there hadn't been plenty of lively young darlings in the interim, as there had been while she was alive, but even the jolliest of dalliances wasn't quite the comfort of a wife.

He muttered to himself, "Ye're gettin' demmed domestic in yer dotage, Billy," pushed his nightcap back out of his eyes, fumbled the bed curtains open, snatched the little silver bell off the night table and gave it a tinkle. When that elicited no noticeable response, he gave it a good clanging, then bellowed: "Horace!"

After a moment there was a clatter on the stairs and Horace appeared in the doorway holding a greasy silver salver with a cup and napkin balanced precariously upon it. Horace had been promoted from footman to valet when old Adam grew too old to be running up and down the stairs, and he was shaping up to be a disaster. After six months of valethood he still walked like a Dutch farmer's son, dressed like a Dutch farmer's son, and smelt like a Dutch farmer's son.

Watching Horace gallumph toward the bed, Johnson seriously considered sending back to the Auld Sod for a real gentleman's gentleman—or, better yet, to London. Reluctantly, he let the notion go. Any real gentleman's gentleman would quiver in his silken hose at the idea of coming to dwell among the wild Mohawks.

Horace said, " 'Morning, Mr. Johnson," and set the salver down on the night table.

"And the grandest of good bleedin' mornin's t'ye, too, Horace." As Horace tied back the bed curtains, Johnson jingled the bell daintily, pointing at it with his free hand to direct Horace's attention. "Bell, Horace? Ye remember? Tinkle, tinkle, and Horace comes pell-mell to earn his princely bleedin' wages?"

"I were in the kitchen, sir, and couldn't hear."

"Ah. Ye couldn't hear. I see. P'r'aps I ought to get a bigger bell. P'r'aps I ought to buy the bleedin' big boomer out of the church steeple and run a pull rope to me bed."

Horace surveyed the room gravely. "Don't reckon you'd have the room to hang 'er in here, sir. And them ceiling beams wouldn't take the weight." He handed his employer the napkin and the cup, spilling only a few drops along the way.

Johnson hoisted the cup to his lips and took a sip, which he immediately spat out again. "Ye call this bleedin' chocolate?"

Horace raised the cup to his hay-fevery nose and sniffed at it, then muttered: "Reckon I forgot."

"Forgot? *Forgot?* Six months of brewin' chocolate every demmed morning—that's ... one hundred and eighty mornings, give or take bleedin' February—and ye *forgot?*"

The back of Horace's straw-thatched head nodded up and down as he carried the cup toward the fireplace. "Yep, reckon I did." He topped up the cup from the decanter standing beside his lord and master's reading chair and stirred it in with his finger. Johnson shuddered to think where that finger might have been, but consoled himself with the thought that the brandy would purify anything.

The brandy also served to loosen his bladder. As Horace busied himself in the closet behind the lord of the manor's dressing screen, Big Billy heaved his aging bulk out of the voluminous feather mattress, padded over to the commode, and pulled out the chamber pot. It hadn't been emptied from the night before. "Horace!"

The haystack head poked out beyond the dressing screen. "Oh. I pondersized on coming in last night to empty 'er, but reckoned I oughtn'ta disturb you."

"Disturb me? When I am happily snorin' away in the land

of bleedin' Nod behind those bleedin' draperies, ye couldn't bleedin' disturb me with the Grenadier Guards Band! And when I'm *not* happily snorin' away ye won't be bleedin' disturbin' me, will ye?"

"Reckon not, sir."

Johnson sighed and held his breath and added a sharp new pint or so to the pungent old. He shut the chamber pot away and padded toward his dressing screen, scaling his nightcap in the general direction of the bed. Horace was just finishing laying out his master's military uniform: cavalry boots, sword and baldrick and all. "Horace—what the sufferin' Judas d'ye think ye're about? The demmed Frogs declare war again while I was snoozin'?"

"Ain't it the day for the parading of the militia? I reckoned you'd want to get dressed up in your red-and-gold rig."

"Ah—so it is. Reckon I forgot."

Bewigged and booted and sporting his red-and-gold rig, Johnson thundered and clattered downstairs, salivating for breakfast. The dining room, with its buff-waxed, mile-long table, gleaming silver, and cabinets sporting Wedgwood like the shields on a Viking ship, never failed to make him smile. "Ah, Billy Boy," he said to himself, "it's one demmed long way ye've come from a bog-trottin' poor relation."

What didn't make him smile, though, was that Mary and Ann and their governess were at the table, instead of breakfasting in their room across the hall from his. The girls chirped tentatively: "Good morning, Papa."

"Good morning, girlies."

"I thought, sir," the governess said softly, "that since it was field day and there will be no lessons—"

"We're going to visit Mama at the old house," Mary piped up.

"And bring her some posies," Ann chimed in.

"Demmed thoughtful of ye. Extend m'regards. Now run along with ye. And ye will see to it," he added to the governess, "that the girls don't go tallyfobblin' about on their own amongst the revelers . . .?"

"Of course, Mr. Johnson." Her voice was breathless and misty, with her colorless eyes rolling under lashless lids. Johnson shocked himself by feeling an actual carnal twinge for that sunk-shanked, watery-eyed, goose-necked, waxen imitation of a woman. He had definitely been unmarried too long. Perhaps he should start giving serious consideration to putting Horace and his brimming chamber pot out to pasture in favor of a chambermaid.

But then, Horace did provide one estimable service no chambermaid was likely to provide. For all that he was a good hand span shorter than his lord and master, and some fifty pounds lighter, the gallumphing barge boats at the ends of his legs were exactly the same size and shape. So long as Horace remained a house servant at Mount Johnson, William Johnson would never have to break in a new pair of shoes again.

Johnson went to the sideboard and filled a plate with beef kidneys, pork sausages, a few rashers of bacon, fried eggs and potatoes, toasted bread with a few spoonfuls of strawberry preserve, and three or four buckwheat pancakes drowned in butter and maple syrup. He hesitated in front of the salver of venison chops and decided to wait to see whether his eyes were bigger than his stomach. The kitchen maid brought him up a tankard of light ale to wash it down.

A footman came in to say that the plantation overseer and the chief clerk from the trading store were waiting to see him. "Well, send 'em in—provided they ain't bringin' any news that's liable to disturb me digestion."

The clerk was disturbed that the annual presents to be distributed to the Mohawks today cost somewhat more than what the Colony of New York had allotted. Johnson said: "I don't care what the demmed account books say. I never kept bleedin' accounts m'first fifteen years here. Me uncle kindly sent me a packet of ledgers, and I fed 'em to the field mice. Keepin' the Covenant Chain greased up and polished is worth a demmed sight more to us than a few numbers in a ledger."

The overseer's problem was somewhat more grave. It seemed that with all the events scheduled for the day, there was some doubt as to whether there would be time for both the greased pig chase and the scolding contest. The scold's, or fishwife's, contest was dear to Johnson's heart, as he'd hatched it up himself over the winter, and this was to be its inaugural year. Women with reputations for sharp tongues were to pair off face-to-face, and whomever was left still spewing venom at the end took the title for the year. Johnson was expecting it to be at least as much of a success as the ever-popular Indian versus white women's wrestling, or the annual prize for the most contorted grimace in the Mohawk Valley. He pondered upon it between mouthfuls, and finally decided: "Run 'em both at the same time in different places. What's our prize for the fishwife contest?"

"Three silver buttons."

"Better add in a couple of pullets. Best to sweeten the pot until we've built up some tradition. Well, gentlemen, if that's all, I'll proceed with me breakfast."

He was just chasing the last bit of kidney around the slippery lake of maple syrup and meat juices when the footman came back in to announce that he had visitors. "Of course I've got bleedin' visitors! We're expectin' several thousand for luncheon."

Before the footman could elucidate further, a little, green-eyed Indian boy came hurtling past him and hurled himself onto Johnson's ample lap. Big Billy laughed and pinched the brown cheeks. "How d'ye do, Willy m'lad? Taken any scalps lately?" Willy began to spout in Mohawk. "Now, now—in English, boyo." Johnson had a basic command of Mohawk, but it was a devilish complex language.

"Papa buyed me—I mean my other papa—he buyed me a pony, and I rided it here!"

"Ye *rode* it here."

"I *roded* it here."

"Well that's a grand thing. What a lucky laddy to have two daddies. Ha! Hearken to your pater the poetaster. P'r'aps I'll go in for scribblin' sonnets in me dotage. A grand good morning t'ye, Hendrick."

King Hendrick had followed Willy at a much more dignified pace—posing in the dining room doorway with his blanket draped around him like a Roman senator's mantle. But Johnson had had enough dealings with the old rascal to know that he didn't get that scar across his face by standing on his dignity. For the first ten years Johnson had lived in the Mohawk Valley, Hendrick claimed not to know a word of English, leaving Johnson no choice but to try to do business in Mohawk. After Big Billy had spent ten years wrestling with when to say "the canoe paddle" and when "the canoe paddle itself," Hendrick had sauntered in one day and said in perfectly fluid

English: "A grand good morning to you, William Johnson. I think you know enough Canienga now."

Hendrick raised his arm and pronounced sonorously, "Good morning, Warraghiyagey," which was the name the Mohawks had given Johnson when they adopted him. In typically maddeningly allusive Mohawk manner, it meant several things in English: "Man Who Gets Business Done," "Man Who Tries Big Things," and probably several other connotations Big Billy was better off not knowing. He supposed they could have called him worse names. Others had.

"Sit ye down, Hendrick. Might I offer ye a cup of tea? Or p'r'aps a mug of ale?"

"A taste of ale would not be unwelcome."

Big Billy bellowed for the kitchen girl, and discovered she was already standing at his elbow clearing the table. "Fetch a mug of ale for Mr. Hendrick, m'gel, and another for m'self—it's demmed dry work orderin' the regiment hither and yon across the greensward." He watched the girl sashay away and down the trapdoor to the scullery, noting that those spindly girl hips had ripened like a pumpkin while he wasn't looking. He cleared his throat and turned back to Hendrick. "It won't be time for polishin' up the old Covenant Chain till afternoon. Did ye bring Willy along early for to see the martial show?"

Hendrick said gravely: "I thought it would be good for my son to see the great war chief, his other father, parade his mighty warriors."

"Don't be sellin' those bumpkins short. They may not march like a Regiment of the Line, but they're a demmed sight better shots. If Monsieur Froggy ever gets a notion to come pokin' 'is nose down the Mohawk Valley, he's goin' to get the surprise of 'is life."

"The French came poking their noses into Canienga country long before there was a white militia here, and got the surprise of their lives."

A hubbub of voices, wagon wheels, and hooves built up outside, but Johnson stayed chattering with Hendrick and feeding Willy the occasional slurp from his ale mug until the captain presented himself with: "Regiment all assembled and ready for inspection, Major."

"Demmed punctual of 'em. Do we have much of a crowd turned out for the show?"

"Upwards of a thousand so far, sir. A good many of them are Mohawks. It should be educational for them to see a demonstration of discipline."

"Discipline, ye say? I'll tell ye a tale of *discipline*, Captain. Up around Oswego lives a white trapper who partnered with a Mohawk for many years—and a grand rack of profit they made for me through all those years. One year the Mohawk seemed particularly anxious to get back from their trap line as soon as the season was over. When they got near the town where the Mohawk lived, three Oneidas came running at him with tomahawks. The white trapper raised up his gun, but his partner stopped him and explained.

"Seems the summer before, the Mohawk had killed an Oneida woman in a fit of jealousy. The council had decided that it wasn't a matter as could be wiped away by payin' a blood price in wampum—the only fittin' blood price was that the Mohawk forfeit his life to the woman's family. The Mohawk had asked the council to let him spend one more winter out trapping with his white friend, to accumulate a bit of a stake for his children. The council had agreed. Now the winter was over. The three Oneidas with the tomahawks were the dead gel's brothers. And with that, the Mohawk shook hands with his partner, walked to the Oneidas, and they chopped 'im.

"Ye'll not get a 'Yessir' or 'By yer leave, sir' out of a Mohawk warrior, but we've precious little to teach 'em about discipline.

"Speakin' of which, we'd best get out there before the lads decide they've been standin' in the sun too long." He shifted Willy down off his knee, stood up and straightened his lace jabot in the sideboard mirror, jammed his gold-braided tricorne down over his crisp white wig, and marched out with the captain, with Hendrick and Willy and the house servants bringing up the rear. A footman was holding the captain's immense, stamping black stallion and Old Knobby, Johnson's somewhat less fractious bay hunter. They mounted up and trotted over to the parade ground.

The cows that occupied the parade ground when the militia wasn't conducting exercises had all been herded into the barn, and were making their displeasure known over the fairground racket of the civilians. The fence around the pasture was crowded with the wives and families of militia members,

Dutch and English clergymen come to show the support of the Lord of Battles, field slaves who would never be allowed to shoulder a musket, patch-coated farmers from German Flats, and a brightly dressed array of curious Mohawks. Two factions that were unlikely to be impressed by the martial display were the off-duty regulars from Fort Hunter and those of the major's tenants who'd immigrated after careers in His Majesty's Highland Regiments.

In the middle of the pasture stood three long lines of men wearing everything from fur hats and homespuns to broadcloth knee breeches and buckled shoes. The only red coats in the regiment were the major's and the captain's, who'd become captain largely because of his willingness to lay out ten shillings for a uniform.

The men clapped their muskets smartly to their shoulders as their officers trotted through the gate. The major reined in his horse in front of them and told the captain to carry on.

In an hour of right-wheeling, by-the-left-turning, and forming squares, there were only two incidences of one file marching head-on into another, only three occasions when the captain resorted to profanity, only half a dozen times when a marcher got his feet entangled with a comrade's, and only once when a musket went off by accident. The onlookers called out encouragements such as: "Pick yourself up and try again, Clell!" or "I cautioned you to wear boots in a cow pasture, Nathan!" But they broke into cheers when the parade ended with three blank volleys fired in relays over the river.

Major Johnson clucked Old Knobby forward to the Mohawk Valley Militia, standing at something resembling attention. "Well, lads. Last night I debated with m'self whether such a ragtag gaggle of louts was worth wastin' a barrel of beer on. Bein' of a parsimonious turn by nature, it cut against me grain to be givin' away the products of me own splendid brewery. So I told m'self I'd keep the barrel for m'self unless ye did one demmed fine job of showin' me some soldierin'. I regret to say," pausing to let out an agonized groan, "the barrel's in the barn, boys."

The captain called out: "Three cheers for the major, boys!" But he only got two and a half—the third was cut off by the rush for the barn.

The major and the captain trotted their horses back along the circuit of the fence, making military conversation about who had tripped over whom and how to go about rectifying it next time. Gets Business Done didn't press the business too hard. He was well aware that the purpose of the circuitous route back to the pasture gate was so that the onlookers could admire the splendid figure the captain cut in his red and gold coat on his glossy black charger.

"Captain!" The voice came from a blanket-robed Mohawk girl perched on the fence. The major and the captain reined in politely. She couldn't have been more than sixteen or seventeen. Her complexion was more olive than copper, and her face was more oval than angular, despite the high cheekbones and slanted eyes. Her sunflower-oiled hair was held back by a headband with a feather in the front, rather than the back, so she was unmarried. And her English was quite surprisingly adroit: "If I get up on your horse behind you, Captain, might I have a bit of a ride—just to see what a big, beautiful stallion feels like between my legs?"

The captain coughed and then chivalrously nodded: "You may." It cost him nothing to say so, since there was obviously no way in hell the girl could come within hailing distance of the back of that horse without a stepladder.

The next thing the major and the captain knew, the girl had sprung off the fence like a jack-in-the-box, to land squarely behind the captain's saddle, reached around him to grab the reins, put her heels to the horse's ribs and was whooping away at a gallop. The black stallion thundered helter-skelter around the pasture like a penned dog set free, with the captain holding on for his hope of salvation and the girl leaning back so the wind blew her blanket out behind her, showing the front of her overdress springing up and down and her dew-bright thighs between the tops of her leggings and the pushed-up hem of her skirt.

After circling the pasture, the girl reined the stallion to a rearing halt beside Old Knobby, slid down over the stallion's rump, picked up the captain's hat, dusted it against her skirt, said, "Here's your hat. Much obliged for the ride," vaulted over the fence and disappeared into the crowd.

"Papa?" The high-pitched voice came from somewhere in the vicinity of Johnson's left elbow. Big Billy blinked his eyes to unfix their focus at the place where the girl had melted away, then looked down. Hendrick was holding Willy up toward him. "Can I have a ride on Old Knobby?"

"Certainly—but not like *that* one." He settled Willy on the pommel of Old Knobby's saddle and then gaped down at Hendrick: "Who the divil was that?"

"Mary Brant. Nickus Brant's daughter, since he married her mother. Young Nickus, not old Nickus."

"Sufferin' Judas. Why the divil haven't I seen her before? If that's a sample of how she carries on by habit, she'd be demmed hard to overlook."

"She has been at school at Schenectady, learning how to be an English lady."

"The divil you say."

"Papa?"

"Hm? Oh, yes, Willy—we'll go for a ride now."

Chapter 14

Miss Mary Brant, recent graduate of the Schenectady Young Ladies' Finishing School, was in the yard stretching a deer hide when she heard two horses approaching from the road behind her. She assumed it was her mother and Carrying News coming back from Canajoharie, so she went on working the hide with the scraper, trying to even it out to approximately the same thickness all over before the sun started to dry it out. There were still a few flecks of brain stuck on it from soaking in the braining tub, but the sun would shrivel them off.

She glanced back over her shoulder as the horses emerged from the trail through the woods. It wasn't her mother and Carrying News after all. The horses were two big, red-brown Irish hunters. Both of them were saddled and bridled, but only one of them had a rider. He was a big, middle-aged white man with a long, straight nose, thick shoulders, and rosy cheeks. Instead of the red and gold uniform and curled white wig he'd been wearing the last time she saw him, he was dressed in a leather riding coat; much-used, floppy-topped boots that came up over his knees; and the square-browed, clubbed brown wig he'd worn with his Canienga clothes the first time she'd seen him. He reined in his horse beside the stretching frame, tipped his hat and boomed out: "A grand good mornin' t'ye, Miss Molly."

"My name is Mary."

"I know that. Ye are Miss Mary Brant, sister of young Joseph, stepdaughter of Nickus Brant, daughter of Someone Lends Her a Flower of the Wolf Clan. And I am William Johnson."

"I know that. If you know my name is Mary, why did you call me something different?"

"It's the Irish in me—Mary, Molly; William, Billy; six of one, half a dozen of another. Whatever yer called, the divil made ye a jockey. I had me doubts whether the poor, gallant captain might not lose more than his hat. Wherever did ye learn to ride like that?"

"Canadiorha—Nickus Brant—has a fondness for fine horseflesh, so I would ride his horses a good deal between school terms. And there was a livery stable down the road from my school, where they would sometimes let me exercise their horses if I asked."

"I don't doubt they would. Somethin' of the same sort crossed m'mind today. I was settin' out for me exercise—endeavorin' to keep the beef at bay—and I says to m'self: 'There's poor Juanita has to languish away in the demmed paddock day in and out while yer bouncin' about the countryside on Old Knobby. Wouldn't she be tickled to get a good canter in from time to time under a light rider like that Miss Molly Brant?'

"And I thought to m'self ye might enjoy it, too. Juanita ain't quite so tall as the captain's black, but she'll take a five-barred gate like puddin'."

Mary was more than a little taken aback, but tried not to show it. It had been fun not to resist the impulse to leap on the captain's horse, but she'd never expected it might lead to such a thing as William Johnson asking her to come riding. She also couldn't help but think of all the stories about William Johnson and Canienga girls. But perhaps his explanation of what had brought him here was all there was to it.

She gazed at Juanita's clean-lined, long legs and spring-muscled rump, then looked back at the half-scraped deer hide. William Johnson said: "P'r'aps ye should ask yer mother."

"She's not here."

"Yer father, then?"

"He's dead. Oh, you mean Canadiorha. He's not here, either. They've all gone to Canajoharie. Except Muskingum—Joseph. His Teacher took him off into the woods." She told herself to close her mouth before she enumerated what the barn cats were up to.

"Then yer all alone here."

Something in his words gave her a twinge of something akin to fear. But she just said: "Yes."

"Then there's no one to tell ye yea or nay."

"No one tells me yea or nay whether they're here or not," which wasn't exactly true, but close enough for a white man.

"Let me give ye a hand up, then."

"Not necessary." Mary took hold of the pommel, sprang up onto the empty saddle and leaned forward to take hold of the reins. It was a long lean. Juanita might not be as tall as the captain's stallion, but she was no pony. She shied a little, feeling a strange new rider, but Mary whispered into her ears and rubbed her neck and clamped her ribs tightly with her knees.

As they trotted down the trail toward the road, William Johnson remarked: "Ye Brants do seem to have a way with horses. Young Joseph ain't big enough yet to tell whether he'll be the rider his sister is, but even Old Knobby took to 'im like a duck to cheese."

"How is it that you know my brother—" She cut herself off just before adding "without him telling me," deciding it would make William Johnson think himself too important.

"I wouldn't say I *know* 'im, but we've passed the time of day from time to time, down to old Hendrick's place. He often plays with me Willy." A great bull moose bellow of a guffaw burst out of his chest. "Dem me, I might've worded that different."

As the narrow trail through the woods opened up onto the

open road, William Johnson snapped the reins against his horse's neck and clucked him into a canter. Mary followed suit with Juanita. The canter became a gallop, with William Johnson kicking at Old Knobby with his spurs. Mary didn't have spurs and wouldn't have used them if she had, but Juanita kept parallel with no more encouragement than moccasined heels. Just when Mary was happily surrendering her last threads of self-consciousness to the surge and thunder of the soft-furred storm she was riding and the feel of the wind blowing up her skirt, a hay wagon lurched over a rise in the road ahead. William Johnson reined Old Knobby back to a trot and then a walk. Mary did the same with Juanita.

William Johnson was puffing and blowing and his cheeks and nose had grown even rosier, but his mouth was stretched wide in a gasping grin. He didn't ride like a man with too much fat on him for even that oversized a frame, or a man whose own hair was probably more the color of the powdered, formal wig than the brown one. He rode like an idiot boy who had yet to learn there was such a thing as caution. Mary was beginning to get the impression that he did everything that way. There was something about William Johnson that made her feel a spring of laughter bubbling between her breasts.

He thumbed a silver snuffbox out of his waistcoat pocket, popped the lid and was about to take a pinch when something seemed to occur to him. "D'ye take snuff, Miss Molly?"

"Of course." She didn't, but it sounded like a boldly grown-up thing to say, so she had to say it. He handed her the snuffbox. She imitated the actions she'd seen snuff users use, tilting the box over the cup between her thumb and forefinger and tapping with a fingertip. It would have been tricky enough without the breeze blowing off the pasture they were passing by, and the roll of the horse beneath her, and keeping hold of the reins at the same time. An alarmingly large brown lump tumbled out onto her hand, but the breeze carried some of it away. She passed the snuffbox back to William Johnson, raised her left hand in the general direction of her nose, twitched her cheek to open up her right nostril and snorted in deeply.

A peppery keg of gunpowder exploded between her eyes. She sneezed and sneezed and fought to keep her seat as Juanita whinnied and balked and shied beneath her.

When Mary finally managed to regain control of her horse

and herself, William Johnson said: "Demmed thoughtless of me. Should've warned ye this is a mixture made for callused palates like me own." He took a hearty snort in through both nostrils, gave out a delicate little sneeze and put the snuffbox away.

His concentration on the snuff ritual gave her the opportunity to observe that—despite the roll of fat under his jawline—his chin was still firm and well-defined, with a clear-cut cleft down the middle of it. And his eyes changed color with the light. Back in the shaded farmyard, they'd been a green-tinted hazel. Now they were gray-green. There was something hawk-like about them, perhaps because of the uptilted eyebrows. And the pupils were misaligned, so that it was impossible to look him in both eyes at the same time. Not that she wanted to look into his eyes, except to show him she wasn't intimidated.

As the hay wagon lumbered near, Mary and William Johnson twitched their horses off the road to let it pass. The farmer called from his perch on the top of the load: " 'Mornin', Major."

"And a grand good morning t'ye, Caleb. How's the wife's gout?"

"Better, thankee. And yours?"

"Comes and goes. Curse of high livin'."

As the wagon creaked and swayed on past, William Johnson turned to Mary and said: "Too much demmed traffic on this road to get a decent gallop in. What say we cut across country?" She just nodded her head, adopting the policy that the best way not to say something foolish was to say as little as possible.

They trotted their horses into the meadow on the inland side of the road. William Johnson swerved his horse to the left and spurred him full-tilt toward the rail-fenced wheat field flanking the meadow. Mary urged Juanita into a gallop. She saw Old Knobby coil his muscles and stretch out to arc over the fence as though the flailing behemoth on his back were so much feathers, then she was concentrated on holding on and leaning into the jump.

Juanita hit the ground with hooves already churning to carry them onward without breaking stride. Up ahead, William Johnson showed no signs of slowing the pace—whipping Old

Knobby's rump on toward the next fence—so Mary let Juanita have her head. The tall grain hissed and crackled and snapped against her moccasins and shins. William Johnson's bellows carried back to her over the drums and rattles of hooves and grain stocks: "View halloo! Look to the hounds!"

They took the second fence as easily as the first. William Johnson slowed to a walk on the other side, puffing and beaming. Policy or no, Mary had to say: "I didn't see any dogs."

"What dogs?"

"You were shouting to look at the hounds."

He laughed. "Old habits, m'dear. I learned to ride goin' fox-huntin', back in the land of decent whiskey."

"You hunted foxes from horseback?"

"Sometimes three or four times a week, if I could persuade me cousins in the manor house to loan me a horse."

Once she'd got started talking to him, she discovered she needn't have worried about sounding foolish, since William Johnson seemed to believe he lived in a glass house. And with good cause, if his hunting habits were anything to go by. She said: "Wouldn't it've been easier to set snares?"

He laughed even louder. "Demmed right ye are—but it wouldn't do near so fine a job of cullin' the ranks of the aristocracy. Dem me, wouldn't it be a sight to see ye showin' those high-toned hunt ladies a thing or two about horsewomanship? Although ladies have to ride sidesaddle. Demmed foolish invention. Ye were made for a man's saddle."

"I don't mind them, but I prefer riding bareback."

"Don't we all. Ahem. Well—"

"What in the name of Jehovah God do you blasted fools think you're about . . ." The strangled shout came from a grizzle-bearded farmer waving a hoe, red-faced and panting as though he'd run all the way from the farmstead on the far side of the field. William Johnson stopped and turned his horse to face him, allowing the farmer to catch enough breath to finish his sentence as he caught up with them. ". . . trampling horses through my wheat field?"

"*Yer* wheat field? It seems to me, sir, that this is still part of me own demmed estates. If ye lose a bushel or two of corn to me horses' hooves, it will just be that much less demmed rent ye pay to me come tithin' time."

"So long as I pay rent, this place is *mine*! And if you or any of your Indian tarts try such a damned fool trick again, I'll dust your hides for you."

William Johnson's boot heels hit the ground like the Flint Giants cracking their drum. "Would ye raise yer hand at *me*, sir? I'll lay ye out like a side of demmed beef, sir! I'll shake ye like a terrier shakes a rat! I'll grind ye up to season me porridge!"

The farmer backed away, tentatively brandishing his hoe as though he might consider using it to defend himself if he had to. William Johnson snatched it out of his hands, broke the haft over his knee, shook the pieces in the farmer's face, threw them down at his feet, climbed back on his horse and said: "If ye stop by me tradin' store and tell 'em I owe ye a hoe haft, they'll give ye a new one. Come along, Molly."

After trotting on a short while farther, he slowed Old Knobby to a walk again, took another pinch of snuff, sneezed and laughed. "Demmed colonials. It's all those demmed Bostonian heretics eggin' 'em on to thinkin' one man's as good as another. I suppose he is, but the day a man can't go for a canter across his own bleedin' estates is the day I leave the land behind and go privateerin' like me uncle the admiral. I suppose I'd best be gettin' ye home before yer mother gets to wonderin' if the Gypsies took ye."

She didn't say much on the ride back. Not because she'd got back her apprehension about saying the wrong thing, but because she was trying to place an odd feeling. There was something distantly familiar about riding beside a man it was fun to make laugh. And one who also made her certain nothing in the world could harm her.

When they got back to Carrying News's farm, there was still no one there. The deer hide looked to be drying off nicely, even if it wasn't worked perfectly even. Mary climbed down off Juanita and said politely: "Thank you for the ride, Mr. Johnson."

His big, open features clouded over and closed up, as though she'd done something to offend him. She didn't understand what it might have been, so she just held the ends of Juanita's reins up toward him and mumbled: "Here's your lovely horse back."

The cloud burst apart. "Dem me—thought I'd made m'self clear, but I didn't, did I? She's not m'lovely horse, she's yers."

"Pardon me?"

"She needs a rider who'll keep 'er trim and well-oiled, or she'll start goin' blowsy and scant of breath like 'er old master. If I know eggs from carcajous, ye're just the gel for her. And there's demmed little point in me keepin' the saddle and bridle that was made to fit her."

"I can't. . . ."

"Ye can and ye will. But there is a price ye must pay for 'er."

"What is that?"

"Ye must come to sup with me at Mount Johnson. With yer mother and father, of course. Stepfather, I mean to say. And young Joseph, if 'e happens to be about. Are ye willin', Molly?"

"Yes, but—"

"No buts. Give me yer hand on it." She raised her right hand and found her fingers enveloped by five warm, thick sausages that she would've thought felt flabby if she hadn't seen them snap that hoe like a bit of kindling. He leaned far down off his saddle, doffing his hat with his free hand and almost losing his wig, and touched his puckered mouth to the back of her hand. Without relinquishing her hand, he straightened back up with a grunt from the pit of his exceedingly deep stomach and said: "I hope this won't prove to be our last ride together."

She tried to think of what she should say in reply. Before she succeeded, he let go of her hand, said, "I'd best be makin' sure me clerks ain't givin' away free rifles with every bolt of cloth," and trotted Old Knobby away.

She was just finishing rubbing down Juanita and about to put her into the paddock when Carrying News and her mother trotted in from the road, Mother with the cradle board of Nickus Brant III bouncing against her back. Carrying News gaped: "Where did that horse come from?"

Her mother's face pinched in as Mary told them. Mother said: "You must give it back."

"Why? I told him I couldn't take her, but he insisted."

"I don't doubt he did. You don't think a man like that gives away a horse like that for nothing?"

"It wasn't for nothing. He said Juanita was wasting away without a rider, and he'd seen me ride. . . ." She trailed off in the face of her mother's pitying skepticism.

"Daughter, that is just the sort of tale Gets Business Done would tell to make it easier for you to take the horse. He is not a liar, no more than King Hendrick or any other Royaner, but he can spread honey with the best of them."

"Maybe he just wants company when he goes riding."

"Maybe he wants more than company."

"What if he does? I don't remember being taught in the longhouse that girls should be afraid of men."

"The old ways are well enough for girls living in the longhouse. We are Christian now."

"Maybe you are, but that has nothing to do with me."

Mother scooped up a palmful of water from the horse trough and dashed it in Mary's face. Throwing water on fractious children was about as far as Hodenosaune parents went in the way of corporal discipline. Mary wiped her face and said with difficulty: "I am no longer a child, Mother."

"You are a child to William Johnson. Listen to me, Mary, the world is not so simple as when there were only Caniengas in our valley and a woman was secure in her grandmother's longhouse all her life. Young men will come courting you— young men who are as shy and fresh-hearted and unsure of the ways of the world as you are. You and they will learn together. A man like William Johnson has been through love so many times that that which would shatter a younger *onikonhra* wouldn't scratch his. And you will find that men treat a woman very different if they hope to marry her."

"How do you know that isn't what William Johnson hopes?"

Her mother just rolled her eyes, but Carrying News put in from the sidelines: "It may be Mary isn't far wrong. Gets Business Done has been living alone a long time. For him."

Mother said: "She wouldn't want to marry such an old man."

"I didn't say I did. But maybe that's what *he* wants."

"If so," Mother said, "he wants what he cannot have. We will go and eat with him at Mount Johnson, because Mary led him to believe we would. Mary, I do not mean to be cruel with thee."

"I know that, Mother."

"And I know *thee*: do not be such a fool as to make yourself want something just because you've been told it cannot be."

Mary went back to scraping the hide. She believed her mother wasn't being cruel, but it was infuriating of her to take an entertaining little tremor and build it into an earthquake. And what was so terrible if William Johnson *did* want to marry her? He wasn't *that* old. He was wealthy and powerful and funny and kind and stronger than any three young men, and very good-looking in an imposing kind of way. Not that he'd asked her, or that the thought had even crossed her mind before her mother put it there.

She muttered, "Demmed hell," and threw down her scraping stick. She'd scraped right through the hide.

CHAPTER 15

Somewhere in the Adirondack Mountains the boy known as Brant's Joseph was wandering naked and alone. The sun was going down and he'd picked the wrong dry creek bed to follow, winding back up among the mists and crags instead of leading him out of them. His Teacher had brought him three days deep into the mountains, taken his clothes and knife and moccasins, and left him there to find his own way home.

If he found his way home, he would be one step closer to being husk-covered and cease being a child. If he didn't find his way home, he would die in the mountains. That was the way of a warrior.

For two days now Joseph had been retracing the route Little Abraham had escorted him in on. And perhaps he'd even had it right, up until the point he'd picked the wrong dry creek bed. For two nights now he'd been sleeping in scratchy beds of broken-off pine boughs and scraped-together dead leaves, with nothing in his belly but a few elderberries and the taste of poplar bark from the green twigs he'd dandled in his mouth like a farmer's straw. And "sleeping" wasn't exactly the word for the shivering half daze in which every falling pinecone or skittering vole was magnified into the footfalls of a bear or wolf or panther homing in on the smell of his fear.

He couldn't decide whether he should turn around and backtrack or whether he should keep on following the creek bed in hopes that it would lead him to some vantage point above the tree and rock walls of the maze. As he chewed it over in his mind—fraying the question to pieces like the nub of poplar twig his teeth were worrying apart—his numbed feet made the decision for him, crunching onward along the shingled pebbles of the creek bed.

The light was turning redder, stretching a twisted shadow out ahead for him to follow. He didn't need the change of light to tell him night was falling. Even blind he would've known from the chill, as the cold hearts of the mountains took back their skin from the defiling sun. Perhaps it was time he started looking for a place to make a bed, before there was no light left to look with. As his mind mulled over the decision of whether or not he should make that decision now, his feet kept stumbling and fumbling ever farther back into the mountains. Until his eyes were whacked by something that froze his feet to the pebbles.

He stood shivering even more than the chill of the evening could account for. He rubbed his eyes and looked again. The basswood tree that had leered at him was still there and was still leering. No matter how wide he opened his eyes or how tightly he squinted them, the tree trunk still had a face on it—and not the sketchy approximation of a face that might appear out of bark furrows and knots when the light hit them right. This was a distinct, three-dimensional, bent-nosed, blubbery-lipped, slit-eyed face growing out of the living wood.

Joseph's Teacher had told him that although a warrior had to make his own way with or without help, if he were very lucky, one of the spirits of the forest might come to him and give him advice. Joseph hadn't expected that it might be a tree. It didn't look like a face whose advice should necessarily be trusted, either. But at the moment he needed any kind of help that came along.

He shuffled his right foot forward across the pebbles, then his left. The tree's face didn't alter its expression, nor did it show any signs of fading away or melting back into the trunk as he drew closer. He rehearsed in his mind the various forms of address one might use to go about starting a conversation with a tree.

As he moved warily through the hairy-leafed young shoots growing up out of the tree's roots, half expecting them to wrap themselves around his arms and legs, he noticed that there were yellow wood chips and shavings around the base of the trunk. He had heard that the members of the False Face Society had to carve their masks out of living trees, but he'd never seen it done, nor knew of anyone who had. Among the wood chips were a few remaining ashes from where the carver had burned tobacco to ask the life of the tree.

The face's great, splayed nose—twisted halfway across its cheek—and the pain-contorted mouth, would make it Joseph's favorite of the False Faces. Old Crooked Nose had got his name by challenging the Creator to prove he could call a mountain to come to him. He'd heard a sudden rushing of wind behind him, and when he looked back over his shoulder, the mountain hit him in the face. Despite his gruesome features, he was kind enough to teach the True People of Turtle Island how to cure themselves from sickness.

It occurred to Joseph that his Teacher had been right in a way. The basswood tree was one of the spirits of the forest, and it was advising him that the wrong turning at the creek bed hadn't led him all that far back into the mountains after all. If some Canienga False Face man was going back and forth from his home in the valley to this tree, the valley couldn't be very far away.

Joseph did feel a little like he was trespassing, though, looking on the unfinished mask. There was just enough light left to show him a pair of young pine trees a little ways off, with boughs still low enough on their trunks for him to reach. He twisted some of the thinner branches back and forth to break them off, covering his hands with sticky pine blood, apologizing to both trees and thanking them for giving him their arms to keep him warm.

Between the two pines was a cleft in the rocks with a bed of moss. Joseph crawled in and pulled the pine boughs over him. They didn't exactly make him warm, but a little less cold, and they might serve to mask his smell from the night hunters.

He found it difficult to imagine ever having been the Canienga boy his Teacher had led into the mountains so long ago. Now he was just another quivering creature of the pinewoods, hoping that the rain wouldn't come down on his roofless excuse for a den and that a bear or a wolf wouldn't find him. Whether it was because of his fear or because of his hunger and lack of sleep, he heard and smelt things sharply that he'd never known were there.

Still debating whether he should start retracing his steps in the morning or keep following the creek bed onward, he fell into something resembling sleep, and woke up to find a wolf looking down at him. It was sitting on its haunches panting contemplatively, with its head cocked to one side and its long, pink tongue lolling out between the long, white teeth the moonlight gleamed on.

The wolf clicked its teeth together and said with Muskingum's father's voice: "We wolves have as many enemies to fear in our lives as you do—maybe more—but we know better than to let it show."

Joseph didn't know what to do. Perhaps he was only imagining the voice, and those very real teeth would start tearing at him if he didn't shout or whack at the wolf with a pine bough. But if the voice was real, he should reply to it politely.

The wolf rolled its yellow eyes and looked back over its shoulder, as though it had expected more of him, then said: "You'll find if you make a habit of going halfway down a road and turning back, you won't get to many places." It suddenly raised its nose to sniff the air, grinned, said, *"Rabbit,"* and loped away.

In the morning, Joseph took a sharp stone from the creek bed and scored a few gashes in the bark of a birch tree to get some watery sap to drink. He carried on following the course of the creek up into the mountains. It grew narrower, wound halfway up the side of a ridge and then disappeared. The trees and the surrounding hills were too high to get a look at the sun, but from the direction the shadows were being cast at this time of the morning, the ridge must run north-south—unless he'd completely lost his sense of time in the sharpening of his other senses. He kept on climbing, twisting sideways to slip his skin safely between the prickly gooseberry bushes and the poison sumac.

There was a lone pine tree at the crest, its roots somehow drawing sustenance out of the naked rock. He climbed the pine to get above the crowns of the trees growing out of the slope. The bark scratched back at his thighs and arms as he shinnied up with his eyes slitted against the flakes of bark and sharp needles pattering down. When he got safely seated on the lowest bough, adjusting himself cautiously on the sharp-ridged bark, he opened his eyes wide.

To his left the tree-furred hills climbed on and on into the clouds. To his right the ridge curved down directly into the green valley of the Caniengas. A bend of the river glinted blue beside the gray pillars of the cooking fires of Canajoharie Castle.

Rough bark or not, Joseph skittered back down the tree and down the ridge. He still had a long way to go, but the fact that he knew where he was going made his feet lighter. The sun was halfway through its path down the sky when he stumbled into the farmyard halfway between Canajoharie and the Lower Castle, still dripping from swimming the river with a deadfall branch for bouyancy.

Si-isha dropped her milk bucket and came running, calling: "Mother! He's here!" And then he was enveloped in the warm arms of his sister, with her soft waves of hair that smelled of sunflower oil and smoked deer hide and home.

He slept through the evening and the night and half the morning. When he woke up, he discovered that everyone was treating him a little different from before. No one told him to go chop some wood before having something to eat. And when he sat down at the table, there was a plate of steaming apple corn bread and maple syrup in front of him before he had a chance to say he was feeling a little hungry. He surprised himself by eating it all and then asking for more. After last night he'd doubted he'd be able to squeeze anything else into his stomach for at least a week.

Si-isha took his licked-clean plate away. Mother went into the room where she slept with Carrying News and their baby and came back out with a long, lumpy bundle wrapped in moose hide. She laid it on the table in front of him and said:

"He told me to keep it until you started becoming a man." It was his father's gun, shot pouch, and powder horn.

Carrying News took him out behind the cow shed and showed him how to cut a flint and fit it into the lock, how to load, and how to work the cover on the priming pan. Most of it Joseph knew already from watching men do it, but Carrying News liked to be able to show him things, and the fact was that seeing and doing weren't quite the same thing.

The gun was taller than Joseph, and so heavy he could barely lift it, much less hold the barrel steady. Carrying News pointed at a maple trunk almost half as wide as the house, and Joseph lined it up and pulled the trigger. The flare of sparks beside his cheek almost blinded him, the cloud of sharp smoke going up his nose almost suffocated him, the trigger guard almost took his finger off as the gun jerked, and the sudden buck and boom of a deadweight too much for his arms so took him off balance that he ended up flat on his back with the gun pinning him like a wrestler.

Carrying News looked down at him and shrugged: "You'll get used to it."

"Did I hit the tree?"

"Well, you hit *a* tree. Now you load and I'll watch."

After half a dozen more tries, he finally hit the tree he was aiming at. He was getting more adept at loading, but his arms were so tired from trying to balance a gun too tall for him that he could hardly hold the barrel steady to take aim. He was saved the embarrassment of having to ask Carrying News if that wasn't enough for one day by Little Abraham riding into the yard. Carrying News took the gun back into the house, and Joseph and his Teacher went to the fallen oak tree in the woods that made a good bench to sit and talk.

Little Abraham rested his toasted-apple head on trellised fingers and said: "So, now that you are rested and fed, tell me how you lived in the mountains and how you found your way, so I'll know whether I've passed the test of being a good Teacher or if you are just lucky."

When Joseph got to the part about the wolf, his Teacher said: "You may tell *me* of that, but you must speak of it to no one else. Nor will I. When the time comes for you to choose another warrior to be your brother on the war road, you may tell him."

"I already told my sister."

"Ah. It may be that she knows to keep it to herself, but I will speak to her to be certain.

"It is a very powerful guardian who has offered to watch over you. The wolf is the fiercest fighter in the forest, and the strongest, excepting only the panther and bear. But unlike them, your friend cares for his family and his clan. I have seen him rolling about in the sunlight smiling while his children chewed his ears. I have seen him loping through the moonlight like smoke on the water—seeming only to be trotting lazily along, but if you blink your eyes he's out of sight. And I have seen him hunting with his brothers and sisters, driving a moose that was heavier and stronger than they themselves all together, ripping the meat off its bones while it ran.

"If the wolf himself stays with you through your life, you are lucky indeed. But if you disgrace him, or if you betray him by bragging of your powerful guardian, he will leave you alone. I have taught many boys who never found a guardian but still made fine warriors. And I have taught many boys who were lucky enough to be favored by a strong guardian, but never until now a wolf. The wolf can be a hard master, little one."

"Harder than you?"

His Teacher laughed. "As difficult as that may be to believe . . . It is a good thing to laugh when you can, little one—and a very good thing to be able to laugh in the teeth of the wolf. But never forget that those teeth are there, and they can crack your bones like you snap a dry twig."

When his Teacher had gone, Joseph went back into the house and found no one there except Si-isha. He had grown accustomed to other people calling her Mary, but she was still Si-isha to him. During the long two years when he only saw her for one summer and two Midwinter Festivals, he'd barely got a chance to see past the surface changes that had taken place in her betweentimes before she was gone again. But now she had become his sister once more. She could be annoying at times, but there was no denying that it was only since she came home for good that the place had become his home, instead of just the farm that belonged to the might-as-well-be-white Christian his mother had married.

Joseph always found it difficult to understand when other boys talked dismissively of their sisters. But then, the other boys all had other family to rely on. Joseph's father could die, and his mother could marry again and move out of the long-house, but his sister would always be his sister.

While he'd been in the woods with Little Abraham, she had changed into her new festival dress, with its typical Canienga rows of silver broaches that she'd modified by adding on a lot of lace as well. Most of the broaches and all of the lace and the velvet for her leggings had come from the money she'd got helping Carrying News gather ginseng roots in the forest. She had a headdress on of white deer hide, with two beaded ro-settes fixed at the temples to furl it down on either side of her face and frame a few artfully accidental black kiss curls. She was studying the effect in her hand mirror.

Joseph said: "Where did everyone go?"

"To Canajoharie, to leave the little one with Grandmother overnight. We're going to eat with William Johnson. You can come, too, if you like."

"Why would we eat with William Johnson?"

"Because he asked us. He says he's talked with you a few times before."

"Once or twice. When I was little he used to give me rock candy and make jokes about me bashing people's noses for Willy's sake."

"What do you think of him?"

It seemed an odd question. One didn't "think of" people that much older than oneself, they were just there, like the rocks and the trees. He said: "He doesn't speak very good Canien-ga."

"Well, you don't speak very good English." That seemed like an even odder thing to say.

His mother and Carrying News came back and went into their room to wash themselves and change their clothes. Joseph didn't intend to do either. He had no objections to going to Mount Johnson to eat: one look at William Johnson told the world his cook set a good table. But the few times Joseph had met him in the past didn't suggest that Gets Business Done was the kind to stand on formality.

Joseph changed his mind, though, when his mother came out in her black Sunday dress and said: "If you choose to come with us in your tattered old hunting shirt with your hair all in tangles, I will feel like a slovenly mother indeed." He washed his face and hands and finger-combed sunflower oil into his hair and put on his white linen longshirt over his loincloth and leggings. But the only concession he made to any festive atmosphere was to tie on the sleeve garter Si-isha had embroidered for him while she was away at school.

When he came back outside, Carrying News had saddled four horses. The one thing Joseph had definitely decided he would do when he became a man was own a lot of fine horses. But for now he had to settle for any chance that came up to ride his stepfather's.

Among the four was a new, big, beautiful bay mare with a new English saddle. Joseph oohed and aahed over her and began to get acquainted, brushing his fingertips down the soft, whorled mat of hair growing out of the hard plate of bone above her eyes. But when he asked Carrying News where he'd got her, the reply was: "I didn't. William Johnson gave her to Mary."

"To Mary? Why would William Johnson give her a horse?"

"Ask William Johnson."

The ride downriver to the ferry was perplexing. Si-isha kept chattering away like she was going to a Green Corn Dance, bouncing along on her big new horse. For all her chattering, she didn't say much of anything. Her eyes had a glassy sheen and her cheeks were flushed, so that she looked more like a glazed porcelain doll than a girl. Finally Joseph had to ask her: "Why did Gets Business Done give you a horse?"

"I guess because he wanted to. I think that's why Gets Business Done does everything he does."

The ferryman said to Carrying News: "Big doin's on t'other side of the river, Brant?"

"We go to dine with William Johnson."

"Oh. Eatin' with him's one thing, but don't be drinkin' with him. I tried matchin' him jug for jug the oncet, back when I was young and limber, and still ain't full mended."

Several scruffy-looking men in green coats were lounging about the front steps of the big stone house. They knocked their pipes out and sauntered forward to take charge of the horses as the Brant family dismounted. Joseph could hear music of a sort coming from inside.

The big front door was opened by a man with straw hair and sagging hose. He led them into a tall, wide hallway—walking as though his shoes hurt—and gestured them through the first doorway on the left. There was a bright-painted room with perhaps a dozen people in it. A copper-haired girl in a green dress was standing playing a silver sideways flute beside a larger version of herself sitting at a wooden box with teeth that made a grating, tinkling sound. The other people sat in listening postures on the padded chairs and couches dotted around the room. Green-eyed Willy was there; and a yellow-haired boy with a pouty face; a goose-necked, pale woman with watery eyes; a couple of white men in dark broadcloth; and William Johnson—who sprang up and came sweeping toward the doorway in silk brocade and lace, booming out in that chesty voice that sounded like boulders rolling down a hill, "Demmed glad to see y'remembered the way, Brant, I was beginnin' to despair of ye," and a horde of other English words Joseph couldn't follow.

Willy scrunched himself sideways in his chair so there'd be room for Joseph to squeeze in beside him. A servant brought a tray of little cakes and a glass of yellow liquid. Joseph tried a bite of one of the cakes and found it so sugary he could hardly choke it down. The liquid wasn't much better. He whispered to Willy in Canienga: "Who are all these people?"

"The girl playing the flute," Willy whispered back, "is Mary my sister. Sort of sister, 'cause her mother was—is—my father's German wife. The other girl is Ann, her sister, and the goosey-necked woman's their Teacher. Then there's their brother, John. Everybody thought he'd still be at school in New York Town, but he came back of a sudden yesterday. Gets Business Done is always sending him off to a school somewhere, and he's always coming back of a sudden. Looks like he'll stay here now until my father can find another school."

"And the two white men?"

"Clerks in my father's fur business. There's so many of them, I can't ever remember which is which."

"White men all look the same."

They both started to giggle, but then Joseph's mother shot him a glance that showed they were making too much noise for politeness while the music was playing. So he hissed: "We better be quiet" at Willy, and sat trying to look like he was pleased to be in William Johnson's house.

He'd never had any reason to dislike Gets Business Done. William Johnson had always impressed him as the apt white yokemate for King Hendrick—bigger and bluffer, but without that awesome dignity. But there was something off-putting about William Johnson today. The way he'd patted the chair seat Si-isha was to sit on was almost obscene. As for Si-isha, Joseph could see she'd put on the same false bravery as when Grandmother asked her to lead the girls in singing, although he couldn't see why.

When William Johnson's daughters finished playing, everyone patted their palms together. The girls put their hands on their skirts and made odd little ducking motions. Their Teacher took them each by the hand and led them out of the room. Watching them go, Joseph noticed that the one who'd been sitting at the jangling box was almost as tall as Si-isha. He didn't know why that should offend him, but it did, as did the fact that John Johnson looked to be just about exactly as old as he was himself.

The smells of real food began to emanate from another part of the house. After an interminable time William Johnson announced that they could eat now and led the way, with Si-isha's arm in his, as though she couldn't walk across a hallway without help. They came into another big room, with a long table where Joseph got sat down between Willy and Si-isha, next to William Johnson at the head of the table.

In front of Joseph was an array of brightly colored plates and bowls flanked by files of silver knives and forks and those silly little English spoons that you had to dip ten times to get as much as one scoop with a good Canienga spoon. Si-isha whispered to him: "Just start from the outside and let them take the dirty ones away with each bowl or plate."

"Why don't they just make one good-sized spoon instead of all these little ones?"

"That's just how they do it."

Joseph had eaten English food before, but never so many different kinds at once. White-wigged black servants kept taking away his dish before he was finished and filling a fresh one from the platters that other servants carried up through a hatchway in the corner. When there was more than one kind of food on his plate, he noticed Si-isha glancing at him impatiently as he spooned up each kind separately instead of mixing them on a fork as she did.

He didn't like the fact that William Johnson's daughters didn't appear at the table, as though the guests were too crude for them. He didn't like the way John Johnson's eyes glided over Willy, as though he were a stranger instead of his half brother. And he didn't like the way William Johnson's eyes lingered on Si-isha. Her blushes should have made it obvious to anyone with good manners that she found it embarrassing.

Although Joseph's ear for English wasn't developed enough to be certain at first, it seemed that William Johnson used an odd name when he spoke to Si-isha. After it had happened several times, he whispered to her in Canienga: "Why does he call you 'Molly'?"

William Johnson chortled, "It's the Irish in me, Joseph," whatever that was supposed to mean.

After the food was all gone, although half of it hadn't been eaten, they all went back into the room they'd started in. Si-isha surprised him by sitting down at the box with teeth and making music of a sort. William Johnson squeezed onto the bench beside her and hammered out a melody while bellowing:

"In Dublin's fair city,
Where girls are so pretty,
I first laid my eyes on sweet Molly Malone . . ."

Joseph found it painful to watch Gets Business Done lose what dignity he had, and poor Si-isha having to indulge it, so he let his eyes drift around the room. Among the pictures and musical instruments hung on the walls were Canienga headdresses and painted war clubs from other nations, as though the purpose of the True People of Turtle Island were to provide toys for William Johnson.

William Johnson appeared to have more toys than any spoilt child. There was a glass-domed contrivance with a fan-bladed thing inside that William Johnson set whirling with a hand crank. When Si-isha politely obeyed his instructions to take her headdress off and put her hand on the glass, her hair stood out in all directions like a frightened porcupine. Si-isha whooped with alarm, Carrying News whooped with laughter, and Joseph's mother muttered a Canienga deflection against witch-craft.

It seemed to Joseph that everyone was going a bit far to give William Johnson the impression that his toy was remarkable. Particularly Si-isha when she let him put his big, fat arm around her as though she needed reassuring.

The people in the room came and went throughout the evening, either to the little house in the bushes or to look out from the front step at the ring around the moon, or elsewhere. At one point Joseph noticed that Si-isha and William Johnson were both out of the room at the same time. They came back into the room a few minutes apart, but they both had the same shade of pink brushed into their cheeks, despite their differing complexions. Although he couldn't have said precisely why, Joseph found himself increasingly certain that it would feel good to smash a baggataway stick across a certain big, long nose.

CHAPTER 16

Billy Johnson wasn't certain whether he was in love or in lust, but he was definitely up to his nostrils in one or the other. As if it weren't enough that the demmed gel was extraordinarily lively and quick-witted, with bright black eyes in an exquisitely high-boned set of features, a taut young body under those floppy Indian dresses, and an education that had prepared her for the rigors of the formal dining hall or the music room—she had to go and have that extraordinary self-possession as well. And it wasn't the brittle arrogance of youth, either, waiting to shatter at the inevitable revelation that its possessor was as much an ass as any other human being. There were moments when it was dead obvious that she was just brazening it out without feeling sure of herself at all— which made it all the more remarkable when she carried it off.

He was also well aware there were advantages to having a wife whose people he did business with. If it hadn't been for Catty Weisenberg, the farmers at German Flats would probably have remained as suspicious of him as of those marble-mansioned thimbleriggers in Albany and New York Town. And Yellow Shoes had done an admirable job of smoothing the road between the Mohawk castles and Mount Johnson. But at the moment, business and political considerations weren't at the top of his list.

He was under no illusions that he was any young girl's dream of a romantic lover. Ten years ago, perhaps, but tall, dark, handsome Big Billy had crammed a lot of living into forty-two years, and the strain was beginning to show. He knew that he was cheerful-enough company in a bombastic sort of way, that he was still a long ways from his dotage and was well set up in the world and getting more so every day. Not exactly a romantic set of credentials, perhaps, but there was more to marriage than romance. And when he'd whispered in his moment alone with Molly on the back steps that she'd make a demmed fine ornament to the dinner table at Mount Johnson *every* night, she hadn't thrown up her hands and run screaming.

The devil of it was that with a Mohawk girl it wasn't just a question of getting the girl to acquiesce, or even her family. Not that the Iroquois were overpriggish when it came to affairs of the heart and other organs. In the days when he'd been ranging about Iroquoia with a canoeful of trade goods, they used to send him beautiful young creatures in pairs to warm his pallet in the longhouse. But marriage was a different matter, especially marriage to a white man, as he'd learned the hard way when he made what he'd thought was a simple proposal to poor, dead Yellow Shoes. The notion of a woman leaving the longhouse, and taking her potential children with her, put the whole community in such a flap that everyone had to get in on it.

On the morning a council fire was kindled at Canajoharie, so the Mohawk Nation could discuss matters likely to come up at the annual fall council, Gets Business Done selected a belt of white wampum from the trunkful in the attic. And not the

cheap glass imitations that had ruined wampum as currency
when New York was still New Amsterdam, but the genuine,
old, hand-drilled-from-seashells wampum. Then he mounted
Old Knobby with about as much enthusiasm as though there
were a gallows waiting at the other end.

The ceremonial longhouse at Canajoharie Castle was
jammed to the roof poles. Although only councillors could
make speeches, any member of the tribe was free to listen.
Johnson would've been damned hard-pressed to squeeze his
beef-fed bulk inside if it weren't that there was a mat set aside
in the inner circle for Gets Business Done. He grunted down
onto the mat as Hendrick crumpled tobacco onto the fire to set
the council in motion.

There were one or two matters of more pressing general interest than the matrimonial fate of Molly Brant. The Senecas
had sent a cluster of red-painted strings of black wampum, inviting the Canienga to join in wiping out the new French forts
that were choking off trade between the Six Nations and the
Ojibway. The Ojibway trade was more than just a question of
middleman fur trade profits, but of one of the staffs of life—
birchbark canoes. An Iroquois paddler could make a birchbark
canoe stand on end and do pirouettes, but they'd just never got
the knack of making them as well as the Ojibway—probably
because the paper birch didn't grow as well in Iroquoia as in
the country north of the Great Lakes.

What with the war proposal and other matters, not to mention the fact that each Royaner or Oyander who had something
to say on the subject had to say it all before passing on the
wampum representing that particular matter, it was evening by
the time Johnson felt it might be appropriate to present his little personal matter.

He heaved himself up to his feet, took the white wampum
belt out of his pocket and began to speak in Mohawk. He'd often had the thought that the measure of the Iroquois' self-
discipline, and the solemnity of the councils, was that even the
children standing on the wall benches managed to keep their
faces straight in the face of his butchered attempts at their language. It was demmed hard to express one's self in a language
that didn't have a word for "demmed."

"Brothers and Sisters—I, Gets Business Done, have been
given many gifts and shown much kindness over the years by

my friends the Canienga. I believe I have given back somewhat in return—and I believe you believe so, too. Else you would not have done me the honor of trusting me enough to give me a voice in your councils, and of allowing me to take to wife one of your daughters. You mourned with me when she walked the road where the strawberries are always growing.

"It has been three years now I have lived without a wife. And I am not an old man yet . . ." There was a low murmur of deep, chesty chortles and bell-like titters. It was permitted to laugh around the council fire—even obligatory—provided that the person speaking said something intended to amuse.

Big Billy cleared the frog out of his throat and launched into the heart of the matter. "There is among you a young woman, a daughter of the Wolf Clan. . . ." He knew he didn't have to specify further. The little bird Tskleleli had undoubtedly been flitting about Canajoharie and the Lower Castle since the first day he and Molly had gone out riding.

"Although she is a woman of the Canienga, she would not feel out of place at Mount Johnson. She has lived among the English at Schenectady, and I only hope my daughters grow up to know as much about how to be an English Oyander as she does.

"Many English Royaners, Oyanders, war chiefs, and men of business visit Mount Johnson. Were the woman of the house a Canienga, they would come away knowing you much better than only hearing of you through me. And a sister of yours whose hearth fire warmed those travelers would know better than I how to tell you what manner of men they are. The Hodenosaune and the English have stood together for a long time, and have come to understand each other a little—but still not as much as we should. Every link added to the Covenant Chain makes it stronger.

"Were she to come to Mount Johnson as my wife, I would do all I could to make her life a happy one—although I doubt as happy as she would mine. She makes me young again."

He laid the wampum belt down beside the fire and creaked his stiff joints back down onto the mat. For some reason, he'd come all over asweat, and he would've given his left foot—the goutless one—for a mug of ale. Or better yet, a flagon of brandy.

Hendrick picked up the belt and proceeded to orate, acting

out the words as much as speaking them. An accomplished Royaner could make his audience feel white water around them by miming how he'd paddled his canoe through the rapids. He began by repeating his brother Gets Business Done's speech, almost word for word, only a good deal more elegantly. In the Indian manner of speaking by metaphor, "she would not feel out of place" became "she would not be a doe in a cow shed."

Johnson had long since ceased to wonder at the uncanny ability of Iroquoian councillors to remember each other's speeches. It came partly from spending a large part of their lives around council fires, and partly from that habit of repeating the pertinent parts of a preceding speech as stalking horses. It did stretch matters out, but they came away with a better understanding of what had transpired than they would from yelling into each other's faces while a clerk scribbled it down for posterity.

At the moment, though, Big Billy would have gladly traded better understanding for a quick verdict. It occurred to him that Hendrick's tomahawk scar looked suspiciously like someone had tried to cut his mouth off.

Hendrick finally finished improving on what his brother Gets Business Done had said and turned to him. "Gets Business Done, we hear the words which you have spoken, and they weigh heavy on our ears. You have been a good friend to us. And, through that friendship, you and we have made each other rich in many ways. We all of us rejoice when a man and woman are brought together as they should be. And rejoice even further when the day comes that he becomes part of her mother's longhouse.

"But you, Gets Business Done, are not asking that of us. You are asking us to let you take this daughter of the Wolf Clan away from us. Although it is true that her mother and Carrying News choose to live in a small house outside the walls of Canajoharie, their *onikonhras* remain inside the longhouse. Mount Johnson is another matter.

"When you asked us before for one of our daughters, we struggled with this question long and hard before saying yes. And even then, some still thought it was a mistake—although once the question was decided, they kept their doubts out of their mouths, as it should be. We gave to you one of our daughters and you gave back to us your son. But our daughter lived such a short time. Perhaps it was not meant for the True People of Turtle Island to live as the English do. Our *orenda* was made weaker by the losing of her."

Orenda was one of those words, like *onikonhra*, that Johnson knew he only caught the simplest gist of. It had something to do with the power or spirit of a clan, hence of a nation and the Six Nations as a whole.

Hendrick went on, naturally. "If the loss of a man to us weakens our *orenda*, how much more so a woman—who takes with her all the yet-unborn men and women carried inside her? Because you are Gets Business Done, and not some other Englishman, we agreed once that one of our daughters could go with you. But now you ask us for another. Were you not Gets Business Done, I would say no now, full certain that I speak for all who are assembled here. But since you are our old friend and brother, I think that we should talk this over some little time amongst ourselves before giving you an answer. I think not tomorrow—perhaps the next day."

Big Billy nodded stiffly and climbed even more stiffly back to his feet. He headed for the longhouse door, leaving the wampum belt behind. It would be delivered back to him along with the verdict. The smoke was stinging his eyes something fierce. Just before he stooped out the doorway, he thought he caught a glimpse of glittering black eyes framed by a white deerskin headdress among the women, but he couldn't be sure.

CHAPTER 17

Mary Brant was in a welter of confusion. It was more than a little heady to see a man like Gets Business Done—as though there were any others like him—humble himself in front of the council to ask for her hand. She would be forever famous among the Hodenosaune just for that.

During the past two years, the only point in the future she'd looked toward was the day when she could walk out the school door for the last time. Since that day, she'd begun to wonder what was going to become of the rest of her life. If she were to marry William Johnson, her future would be assured almost before she'd started worrying about it. Not any of the proud white girls at the Young Ladies Finishing School could aspire to marrying a wealthier man than William Johnson.

On the other hand, she wasn't as certain as William Johnson seemed to be of how easily she'd fit in at Mount Johnson. Two years of schooling didn't change the fact that she hadn't even seen a porcelain teacup till she was thirteen years old. And while other girls her age would be flirting with young men and gradually learning to be women, she would be thrown immediately into the role of a grizzled giant's wife.

On the other hand, there was more to William Johnson than his wealth and age. It was impossible not to enjoy his company. But it was also impossible not to be just a little afraid of a man of such ferocious passions.

There was something physically exciting about that passion and power. But she couldn't help but wonder whether her half-formed *onikonhra* wouldn't get swallowed up in his before it had a chance to bloom.

All in all, Mary was glad the decision wasn't hers to make. She sat down beside her grandmother and behind her mother in the evening council of the Clan Mothers. As in the men's councils, those sitting in the inner circle could have whispered conversations with the advisers behind them, but otherwise no one was permitted to speak except the councillor holding the wampum denoting the matter at hand. There were several important matters to be discussed that night, most importantly—at least to everyone but Mary Brant—the red war strings the Senecas had sent.

Although war was men's business, if the Clan Mothers decided a particular war had gone on too long or was ill-advised, the women could put a stop to it. No man could stay on the war road long without a pouchful of spare moccasins and a bag of cornmeal.

Mary was confused by the message the Canienga Clan

Mothers agreed to send to their Seneca sisters. It said that as long as the Keepers of the Sunset remained friends with the French, the French would keep giving them presents for discouraging the Keepers of the Dawn from scalping Frenchmen. She whispered to her grandmother: "I thought the Covenant Chain made the Hodenosaune friends with the English, who are enemies of the French?"

Her grandmother whispered back: "Friends and enemies may change; the Tree of Peace remains."

The presiding Oyander picked up the white belt that William Johnson had left with King Hendrick. "Sisters—in the usual course of things, we of the Turtle Clan would not presume to speak to our sisters of the Wolf Clan on a matter concerning one of their daughters. But we believe that this wish of Gets Business Done to take your daughter away from us is unfortunate. It is hard to say no to a man who has been such a good friend to us for so long a time—although his friendship has not been entirely without profit to himself. . . ." There was a ripple of laughter. "But a man must be said no to from time to time, as hard as it may be. And a man of his age must have heard the word before."

There was a good deal more laughter. When it was done, the Oyander went on in a softer tone: "Who among us does not wish to see that old stag of a man happy? Is there any among us does not feel something for a man who has had to grieve for two wives already—one dead and one hovering on the lip of death for years—and yet who still has the heart to take the chance of grieving for a third?

"But I say: let him find a woman of his own kind. In the towns and farms of the white people I have seen many a patch-dressed young white woman who would be glad to marry an aging rich man in hopes that he would eat strawberries while she was still young. We Canienga have given Gets Business Done one of our daughters; that is enough. If he is not friend enough to us to be told no from time to time, he is no friend at all." Then she stepped around the fire to put the wampum belt in the hands of Someone Lends Her a Flower and squatted back down on her mat.

Mary's mother stood up. "My daughter spent two hard years in the English school away from us. But she bore it, for our sakes. Because we together had determined it would be a help to us. She gave us those two years we asked of her, and she suffered the English schoolteachers to order her about—with all the meekness and mildness that is in her nature."

There was a murmur of knowing chuckles. Mary felt like a calf listening to the farmer and the butcher talk about the weather.

"My daughter gave us those two years so that in future years our councils would have the benefit of what she'd learned about the English and their ways of thinking. Although it might seem like a boastful thing for a mother to say, her *onikonhra* would be even more of a loss to our *orenda* than losing *any* girl about to become a woman. I am sorry for Gets Business Done. But I say my daughter should not have given us those two years—and two years is a long time in the life of a girl—only to have us give her away."

Someone Lends Her a Flower moved to hand the white belt back to the Elder Sister of the Turtle Clan. Mary could feel it slipping through her fingers, and knew what she wanted. She sprang on her feet and snatched it, shouting: "This is *my* life!"

She found herself standing by the council fire with the belt held over her head, surrounded by the aghast faces of the inner circle. The usually slitted mouth and eyes of the Elder Sister of the Bear Clan were bugged out round like a Corn Husk mask. The Elder Sister of the Turtle Clan had clapped her hand over her eyes.

"Forgive me, Oyanders—mothers and grandmothers and sisters—but this *is* my life." What to say next? No one tore the belt out of her hands or spat on her or stood up to shout her down. Her mother looked like she wanted to crawl under the nearest rock. "I don't mean to disgrace my mother, but I must say something. . . . After that, I will live by whatever you decide."

Mary closed her mouth to moisten it, then opened her lips again. "It isn't easy for me to think of me as just something useful to you, and a part of our *orenda*. Maybe I should, but I think there are other girls my age who also have other things on their minds besides council fires." Her grandmother laughed out loud and the presiding Oyander covered her mouth to hide a smile. Mary wasn't certain whether they were laughing at her or whether they thought she'd said something witty, but she still felt a pinch less terrified. "But I do understand—please believe me—the reasons you've said what you've said. As much as I can . . . I understand well enough to know that me marrying Gets Business Done would be a help to you, and the whole League of Peace. Or so it seems to me.

"You wanted me to go to school in Schenectady so I could help you understand the whites better. Would it not be so much more so if I were married to a white man? And not a white man who would take me away to live in a white town, but one who lives nearby, one who in fact has been so close to the Canienga that we gave him a voice in our councils. And, as Gets Business Done said, the English Royaners and Oyanders always stay in his home when they pass by this way. I would be there, and I would hear what they say among themselves, and I would be able to tell you if it's different from what they say in their speeches to us.

"Were I the wife of Gets Business Done, I would still be part of the longhouse. Mount Johnson is hardly farther from here than Carrying News's farm. And Gets Business Done would not keep me tied to a chair in his kitchen.

"Each year brings more and more white men to our valley, and they all look to William Johnson as their chief. When a white farmer starts to clear away part of our forest without asking, is it not William Johnson who invokes the English law to make him stop? Is it not Gets Business Done who tells the white Royaners in New York Town what they must do to keep the Covenant Chain intact?

"Would it not be a help to thee—mothers and grandmothers and sisters—to have one of thy daughters always by the side of the man who is the hand of the English king on our part of Turtle Island?"

She was afraid of what was going to happen when she stopped talking, afraid she'd talked too long, afraid that she hadn't yet said what she needed to say, afraid that if she paused too long to think of what else she should say, they would take the opportunity to take the wampum belt away from her. "That is all I have to say . . . except this! In all the old stories, it is the young girl who begs the council *not* to make her go with the old chief of the neighboring tribe for the sake of her nation—not the other way around."

She stooped down to drape the belt across the lap of the presiding Clan Mother, muttered, "Forgive me, Oyander," and shuffled back to her place with her head bowed for the ax.

The Oyander lifted the belt, peering at it like she'd never seen it before, and said to it: "Were I Gets Business Done, I'd make sure to keep her tied to a chair in the kitchen."

CHAPTER 18

Big Billy and his Molly were married according to the rites recognized by those who dwelt under the Tree of Peace. As to the blessings of the Church of England, she said she didn't know what the hell such a fusspot of a god had to do with a man and woman bedding down together. Demmed headstrong when she got the bit in her teeth, but that oughtn't to've come as a surprise. In this case he was just as glad. A registered church marriage would have entailed some complications that he wasn't quite sure how he might've resolved.

When he brought his bride home from Canajoharie, he instructed Horace to light the bedroom candles and then go to bed. In the parlor he poured out a good quaff of brandy for himself and a smaller one for Molly. He clinked glasses with: "May I see ye gray and combin' yer children's hair." She blushed and sipped and wrinkled her nose and then sipped again. He blew out all the candles except the one to light their way to bed and said: "Well, m'dear?"

Horace had practically set the bedroom ablaze with candles, not to mention the Guy Fawkes conflagration in the fireplace. Johnson carried his candlestick toward his dressing screen, pointing at its newly installed companion on the opposite side of the hearth: "That's yer dressin' screen, m'dear. Tomorrow we'll take a jaunt over to the seamstress's in Schenectady and make a start at fillin' up the closet behind it."

Behind his dressing screen he gratefully set his wig on its stand and gave his itchy scalp a good scratch with the fingertips of both hands. Once in his nightshirt, he reached automatically for his nightcap and then hesitated. It was a question of which looked more ridiculous: the tassled nightcap or his own grizzled, balding, close-cropped brush of hair. He decided to forgo the nightcap. Better she should know the worst at first. Besides, he didn't expect to have to worry about catching a chill within the bed curtains tonight.

When he came out from behind his dressing screen, she was standing beside hers looking down at the floor. She'd taken off her headdress and combed out her glorious, waist-length raven wings of hair, but other than that the only clothing she'd removed were her moccasins and leggings. He said as gently as he could manage: "Not ready for bed yet, Molly?"

Without looking up at him, she said: "I'd thought ... I didn't think to bring a nightgown. I haven't worn one since Schenectady. It's packed away with all my other things being sent over tomorrow."

"I'd've been demmed disappointed if ye had. For a saggy old warthog like m'self, a nightshirt's a courtesy to the eyes and digestion of other human bein's. But *ye*, m'dear—here, let me help ye. ..." He unbuttoned the neck slit on her overdress with surprisingly fumbly fingers and pulled it off over her head as she raised her arms. Her breasts were high and rounded rather than pointy, and they danced when she shook her head and ran her fingers through her hair. He reached for the leather bow dangling on the hip of her estimably pragmatic Mohawk skirt—one tug on the drawstring and down it came.

He stepped back and looked her up and down—the smooth, taut thighs and neatly nipped-in waist which his hands itched to discover if they could encircle completely; the nipples poking out through the curtains of hair; the chin raised in a kind of defiant "all right, if you want to look me over, do and be demmed t'ye." In the yellow candlelight she was a gold-and-ebony statue of Venus rising from the waves of the skirt puddled around her feet. He whispered, "Sufferin' Judas," then reached out to take her hand. "Come to bed before ye catch a chill or I have apoplexy."

One factor he hadn't considered was that he couldn't feast his eyes on her once enclosed in the drapery cave of the bed.

It was probably just as well, for the sake of his heart and her stomach, until they got used to the sight of each other.

It was astounding how sweet a human mouth could taste when it hadn't taken in several decades of tobacco and Madeira and roast beef. He proceeded as slowly as he could manage, skating his fingertips over the silky hills and hollows of her body. But he was also aware of the danger, if he proceeded *too* slowly, of finishing before he'd begun.

The last thing he'd expected to encounter—given the ribald strain that ran through some of her banter, and the Mohawks' general neglect to inculcate their children with the doctrine of Original Sin—was a hymen. But before his guiding principle had poked much more than its head inside her, there it was. When he broke it, she let out a howl like a bobcat on fire. A moment or two later it was his turn to howl. He heaved himself out of and off of her, flopped onto his back and plunged straight into a sleep deeper than the riverbed of the Styx.

He woke up cold and alone.

An excessively sharp crack of sunlight was forcing its way in through the gap between the bed curtains. He flung the curtains wide, snatched up the little silver bell and gave it hell, then automatically opened his mouth to bellow for Horace. Before the bellow left his throat, the door opened and Horace entered—with his hair combed almost cowlickless, his hose unwrinkled, and the morning cup balanced perfectly on a salver polished so bright the sunlight paled by comparison. "Good morning, Mr. Johnson, sir. Which suit of clothes should I be a-laying out for you this morning, sir?"

Johnson blinked at him suspiciously and sipped his chocolate. It was exactly right: not three-quarters of an ounce of brandy, not an ounce and a half, but one precise ounce. Or so demmed close he couldn't tell the difference. Perhaps he was still asleep and dreaming.

Horace said: "Which shall it be, Mr. Johnson?"

"Which? Which what?"

"Which suit of clothes?"

"Oh. What say . . . the brown one with the yellow what-ye-may-call'ems."

"I'm afraid I can't do that, sir."

"Why the bleedin' hell not?"

"Miss Molly has packed it up with the other clothes as need laundering, sir. Said something about a gravy stain . . ."

"Well, the demmed suit's brown and so's gravy. . . ."

"Maybe it were on one of them yellow what-ye-may-call'ems."

"Well . . . lay out m'green one, then."

"Which of the green ones would you prefer, sir?"

"*Any* demmed green one. Suit yerself. Or suit me, more like. Ha ha—suits me . . . Oh, go on about yer business."

The chamber pot had been emptied and scrubbed to a sheen. There seemed to have been a lot of activity going on about the master bedroom while the master was snoring away.

When he came downstairs, the kitchen maid looked up from fussing with the table settings and said: "I'm very sorry, Mr. Johnson, sir, but your breakfast'll be a little late. Mistress Molly said only a few moments longer, sir."

"Where the divil is she?"

"In the kitchen, sir."

"What the divil is she doin' in the bleedin' kitchen?" It was a rhetorical question, directed at the sideboard as he flung open the trapdoor to the scullery and tromped down the steps, scuffing his shoulders on the hatchway frame. Molly was at the hearth, flipping rashers of bacon in a skillet. "What the divil are ye doin' in the bleedin' kitchen?"

"Cooking your breakfast."

"I can see that. We have a cook to do the demmed cookin'."

"Not anymore we don't. This place was a pesthole—with meat rotting in the larder and mouse droppings in the flour bin. When I pointed that out to the cook, she replied disrespectfully. She's upstairs packing her traps together. I know of a very good cook in Schenectady who would be more than happy to leave her present situation."

"Well I'm demmed. Shoot a few for an example, hm?"

"Pardon me?"

"Nothin', Miss Molly—just an old military expression. If ye want me for anythin', I'll be waitin' meekly at me station in the dinin' room."

CHAPTER 19

Miss Molly set out on a solo expedition to explore her domain. Her husband had been called away to Fort Hunter. He'd fumed curses about being dragged away the morning after his wedding night, but said it couldn't be helped and expected to be no more than an hour or two.

She'd already seen the cellar, with its cooking hearth and aisles of bins and barrels, so she decided to go up to the top of the house and work her way down. As she was going up the stairs to the second floor, a servant bearing a basket of laundry was coming down. Perhaps among its contents were the bloody sheets from the master's bed. "G'morning, Miss Molly."

"Good morning." There were so many of them, it would only be over time she learned their names. They seemed to have no trouble accepting her immediately as mistress of the house, but perhaps that was only because the story of the cook had got around. Perhaps it had been a wise strategic move to fire the cook, but it had only happened because she'd lost her temper when the cook said: "I ain't about to take lessons on keeping a clean kitchen from a squaw."

Another servant was scrubbing the floor of the broad second floor hallway. "Excuse me . . ."

"Yes, Miss Molly?"

For all the servants' deference, "Miss Molly" couldn't quite forget the fact that all of them knew what had happened in their master's bed last night, at least in general terms. Most of it had been pain, some of which came back every time she raised a leg to climb a stair. But just before William had stopped, she'd felt the beginnings of a very interesting, dilated,

149

filled feeling. She hoped that the next time that feeling would start a little sooner, or William would stop a little later.

Trying to keep herself from blushing, she said to the floor scrubber: "Would I need a candle to see in the attic?"

"Ain't nothing up there to see, miss, but servants' quarters and storage."

"I know, but I want to see all the house for myself," although as soon as she'd said it, she wondered if it wouldn't be an intrusion on the servants' privacy.

"Of course you would, miss. At this time of day there should be plenty enough light coming through the attic windows."

"Thank you."

"Miss Molly . . . ?"

"Yes?"

"I know it ain't my place to say, but we're all of us glad to see Mr. Johnson happy."

"Thank you. Thank you very much."

On her way up the attic stairs she realized she finally had a name of her own. William Johnson might've given it to her, but it was more hers than the one her mother had picked out of a Bible or the name she'd worn as a child.

The attic was a wide cavern with servants' cubicles and trunks and crates piled up to the slope of the roof. Molly took a cursory glance from the head of the stairs and went back down to the second floor. At the back end of the hallway was a door on either side. One of them was open, disclosing a narrow room with two beds and trundle beds and the impersonal look of a guest room. The other door was closed. Molly knocked, and when no one answered, turned the knob. It was another narrow little room, this one with a bed, a desk, framed pictures on the walls, and various boy's things scattered about. It had to be John's room. Neither one of the back rooms had hearths, so Molly suspected they didn't get used much in the winter except to jump under a mound of quilts and furs as quickly as possible.

In front of John's room was the big master bedroom, which she was already acquainted with. That left one door, across the hall from the master bedroom. She went and knocked, then tried the knob. It turned, but the door wouldn't open. She turned to the servant scrubbing the floor. "Why is this door locked?"

"That's Miss Ann and Miss Mary's room, Miss Molly. And their governess. She always locks it when they go out to take the air."

Molly didn't like the idea of a locked room in her house that she didn't have a key for. Oddly, she could hear the sound of twittering birds from behind the door. But then, everything related to William's daughters seemed a little odd. Or maybe it was the way their father related to them.

On her way back downstairs Molly glanced over her shoulder at the woman huffing and puffing over the scrub brush. It felt a bit uncomfortable to see a hired woman doing her housework. The Ladies Finishing School should've accustomed her to servants doing all the work, but that hadn't been her home.

Below John's room and the guest room were two other narrow rooms. One was another guest room, and the other had the look of an office. The windows in both of them looked more like the loopholes in a fort.

Molly had already seen the parlor and dining room, with their big front windows and high fireplaces, so she went out the back door to explore the grounds. She went first to the hedged-in outhouse that she'd only seen by candlelight before. It had curtained windows and a roof shaped like an onion. Its capacious interior was wainscoted with the same artfully beveled, painted paneling as the parlor and dining room. As Gets Business Done had said: "What with one thing and another, a man can end up spendin' a good portion of his life out there. Might as well be comfortable."

She came out of the hedge debating where to scout next. The estate called Mount Johnson stood between the hill called Mount Johnson and the river. She turned toward the river and walked across the lawn, skating her fingers along the top of the stone wall that stood between the front of the house and the riverbank.

The lawn was bounded on the east by a pretty creek. Beyond the creek were pastures mottled with fat cattle, and a cornfield where the eldest of the Three Sisters stood in lonely ranks with no younger sisters to cling to her.

To the west the lawn ended at a fenced garden with rows of fruit trees down the middle and flanking both sides. Some of

Mount Johnson's black slaves and white farmhands were up on ladders picking apples. Horace the valet was leaning across a fence rail watching them. He straightened up when he saw her coming and took the grass stock out of his mouth, then glanced at the sun and said: "Afternoon, Miss Molly."

"Good afternoon, Horace. It looks as though we'll have a lot of apples to keep us through the winter."

He shook his head dourly. "Be a lot sweeter if'n they'd leave 'em on the trees a few more days. They oughtn't to be takin' anythin' but windfalls for cider yet, but that old overseer don't listen to nobody."

"You seem to know a lot about farming for someone who spends his days inside."

"I never had it in mind to be a house servant, miss. That were my father's idea, and Mr. Johnson's. I do have to admit the wages are better'n a fieldhand's."

"I expect you know a lot about this place."

"As much as anyone, miss, includin' that dang fool of an overseer—beggin' your pardon, miss."

"Perhaps you'd care to show me around, while you have an hour when you don't need to fetch and carry for Warraghiyagey—Mr. Johnson."

"Don't mind if'n I do, Miss Molly. But I'd best not be draggin' these shiny new shoes through the mud or Old Gory'll skin me."

"Old who?"

"Ahem, um, Mr. Johnson, that is. Just you wait here a minute, miss. I won't be more'n two shakes."

He went into the house and came back out a few minutes later with scuffed boots on his feet and a smile on his face. "Well, you've already seen the garden, Miss Molly—that is, I could spend all day showin' you 'round the garden, but I reckon you want to see the rest of the place as well. If'n you'd care to just follow along this path here . . ."

Set back behind the house was a clutch of smaller buildings. Horace pointed as they ambled along the path. "That there's the cooper's, and the bakehouse, and the big one's the mill. You can see the ackyduck that carries the water down from the millpond. She's got a few seams gettin' sprung in 'er, but that man don't think of seein' to nothin' till it's broke but good.

And that there towery kind of thing's the pigeon house—or dovecote, they calls it."

As they rounded the corner of the cooperage, a glimpse of pink chintz and green silk disappeared through the dovecote door. Horace stopped and said: "If'n you want to have a look at the birds, Miss Molly, I'll wait for you here."

"Why is that?"

"That was Miss Ann and Miss Mary goin' in there. Mr. Johnson don't like no men bein' around them, 'ceptin' hisself and young Master John."

"That doesn't sound very pleasant for them."

"Beggin' your pardon, Miss Molly, but if'n *you* want to say that to Mr. Johnson, you just go right ahead. Me, I like my head settin' right here on my shoulders where it belongs."

Miss Molly approached the dovecote and opened the door. The inside was a rounded tower going straight up to the turreted roof. The air was warm and thick with the cooing of iridescent birds half the size of wild pigeons. The floor was carpeted with straw and down and pigeon droppings. Shafts of light slanted in through the loopholes in the walls.

The girls and their governess turned to the doorway from cooing over a clutch of chicks in a lower roost. It occurred to Molly that every time she'd seen her husband's daughters, they'd been wearing pink chintz dresses and green silk petticoats. The only difference now was that they both wore hooped silk bonnets to shield their delicate complexions from the sun. Between the two of them, they didn't have a chin to call their own, but that was almost made up for by the gold and copper hair hanging down their backs.

Molly said: "Good afternoon."

The governess, whose eyes had grown redder and more watery since Molly last saw her, said: "Good afternoon." The girls said nothing.

"Well, I just thought I'd come and see your lovely birds."

Ann said: "These aren't our birds. Our birds are in our room. Finches and canaries and a thrush." Ann couldn't have been more than two or three years younger than her new stepmother, but her manner was still that of a little child, as though the growth of her *onikonhra* had been stunted like an ornamental shrub.

Molly said: "Ah, those were the songs I heard in the house. I'd like to come see them sometime."

The governess sniffed: "I don't see when. In the afternoon they have their half hour with their father. Mornings are Bible readings, and then their books of history and literary romance. In the summer they have their flowers to tend, and in the winter sleigh rides for fresh air, and chess and shuttlecock for recreation. And then there is their needlework . . ."

Molly couldn't decide whether the governess was being intentionally rude or whether that was how she spoke to everyone except her employer and her charges. It couldn't have been very pleasant to suddenly discover that another woman was going to be wedged in at the top of the household. So Molly just said to the girls: "What kind of needlework do you do?"

Ann replied: "Ornamental pieces for ladies' dresses. Collars and cuffs and bodices and—"

"Is 'bodices' vulgar?" her little sister interjected.

"Not in its proper context," their governess pronounced.

Molly said: "I bet you look pretty in them."

Little Mary wrinkled her forehead. "We don't wear them—just make them."

"Oh. Would you show them to me sometime?"

Ann said: "If you'd like." Molly decided that was enough of an advance for one day and left them alone with their rock doves.

When she came out of the dovecote, she discovered a balding man in a brown broadcloth suit standing a little ways off. She knew him to be a German employed by the Pennsylvania Indian Office, sent to William Johnson a year ago to learn how to communicate with the Six Nations. He now spoke Canienga nearly as well as William Johnson, but for some reason, he still hadn't gone back to Pennsylvania, choosing instead to remain a boarder at King Hendrick's farm on a corner of the Johnson estate. The only piece of Daniel Claus's conversation that had stuck in Molly's mind from her first dinner at Mount Johnson was that, for all his facility with languages, he said "dachshunds" for "dozens." At the moment, he appeared to have discovered something intensely fascinating about the shingles on the mill-house roof.

As Horace continued her tour, Molly glanced back and saw the girls and their governess emerging from the dovecote. Daniel Claus continued his study of the mill-house roof, but cast calf eyes at Ann whenever her governess wasn't looking.

Horace led Molly along the road that wound behind the house and crossed the creek before continuing on toward Schenectady, the same road she'd traveled with Carrying News four times a year, seeing the back of the big stone house framed by gold leaves or green or hoarfrosted branches. Horace stopped on the other side of the little bridge and said: "The building back there's the barn and stables—I guess you can see that well enough without me sayin' so. The littler one beside it's the sheep house. There's another barn farther along this road, behind the old house where Mr. Johnson used to live."

"Who lives there now?"

"Oh ... just a German lady and her mother."

"What German lady?"

"Oh ... Catty—Catherine, that is—Weisenberg."

"I see. Would you ask one of the grooms to saddle Juanita for me, please?"

"Oh, I can do as good a job of that as any of them fumblefingers. Where do you figure on goin' ridin', miss? Just so's I can tell Mr. Johnson if'n he gets home afore you."

"Over to the old house."

"Oh, well now, Miss Molly ... I don't know if'n you'd really want to be doin' that...."

"I do." What she knew was that she didn't really want to be doing that, but that she couldn't live out the rest of her life pretending her husband's first wife and the mother of his children wasn't living just across the hill. The longer she put it off, the harder it was going to be. And she suspected that if she didn't take advantage of a sudden inspiration while William happened to be away, he would argue against it.

Instead of following the road, she guided Juanita up the side of Mount Johnson. It was steep, but Juanita was sure-footed and the sheep had sheered away the undergrowth. When she got to the summit, she stopped and looked back. What with the turreted dovecote, and the gables and chimneys poking out all over the steep roof of the house, her new home looked like a castle from the illustrated *Morte d'Arthur* in the school library at Schenectady. A mocking voice in her head said she could never pretend to be Queen Guinevere. She replied to it that she had no intentions of pretending to be anybody; she *was* Miss Molly.

The house on the other side of the hill was much smaller. It had a border of flowers, but no vegetable garden. The barn on the other side of the road was lively with pigpens and chickens and fieldhands, but there was no path beaten between the house and the farmyard.

The curtains in the front window twitched as Molly dismounted. She hitched Juanita's reins to a porch post and knocked on the door. It was opened by a shriveled chicken wing of an old woman in a black dress, who said in a heavy German accent: "What do you want?"

"How do you do? I am—"

"I know who you are. What do you want?"

A slightly less thick accent shouted from the interior: "Who is it, Mama?"

The old woman bellowed back over her shoulder: "The new one!"

"What? What does she want here?"

Molly said: "I only came by to visit, to meet ... your daughter."

"Mama! What does she want?"

"She says to meet you she wants!"

There was a pause and then the voice from inside called back: "Well, let her."

The old woman stepped back from the door, closed it behind Molly and pointed to a chintz-curtained doorway on the other side of the parlor. Beyond the curtain was a bedroom and a woman in a frilled nightcap. She was so fat that it was difficult to tell where the feather mattress ended and she began. She was playing patience with a deck of cards streaked here and there with strawberry jam from the plate of cakes on the bedside table.

Molly said: "How do you do ... Miss Weisenberg."

"How do you do, *Miss* Brant. He will never you marry, you know, my children to disinherit."

"We are already married."

"What?"

"We were married yesterday at Canajoharie Castle."

"Oh, that!" The frail invalid whooped with laughter. "*That* he would do. But in a church he never will you marry."

"I would never marry him in a church. If I were to become a white man's possession and take his name, I could never sit among the Clan Mothers."

The flesh-pouched blue eyes squinted. "You joke with me."

"I do not. It is a fine thing to carry the keys of Mount Johnson, but I am still a woman of the Wolf Clan of the Canienga, and someday I will be asked to add my voice to the council circle." It seemed like a presumptuous thing to say, but all the signs seemed to be pointing in that direction, and Catty Weisenberg was unlikely to be passing on what she'd said to any Caniengas.

"Huh. Would you like strawberry cake a piece? The doctor tells me it does me bad, but I have done enough years of working good and being good."

"Thank you." She didn't want one, but she took one off the stack and nibbled for the sake of politeness. Catty Weisenberg patted the side of the bed, and Molly perched on the edge of the frame. Up close it was still just possible to discern the structure of a pretty face within the rolls of dough. "I just spoke to your daughters."

"They come for visiting some days. Good girls they are."

"It doesn't seem as though they're allowed to have much of a life."

The suéty shoulders and flour sack breasts shrugged. "Wilhelm does as he sees fit. And he always will. With kitchen girls, schvartzes, Dutch farmer's daughters, brown savages, fieldhands' wives—right under your nose. So he is and will not change. I tell to you, Molly—see your time with him as a summer that will pass. When he tires of you, he will see you and your children do not starve. *If* you have not caused him annoyance. Without Wilhelm I would still be scrubbing chamber pots today." Another slice of strawberry-striped pastry disappeared into the pink-lipped maw. "And sometimes, my girl, he still gets a yen for a bit of fat on his table."

Molly's mouth had gone dry. But she said: "Anyone can see that from one look at him. I intend to put him on a healthier diet."

"If you think to control *his* appetites, you are a fool."

"We Caniengas do not prize chastity the same way white people do. In men *or* women."

Catty Weisenberg cocked her head at her and then chuckled.

"My my. I wonder if Wilhelm did know what he was getting into this time."

Gets Business Done was home when Molly got back—pacing the parlor with his fiddle and bow dangling from one hand and a tumbler of Madeira in the other. Those immense, thick-fingered hands looked different to her after so reverently caressing her body last night. She had an instant's picture of them kneading Catty Weisenberg's tremendous udders and wiped it away.

"Ah, there ye are, m'dear. Did Juanita give ye a pleasant canter?"

"Yes."

He said, "That's good, that's good," but it seemed he hadn't heard her.

"Did your business not go well at Fort Hunter?"

"Hm? Oh, it wasn't 'business'—though I suppose it all comes down to business in the end. Seems some demmed Virginia bumpkin, name of Washington, set out with his militia to drive the demmed Froggies out of their new fort down the Ohio, and Sir Froggy gave 'im a demmed sound thrashin'. There's talk of war."

"Because of this Washington?"

"He's just a spark. Whether it catches or not remains to be seen. If it does come, m'dear, it'll come for the same reason civilized people always fight wars. Money."

"We have all the money we'll ever need."

"Ha! T'ain't no such thing. The men in London whose foundries make the ax heads we trade for furs could buy and sell me like a wedge of cheese, and *they* don't believe they have all the money they need. All over the demmed globe—from Calcutta to Hudson's Bay—there's a Frenchman and an Englishman both tryin' to sell an ax head to the same benighted savage for his furs or spices or gold. If it comes to a war, there'll be a Frenchman and an Englishman hackin' away at each other in every corner of the world."

"Even here?"

"Don't worry, m'dear—if Monsieur Froggy starts down the Mohawk Valley, we'll give 'im a sound thrashin' long before he gets this far."

"Just like that Washington did?"

One hawkish eyebrow jerked upward and the gray-green eyes shot out at her. He set down his fiddle, recharged his glass, and poured a smaller one for her. "When I had m'visit with the girls this afternoon, they said ye'd spoke to 'em in the dovecote. I think it's a demmed fine notion of yers to go up and pass the time of day with 'em from _time_ to time."

"I don't always have to go *up* to visit them. They could dine with us from time to time."

"They never dine downstairs. After ye've seen a few more evenin's at Mount Johnson ye'll know why. Ye never know who's goin' to appear at the door while the table's bein' set: fur traders, war chiefs, military officers. . . . They can get to be a rough lot when the decanters start goin' 'round. Ye can hold yer own in any company, but the girls . . ."

She felt a little thrill of warmth that he was so offhandedly confident in her, shaded with apprehension as to whether she could live up to it. It seemed best to let the matter of Ann and Mary lie for the moment, but she was determined to find ways to gradually change the situation. They were part of her household now, and the way they were being raised wasn't healthy. Oddly, her determination came more out of concern for their father than them. The day would come when his cage-raised songbirds would feel the urge to fly on their clipped wings. The great Gets Business Done was blindly stumbling toward a heartache she might be able to prevent. She rather liked him the more to see a way she could care for him.

"Besides," he added, "though I sent downriver to yer old schoolmaster to buy— What was her name again?"

"Juba."

"Lucky I wrote it down. I'm sure he'll be more'n glad to skin me for 'er, but it'll take a few days at the least. In the meanwhile, ye don't want to be makin' extra work for yerself by cookin' sit-down dinners for the girls as well as me and John and yerself."

"Oh!" She banged down her glass almost hard enough to crack it. With all the new things that had been thrown at her since she'd sent the cook packing, she'd forgotten that if anyone was going to sit down to dinner, she was going to have to cook it.

She jumped up and scurried across the hall to the dining room, with her husband's voice echoing rhetorically behind her: "What the divil's got into ye this time?" The hatch down to the scullery was closed. She flung it open and scampered down the stairs.

The two kitchen girls jumped up from the table as she came down. "Oh, Miss Molly—we done the cleaning you said, we wasn't lazing. . . ."

"I know. Quick, what does he like for dinner?"

"Anything, so long as there's lots of it and it ain't finicky to eat."

There were a hundred good Canienga dishes she could've made for him, but they all took time. Especially in a kitchen that didn't keep articles like dried pumpkin and parched corn on hand. The only experience she'd had of English cookery were her periodic banishments to Juba's kitchen. She looked in the larder and found bread fresh from the bakehouse, fresh chicken eggs, a hanging quarter of beef, and, blessedly, a basket of new potatoes that wouldn't need peeling. She remembered something Juba used to make for the schoolmaster.

She set one of the girls to slicing up two loaves of bread and the other to carving steaks off the quarter of beef, while she built up the fire in the big cooking hearth and dipped water into a pot to hang over it. Then she took down a string of onions and began to slice them up. She wasn't sure it was the onions bringing tears out of her eyes or frustration and annoyance at herself for airily dismissing her husband's cook and then forgetting until the last minute.

"Both loaves is sliced, Miss Molly."

"Good. Now get a wineglass—not too wide a one—and make a hole in the middle of each slice. Oh—what do we do about dinner for Mr. Johnson's daughters?"

"They only take bread and cheese of an evening. I do that up and take it up to them."

"Thank you."

By the time the onions were sliced, the water was boiling. Molly dumped the potatoes in, pushed the fry grate in over the coals, larded up a skillet and threw in two steaks with onions. Once the steaks were fried bloodless, the way Englishmen liked them, she realized she had another problem. "How do we keep food warm?"

"There's a warming oven on the side there, Miss Molly. Behind that iron door."

When the warming oven was filled with fried steaks, she proceeded to fry up pieces of bread with an egg broken into the middle of each one. By the time both loaves were done, the potatoes were boiled. Molly washed her face in the water barrel and went back upstairs to announce that dinner was ready.

True to William's word, visitors appeared at the door as the table was being set. In this instance they were King Hendrick and Willy. Molly sat at the foot of the table and left it to the servants to serve up. As the three platters settled onto the table—nothing but singed beef and boiled potatoes and eggs fried in bread—Molly's insides turned to lead. She could see John Johnson making a face at the platter of eggy bread.

William Johnson pointed at that platter and boomed: "Toad in the hole! I ain't seen toad-in-the-bleedin'-hole since I left Ireland! Me mother used to make it every Sunday. Ye rag me about British cookin', Hendrick, but wait'll ye taste this!"

Molly didn't know whether he might be lying through his teeth about his mother and toad-in-the-hole, and she didn't care a bleedin' dem.

After the table had been cleared away and the pipes came out, Hendrick said: "There is to be a council fire at Philadelphia this winter, to untangle the matter of the Wyoming Valley on the Susquehanna. It would be a great help to those of us who go to speak at Philadelphia if we could have someone with us who could translate not just the words, but the thoughts of the English."

William said: "Ye know I'm always willin' to do what I can, but there's some matters heatin' up that might mean I have to travel elsewhere this winter."

"I was not speaking of you, Gets Business Done, but of your wife."

William threw back his head and laughed. "Dem me— barely one day married and already I'm reduced to a bleedin' consort. Well, Molly, it's up t'ye to jaunt along or stay as ye choose. I'd rather have ye at home, of course, but I don't even know if I'll be home m'self. I just hope Wyoming ain't so div'lish complex as the Stevens Purchase." He laughed again, and Molly could swear she saw an upward twitching in King Hendrick's grinning scar.

She said: "What's the Stevens Purchase?"

William wiped the laugh off his face and said soberly:

"That's how we came to own twenty thousand of our acres. It grew complicated by the law what says no white subject of His British Majesty can purchase more than one thousand acres from his red brothers."

"And a wise law it is, too," Hendrick intoned. "The king is always willing to pass laws to protect us, whether we ask him to or not."

"Bleedin' right. And laws were meant to be lived by the letter of. So, of the twenty thousand acres, one thousand was purchased by me interpreter Arent Stevens, another thousand by me tenant Miles MacDonell, another thousand by . . ." He started sputtering and had to take another quaff of Madeira.

Hendrick took up the thread, and they traded off telling her the rest of the story. Some of the Indian commissioners at Albany had taken exception and whispered to some Royaners who complained to Hendrick that the deal he'd agreed to was a swindle. Hendrick promptly took the great Peace Belt to Albany and threw it in the commissioners' faces. He said that if the English law was only there to help Englishmen swindle Canienga land, the Six Nations might just as well break the Covenant Chain and make a new one with the French. The Royaners had been satisfied that Hendrick had the matter well in hand, and the commissioners had been terrified.

"So," Hendrick went on gravely, "the Albany men quickly kindled another council fire, in hopes of saving the Covenant Chain. At this second council Gets Business Done presented new documents."

"Which," William put in, "ye hadn't seen before."

"Did I forget to say that? Yes, documents I had not seen before. Documents which proved that any odor of trickery had only been the little bird Tskleleli singing. I was overcome with surprise and relief and everyone was happy: the Canienga got to keep William Johnson's money, William Johnson got to keep his twenty thousand acres, and the Albany commissioners got to keep the Covenant Chain intact."

"Speakin' of gettin' and keepin', Hendrick, have ye got around yet to clearin' off yer back five hundred for a horse pasture?" And then the great chiefs King Hendrick and Gets Business Done erupted in the kind of laughter that puts dents in chair arms. Miss Molly Brant was beginning to get the distinct impression that two years in Schenectady had only been the bare beginnings of her education.

Chapter 20

Juba sat in the back of a wagon along with the other articles being freighted from Schenectady. A hard rain had been plummeting down since dawn. The drover had rigged an awning over his wagon seat, and the rest of the freight was under a tight-lashed tarpaulin, but Juba had only an old blanket to cover her head, her dress, and the knotted kerchief holding all her possessions in her lap. She was soaked to the shivering point, but she'd felt worse before, and where she was going was bound to be better than trying to satisfy two dozen picky-mouthed girls and a mistress who liked to make as much profit off their board as their education.

The news that Sissy Brant had married William Johnson had gone through the school like onion through milk. Juba had heard the schoolmaster snort that "marry" wasn't the word, but there'd been a vein of pure green in his voice. Over the years, Juba had heard and overheard a thousand stories about William Johnson, leaving an impression of the Philistine Goliath with King Solomon's wealth. She didn't know what to expect of him or his household, but she'd learned long ago not to expect: you got what they gave you, and there was nothing you could do about it.

The road wound around a steep hill and into an estate behind a stone house even bigger than her first master's, outside New York Town. The freighter clucked his horses off the road and up a side trail to the back of the house. He reined in by the door and bellowed, "Hello the house!" then bellowed it again.

The door was opened by a white man with strawlike hair who stood back beyond the curtain of rain skirting the threshold. "What do you want?"

"I got a article to deliver to William Johnson what has to be signed for."

"I'll sign for it."

"You William Johnson?"

"You cracked? No, I ain't William Johnson." The blue eyes under the haystack mop drifted across the wagon, and it seemed to Juba that the mouth below them tightened when they touched on her.

"I need William Johnson to sign for it. I ain't got all day. I got to be in German Flats 'fore nightfall."

"He's out in the paddock a-lookin' over his horses."

"Well fetch him. I ain't got all day."

"You want me to fetch Mr. Johnson?"

"That's what I just said, ain't it?"

"I heared you sayin' it, but warn't sure if that war truly what you wanted."

"I wouldn'ta *said* it if that weren't what I wanted!"

"Well, keep your britches on." The door closed and then opened a moment later. The straw hair was now covered with a shapeless, broad hat, the pointy shoulders with an oilskin cape, and the shiny, buckled shoes had been replaced with ancient boots. Juba watched him disappear through the rain down the road they'd just come up, and then sat shivering and listening to the crackle of raindrops on the drover's awning and his muttered cursings against wooden-headed servants and uppity Irishmen.

The wooden-headed servant came back in company with a monstrous figure in a leather cloak and a tricorne hat pulled down tight over his eyes. As the figure loomed into focus through the mist and rain, the freighter called: "You William Johnson?"

"I ain't yer dotin' granny."

"That there's the cook you bought from—"

"That *there* is a woman halfway to pneumonia. Horace, take 'er inside and sit 'er by the fire."

As Horace rattled the chain pins out of the wagon gate, the freighter roared: "Not till you signed for her!"

"I'll sign yer bleedin' face with the back of me hand. Horace, take her inside."

As Horace's surprisingly strong hands lifted her down off the wagon and helped her up the steps, Juba heard behind her: "If she takes ill, ye'll wish to Christ ye put yon awning up in back and let yerself be soaked."

"My contrack don't say nothin' about health, just breakage."

"I ain't talkin' about the *law,* laddy-buck."

Then the door closed and Juba was in a long, wide hallway with no rain coming down. Horace kept his hand on her elbow and walked her into a room with a long dining table and a raging hearth. He pulled a chair out from the table, sat her down in front of the fire and said: "I'll call one of the kitchen girls to fetch you something hot to drink. You got a dry dress to change into?"

"This here's the onliest I got."

"I'll fish you one out from the slop chest when I show you your bunk."

"Thank you, suh."

"Don't be callin' me 'sir.' I ain't but just Horace."

A door slammed and a rumble of boots and grumbling curses approached. William Johnson came into the room, still in his hat and cloak and boots. Horace looked at the trail of muddy footprints and the water dripping on the carpet and clucked: "Mr. Johnson . . ."

"What? Oh, bloody hell. Molly'll skin me alive if this ain't cleaned up before she's home." He handed his cloak and hat to Horace and flopped into a chair, raising his foot for Horace to tug off his boots. Juba could see his face clearly for the first time. It was handsome enough, in a large, ruddy way, but it bore the marks of a lot of hard living in a world where Schenectady schoolmasters would get ground up like chicken dumplings. She tried to imagine the face of a certain dewy Mohawk girl on a pillow beside that rough, heavy-looking one, and couldn't.

The green-brown eyes turned straight on her—or almost straight; there was something askew about their centers. "Are ye sure ye're Juba?"

"I'ze positive, Mr. Johnson, suh."

"Molly told me Juba was an old woman."

" 'Molly,' suh?"

"Yer new mistress. Don't ye remember her?"

"I surely do, suh, but at school they called her Sissy."

"Must've been a batch of blockheads at that school to think there was anything sissy about *her*. Ye're sure they didn't flummox ye up with some other Juba? Ye're no old woman."

"I s'pose I looks old to her, suh."

A flicker of something crossed his face, as though she'd said something he didn't want to hear. It was only a hint of a flicker, but wise slaves learned to read the slightest traces. He said: "Ye'll have to settle for the kitchen girls showin' ye the lay of the land; Molly's down to Canajoharie takin' advice from her granny on somethin' or other. Bleedin' lucky for that oaf of a teamster. Molly tells me ye're a paragon of cooks."

"Thank you, suh." Juba wasn't quite sure what a paragon was, but it sounded like a compliment.

"We eat hearty at Mount Johnson, but not prissy. I'll have no fancy syllabubs or airy what-ye-may-call-'ems on me table."

"No, suh. Do you like pepper?"

"Pepper? Don't mind it. Anythin' to cut through the callus on m'palate. So long as it don't do the same to m'belly. Well, I thank ye for comin' to Mount Johnson and givin' me m'wife back again. Seemed like I'd barely got 'er home and she was spendin' half her time in the bleedin' kitchen. And between you and me, Mohawk succotash and hominy ain't m'first choices for a steady diet."

After Juba's outsides had been warmed a little by the fire, and her insides by the second cup of tea she'd drunk in her life, Horace showed her up into the house servants' quarters and found her a dry, nearly new calico dress that was baggy enough for a body that had borne ten children in its first ten years of fertility. The kitchen seemed like a low, stone-walled cave, but it was bigger and better equipped than the one in Schenectady, and the kitchen girls seemed eager to please. Juba found it hard not to gape when they informed her that the larder was limited to whatever could be grown or raised on the estate, or bought from local fishermen and hunters, or imported through New York Town.

She was happily stirring a stew of peppered chicken when the kitchen girls behind her said in unison: "Good evening, Miss Molly."

Juba propped her spoon in the pot, cricked her back straight and turned around. Standing on the cellar stairs, with one hand propped up on the rim of the hatchway, was a young woman who couldn't possibly be little Sissy. The slanted black eyes were the same, but they had a gleam that wasn't a part of that fiercely lonely little girl. The egg-shaped face and high cheekbones looked the same, but the olive-cream skin that covered them had a blush of pink brushed in. She was wearing Mohawk clothes like Juba had seen Sissy in on the first and last days of every school term, but these were blazing with silver broaches and silk embroidery, with glints of gold at her wrists and ears. Of course, she wasn't a virgin anymore, but Juba's memory of before and after that was hardly likely to explain this. The young woman on the stairs looked like the Queen of Sheba.

Juba said: "Evenin', Mizt'ess Molly."

Her new mistress smiled like the sun coming up and said: "Hello, Juba. It's a great relief to me to see you in our kitchen. And, were the truth known, probably even more of a relief to Mr. Johnson. I can see you're busy. I'll come down and have a cup of tea with you after dinner."

After the trapdoor closed again, one of the kitchen girls imitated flutingly: " 'And, were the truth known . . .' Lawks a mercy, ain't she the grand lady of the manor?"

Juba said: "That's what she *is*, ain't she? Here, scrub out this skillet." But she wasn't sure it was such a good idea for the lady of the house to be so familiar with the servants as to be having tea with the cook.

Juba had her own dinner at the scullery table while footmen and serving girls ferried platters and plates up and down the stairs. It was good to be able to eat something with some bite to it again, but she hoped it wasn't too much of a bite for Mr. Johnson.

After the dishes had been cleaned and the scullery maids let out for a bit of air, Mistress Molly came down into the kitchen and Juba poured her out a cup of tea. "You were a great success, Juba. I knew you would be."

"Not too spicy for Mr. Johnson?"

"Well . . . he liked the taste, but I don't think his stomach is up to that much pepper more than once a week or so. Are you sorry I stole you away from Schenectady?"

"Lord, Mizt'ess Molly, I'd say we both done landed in clover." She watched the corners of the slanted eyes and bow-curved lips for signs there might be a thorn or two, and saw none. "All that time at school, I thought you was just a lost little Indian girl. . . ."

"I was."

"Maybe, but look at you now."

Miss Molly shrugged and blushed and whispered conspiratorially: "Maybe I still am, but don't tell the servants."

They gossiped and giggled about the Young Ladies Finishing School until Juba wondered whether her new mistress hadn't wanted a new cook as much as someone in the household she didn't have to be Miss Molly to. "I hope you remember, Juba, the stories you used to tell me—I mean the good ones, about Africa—so you can tell them to my children."

"I couldn't never forget them, Mizt'ess Molly." The fact was, Juba had been so young when they put her on the slave ship, she wasn't sure how many of the stories were her own memories and how many had been borrowed from other slaves. But if her owners found them entertaining . . .

After enough gossip and chatter that it seemed once again they were just the school cook and a naughty girl banished to the kitchen—except without the potato-peeling—Juba felt secure enough to venture: "Your Mr. Johnson, when I first laid eyes and ears on him today, I thought, 'Lord, Juba, you done landed in the lion's den this time.' But I soon seen, for all his roaring, he's a kind man."

"He is. Sometimes too kind. Oh, anyone that offends him regrets it pretty demmed quick, but it would never occur to him that the poor tenant who never seems able to pay his rent might be hiding the money away." She went on like a millrace about the funny thing her William had said yesterday, and his eccentric habit of raising his glass with lyrical Irish toasts, and how he'd heaved a deadfall out of the creek mouth after all the fieldhands had given up. . . .

Juba finally saw the explanation for the Queen of Sheba on the cellar stairs. It didn't have all that much to do with gold bangles and stone mansions after all. Little Sissy was moon mad in love.

CHAPTER 21

Brant's Joseph hadn't really been pleased by anything for a long time. He didn't spend a lot of time sitting around thinking about it, but he did have a vague notion that there once had been a boy named Muskingum who'd found a good deal of joy in everything from climbing a tree to curry-combing his stepfather's horses; and now there was just Joseph, who dutifully performed the tasks his Teacher set for him and did his best at baggataway because that was what was expected of him.

His sister had been living at Mount Johnson for three phases of the moon when the invitation came to Brant Farm to come to tea. Joseph snorted: " 'Come to tea'—maybe me and Carrying News ought to put on white wigs and buy snuffboxes." His mother pursed her mouth but didn't say anything.

There were no footmen lounging about the front steps of William Johnson's house this time—they were standing smartly at attention. The horses were taken in hand and led away almost before there was time to get down off the saddle. The same straw-haired servant who'd ushered the Brants into the music room the first time did so again, only now he didn't look quite so much like he'd come fresh from stacking hay.

John Johnson wasn't there this time, but his sisters were, along with their goose-necked Teacher, whose eyes weren't colorless anymore but quite pink, as though she spent her nights weeping. Willy was there, and so was the awesome King Hendrick, which should have made Joseph more than glad to be there but didn't. William Johnson was there, bellowing his big, bad-mannered, white man's laugh. And William Johnson's wife was there, squeezed into a red velvet gown cut on the constricting pattern of white women's dresses, pushing her breasts up unnaturally.

She was a stranger to him: someone who lifted a finger to beckon servants and laughed overloud at jokes he didn't understand. The Left-Handed Twin behind William Johnson's False Face was bitterly obvious now. Joseph couldn't believe that the grating voice and looming leer had once actually seemed pleasant. Mother and Carrying News and even King Hendrick didn't seem to notice. Or perhaps they, too, saw nothing but his money and his big house.

Along with the tea there were some slices of meat between pieces of bread and a profusion of those little cakes made from white sugar that tasted of nothing but sickly sweetness. The conversation was boring and difficult, with everyone talking in English for politeness's sake. After Joseph had endured it for an interminable time, Si-isha said to him, in Canienga: "You must come outside and take a look at our horses."

"Our?"

She flushed, but just beckoned: "Come along." He went along not too grudgingly. At least it would be better than sitting in a stuffy room struggling to pick up one word in five. Not to mention having to watch William Johnson's habit of settling his fat hand on Si-isha's shoulder or her knee.

The barns and stables were set a long way back behind the house, on the other side of a small creek. Joseph and his sister walked all the way there without saying a word. The only sounds they made were of his moccasins and her silly, raised-heeled shoes crunching through the fallen leaves. There was a groom in the stableyard, filing the hooves of a bulging, bob-tailed draft horse. "Afternoon, Miss Molly."

"Good afternoon, Caleb. Did you brush down the colt?"

"Polished him up like a silver teapot, miss. He's out a-frisking in the paddock. 'D'ya like me to fetch him for ya?"

"No, thank you, Caleb. Juanita will come for sugar."

There were a number of horses gamboling or grazing in the pasture behind the stables, and two in the smaller enclosure of the paddock: the bay mare William Johnson had given Si-isha and a fawn-legged colt bouncing along in her wake. The mare came toward the fence when she saw them approaching.

Si-isha took two lumps of rock sugar out of the pocket of her dress and handed one to Joseph while she held the other out for the mare. Joseph put his right arm between the fence rails with the sugar in his half-cupped palm. The colt held back, then came forward cautiously and snuffled his nostrils into Joseph's hand. Joseph reached his left hand out slowly and stroked the fine fur on the side of the colt's neck.

Si-isha said: "Has he given you any ideas yet of what to name him?"

"Name him? That's up to you."

"No it isn't. He's yours. His mother died and he adopted Juanita in her place. William said that the colt choosing Juanita must mean he wanted to belong to me, but I can only ride one horse at a time. William says that if he takes after his real mother, he'll be even taller than Juanita."

Joseph was tinglingly aware that the colt's nose was still happily snuffling in his palm even though the sugar was long gone, and that his legs did appear to be even longer than most colts at the gangly stage. But what he said was: "That is very generous of you, Mrs. Johnson."

"I am *not* 'Mrs. Johnson.' I am still Molly *Brant*."

"What happened to Si-isha?"

"That's a child's name, I'm not a child anymore."

"You must have been very busy growing up, that it took you from new moon to waning to invite us to your fine new home."

"You must have been very busy *not* growing up that it took an invitation to bring you. What's come over you these days? Well, the colt's yours to do with as you choose. You can sell it if you want. You can stay out here and beat it with a stick if that'll please you; I'm going back inside."

Joseph waited until he thought it was close to time for the guests to be heading home before he went back into the big stone house. William Johnson's daughters and their Teacher had left the music room, but everybody else looked up as he came in. He squatted down on the floor beside the chair he'd been sitting in.

His mother said to him in Canienga: "We have been talking of you while you were gone. Of you and Willy. The white farmers around Canajoharie have banded together their money to start a school for their children. You are learning a great deal from your Teacher, but in the coming years it will no longer be enough simply to know how to be a Canienga warrior. We think you and Willy should go to the new school. Of course, we will have to talk this over with Little Abraham first. But I think there are not so many hours spent in the white schools that you would not have time to learn from your Teacher as well."

He looked around at all those alien faces above him, once so familiar but now like painted acorn husks on the fingertips of William Johnson. All except Willy, who looked like the white school was a whirlpool he might be able to steel himself to jump into, but definitely not if no one else was going to jump.

It seemed like head-patting to Joseph that his mother was explaining reasons as though he had some choice in the matter. Little Abraham had told him that the first thing a warrior had to learn was: that which cannot be changed must be endured without flinching. So he just said flatly: "If all of you think that is what Willy and I should do, then it must be the thing that we should do."

CHAPTER 22

Molly sat watching the first snowflakes of the season flutter down past the music room windows. A voice she could feel inside her rib cage rumbled from the doorway: "Well, I'm off to the races, m'dear. Ye haven't had a change of mind about comin' along . . . ?"

She turned her head to see around the brocaded back of her chair. Her enormous, silly, mesmerizing husband was standing there in his weathered, hueless riding clothes and the boots she'd tried to polish and gave up on. She said: "You don't want me to be getting between you and your horses and grooms and jockeys and odds makers. From the look of the weather, it'll be the last meet of the season. So go along with you, and I'll have Juba wait dinner till you get back."

He wandered away, with the hallway echoing the thump of his boot heels and the thwack of his riding crop against his boot tops and his cavernous mutterings: "I wouldn't have to pay no bleedin' jockeys if she'd do the ridin'. No, I suppose we'd never bind 'em up tight enough to keep 'em from bouncin', and then all bets'd be off. . . ."

She heard the back door boom shut and went back to gazing out at the snowflakes dancing around the two head-high black walnut trees he'd planted in the lawn and christened Billy and Molly. She felt a niggling prodding to jump up and be doing something, but assured herself that there was no reason why she couldn't just sit sipping sherry and looking out the window.

After three months at Mount Johnson she was reasonably satisfied that the place had been put in working order. There had been so many frayed edges to knit together, it was a wonder they hadn't all unraveled years ago and left poor Gets Business Done naked. His clerks had been robbing him blind; not out of any malevolent plan to line their own pockets, just out of slovenliness. His field hands had got into the habit of spending half the morning in the barn debating whether it was going to rain or not, while the barley rotted in the fields. His house servants had been living under the impression that they were being paid to hatch out ingenious schemes for siphoning off his liquor.

All of them, even down to the slaves, had only needed to be informed that jolly old Mr. Johnson now had someone to look after him. She probably never would've had the temerity to yank on the reins of so many people so much older than herself, except that it made her angry to see anyone taking advantage of him.

When it came to Horace, though, she couldn't do much beyond cosmetics. In his heart he would always be a farmer, not a valet. In his off hours he could always be found loitering wistfully about the fields or barn, tasting the soil and squinting at the sky. But William got so much pleasure out of grumbling about him that she didn't have the heart to suggest a change.

She took another sip of Spanish sunlight and lolled her head back against the top of the chair, feeling the warmth from the hearth fire on one arm and the coolness coming off the windowpanes on the other. It crept into the forefront of her mind that she was happy and had every reason to be. She immediately reached down to the side table and knocked on wood like William did, then followed her own custom of trying to think of things that made her life less than perfect.

She could only think of two: her brother and her stepson. In the rare times she saw Joseph, he was still surly. Her mother said he was the bane of the schoolmaster's life: picking up the lessons like a sparrow picking up seeds, but refusing to admit that he'd learned anything.

John Johnson wasn't exactly surly, but he made it abundantly clear that he found it ridiculous to have a stepmother only five years older than himself, especially with his own mother still living just across the hill. John was at Mount Johnson all the time now. The new school he'd been sent to hadn't worked out any better than the old one, so it had been decided that he would have a private tutor until it came time to send him to England to finish his education.

She started to take another pensive sip and giggled to discover one more imperfection to ward off bad luck: her glass was empty. She went to the sideboard to refill it, then decided to fill another glass and take it down to Juba.

She found Juba sniffling and drying her eyes with her apron, and nary an onion in sight. "Juba—whatever is the matter?"

"Oh don't mind me, Mizt'ess Molly. Sometimes I just gets melancholic thinking on Jemmy."

"Jemmy?"

"My mother and I uz sold together and she made many, many children—lots more'n I did—on that place we uz at together. Most of 'em got sold young. But my babiest sister Jemmy stayed with us for the longest time. She's maidservant for a lady in New York Town, and sometimes I thinks of Jemmy so far away and gets melancholic. Sometimes I thinks of the winter coming on and gets melancholic. That's just life."

"She's a lady's maid, your sister?"

"Oh, I wouldn't say she uz anything so grand as that." Juba let out a cackle of laughter. "I'd say she's prob'ly about as much a ladymaid as Horace is a valet."

"Do you know the name of this lady in New York Town who owns her?"

"The schoolmaster wrote it down for me. I got it in my trunk upstairs. But there ain't no use in you writing me a letter for Jemmy—she can't read nor write no better'n me. *There*, I done my little weep about it and now my eyes is dry again."

Footsteps castanetted across the dining room floor above their heads. A pair of shiny, buckled shoes and silk hose appeared on the cellar stairs, then the rest of John's tutor: with a chalky face and a split lip. "Miss Molly, I can no longer endure . . . He threw his Cicero at me. If he were *my* son, or a pupil in my school . . ." He held up his vibrating hands. "But Mr. Johnson has forbidden me to . . . I would not for the world leave you in the lurch, Miss Molly, but I can no longer endure."

"I'll speak to him."

"Miss Molly, I can no longer endure. I fear that if such a thing should happen again, I shall—"

"It won't happen again."

She brushed past the tutor and went upstairs. John was leaning in the doorway of Ann and Nancy's room. In repose, there was something ethereal about his delicate features and gold hair. But at the moment said features were contorted into something resembling Old Crooked Nose, as he made faces at his sisters while their governess was trying to teach them some fiendishly complicated old English hymn.

"John." He turned toward her. "I heard what you did. You will go downstairs and apologize, and promise never to do such a thing again."

"I don't have to listen to you. You ain't me mother."

"I am your father's wife."

"Ain't nothing of the kind. You're me father's doxy."

"You muck-assed little shit-tongued puppy! You think because your father owns a Persian carpet for you to crawl over, it makes you anything more than a puking infant? The stupidest boy ever born into the flea-bittenest backwoods tribe in the swamplands has some dignity by the time he's half your age. Horace!"

John's pop-eyed shock had only managed to come out with "How dare you—" when Horace clattered up the stairs.

"Horace—I want you to make it known to everyone in the household that this *boy* has no voice until I say different. If he asks the cook or the kitchen maids for something to eat, they don't hear him. If he wants to go riding, the grooms may amuse themselves watching him trying to catch a horse and saddle it for himself. If he wants a warming pan for his bed at night, that's his lookout."

John shrieked: "Horace!"

"Yes, Master John?"

"You are not to listen to a word *that woman* said."

"But, you see, I already heared it, Master John."

"Well . . . disregard it."

"Oh, I couldn't be doing that, Master John."

"Why the devil not? Am I or am I not the son of this house?"

"That you are, Master John. But she's . . . well, she's Mistress Molly."

Mistress Molly said: "All you have to do, John, to put things back the way they were, is apologize to your tutor and promise never to do such a thing again. A gentleman keeps his promises."

"How would you know? You'll see what's what when my father gets home."

"So we shall." But it did put a bit of a chill up her back. William might fume and grumble about John at times, but John was still his son and heir. Molly couldn't quite grasp why white men held firstborn sons more sacred than all their other children put together, but she knew they did.

She was in her husband's book-lined office toting up the household accounts when she heard a troop of horses coming up the drive: Gets Business Done and his grooms, racehorses, and jockeys. The back door slammed as John ran outside yelling: "Father!" She finished her column, waited for the ink to dry, closed the ledger and went to find out whether she was William Johnson's wife or his doxy.

He was sitting in the music room sipping a large glass of Madeira wine and looking pensive. She said: "Did John speak to you?"

"Hm? Oh, yes—said ye two had a bit of a set-to and he wanted me to put ye in yer place. I told him ye already were in yer place and he'd best get used to it. Hope he wasn't too demmed cheeky."

"Not so much." But it was difficult to say it evenly, after

he'd so offhandedly proven once again that she couldn't have found a safer place to invest her heart than in Big Billy Johnson.

He muttered, "That's good," and went back to staring into his glass and sucking on his cheeks.

"Did you not have good luck at the races?"

"Hm? Oh, won here, lost there . . . in the end came out two shillin's ahead." A two shilling net gain would usually cause him to wax even more expansive than usual, distributing many shillingsworth of ale among the servants so they could toast his good fortune. "Every bleedin' soul that came out to watch the horses run is takin' it as a given that there won't be much of a racin' season next year 'cause we'll be too busy fightin' the French. . . .

"When the time comes for ye to travel with Hendrick and his cronies to Philadelphia, ye might try and keep an ear peeled for what the Royaners think the Six Nations ought to do if the storm crows prove right."

"I'll try."

"And I'll have to go to bleedin' New York Town when they convene the Provincial Council. Ain't sat down with m'fellow councillors for years. Seems demmed ridiculous for a man to go to all the trouble of buildin' 'imself an estate and then have to leave it to go tallyfobblin' about from one demmed council to another. But I'm afraid this time it can't be helped."

"While you're in New York Town . . . I've been looking at the household accounts, wondering if we could afford a certain expense. . . ."

The muddy green eyes glinted at her and the broad slash of a mouth grinned. "Ye know bleedin' well, Molly, that when ye stretch out yer legs and tap yer finger on yer lips like that I'll buy ye the bleedin' moon and be demmed with the ledgers. What d'ye want?"

"Do you think I might have a maid, as you have your valet?"

"If ye want a maid like Horace, I have to wonder what kind of berries ye've been chewin'."

"There is a lady's maid in New York Town I know of, name of Jemmy . . ."

CHAPTER 23

Major William Johnson, commanding officer of the Mohawk Valley Militia, was engaged in a feat of military engineering: constructing a snow fort with John and Molly and the girls. He stepped back to get an overview of the rising battlements as the troops carried on with the spadework.

He found himself not looking at the fort at all, but at his family. It was demmed remarkable how smoothly John had adjusted to Molly's position in the household once it had been spelled out to him. But then, she'd had the sense not to rub John's nose in it. As for the girls, Johnson had to admit it was pleasant to see them capering and laughing freely and throwing snowballs at their brother. He'd just never known what to *do* with them, except keep them sequestered from anything rough or coarse, and come visit them on his best behavior once a day. Had he ever made a wiser move than bringing a certain high-spirited Mohawk girl to live at Mount Johnson?

Molly looked up from stamping down the floor of a bastion—with snowflakes spangling her blue-black hair and sable cape—and said: "What are you grinning at?"

"Nothin'. Can't a man stand around grinnin' at bleedin' nothin' if the notion takes him?"

"Not while there's work to do."

"Ye seem to have it well enough in hand." She hove a snowball at him. Demmed deadly aim for a female.

Out of the dense fog of gently wafting snow, a shadowy horseman began to coalesce. As the horseman drew closer, he revealed himself to be the ensign from the little garrison at Fort Hunter, bearing a dispatch case. "Some dispatches have arrived for you, sir, from New York Town."

"For me? Must be demmed important to send some poor divil poundin' down the high road in this weather. Probably the governor wants a new fur hat. Well, come inside and warm yer toes."

Molly fell in with them, tossing over her shoulder: "John, if your sisters' lips start turning blue, you send them back inside."

"Yes, Molly."

"And the same goes for you."

"Yes, Molly."

The cook, bless her, had brewed a bowl of mulled wine and propped the end of the poker over the hearth grate. Johnson took the poker out of the fire and dipped it in the bowl to make it sizzle, then ladled out three cups and settled down to read his dispatches while Molly kept the ensign entertained.

There were two dispatches, the first one from the Royal Governor of the Province of New York. Johnson had to read through it twice to make sure it was as nonsensical as it appeared to be. It was a general's commission in His Majesty's North American land forces. Perhaps the second dispatch would make some sense of it.

The second one was sealed and marked MOST HIGHLY CONFIDENTIAL. It informed General Johnson that General Braddock and two Regiments of the Line would embark from England in the spring to secure His Majesty's North American possessions in the event of invasion by a foreign power.

Johnson took another quaff of punch to calm himself, then remarked: "Seems I'm by way of bein' a general."

The ensign said: "Allow me to be the first to congratulate you, sir." Molly said nothing, just flicked her black eyes at him once.

The ensign loitered about awhile longer to pick up any further scraps of news that might fall off the table. When it became evident there weren't going to be any, he took his leave. As soon as he was gone, General Big Billy stormed out of his chair, brandishing the second dispatch at Molly. "Two regiments! Two regiments couldn't defend His Majesty's North American possessions from me granny's whist circle! Not that the French or the Spaniards have any more troops, but they can strike at Virginia while our two blessed regiments are guardin' New York, or vicey-versey.

"And *this*," switching his brandishing to the hand holding his commission, "*me* a bleedin' general! I've never even seen a bleedin' battle!'"

"I thought you and Hendrick led the Canienga in the last French war? I heard the stories of you in loincloth and war paint dancing them all the way to Albany."

"We led 'em *to* the war. What with ditherin' and bickerin', by the time His Majesty's generals and governors decided where we ought to fight, His Majesty's ministers were already makin' peace in Europe."

He began strangling his commission. "And the only troops at me disposal is me so-called regiment of Sunday-marching farm boys. 'Tain't much of a foundation to erect a general on."

"Maybe the king thinks you already have another army here."

Something along those lines had already occurred to Big Billy, but he said: "How's that?"

"The Hodenosaune and the other nations in the Covenant Chain."

Johnson put down his dispatches and refilled his cup. It was perfectly possible that the gentlemen in London interpreted the Covenant Chain as meaning William Johnson could snap his fingers and bring the Six Nations and their allies running. Perhaps he hadn't been laggard over the years in encouraging that impression in official circles.

"What're they sayin' in Canajoharie, Molly?"

"Some are saying that if the French can beat the English in the Ohio country, they can do it here, and that it's best we help the side that's going to win. Some say that if either the French or the English succeed in defeating the other, they won't need to be so friendly to us anymore. And some say we should stand back and let the white men kill each other."

"And that's all they're bleedin' sayin'?"

"No. Some say we should take up the hatchet alongside the English and drive the French off Turtle Island for good."

He grunted back into his chair and settled in to worry at the problem like an old dog with a new bone. It put him off his food. He could barely choke down three little venison steaks and a quart of ale. After supper he went back at it, expanding into speculations on which route the French might be most likely to choose for an invasion, brooding late into the night without hatching anything.

When he finally went upstairs, Molly was still awake, sitting up in bed beading a skirt by candlelight. By the time he'd changed into his nightshirt, she'd put her work away and banked the fire, but she hadn't closed the bed curtains. He climbed in next to her and reached one hand across to cup one soft-flanneled breast. She'd taken to wearing nightgowns since the weather changed, but he was beginning to know her body well enough to see it clearly through the cloth. And it was a simple enough matter to pull a nightgown up above a waist.

He was demmed knackered, but still a long way from sleep. And Molly did have a knack for waking him up. But after he'd been rooting away on top of her for a moment or three, he discovered he was even more knackered than he'd thought. Not much point in sliding a ramrod up and down a barrel if you've forgotten to put in a load.

Molly put her right hand under his left shoulder and pushed. He thought at first she was telling him to stop, but then she pushed with her right thigh against his left hip as well, rolling him over flat on his back while she came up sitting with her knees straddling him. She began to work herself back and forth and up and down, on top of and around him. It was a demmed odd feeling—being rogered instead of doing the rogering. But once he gave in to the oddness, he began to enjoy it.

Molly began to make strange noises. She whipped the nightgown off over her head, threw it aside, and proceeded to give him a demonstration that female genitalia have a life of their own. Sometimes he just lay there as passive as an Englishwoman, watching her bounce around and flail her hair from side to side like a flag in a storm, with her Oriental eyes flaring fireworks. Sometimes he stretched his hands out stiff-armed so she could prop herself against them and he could feel her breasts roll up and down against his palms. Sometimes she leaned forward and planted her hands on his chest, to ease the strain on her thighs and give herself another angle. It crossed his mind that Molly Brant had indisputably come to Mount Johnson, and he began to laugh.

Well well—he'd remembered to load in a charge after all.

CHAPTER 24

Joseph sat gazing out the schoolhouse window at the hoarfrost-filigreed forest and the unmarked snow rolling away between the trees. He could imagine himself marking the top of those cold cloud banks with snowshoe prints, running until he started spitting blood, and then biting off a piece of the horsetail root Little Abraham had taught him to keep in his pouch, and chewing it up to stop the blood while he kept on running.

According to his mother, thirteen summers had passed since she'd first dipped him in the Muskingum. Even though he hadn't been husk-covered yet, he was of an age when he should be out tending a trapline to bring in furs and fresh meat for the family, instead of sitting at a boxed-in desk—with a nursemaid to watch over him.

His deskmate nudged him gently with her elbow, to tell him the schoolteacher was saying something he should pay attention to. Besides him and Willy, Margaret was the only pupil in the class who wasn't white. She was an Oneida whose father had come fervently to the English Bible in his old age and wanted his daughter to get an earlier start. The schoolteacher had sat Joseph beside her so she could help him understand the lessons; Willy had enough English not to need a translator. Sometimes Joseph found Margaret's know-it-all ways annoying; sometimes he found her translucent skin quite interesting to look at, making his fingertips wonder what it would feel like.

Margaret whispered translations of phrases to him as the schoolteacher announced: "When we come back after the Lord's Day, we will each of us, one by one, tell the class what we did on that day. I will begin the exercise and then step aside, and you shall each take my place at the front of the class. It need not be any longer than a minute or two, and you need not invent any fantastical adventures to entertain the class, just try to speak clearly and plainly. When you are grown up you will find that it is the responsibility of citizens to speak in public meetings, and some of you may become schoolteachers yourselves, or even church ministers. Now is the time to start learning there is nothing to be afraid of.

"And that includes you, Joseph. You needn't be embarrassed about your English; it is coming along much better than you think. If you set in your mind what you are going to say, and practice it Sunday evening, you will do perfectly well."

Joseph was already embarrassed enough without being singled out. He could feel his *onikonhra* shriveling up at the picture of himself stumbling out "Me Joseph" at the front of the class, the white children snickering behind their hands, and Margaret hiding her face as he proved the Hodenosaune were just the stupid Indians whites assumed.

When the schoolteacher said, "Class dismissed," the rest of tho olass jumped up and ran squealing for their coats. Joseph plodded to where his blanket coat was hanging and tugged it on over his longshirt and leggings. His mother had sewn him English clothes, and Gets Business Done had given Willy a suit of clothes for school, but Joseph preferred to go to the white school dressed like the Canienga he was, so Willy had done the same.

Joseph and Willy's snowshoes were standing in a drift beside the schoolhouse door, with their belt knives hanging from them. The schoolteacher didn't like his pupils wearing knives in class. They tied on their snowshoes and jogged off through the woods, with Willy chattering away and Joseph grunting replies.

At Willy's home, King Hendrick's farm, Willy dug out the old hatchet they used for practice and they took turns throwing it at the thick plank fixed to the side of the barn. Joseph had to stand farther back to make it a contest, but although Willy was still a hand span shorter, his shoulders were already thicker, and what he lacked in accuracy he made up for with brute enthusiasm. Joseph got some pleasure out of the clean thunk the hatchet made when it struck true, and he laughed along with Willy when it hit with the blunt end and they had to dance out of the way as it bounced back. But he couldn't forget what the teacher had sentenced him to the day after tomorrow.

They decided they were hungry and went inside to get the cook to give them something to eat. King Hendrick was sitting at the kitchen table whittling a pipe stem. Willy said to him: "Do we have to do everything that schoolteacher tells us?"

"Pretty much. Unless it is something that seems wrong to you. What has he asked you to do?"

"He wants us to stand up in front of everybody else and speak. In English. It don't seem fair. If we have to do it in English, they should have to do it in Canienga."

Hendrick laughed. "You are right, Willy, but life is not fair. In this event, not fair to *them*. When you have finished school you will know English as well as you know Canienga, while they will still be ignorant of everyone but their own kind. Besides, Gets Business Done would not be happy with me if I gave him back a grown son who spoke English no better than I do."

"But what is the use," Joseph protested, "of making us stand up and try to speak in English with everyone looking and listening? The schoolteacher only does it to make us look stupider than his white house pets. When we are warriors, it will be a good thing to be able to speak to the English soldiers and read what the English war chiefs write, but that's got nothing to do with making speeches."

King Hendrick turned his eyes on him and held them there, making Joseph uncomfortable. Not that he thought the Royaner meant him any harm, but whenever Hendrick's eyes settled on him for long, Joseph always felt like he was being weighed.

King Hendrick said: "Thy father was but half a man." Before Joseph could feel outraged or shamed, he added: "Although that half was more than most whole men. Tying Snowshoes was a man for the war road, for the hunter's path, for talking and laughing through the night around the hearth. But he was never a man for the council fire—even village councils and war councils where anyone may speak. The voice of his *onikonhra*—even if he could only raise it to Royaners away from the council fire—would have strengthened our *orenda*. But he would not, or could not. When thou art a man, thy voice should be heard—even though you will never be called upon to wear a Royaner's name. This English school-teacher is giving you a chance to practice, just like you and Willy practice with my rusty old hatchet."

"But . . . I don't know how."

"Who does? The only useful piece of advice ever given to me was from an old woman I knew when I was young—yes, I was young once—and I will give it to thee. Whenever you fear you are speaking too slowly—speak slower."

Joseph didn't feel any more comfortable about the prospect, but at least now it seemed like it had some purpose. He helped Willy and the Royaner devour a loaf of bread with honey from the old man's beehives, and was just thinking of going home when the back door opened and Little Abraham came in. King Hendrick's way of greeting his brother was: "Too late, we ate it all. You'll have to beg your wife to cook for you again."

"At least what my wife cooks she also has to eat herself, un-like your hired cook."

"Your pupil here is weighed under with a task his other Teacher has set him—the white one."

"What task is that?"

They told him. Little Abraham said: "My brother is right—as difficult as that is to believe—that it is a good thing for you to learn. But you will be spared this time, because you will not be going to school that day. Because you will be husk-covered."

Hendrick said, "In the *winter*?" and then reined to a more measured tone of voice. "Of course, a boy's Teacher knows best what is best for him."

Joseph could feel Willy's eyes wide on him, so he endeavored to keep his voice matter-of-fact: "When does it start?"

"Now. Come with me."

As Joseph rose to his feet, King Hendrick said pleasantly: "If I know my brother, you will wish you were being made to speak in English to twelve schoolfuls of English people."

Joseph followed Little Abraham on snowshoes. They headed for the valley wall and up into a cleft in the hills. There was a small, steep clearing beside a frozen stream. The remnants of a fire smoldered in a circle of stones. Little Abraham stopped there and said: "Give me your coat and longshirt and snow-shoes."

Joseph did as he was told, trying not to shiver as the cold air hit his skin. Little Abraham took a blanket out of his bulging shoulder pouch and handed it to him. Joseph stood holding it as Little Abraham stuffed his coat and longshirt into the pouch and picked up his snowshoes. Little Abraham straightened from stooping for the snowshoes, saw Joseph still holding the folded blanket and said: "Wrap it around yourself. A warrior has enough discomfort in his life without looking for more."

"Yes, Teacher." Joseph gratefully did what he was told. "Where is the husk to cover me?"

"You will have to make one. You have a knife, that is all a warrior needs."

"Will you come every morning and set me tasks to do?"

"Who told you that?"

"My sister."

"Maybe you and your sister tell each other too many things."

"Not anymore."

"The husk-covering of a girl becoming a woman is not the same as that of a boy becoming a warrior. The dangers to a woman's life come from inside her body and outside her *onikonhra*; the dangers a man must face are the other way around. The only task I set you is to stay alive. But every morning, you will take a twig out of the fire, blow the flame out, and press it to both your arms to make a burn, starting here." He touched both Joseph's arms just below the shoulder. "And then a finger's breadth below each morning. And that way you will know how many days you've been here."

"How many days will that be?"

"We will ask your arms when the time comes." Little Abraham turned and started back down the trail they'd made with their snowshoes. He stopped just long enough to point back at the fire and say: "He is your only friend. Make sure you keep him well fed." Then he was gone.

The sun was going down, but the snow meant Joseph could still see in silhouette, and a full moon would be rising soon. He went looking for firewood, floundering as his moccasins sank into hip-high drifts. He soon discovered he couldn't cut and carry pine boughs with the blanket shawled around him, and if he dropped it, it would be covered with snow when he put it on again. So he tied it around his waist. He found that by grinding his back teeth together he could keep his arms from shivering too much to do their work.

When the first pine bough flared up, he cowled the blanket over his head, back, and arms and leaned in close to the fire. Eventually he stopped shivering, but he knew he couldn't crouch there forever feeding quick-burning pine boughs to the fire.

He left the blanket on the stack of boughs and went to wrestle out a deadfall he'd seen poking up through the snow. When the cold began to conquer the warmth his body had soaked in from the fire, he heard his Teacher's voice in his mind: "The cold is there, the pain is there, the hunger is there, there is nothing you can do to keep them out." He let the cold penetrate his chest and kept on working.

He propped the wide end of the deadfall in the fire, leaving the bulk of its length sticking out on the snow beyond the stone circle. As the end burned down, he could keep feeding it in. With the fire fed for now, the next thing to see to was the husk to cover him. There was a wind coming up that would make husk-covering more than just a matter of fulfilling custom.

But first he crouched beside the fire till he felt warm again. Little Abraham had shown and told him many times that a man can keep going on even the coldest or hottest of days, provided he has the sense to pause to warm or cool himself from time to time. He took a small handful of snow to wet his mouth—too much and his belly would cramp up.

There were some poplar saplings beside the stream. He cut down four of them to make a framework for a lean-to and trimmed them by the fire. The wind was blowing through his blanket like it was a fishnet, and he kept having to warm the numbness out of his knife hand.

When all four poles were trimmed, he looked at them and a mountain hit him in the face. He had nothing to lash them together with. The snow was too deep to try scooping it out blindly looking for spruce roots. If he cut long-enough pieces off his blanket or his leggings, he'd be even more naked to the cold.

Hopeless whimpering noises began to come out of his throat. He told himself, "You are a Canienga warrior, you are a Canienga warrior," tightened his jaw and looked at the poles again. He worked his knife down crosswise about a hand's breadth deep into the ends of three of the poles, then wedged the crosspiece tightly into the splits. He wasn't sure whether it would hold, but he couldn't think of what else to do.

He stamped down a bed-sized patch of snow beside the fire circle, tunelessly chanting a Midwinter Moon dancing song to keep his feet moving. Then he wedged the ends of the three poles into the deep snow and went to cut armfuls of pine and spruce boughs.

By the time his husk was ready to cover him—an evergreen awning facing the fire, sheltering a thick mat of pine and spruce boughs—the moon was going down. He wrapped himself in his blanket, making sure to leave enough slack to pull over his head, and climbed in among the boughs. He didn't feel particularly proud of or pleased with what he'd accomplished; he'd only done what he had to do. He told his shivering body and gnawing stomach: "You are a Canienga warrior."

In the morning, he built up the fire around the last chunk of the deadfall, stripped the needles off a twig, and sat cross-legged staring into the fire. He remembered Little Abraham saying: "Waiting for the pain to come only makes you feel it before it comes." He thrust the end of the twig into the fire, blew the flame off once it caught, shrugged the blanket off his shoulders, straightened his back and pressed the red end of the twig against his left arm. He gasped aloud as the fire bit into his flesh, but forced himself to hold it there while he counted three, hissing his breath out with each number.

When he went to burn his right arm, his left hand was shaking. He realized Little Abraham had known what he was doing when he told him to burn both arms. If it had only been one, he might've been able to forget from morning to morning what it was going to feel like.

By the fourth morning he could do it while breathing calmly and evenly through his nose. He'd grown accustomed to constantly feeling hungry, but found enough to eat to keep himself on his feet. He found a few bedraggled, frozen berries, ate most of them and saved a few to bait a trap. The trap was made of a square of bark with a round hole cut in the middle, and a tiny noose made from a sliver-wide strip cut from Joseph's leggings. Brother chickadee could easily thrust his head through to get at the berries, but when he tried to pull his head back out, his neck feathers caught on the noose.

When Joseph dropped a stone through the ice to get drinking water, he noticed that the stream looked maybe deep enough for fish to live in through the winter. A few more stones made a big enough hole to spear fish through, and incidentally a dam to slow down brother fish and confuse him. A three-pronged sapling presented itself to be trimmed and sharpened for a fish spear. When the first fish appeared, Joseph had been crouched for so long, with his fish spear poised and the rough blanket chafing the burns on his arms, that he'd come to believe he was waiting for nothing. He was so surprised to see the flicker of silver in the water that he stabbed too late.

He got the next one, though. It wasn't a very big fish, but it was the biggest one he'd eaten lately.

At night he would sit beside the fire singing a song he'd made up to ask his Guardian to come and help him. But the wolf never came.

The days and nights faded together until he wasn't sure when he was in the dreamworld. The worst dream was of a Flint Giant who'd stolen something precious from him and laughed at his feeble attempts to get it back.

But even in the dreamworld, living things had to do what they had to do to stay alive. He was poised on the edge of his fishing hole again, dully gazing at the hypnotizing ripples, when he heard a crack below him and plunged down and forward. He threw his arms up in front of his face as the ice on the other side of the hole leaped at his eyes. He crashed through and scrambled to plant his hands and knees on the stream bed.

He got back on his feet and thrashed to the shore, but he was soaked through. He knew he had to get to the fire. By the time he got there, half his blanket was frozen so stiff he could stand it up beside the fire stones.

He threw on all the firewood he had, but he'd been planning to replenish the pile after he'd done fishing. He yanked boughs out of his bed and added them on, then crouched with his elbows and knees spread around the fire and his eyes screwed tight against the smoke. He couldn't keep his teeth from clacking together, with nonsense syllables moaning out in between.

He turned himself back to front to the fire like a pigeon on a spit, still feeding pieces of his bed onto the flames. He seemed to be sinking into the snow, ever deeper into a soft, white, feather bed that had no bottom.

He woke up in his husk, wrapped in furs. Little Abraham was crouched beside a crackling fire with a pot of something that smelled of meat propped on the stones beside it. Little Abraham said: "So, now you live again." Joseph tried to ask what had happened, but his mouth was still in the dreamworld. "I have been watching you, and saw the ice play its trick on you."

"You . . .?"

"I couldn't come close without leaving tracks in the snow, but . . . " He held up a little brass telescope. "Husk-covering may have nothing to do with white men, but still, white men's things can be useful."

"I must have . . ." Joseph had to pause to massage his cheeks and mouth with his teeth. "I must have done something to offend my Guardian."

"Why do you say that?"

"I asked him every night to come and help me, but he never did."

"Did I not tell thee many times that just because you cannot see the wolf doesn't mean he isn't there? *Someone* kept you alive these eight days."

"Eight . . .?"

"Count your arms." Joseph looked down confusedly at the furry swaddling around his body. "Not now. But when you are warmed enough to unwrap, you will see you still have two arms, but each has eight scars. By the time you're my age, they will have gone away."

"So . . . so now I am a warrior?"

"No. But you are ready to find out if you are when the time comes."

CHAPTER 25

When Molly set off with King Hendrick for Philadelphia, she did so as Degonwadonti—One Against Two. A woman with a household of her own was obviously too old to carry a child's name any longer, and in fact, she would've ceased to be Si-isha earlier if she hadn't been away from the longhouse at the white man's school. The Name Giver of the Canienga Wolf Clan had spent a long time sifting through his memory of women's names that belonged to their clan, looking for one no living woman was wearing and whose previous owner had been eating strawberries long enough that there was no flesh left on the name's bones.

The delegation of Royaners traveled in cutters provided by the British army, with an escort of British officers. The largest white town she'd ever been in was Schenectady, and it was a hunter's wigwam compared to Philadelphia. Despite the buffering cocoon of grizzled Royaners and red-coated officers, she found herself feeling as she had at school: naked in an alien place where all eyes were judging her. She had forgotten that feeling in the months since William Johnson had lifted her so easily to carry her across the threshold of Mount Johnson.

If the Pennsylvania Provincial Council thought it ridiculous to meet a delegation that included a seventeen-year-old girl, they were too polite to say so. For her part, she sat and listened to the speeches and kept her mouth shut and wondered what she was doing there.

The Pennsylvania Provincial Council hoped the Six Nations would solve for them the matter of the section of the Susquehanna Valley called Wyoming. By all reports it was a beautiful piece of country and many Pennsylvanians had settled there.

191

But the Colony of Connecticut claimed it was theirs, both by Royal Charter and because the Delawares had sold it to them.

In the inn where the Hodenosaune delegation was being put up, Hendrick shook his head and muttered: "I do not understand. The Pennsylvanians keep repeating that we long ago made the Delawares as women and put petticoats on them. And so we did. But they just keep saying it over and over, as though that should knock Connecticut on the head. I do not understand."

Molly said: "When the council at Onondaga declared the Delawares were women and dressed them in petticoats, what did it mean?"

King Hendrick blinked at her, but he explained patiently: "It meant if there is a foolish war between neighboring nations, the Delawares can go in unharmed—as though they were women and not warriors—and talk peace to both sides, as Clan Mothers."

"What the English think it means is that we Hodenosaune have such contempt for the Delawares that we stripped their breeches off and made them mere women, who must do what we command."

"No . . ."

"That is what the English think."

Hendrick ran his forefinger up and down the scar on his cheek and said: "Little One Against Two—I have done many foolish things in my time, but asking thee to come along to Philadelphia was not one of them."

When the military escort delivered the Canienga councillors back to the Mohawk Valley, William Johnson was away from Mount Johnson at the council in New York Town. He came home a few days later, and Molly immediately had to leave to spend a few nights in her grandmother's longhouse. A mat had been set aside for One Against Two in the inner circle, giving her a right to speak among the Clan Mothers. As her grandmother had said: "It was either that or tie a gag on you." The Hodenosaune believed in throwing a little mockery at people who were elevated to positions of importance, lest they forget it was the Tree of Peace that was important, not them.

In this case, Molly's grandmother needn't have worried. Molly had no doubt the Clan Mothers had given her a voice so young only because she knew something of white people and now sat at the right hand of William Johnson.

The subject of the current council of the women of Canajoharie was the impending war between the English and the French. Molly knew she was going to be called upon eventually, to tell them what the matter looked like from inside Mount Johnson. So she waited patiently—well, patiently for her—while the Oyanders around her expressed their opinions.

So far the overwhelming majority were of the opinion that the *orenda* of the Canienga had already been weakened dangerously by the white man's diseases and the white man's rum. It would be foolish to weaken it even further by joining in the white man's war.

An overwhelming majority didn't mean the question was decided. The Hodenosaune didn't decide questions by vote like the English did, but by consensus. A matter had to be talked over until it could be put into a speech that everyone agreed to. Which was why persuasive speakers like Hendrick and Molly's mother were valued higher than the bravest warrior.

The wampum strings finally passed into the hands of One Against Two. Molly rose to speak. Since the day she'd got back from Philadelphia, she'd known this moment was coming and had rehearsed it in her mind a hundred times. But now that the faces of the Clan Mothers were all turned toward her, she wondered whether the words she'd rehearsed were for the good of the Canienga or the good of William Johnson. She brushed it aside: Gets Business Done was a Canienga, too, and what was good for one was good for the other.

But that didn't help the fact that as soon as the wampum settled into her hand, she felt the same light-headedness and fluttering heart as when she'd snatched the white belt from her mother. Just before she began to speak, she heard the echo of a rasping whisper: "What're they sayin' in Canajoharie, Molly?"

"Sisters—Mothers and Grandmothers and Elder Sisters—from what passes through my ears and eyes among the English, I can tell you that they have it in their hearts that this is a war they have no choice but to fight. As it was with the Hurons and the League of Peace, so it has become between the English and the French.

"Some in the circle around today's fire hope that the English and the French will destroy each other and leave Turtle Island to its true people. But in the Huron war—did the Hodenosaune and the Hurons destroy each other? Or did not the Hodenosaune destroy the other and become that much stronger by devouring our great enemy? And when that war was over, did not the Hodenosaune turn upon the Neutrals and do the same to them as we had done to the Hurons?

"If our *orenda* has grown so weak that we cannot fight in this war, how shall we defend ourselves against the victors? If the English win without our help, I do not believe the king would declare a war against us. But who in this circle has not seen a white farmer yearn to burn this longhouse to make a new potato field? Our river would have run red a thousand times if Gets Business Done and the English law hadn't stepped between us and their own people. Why would the English law and judges stand beside us if we leave them to fight this war alone?

"The French have many nations of Turtle Island willing to dig up their hatchets to fight against the English. If we were to join the French, they might win. And what then? The French speak sweetly to us when they need us, but they hate us. Ever since the Frenchman Champlain amused himself by firing his gun into our great-grandfathers, we have made war on the French and they on us.

"I know that some will say I only speak this way because I carry William Johnson's child." There was a murmur of surprise. "But my *onikonhra* remains in the longhouse of my grandmothers. From all that I, thy daughter, have seen and heard at Mount Johnson and Philadelphia, if we do not help the English to win this war, the day will come when we shall see the Tree of Peace cut down and its broken branches scattered to the winds."

She handed the wampum back to the presiding Oyander, who announced that it was time for the Wolf Clan, the Bear Clan, and the Turtle Clan to go off into separate longhouses. When each had talked out a position that represented the will of the clan, they would reconvene in the ceremonial longhouse and discover how far apart or close together their three speeches were.

It took two more days of arguing without appearing to argue before Molly emerged from Canajoharie Castle to discover that

spring had come while she'd been eating smoke. The brown
and gray world she'd left outside the stockade gate now had a
translucent film of bright green.

When she got home, Gets Business Done was prowling
around a new tablecloth draped over the dining table—a huge
map with its springy corners held down by decanters.

"Sufferin' Judas, Molly—y'look like ye've been dragged
behind a horse."

"I feel like I have."

"Sit ye down, I'll pour ye out a tot of brandy. Oh, blast . . ."
The map corner the brandy decanter had been holding down
sprang to try to rejoin its opposite number. "Well, I suppose I
can always roll it out again. Here ye are, m'dear. Here's a
health to yer enemies' enemies. Well?"

She waited a moment for the brandy burn to leave her throat
and the warmth to settle in her stomach. And perhaps there
was a certain wicked little thrill in having the great William
Johnson hanging on her words. She said: "The speech that will
travel with the wampum the Clan Mothers of Canajoharie send
to their sisters in the Upper and Lower castles will say that we
believe the Hodenosaune must go to war on the side of the English."

He slapped his hand against his thigh and expelled: "That's
m'darlin' gel! Blessin's upon thee."

She felt it only fair to point out: "That doesn't mean it's decided. The Oyanders in the other castles may disagree, or the
Royaners and warriors may be against it. . . ."

"So long as Hendrick has a few other voices to give his le-
gitimacy, it's a sold horse. That man could talk the skirts off a
mother superior. This calls for a bottle of champagne. Horace!
Horace! Where the bleedin' divil are ye?"

"I *was* on my way down-cellar, Mr. Johnson, sir, to fetch
you a bottle of champagne like you was bellering for. And
then I heard you a-bellering again and so I come back right
smart—"

"Well how the divil am I supposed to know ye've *heard* me
bleedin' bellerin' unless y'shout out smartly: 'Yes, sir!'"

"Yes, sir! I'll be a-fetching of that bottle now."

Two ham-sized hands slapped down on the arms of Molly's
chair, not quite cracking it asunder, and her husband's face and
shoulders filled her vision as the tip of his long, Roman nose

touched hers. "Who's the bleedin' savior of His Majesty's
North American colonies but a little Mohawk gel?"

She tried to wave away his preposterous exaggeration, but
nonetheless felt like she was giggling between her legs.

The champagne bottle had barely been popped when a foot-
man ushered Molly's mother in, looking more wrung-out than
Molly. She said anxiously: "Has your brother been here?"
Molly shook her head. "The schoolmaster came to Carrying
News two days ago to ask him why Joseph hadn't come to
school. Joseph didn't come home that night, or last night. Little
Abraham knows nothing of where he might be."

William said: "Have ye asked Willy? The two of them are
as thick as Damon and what-ye-may-call 'im."

"He does not know, or will not say. Willy would not lie out-
right, but he would keep a secret under torture if Joseph asked
him."

William said: "I know it's small comfort, Mother Brant, but
I'll lay ye ten to one he just got a whim to see if the bass are
bitin' upriver yet. Ye know how thoughtless children can be.
Joseph can live in the woods like a little ferret." But it seemed
to Molly like he was just trying to get them not to worry about
what worrying couldn't change.

Molly's mother went back home, leaving Molly feeling like
the air that had been pumped into her had been let out again.
When the champagne was drunk and William gone off to put
in an appearance at his trading store, she dragged herself upstairs to try to sleep before dinner. She was just stripping off
her leggings when a knock came on the bedroom door.

"Come in."

Horace poked his straw-thatched head in and then shuffled
his barge-boat feet along after it. "I'm sorry, Miss Molly—but
I don't rightly know what to do with him. . . ."

"Him?"

"Him out there on the lawn. He won't come in and he won't
go away."

She went to the window. In the middle of the carpet of
spring-glistening green, a scrawny, tangle-haired figure in
breechclout and moccasins was sitting cross-legged with his
chin on his fists, staring at the front door.

"I'll see to it, Horace, thank you."

"Yes, miss."

"You were right to come and tell me."

She put her moccasins on again and went outside. The grass was wet with a winter's worth of thawing frost. As she got closer to him, she could see that he was shivering. She stopped in front of him and said: "It's warm inside."

He said nothing, just raised chipped-glass eyes to cut against hers. She tried again: "Our mother tells me your Teacher says you did well when you were husk-covered. I remember when I spent my husk-covered time on the Ohio, I thought I'd never live through it. That old woman would point me out a mountain of firewood to chop in one day with a dull ax, or a hill of corn to pound before sunset, or—"

"The husk-covering time of a girl is hardly the same as for a young warrior."

"What do you want here?" His face pinched up as though she'd spat on him, then it froze back into its stoic rictus. She wanted to pick him up and shake him until his eyes bugged out; she wanted to wrap herself around him until he stopped shivering; she wanted to cry.

He said: "In the English school we learned a little of how English law works. I think I may lay a charge against Mr. and Mrs. William Johnson for the murder of Si-isha."

"Stand up."

"I'm not one of his servants."

"I just want to look at something. Stand up."

He did it grudgingly, but then that seemed to be how he did everything these days. Despite how small he looked when sitting coiled together, he was a good half a head taller than she already, almost as tall as the average full-grown man. She said: "You don't want to be a schoolboy anymore? You think you should be treated as a young warrior? There is a war coming. Either go to school or follow the warrior's road."

He glared down at her a moment longer, then turned and loped away.

As the summer ripened, so did the child in her belly. Her mother and grandmother seemed doubtful whether it would be safe for her to travel when the time came for the Great Council of the Six Nations at Onondaga. Molly knew she would have to go regardless, to speak for her husband. Adoptive Canienga or not, it would be unwise for him to go to Onondaga to speak for himself without the council's invitation. Especially this year, when the last thing Hendrick needed was for the other five nations to get the impression that the Caniengas had become the hunting dogs of the English.

General Johnson traveled to Virginia to meet with General Braddock, grumbling and cursing at being forced to leave Mount Johnson. He came back crowing: "We're out of the fur business, m'dear!"

"Pardon me?"

"The good general brought commissions from the king for two superintendents of Indian Affairs: northern and southern. I'm the northern superintendent."

"What does that mean?"

"A lot of things. For one, yer Six Nations' Confederacy won't be havin' to deal with a rats' nest of different colonies' Indian commissioners. When they speak to me, they'll be speakin' directly to His British Majesty, and vicey-versey.

"'Course we can't have His Majesty's representative to the Indians also carryin' on private commerce with the Indians. That's why we're out of the fur trade."

"Then how will we live?"

"Even better'n before. The royal exchequer's very generous to those who represent the British Empire in foreign lands. Who'd've ever thought things could come to such a pass: Backwoods Billy Johnson from County Meath representin' the king?"

She put her hand up to his cheek and said: "It will be very reassuring to the Hodenosaune that the king and his ministers can be so wise."

"Couldn't've put it better m'self." But she could see she'd pleased him.

"Did General Braddock say anything about his plans for the war, or did he just invite you down there to talk about Indian Affairs?"

"Same bleedin' thing at this point. Braddock and the Froggies are at even odds—it's a question of who can call up the most benighted savages to tip the balance."

Mount Johnson became Fort Johnson. The windows in the parlor and dining room were bricked in. The little wall between the river and the lawn grew into a parapeted, gated barracks to house the garrison from Fort Hunter. The sheep house was torn down and a blockhouse built to guard the back of the house.

All the activity and noise of construction seemed far away to Molly. The baby growing inside her, which had seemed to grow so slowly for the longest time, suddenly began to swell her belly out like rising bread dough. At the same time, she miraculously lost the need to run for the nearest commode whenever she caught a whiff of frying bacon. Now that she could keep food down again, she made up for it with a vengeance.

She stopped wearing her white-style dresses, even when the Royal Governor of New York paid a visit to Mount Johnson. In a comfortable Canienga overdress, a woman didn't show until her belly stuck out farther than her breasts. Not that she was ashamed of being pregnant—just the opposite—but she thought perhaps it looked grotesque to white men.

The nights grew warm, but she still went behind her dressing screen to don her nightgown before coming to bed. One night as she settled blissfully onto back muscles unaccustomed to lugging that kind of weight around, William said: "Are ye feelin' a bit of a chill?"

"No."

"Then why d'ye wear that frippery tent? What the divil's the use of a man fatherin' a child without bein' able to see it growin'?"

She took her lower lip in her teeth and squinted at him to see if he meant it, then furled the hem of her nightgown and elevated her hips to raise it to her waist. He put his hand under her back to help her sit up so she could slough it off over her head.

She lay back down, blushing. Not long ago, one of his hands would have stretched across her from hip to hip; now it just barely covered the summit of her belly, the calluses at the base of his fingers scratchy against her tautened navel. He said: "The child will be of the best—or female—kind."

"How can you tell?"

"Because she makes her mother as lovely as any two females put together."

An impromptu council convened itself around the kitchen table of Fort Johnson. Molly sat down to tea with her mother and grandmother and Juba and the Scottish midwife who was one of William's tenants. Juba's baby sister Jemmy was there as well, but she had nothing to contribute except a round-eyed stare at the grown women talking about women's things. She didn't contribute much as a lady's maid yet, either, but she was learning, and her presence in the household made Juba happy. As William said: "A sound roof don't mean as much to a house as a happy cook."

Juba began the council with: "From now till the baby's come, Mizt'ess Molly, you don't want to be sharpening no knives, or the cord might cut before its time."

The midwife just rolled her eyes at such nonsense. Molly's grandmother said: "At the last full moon before your time, we will build a birth hut in the forest."

The midwife said: "She has a fine, warm, cozy house to give birth in."

"Yes," Grandmother agreed, "a fine house with no place to build a fire except stone boxes. If her afterbirth does not come, how can we build a fire of corn husks to pass her body over?"

"That's little reason to make her suffer through her labor on the cold, cold ground instead of lying in her own bed."

Mother said: " 'Lying'? What kind of torture are you thinking of? A woman gives birth squatting down, with a good, strong pole over her head to hold onto."

The more they talked, the more confused Molly became, and terrified. None of their authoritative contradictions seemed any more or less ridiculous than the doctor's pronouncements about infusions of sulfur. It must've shown on her face, because her grandmother leaned across the table to pat her hand and smile: "It *is* something to be a little afraid of, granddaughter. But young women and their babies have been doing what they have to do since the dawn of time, while old women prattled on."

A few weeks before the Canienga Oyanders and Royaners were to start their journey to the Fire That Never Dies, Molly waddled downstairs to find William slumped gray-faced in his chair with a sheaf of crack-sealed papers slipping from his hand. His eyes had rolled up and his breathing sounded like a clubfoot dragging across gravel.

She hurled the top off the brandy decanter, forced its lip between his teeth and ripped his neckband open. When he came back to himself, she said: "What happened?"

"Happened?" he croaked. "Ain't it obvious? I'm a demmed spavined old relic. Sorry."

"You are nothing of the kind. You just had a bit of a twinge in your heart, but it's passed now. Isn't it?"

"Seems to be."

"What set it off?"

"Braddock . . . fool . . . demmed bleedin' fool . . . Told 'im in Virginia that if he took Niagara, Sir Froggy's Indian friends were cinched off like a bullock's ballocks. Seems Braddock believed me. Only instead of takin' 'is army on a Sunday stroll up the Mohawk Valley and across, he decided to go by way of the Ohio and clean out the French outposts along the way— just like that pup Washington last year. But he had to go Washington one better."

The blue lips took in another sip of brandy and the green eyes focused a bit more clearly. "So now our shield and bulwark General Braddock is lyin' molderin' on the banks of the Monongahela River with a pound or two of French musket balls in 'im—along with most of his glorious two blessed regiments. And there's a French army marchin' south from Montreal. Ye shouldn't've wasted two years learnin' English, m'dear."

CHAPTER 26

Joseph was in the ceremonial longhouse, currently occupied by the Warrior's Society, and his Teacher and stepfather were plucking the hairs off his head to prepare him for the war road. Just like his father, he'd decided, Joseph would have his head plucked clean except for the little circle at the crown.

The roots of his teeth began to hurt from gritting his jaw to keep his features impassive as Little Abraham and Carrying News worked away with their thumbs clamping strands of his hair against the rims of mollusk shells and yanking. It helped that Willy was sitting and watching him with his mouth open. It was easier to keep up an impression of manfully enduring pain when there was someone to be impressed by it.

It also helped that all around him there were old war stories to listen to, and war songs, and the thrilling, glistening sounds of sharpening blades. Vibrating under all the songs and stories was the deep bass rumble of King Hendrick. Joseph tried to hold on to the fact that Hendrick had once been a boy like him, with the same terror of how he might react to his first battle, and the same inexperience with pain. But he couldn't quite believe that King Hendrick could ever have been like him.

Little Abraham and Carrying News paused to rest their fingers, but he knew it would just hurt all the more when they started again. King Hendrick loomed in front of them and stooped to run his hand across Joseph's tingling scalp. Joseph could feel the Royaner's hand scratching his skin all the way back to the beginning of his scalp lock. It was half done.

The barrel bass voice thrummed: "Your father and my oldest son were made warriors together, sitting face-to-face while their heads were plucked. I thought my son would be the one to put a better face on it, but A Man Tying on His Snowshoes, the son of a bitch, he started singing.

"In these days, though, there is no need for such barbaric practices." He produced a short pair of shears from the folds of his blanket. "I would say that if you cut the back part short, your scalp lock will stand out just as well."

Joseph pried his top teeth out of his lower teeth and said: "If you think that would be best, Royaner . . ."

It only took a moment with the shears. When it was done, Carrying News handed Joseph a new hatchet, the kind with a hollow handle and a pipe bowl behind the blade, and said: "This is only for war. It is permissible for you to practice throwing it and accustom yourself to the feel of it, but otherwise you bury it at the end of a war and do not dig it up until the beginning of the next. It is only for killing enemies of the League of Peace. If another man of the Hodenosaune should get angry at you and come at you with a knife, and you happen to have this hatchet in your hand—better you should die than have the blood of one of your own on a weapon of war."

At Fort Johnson, General Johnson was trying on his spanking new general's coat, shading his eyes against the mirrored blaze of gold and scarlet. Molly was on her knees in front of him, trying to fasten it around his midriff. She said: "It doesn't fit."

"'Tain't meant to fit—not around the front, at least. It's meant to hang open and show off m'brocade waistcoat and lace jabot."

"It won't keep you very warm."

"That's what God made rum for." He gave her a hand up and marched downstairs in his martial splendor to sit down and inspect his paper army once again. Their numbers hadn't changed while he wasn't looking. The various militia companies from the Mohawk Valley came out to a grand total of eleven hundred men. Another two thousand militiamen from the New England colonies were supposed to rendezvous with them at Albany. One never knew with militia. At the first shot they might suddenly decide that they'd rather be back tending their farms. He would have to din into their heads that if the French and their Indian allies ended up owning North America, the few English farmers who didn't get slow-roasted wouldn't have any farms left to tend.

A footman announced: "The King of the Iroquois."

Hendrick paused in the doorway and squinted at Big Billy's appearance, then moved on into the room and took a chair. Johnson called Horace to pour out some Madeira, then said to Hendrick: "Well?"

"Perhaps fifty to a hundred to go with you now. I will stay and follow after you with the rest. Hodenosaune running down the war road can catch up with marching white men easily."

"Ye're no more fit for runnin' than me granny's uncle."

"I have a horse that can run for me."

"How many is 'the rest'?"

"Perhaps—if I talk well—perhaps two hundred."

"That's all?"

"Without the council at Onondaga rendering a decision, all the king can expect is those Caniengas—and perhaps a few Oneidas—who are willing to take the war road just on my say-so." He squinted at Big Billy again contemplatively. "I have word about the French. They are coming with eight thousand white men—six thousand of them uniformed warriors from across the ocean."

"Huh. Even allowin' for the natural boastin' and vapors of Sir Froggy, we'd seem to be outnumbered."

"With them, too, will come some seven or eight hundred warriors of Turtle Island."

"Sounds like the warriors of Turtle Island like the French better'n the English."

"The Men Who Wear Dresses and their neighbors are quick to fly to arms—and just as quick to fly from battle. Among the Hodenosaune these things take time. But once the decision is made to dig up the hatchet, we do not yelp and run away. Be thankful that you may have two hundred. What do you know of the French war chief?"

"They ain't been kind enough to inform me who's goin' to lead their expedition. But the French commander-in-chief for North America's the Baron Dieskau. He's fought and won more battles in Europe than I have in bed."

Hendrick seemed to have stopped hearing him. His cattish eyes had narrowed again into that riveted squint fixed somewhere below Billy Johnson's second chin. "It is an odd thing, Gets Business Done . . . I had a dream last night. . . ."

" 'Tain't odd at all. Most men has dreams most nights."

"But in *this* dream I wore a coat . . . a red, red coat with much gold on it. A coat just precisely so much like the same coat I see you wearing."

Johnson choked on his current throatful of Madeira, sputtered, swallowed, cleared his nose and wiped his eyes and said: "The divil ye say."

"I say nothing about devils. But I do say I dreamed that coat."

"*This* coat. . . ?"

"That very coat."

It was Big Billy's turn to squint, but it was impossible to read the old rascal when he put his Royaner's face on. Among the Hodenosaune, anyone who had it in his power to grant someone the substance of a dream and didn't, was doing the equivalent of refusing water to a child dying of thirst. He was reasonably sure that even cardsharping Hendrick wouldn't lie about the dreamworld to fool another Indian, at least not another Hodenosaune. But he might to a white man. Nevertheless . . .

General Johnson set his glass aside, stood up, lifted off the baldrick holding his ivory-handled general's sword, stripped off his general's coat and handed it to the dreamer, saying: "If thee dreamed it, then it must be so."

"Gets Business Done is generous." Hendrick stood to shrug off his blanket and slip his arms through the sleeves of the coat. The shoulders bagged on him a little, but the cuffs didn't quite cover his hands. He looked down at himself, slapping his hands against the gold frogging across his chest. "Damn fine coat."

"Don't worry if ye can't get it to button across the front. 'Tain't meant to."

Two days later, when the pastures around the half-built blockhouses were sprouting militia tents, Hendrick came to Fort Johnson to find out when the general would be ready to march. The general had been reduced to his old major's coat, which was still sufficient martial splendor to cut a figure among the militia. But it wasn't a patch on Hendrick, with his gold and scarlet acme of military tailoring worn shirtless to show off his tattoos and old scars.

Johnson said: "Odd thing, Hendrick—I had a dream last night."

"Did you, now?"

"That I did. Ye know that lovely little meadow just past the southwest border of me estate? The one me trout stream flows out of?"

"I do."

"I dreamt it was mine."

Hendrick looked at him a long time before saying slowly: "If thee dreamed it, Gets Business Done, then it must be so. Write me up a piece of paper and I will put my name to it."

"Odd thing—Molly's just copyin' out a deed in the other room."

"I think, Gets Business Done, that Hendrick will dream no more."

The next morning, the little army of the Mohawk Valley lined up in front of Fort Johnson: the militia with their train of baggage wagons, and the Mohawks carrying all they needed on their backs. General Johnson said good-bye to his family on the front steps of his house—all except John, who was coming along. Carrying News and Joseph came out of the Mohawk line to say good-bye to Molly, although it looked to Johnson that Joseph was being brought rather than coming forward with a good grace. He certainly had turned into a surly pup, and looked like a parody of a warrior, with his new scalp lock and matchstick arms. Molly said to them in Mohawk: "May thy guardians bring thee home safe with the scalps of our enemies dangling from thy belts."

Carrying News said in English: "Pray for us, Mary." Joseph just grunted and turned on his heel.

Johnson said: "Well, Molly m'gel—if I can manage this army half as smooth as I know ye'll manage things here, we should be back in jig time with a barrelful of Frog's legs."

Molly didn't say anything, just raised her hand up to his cheek. He put his hand on her blossoming womb and said: "Ye'll be as much at risk as I will—likely more. Remember ye have servants to do the liftin' and stoopin' for ye, and ye won't dent the treasury if ye call in the doctor and midwives at the least twinge."

He heaved himself up onto Old Knobby and told the captain to give the order to march. Someone struck up that contagious piece of nonsense, "Yankee Doodle." Trust the colonials to take something meant to mock them and make it their own.

As he and John trotted out the gates of Fort Johnson, Big Billy looked back over his shoulder at the barbarically dressed, black-haired girl standing on his doorstep. She raised her arm and he raised his hand. He'd waved good-bye to more women than he could count, often with a twinge of regret, but never with this feeling of being wrenched apart. He hadn't realized how much she'd become his life until he had to face the possibility he might not see her again. But then, men were born fools.

Joseph didn't quite know what to make of these militiamen. Some of them were heavy-footed farm boys, some of them looked like they'd be more at home in a pulpit or behind a schoolmaster's desk, some of them were bearded men in greasy buckskins who carried long rifles and spat tobacco in all directions, and some of them were old men in checkered skirts who marched behind a squealing instrument that drowned out "Yankee Doodle." Some of the militia were on horseback—everything from glossy thoroughbreds to plough horses—but most of them walked. They didn't walk very fast. On days when it was known in advance where the army would camp that night, the Canienga contingent would jog ahead, leaving the militia plodding behind.

Those were the best days, when Joseph could show that his meatless, thirteen-year-old legs could carry him loping along the trail as well as any grown man's, and he could join in the laughter when the people on the white farms by the road dropped their hoes and gaped or ran into their houses at the sight of fifty painted warriors coming down on them. After a few hours his heart and lungs would start to feel like they'd been used to line a hearth, his father's musket began to feel like an anvil chained to his arm, and the slapping of his fire bag, blanket roll, shot pouch, powder horn, and food pouches against various parts of his body began to feel like they were flailing his skin apart; but he still managed to keep up with the pack.

The best thing about those days, though, was that he wasn't marching behind William Johnson and his ornamental son. Joseph hated the thought that the people watching the column pass by would think that he and all the Canienga Nation had become as much William Johnson's property as his sister was.

They camped on marshy ground outside Albany, but as far as Joseph could tell, there was no other kind of ground around Albany. Trust a white man to build a town in a swamp. It seemed they were to wait there for the militias from the colonies east of the Adirondacks. Joseph watched the militia camp sprout more and more tents, until it was three times its original size, but still they waited. When he asked Carrying News why, Carrying News said: "I don't know."

Joseph snorted: "Maybe Gets Business Done should've stuck to doing business." Carrying News looked like he was about to say something in reply, but didn't.

When they finally set off marching north along the Hudson, there were about three thousand militia, more armed men than

Joseph had ever seen together. When they reached the north bend of the Hudson, a third of them were left behind to build a fort, while Joseph and the rest of the army cut a road through the forest to a beautiful lake that the French had named Lac Saint Sacrement. Joseph sat under a tree and watched William Johnson step into the water with his sword drawn and bellow ridiculously: "In the name of His British Majesty—literally—I christen this Lake George."

They encamped on the lakeshore, and the next morning went to work clearing the trees in front of their camp. Joseph hacked away viciously with a felling ax, wondering why he'd bothered to bring his war hatchet. He paused for breath and grumbled: "We are spending all our time killing trees instead of enemies."

Carrying News stopped chopping to say: "There is more to war, Joseph, than screaming out of the forest with scalping knives. We are killing these trees to do the same thing our grandfathers did when they cut clearings to funnel deer to the hunters. Do you think Gets Business Done chose this place to make a camp just because it's where we happened to come out on the lake?"

As a matter of fact, that was exactly what he'd thought, so he just shrugged.

"You must learn to look around you, Joseph, if you hope to have a long life as a warrior. On our left side is that hill with our cannons on it, on our right side the marsh. An enemy will have to come straight down the slope between them, with nothing to hide behind once we have killed all these trees. Gets Business Done may not have any battle scars, but he learned somewhere that preparing for a fight is even more important than fighting hard."

Joseph shrugged and grunted and hefted his ax again. Carrying News could say all the fine things he wanted about Gets Business Done; Joseph suspected that "General" Johnson would still be making preparations when winter descended. Or the French.

There were increasingly unhappy murmurings around the Canienga campfires about the fact that many Men Who Wear Dresses were accompanying the French army. Joseph said to Carrying News: "Why should Canienga warriors be afraid of Men Who Wear Dresses?"

"Do not be fooled by the name, Joseph. Although they chose to follow the French priests, they are still Hodenosaune warriors. It would be a terrible thing if Hodenosaune war weapons drank Hodenosaune blood."

The next morning brought cheers and cannon salutes as King Hendrick appeared down the new-cut road, with his silver hair shaved to a scalp lock and two hundred Canienga and Oneida warriors jogging behind his horse. A few nights later there was a bustle of scouts coming and going. Joseph wasn't privileged to hear what the scouts said to the war chiefs and officers, but from the strange glint in the eyes around the campfires, he could guess.

General Johnson's staff convened around the table in his well-appointed campaign tent: provincial militia officers, Mohawk chiefs, and the only two regular officers in his command—the engineer and the commander of his pitiful little artillery battery. As Horace poured out rum punch, Big Billy said: "Well, gentlemen, we know Monsieur Froggy's bivouacked within a mornin's march, and we know 'e ain't quite made up 'is mind yet whether to come at us here or sneak down to the Hudson and ambush our comrades in their half-built fort.

"What seems our best response is to set half our force to buildin' a barricade here at first light and send the other half out in two columns: one to warn and reinforce the lads back on the Hudson, the other to burn Monsieur Froggy's boats behind 'im. . . ."

As he went on outlining his strategy, he noticed Hendrick murmuring something to Nickus Brant. Brant slipped out and came back with something hidden under his blanket. Hendrick said: "How many soldiers, Gets Business Done, did you say would be in each column?"

"Five hundred, give or take."

"Five hundred," Hendrick repeated thoughtfully. "Does it not seem to you, General Johnson, that if they are to be killed, they are too many, and if they are to fight, they are too few?"

"Ah. Well . . . when ye put it in those words, Hendrick, demmed if it don't seem as y'have a point. But we can't very well just squat behind our barricade and leave our brothers to the French."

Hendrick held out his hand to Nickus Brant, who put two sticks in it. "Break these sticks one by one, Gets Business Done." Johnson snapped them with his fingers. Brant put two more sticks in Hendrick's hand. "Now, Gets Business Done, hold these two sticks together and break them at once."

Big Billy probably could've, they weren't that thick, but he got the point. It was the old trick the Peacemaker and Hiawatha had used to show Atotarho that the nations would be stronger together. "If tomorrow," Hendrick continued, "you send both your parties of five hundred together to warn the men building the fort, I will lead my warriors in front of them."

"Demmed fascinatin' bit of philosophy there, Hendrick— with the sticks and all. . . . What I propose is that tomorrow we send a thousand militiamen, along with Hendrick's warriors, to reinforce the fort. The rest of us will construct a barricade here, and leave the French boats for another day."

"I think, Gets Business Done, that the king made a wise choice when he picked you for a general."

When his staff had departed, Big Billy hung up the baldrick of his bright-bladed general's sword, rummaged in one of his traveling trunks and came out with a squat old navy cutlass. With more bravado than he felt, he said to his son: "Those demmed, pretty, nickle-plated toothpicks are well enough for parades, John, but when it comes to a fight, a man wants a weapon in his hands."

"And which weapon shall I use?"

"Weapon? Ye ain't doin' any fightin'. Ye're still a boy. At the sound of the first shot, ye're to run pell-mell back to the baggage train and watch from there, for the purposes of yer eddication."

"Joseph's no older than I am, and he's fighting."

"In case ye ain't noticed, Joseph's an Indian. Ye're a British gentleman—or will be if ye live long enough. Don't worry, son, ye'll get plenty of time for soldierin' when yer time comes." He didn't mention that it well might come tomorrow, if the French managed to break through the barricade.

In the Canienga camp, Joseph lay staring at the stars, with every string and muscle in his body vibrating like a kicked harpsichord, waiting for the morning to come and get itself over with. He didn't know how many of the blanket-shrouded lumps around him were also lying awake, but from a neighboring campfire he could hear the deep, sonorous snoring of King Hendrick.

At the first tinge of pearl-gray in the sky, the snoring stopped abruptly. All around Joseph the fires came alive again, flickering on warriors streaking each other's faces with ocher and vermilion and ashes. Carrying News squatted across the fire from him with a birchbark bowl of pigment, and they took turns daubing each other's cheeks and foreheads. Carrying News said: "Best you don't eat this morning." Joseph was ecstatic he wasn't expected to.

When the two tuneless boys who made up the fife and drum corps let fly with reveille, General Johnson grunted up off his camp cot, tugged on his boots, shrugged on his major's coat and cutlass baldrick, shoved a pair of pistols in his belt and reached for his periwig. On second thought, he probably made a much more scarifying figure without it.

Hendrick was standing at the tent door in his general's coat. "There is an old Indian saying, Gets Business Done, 'This is a good day to die.' Me, I don't think there is any such goddamned day."

Joseph fell in behind Carrying News in the line of warriors following King Hendrick's horse. Behind the single file of warriors came the militia marching five or six abreast. They followed the road they'd spent the last few weeks cutting through the woods, hemmed in on both sides by tangles of felled trees with the leaves still withering on their branches.

They hadn't gone far before the militia colonel called a halt to reorder his ranks. The message was relayed up the line to Hendrick, who replied that he and his warriors would forge on and leave the militia to catch up. Without the militia to slow them down, they broke into a trot.

There was a gunshot up ahead, and a voice called out of the woods in oddly accented Canienga: "Who is it that travels down this road?"

The warriors began to crowd up toward the front of the line, carrying Joseph along with them. King Hendrick's voice, wrapped in Royaner's dignity, replied: "We are the Six Confederate Nations, the Elder Brothers of all the nations of True People of Turtle Island."

There was a moment's silence, then all along the entanglement of fallen trees and living forest scalp-locked, feathered heads and painted torsos poked up. A blue-striped head with a roached mane pronounced: "We are the Seven Nations of Canada, and we come with the soldiers of our Father, the King of France, to fight his enemies, the English. We come to fight against the English only, not to trespass against any nation of the True People. We tell thee, leave in peace, lest thee and we come to a war amongst ourselves."

As calmly as though he were striding back and forth beside a council fire, King Hendrick said: "We have come to help our brothers the English stop the French, who are already pushing our people off the Ohio and would take all of Turtle Island if they could. The Seven Nations of Canada should join with us, for the sake of thine own people—or leave in peace and let us fight the French."

Before the crested head in the thicket could reply, the warrior standing next to Joseph threw up his gun and fired at it. The faces in the woods disappeared. There was another instant's silence, except for the twittering of a wren, and then the thickets erupted with gunfire and war cries.

When the roar of gunfire hammered against his ears, Joseph's ankles started to twist around to run away. The warrior beside him sat down with a surprised expression on his face and blood gushing out of his mouth and stomach. Joseph grabbed onto a poplar trunk and hugged it with both arms as the bullets chipped bark into his eyes. His feet kept churning backward, trying to build up enough momentum to uproot the tree and run back down the road with it.

General Johnson's barricade of overturned wagons interlaced with felled trees was only partially completed when he heard gunfire—at a rough guess perhaps three or four miles away. It seemed to be getting closer, which meant the column in the woods was retreating. He sent a company of three hundred militia to reinforce them and carried on bellowing at his work crews to fetch more tree limbs and overturn more wagons.

The mouth of the road suddenly vomited a river of militiamen and Iroquois. They ran across the meadow of pink-toothed stumps and scrambled over the barricade. Some of them were shrieking that the French were going to kill them all. Panic took hold.

General Johnson strode back and forth along the line, bellowing, "Remember ye're Britons, not some cowardly foreign rabble! Think what they'll do to yer wives and daughters if we don't stop 'em here! Look to yer guns and aim straight!" and God knew what other manner of nonsense. He also applied the flat of his cutlass to the knee of the occasional militiaman trying to run past him.

He wasn't the only one striding back and forth behind the barricade. Former Pipe Major MacCrimmon was assaulting the sky over Lake George with "Scotland the Brave." Johnson was moved to shut him up so he could make himself heard, but one look at those claymored old relics straightening their spines made him change his mind.

It seemed impossible that the French hadn't come pouring out of the woods already. Perhaps the officer Baron Dieskau had sent to lead the invasion didn't know enough about human nature to understand that once your enemy's on the run, you want to keep him that way.

Finally, a double file of white-uniformed men marched out of the road through the woods, splitting off to either side, their bayonets glistening in the sun. The line never seemed to end.

"Hold yer fire, lads—they're out of range of us and we of them."

The clattery beat of two drummer boys—perfect miniatures of the professional killers emerging from the woods—kept time while the French soldiers lined up calmly in three ranks. The drumbeat changed and the white lines began to advance step by step, the first rank kneeling to fire, then standing to reload while the next rank stepped past and fired by the numbers. The cannon on the hill boomed, but only managed to decapitate a few trees. Johnson shouted between French volleys: "Stand to, boys—them Froggy muskets're just pissin' in the wind from there!" He waited until the soldiers of His Most Christian Majesty had come halfway down the funnel, then roared: "Give 'em hell, boys!"

There was a more or less coordinated volley that segued into desultory gunshots as the various militias vied to prove who could reload and aim the fastest. The white-uniformed ranks turned and marched away, leaving white and red blossoms scattered among the stumps and wildflowers. The drumbeats changed and changed again as the professionals reformed calmly and advanced once more.

Big Billy felt a twinge of hopelessness. Never in human history had a rabble of farmers and carpenters and innkeepers stood up to soldiers-of-the-line and lived to tell the tale. Those ranks of bayonets would just keep mechanically falling back and reforming and advancing a little farther each time, like the hands of a clock driven inexorably by the ticking of the drumbeats. . . .

He jumped forward to lay hands on the nearest militiamen, shouting: "When they get within range this time, shoot the drummers!"

"Those little boys?"

"*Kill* 'em!"

He moved back to a rise of ground where he could see over the barricade. The French front rank stepped over the last of their comrades to be shot down in the last advance. As he swung his head from side to side to see who needed bellowing at, his gold-braided tricorne hat—made to fit a head swollen by a periwig—bobbled down across his nose and then fell off. He stooped to pick it up. An ounce or two of half-molten lead punched into his left buttock, knocking him ass-over-teakettle. He lay on the ground for a moment convincing himself that he had indeed been shot in the ass. Then Horace was there, trying to help him back up. "Mr. Johnson, sir! General Johnson! Can you stand?"

"Yes, I can bleedin' stand! Or I can stand bleedin'. Hand me that." He pointed to a musket lying beside a militiaman who obviously didn't need it anymore. He tried stumping around using Horace as one crutch and the musket as another, but every step hurt like billy-o and his left boot began to fill with blood. "Take me to the surgeon."

The surgeon peeled back Johnson's breeches and clucked: "The bullet's deep. I'll have to probe the wound."

"Leave yer bleedin' probin' till the battle's over. Bandage me up and staunch the blood."

When he hobbled back out to the barricade, still clutching the musket to take the weight off his left leg, the French were retiring from another advance, so the defenders had time to turn and cheer his reappearance. Some of the cheers seemed to be of a rather rude nature.

It did seem odd, now that he'd had time to pause and think about it, that the only enemies in evidence so far were the white-coated Regulars. He stumped toward the willow bog at the right end of the barricade, tugging a pistol out of his belt with his free hand.

There was a crackling in the bush. A painted face above a silver crucifix leaped out at him. Johnson pulled the trigger and the painted face disappeared, only to be replaced by a bearded one above a bayonet-tipped musket. He threw his pistol at it, buying enough time to draw his cutlass. He swung at the Canadian and missed, then looked down at the bayonet driving for his belly.

Something whistled past his ear and the beard and bayonet disappeared. Then a ropy-armed, half-naked little demon sprang past Johnson's shoulder, knelt on the beard-wreathed chest to pry his tomahawk free, and bounded whooping into the willow bog, with a wave of warriors and militiamen following behind him.

"Well, I'm demmed," Big Billy said to himself, "he's got a bit of his sister in him after all."

While the right flank of the barricade's defenders charged into the marsh, the center and the left flank were clambering over the trees and wagons. Their commander-in-chief went to see the white-uniformed professionals showing their heels.

General Johnson intended to leap over the barricade, but it turned into a sort of jackknife flop, coming down on his tenderest portions. He jacked himself back up with the aid of his musket crutch and followed his troops, waving his cutlass and bawling like a bull in heat.

Joseph kept on running forward, through the marsh and into the woods. He had no idea who he was or what he was doing, only that he'd already killed one for certain and there were more ahead of him. A shout went up around him, "They're on the run!" which seemed like a perfect opportunity to catch another one or two from behind.

"Joseph!" Carrying News's voice stopped him. "Not this time." He gestured at the white militiamen slumping down and grinning and laughing at each other. "If we go on chasing them alone, they can turn on us." Joseph sagged his back against a tree and slid down it. "Did you have good hunting, Joseph?"

"I killed one for certain!"

"Come show me, and I will show you how to take a scalp."

Now that it was over, Joseph found it hard to get back on his feet. Even later, after the day had faded into night and he sat turning the hoop-stretched scalp in the smoke and hearing the other warriors around the other campfires celebrating and lamenting the day's dead, he still felt sick. Not sick at the smell of blood, but sick with exhaustion, as though his *onikonhra* had blazed itself out like a bonfire and left his body to face the consequences.

He wished his know-it-all Oneida deskmate Margaret could see him sitting among the warriors curing the scalp of a full-grown man who would've killed him if he could. But then it occurred to him that a girl who'd studied the Bible on her father's knee might only consider it proof that Joseph Brant was an ignorant savage. He said to Carrying News: "How is it you can be both a Christian and a warrior?" It had never crossed his mind that Carrying News *was* a warrior until he saw him take the first bite out of the boiled dog's head that King Hendrick had passed around the longhouse to see who would dig up their hatchets to fight the French.

"It is not an easy question, Joseph. Are not the French soldiers Christian? And the militiamen who marched with us? A Christian must turn his cheek when he can, but did not Jesus himself whip the moneychangers out of the temple? A man must defend his home and family, whether he follows the Prince of Peace or the Tree of Peace or both."

Joseph grunted to show he'd heard, and shook his head to show he didn't understand but was determined to work at it. Maybe tomorrow.

The next three days were spent scouring the woods for scalps and prisoners and missing friends. What with the Bloody Morning Scout and the skirmishing on the heels of the French retreat, there were a lot of dead and wounded men scattered through the forest. Among the wounded Frenchmen left to be taken prisoner was their commanding officer: the Baron Dieskau himself.

But there was one lost man the victors of the Battle of Lake George were most intent on finding. On the third day, a wail that went up from the road through the woods told Joseph that his own commanding officer had been found. Across the stump-studded meadow came a crowd of men bearing a large, limp figure in a red-and-gold coat.

From above and behind Joseph's scalp lock a deep voice rumbled hoarsely: "Ye old rascal—ye warned me ye would dream no more."

Joseph had known two men in his life he'd wished to grow up to be, and neither of them could show him any longer what it was to be a man.

When Joseph got control of himself enough to look back and up at William Johnson, he discovered a remarkable transformation had taken place. Somehow the overbearing white giant who'd stolen Si-isha's *onikonhra* had transformed himself back into the old Gets Business Done who used to give him and Willy candy. Johnson's gray-green eyes were rivering unashamed tears for his oldest friend, who'd gone down the long road where the strawberries are always growing.

CHAPTER 27

Through Hodenosaune runners, Molly knew before they knew in New York Town that General William Johnson had beaten back the French at the Battle of Lake George, that he'd been wounded but not badly, and that King Hendrick was eating strawberries. The runners also told her that Carrying News and Brant's Joseph had come safely through the battle. The Hodenosaune who had fought for General Johnson were on their way home, but the general and his militia had to stay and build a fort on Lake George in case the French tried to come the same way again.

The Oyanders of the Wolf Clan began to council immedi-

ately to determine which of Hendrick's male relatives was best
suited to inherit his Royaner's name. In the end, it would be up
to the Clan Mother of his bloodline to make the decision, but
it was too important a matter not to solicit opinions and advice.
So Molly was at Canajoharie when the warriors came home.

Her brother came leaping out of the line, flung his ropy
arms around her and crushed his body to hers. She reeled back.
He sprang away, flustering, "Forgive me—I didn't think . . ."
gaping down at her swollen belly.

"You didn't hurt me—just surprised me."

He took her hands and said: "It is the spring sun to me, my
sister, to see thee again. Once I am settled back in at school,
may I come visit you at Fort Johnson?"

"Of course."

"Thank you."

She watched him dance with a scalp around the painted war
pole that night. The hours of the night belonged to the Left-
Handed Twin, the Destroyer. Her brother danced like the Destroyer himself, leaping and wolf-howling with the same
fervency he'd put into his soft "Thank you."

Nobody had ever told Juba where she could or couldn't go
in the house, but she'd mapped it out in her mind: the kitchen
in the cellar, the servants' quarters in the attic, and the stair-
ways in between. She stood at the top of the stairs on the second floor, looking down the hallway toward the master
bedroom, feeling like there was a line drawn in front of her
toes that would burn her feet to step over. She crossed it anyway and hurried down the hall, trying to make as little contact
as possible between her shoes and the floor.

The bedroom door was open. Jemmy was helping her mistress lay out Indian clothes and fold them into a double-sided
basket for slinging over a packhorse. Juba said: "Mizt'ess
Molly. . .?"

"Oh, hello Juba." Just as though Juba had business to be
there.

"Mizt'ess Molly, I know it ain't my place to say, but I worry
you shouldn't be traveling."

"Of course it's your place to say. My mother said the same
thing. But my husband is fighting a war for us; the least I can
do is put my voice in at Onondaga. Especially now that King

Hendrick won't be there to speak for the English. Besides, you and all the other wise old women are agreed that the baby won't come until well into the winter."

"But to be traveling all that way on horseback . . ."

"I have no choice in that, either. We could travel by canoe, but with the French threatening Oswego it's unwise for anything less than a war party to make themselves a target on the lakes.

"While I was listening to the Oyanders," she added brightly, "deciding whether it would be safe for us to go by canoe, it occurred to me that it might be just that accident of geography that made us 'Mohawks' always strong beyond our numbers. Whoever owns the Mohawk Valley, you see, can easily send warriors by water up into the Great Lakes and all the country around them, or down the Hudson to the sea."

Juba mumbled: "I still wish you wouldn't go."

"I wish I didn't have to. Don't worry, Juba, I'll be back here pestering you to make cherry doughnuts before you know it."

The route the Canienga delegation took toward the Fire That Never Dies was back along the same path that Si-isha and Muskingum and their mother had followed five years and a century ago. It was somewhere past Oneida Lake and not far from Onondaga that Molly began to feel twinges inside her. She managed to stay upright on her horse, but her knees kept jerking inward.

It passed. When they stopped to camp for the night, by a stream with an ancient fire pit dug into its bank, Molly waddled about the forest gathering firewood without feeling she'd suffered anything worse than a slight stomachache. But when she was sitting down among the Oyanders, tossing jerked beef and strips of dried pumpkin into the boiling pot, the rind of her distended belly suddenly shattered like a glass ball.

The women made a circle around her. She heard one of the Oyanders saying they must put up a hut to cover her, and her mother snapping: "There is no time!" Molly held her teeth clenched together to keep from screaming. They raised her up onto her knees and furled up her skirt and overdress as the half-formed child gushed out of her onto its bed of autumn leaves.

The women eased her down on her back. It felt like it *had*

been the shards of a glass ball that had passed through her, but that wasn't why she was weeping. She could hear the scraping sound of dry leaves being mounded together, and sobbed: "I want to see it."

"No!" her mother barked. Mother knelt down beside her and lifted her head and shoulders up into her lap. An Oyander was picking up a ball of leaves matted together with blood. Another Oyander brought a bowl of water and a piece of moss and furled up Molly's skirt again to wash her clean. There was the sound of a spade biting into the earth.

Hodenosaune children were always buried by the side of a path or road, so that their *onikonhra* might enter into the womb of a woman passing by. Little Abraham draped moss over the grave and sang, "Hai, little one, hai hai . . ." but there wasn't much else he could say.

Molly's mother said in English, "Into thy hands, O Lord, we commend this spirit," then turned to Molly. "Now, be thou condoled."

Molly just looked down at her own trembling hands. Even blurred by tears, they were clearly hands that might just as well have strangled their own child.

Mother said: "You must rest here at least a day, and follow after us when you feel well enough to ride."

"No." Tomorrow would bring them to Onondaga. She had already failed Gets Business Done miserably. She wouldn't miss the first day's council.

"What good will it do your man if you kill yourself . . . ?"

"You meant to add 'as well.' Did you not think, Mother, that I might not *want* to spend another day in this place?"

Mother's hand came up to cup the side of Molly's head. "Oh, child . . . it was not thee who caused this. When it happened to me, I hadn't ventured outside the longhouse, and nonetheless—"

"To you?"

"In between you and Joseph. You would have had another brother, but God chose differently. This was no more your fault than that was mine."

Molly nodded, but she knew her mother was mistaken.

When the long file of horses started on its way again at dawn, Molly looked back over her shoulder at the little mat of fresh moss beside the path until it disappeared among the trees.

She rode with both hands propped forward on the pommel and her arms and shoulders locked, to try to take some of her weight off the saddle, grinding her teeth against the torture of Juanita's back rolling up and down beneath her, trying to lock her mind onto what was ahead instead of what she'd left behind.

By the time they came to the beautiful, spring-studded hill that gave the Onondagas their name, Molly could think of nothing but the moment when she would climb down off Juanita. The Canienga party were met at the edge of the cleared land by the Royaners and Oyanders of the other nations. Molly's mother and Carrying News helped her down as a silver-haired Royaner began the ceremony Molly had heard of but not heard before, the condolence for a Royaner walking the strawberry road.

> All along the pathway to this place
> thee kept seeing the footmarks of our Grandfathers,
> and could all but see and smell the smoke
> where they used to smoke their pipes together.
> Can then thy mind be at ease
> when thee came weeping on thy way . . . ?
> Therefore in tears
> let us smoke together . . .

When the ceremony called At the Wood's Edge was done, Carrying News and Molly's mother helped her back to her feet and began to walk her up the hill toward the town. She shrugged their hands off, shaking her head. It wouldn't do for the councillors of the other nations to get the idea she was anything but in complete command of herself. She took hold of Juanita's reins with her right hand, reached her left up to clutch the pommel for support and clucked her tongue. Juanita, bless her, walked on toward the gate, so her mistress could use her as a crutch while giving the impression she just wanted to stretch her saddle-stiff legs.

The inside of the ceremonial longhouse was no longer the hollow drum that had echoed her little brother's gasp at meeting Atotarho. It was filled to bursting with Royaners and Oyanders and war chiefs. There were headdresses of turkey feathers and eagle feathers and partridge plumes and even a few stag-horned crowns that had survived intact from the days of the first Hiawatha and the Peacemaker.

A leathery old Seneca warrior came weeping up to Molly and said: "One Against Two—if a child hears the voices calling from the Land of Souls, no one can stop it from turning back. Gets Business Done and thee will have other children."

She could feel the emotion swelling up through her throat and behind the bridge of her nose. She managed: "Thank you."

When the Seneca had moved on, she whispered to her mother: "Who was that?"

"You don't know? That is the great war chief Old Smoke. Your father used to say that Old Smoke was the only Seneca he would think of following on the war road."

The Younger Brothers of the League—the Senecas, Cayugas, and Onondagas—delivered the final condolence for the death of a Royaner of the Elder Brothers: the Caniengas and Oneidas. The last line of the speech, which had been delivered a thousand times since the planting of the Tree, was: "Now show me the man!" And King Hendrick's baby brother Little Abraham became the living embodiment of one of the nine Canienga founders.

As the red war belt the Caniengas had brought with them passed from Royaner to Royaner, Molly could feel her *onikonhra* shriveling even smaller. She had expected to hear a lot of speeches advising the League of Peace to stay out of the white man's war. She hadn't expected to hear speeches urging the league to dig up their hatchets to help the Delaware and Shawnee drive the English off the southern Ohio, speeches that called up choruses of "Yo!" all around the circle.

When the ashes were raked over the coals to end the council for the day, Molly's mother said: "Now we begin In the Bushes."

"What is that?"

"Not all the work of a Great Council goes on in here. Sometimes we step away from the fire and talk In the Bushes."

In the Onondaga Wolf Clan longhouse where the Brants were to stay, Molly sat slumped beside her mother while her mother talked with other Oyanders over succotash and hominy. She was too wrung out to do much but watch and listen, but she soon got a strong suspicion that more matters were decided In the Bushes than by any flourish of public oratory.

After the next day's council, Molly struck out on her own. She managed to corner an Oneida Royaner and began to talk to him of the Covenant Chain and how the Caniengas who'd taken the war road with Gets Business Done had come home with many French scalps. But she could see he was only being polite.

She could also see he was a stooped old man with a face that made Old Crooked Nose look handsome. She arched her back to push her breasts up and batted her eyes to make them shine more. His attention ceased wandering over her shoulder. She said: "I overheard two of the soldiers at Fort Johnson talking about the five new regiments the king is sending to crush the French."

"*Five* regiments, you say . . . ?"

"Yes, five. And not raw boys, but seasoned warriors." Well, it wasn't technically a lie. She hadn't said there *were* five regiments, only that she'd heard the little bird Tskleleli singing to that effect.

From then on she made a point of hunting up Royaners who were old men with old wives. But not all of them could be flirted out of the suspicion that she only spoke up for the English king's men because her husband was one.

Fortunately she wasn't alone. Carrying News and most of the other Canienga Royaners had lived beside the English for too long to believe their fates could be separated, and Carrying News was the spokesman the Clan Mothers had chosen to deliver their speeches to the Royaners. But the best ally was the ghost of King Hendrick. Molly made a point of reminding every ear she bent that his last act had been to lead the Bloody Morning Scout against the French.

In the end, those who believed that the Hodenosaune should ally themselves with the soon-to-be-victorious French were persuaded differently. But the best the Caniengas could accomplish was that the other five nations would leave their war clubs buried until next year's council. It would be clearer by then how the white man's war was unfolding.

Molly went home to Fort Johnson to wait for her man. It was December before His British Majesty's commander-in-chief for North America allowed General Johnson to leave the new fort he'd built on Lake George. A fine dusting of snow was filtering down when he rode through the gate of Fort

Johnson, sitting Old Knobby a little lopsidedly, with his faithful valet following on a scruffy-looking nag.

She didn't run to him as he climbed down off the saddle. After all that had happened to both of them, it was a solemn kind of joy, and she didn't know how he'd taken the news that she had killed his child. She came down the steps and walked at a measured pace toward him as he limped forward to meet her. His big, hawkish face was gray with pain. He stopped in front of her, put his hand out to cup the side of her head and said softly: "No fear, Molly m'gel—we'll have more children."

"And your wound will heal."

"P'r'aps. I'm still carryin' the demmed Froggy bullet. Surgeon said he couldn't cut it out without cuttin' off half me . . muscle with it."

"Come inside."

When he was settled by the fire in the music room with a hot rum toddy in his hand, he looked around and sighed: "Dem me, it's good to be home. Here's that the face of every good news and the back of every bad news be toward us." The drink washed some of the gray out of his face. "It seems—if the little bird sings true—I'm by way of bein' a sir."

"A what?"

"A baronet. *Sir* William Johnson to ye. For the famous victory of Lake George—bein' as how the only other victory His Majesty's magnificent fightin' forces managed to accomplish in the whole bleedin' year was takin' some piss-pot fort in Nova Scotia. When John reaches his majority, he'll be Sir John Johnson."

"What did John do?"

"Had the good sense to be born first son to a general that won a famous victory."

She sipped her Madeira and considered letting the matter pass, but she couldn't. She said: "They say in Canajoharie you had other sons before John." She refrained from adding: Ah, but they weren't white, were they?

He shot a slit-eyed glance at her, sipped his toddy again and said: "How was the harvest this year?"

They moved on. He could be color-blind in everything except when it came to who was going to take his place in the next generation. It had something to do with growing up a raggedy little poor relation at the back door of the manor house, and no amount of knighthoods or famous victories or estates was ever going to change that. She would have to live with it if she were going to live with him.

They talked and laughed through the afternoon and into the evening. Molly couldn't get enough of him and, most endearing, it seemed he couldn't get enough of her.

When they went up to bed, there was a bottle of champagne waiting. He sighed. "Ah, Molly, y'think of everythin'," and wrenched the cork out with one effortless twist. She carried her glass behind her dressing screen and changed into her nightgown, luxuriating in the domesticity of having no need to hurry or cajole or be apprehensive. When she came out, he sat up and threw the bedclothes back on her side of the bed, shivering out: "Sufferin' Judas, Molly, a warmin' pan ain't enough in this kind of weather."

Once under the covers, she rolled onto her side to face him. His hand scooped onto her hip and moved up and down. He said tentatively: "D'ye have pain still?"

"No."

"That's a blessin'."

His hand moved down. She brushed it away, saying, "There's no need," and there wasn't; she could almost taste him already. She rolled onto her back, wrapped her hand around the scalding pine trunk of his *ohnoru* and pulled it toward her *ohnanerita*. She was so ready for him that he popped in as easily as those monstrous hands could pop out a champagne cork. As the weight of his body settled onto her, pancaking her breasts across her ribs, she remembered what it was to feel safe and owned and in command and whorish and shameless and like a princess, all at the same time.

His hips were built on the same scale as the rest of him, so it was always a bit of a strain to get her legs up around his waist, but she could manage it. But when her left ankle touched his left buttock, he let out a yelp and drove into her like a spurred stallion. She gasped "I'm sorry," and then began to giggle at the thought that the bullet meant she could get him to do that whenever she wanted and she didn't need spurs.

He grunted "What's so bleedin' funny?" but it was in the same tone of voice that he'd been whispering "That's m'darlin' gel" and "Lined like mother-of-pearl, she is."

When he erupted into her, it was like the gorge of the Boiling Kettle in a spring storm. His body settled across hers even more heavily than before. He lay there gasping for a moment as she scratched her fingertips across the spiky stubble at the nape of his neck, then he rolled over onto his back. She rested one hand lightly against his shoulder and lay there with her eyes open to the dark in the bed-curtained cave, which was warm for the first time since the snow came.

Over breakfast—which he pronounced the first decent meal he'd encountered in six months—she asked: "What happened to Thayendenegea at Lake George?"

"To who?"

"Oh—Joseph. He has a man's name now that he's taken a scalp."

"Thayendenegea . . . means 'He Binds Two . . . something-or-others Together,' don't it? Binds Two Sticks Together? Like Hendrick the night before the Bloody Morning Scout?"

"Yes . . . partly . . . It also means 'He Binds Two Bets Together,' like the judge entrusted with the two teams' wagers before a baggataway game. It's a very strong and ancient name."

"I don't understand why ye demmed Mohawks can't have one word mean one thing instead of three or four."

"I don't understand why after all these years you still haven't learned not to call the Canienga that terrible name."

"In this world, Molly m'dear, 'tain't necessarily such a bad thing to be known as 'They Eat Their Enemies.' What d'ye mean 'what happened'?"

"Pardon me?"

"To 'Binds Two,' at Lake George."

"Oh. He isn't the same as he was. Or, rather, he's more like the way he used to be when we were children. He doesn't hiss like a cat when I come near him anymore—if anything, I have to pry his arms from around my neck before he suffocates me. And my mother tells me he's become the gem of his schoolmaster's eye. Ever since he came back from Lake George. What happened to him there?"

"Demmed if I know. Except that he kept somethin' demmed unpleasant from happenin' to me. Boys do have a habit of startin' to grow up eventually. If they live long enough. Maybe poor old Hendrick put a whiff of mortality into 'im. Or maybe God's smiled on 'im."

"Pardon me?"

"Old piece of philosophy from some race of dusky demmed foreigners. Dagos or Jews or Gypsies, I disremember. They say there's two things a man's got to learn before 'is life's worth anythin' to 'im, or to anyone else for that matter: what it is that makes 'im happy, and what it is that he does well. 'And if God smiles on ye, they'll both be the same thing.'"

"What's my brother good at?"

"Choppin' the other fella before the other fella chops him. From what I hear of yer father, he comes by it honestly."

Juba's round of days was centered in the cellar kitchen, where Sir William Johnson never strayed, so it wasn't unusual for her not to see her master from one month to the next, even when he was home. But she heard enough about him, from Molly and from the other servants. When the end of the winter brought the war back to life, it seemed that whenever he wasn't off soldiering, he was prostrate in his bed. Doctors came and went. If it wasn't pneumonia, it was a twinge in his heart or a terrible pain in his side or deep down in the pit of his stomach.

From what Juba heard of how he passed his time away from home, she wasn't surprised. A man half his age would've had his health broken: galloping the militia toward every rumored French attack, squatting for weeks on end in smoky huts trying to sweet-talk the Indians into fighting for the English, wading spring creeks by moonlight with his rifle and powder flask held over his head. . . .

Juba was making green pea soup one afternoon when Molly came down the steps with an evil-looking, humpbacked old woman who appeared to have been hung up in her filthy blanket in a smokehouse for twenty years. Molly said: "I think the girls could do with some fresh air."

Juba turned to the kitchen maids shelling peas and said: "Go along with you now, but not so far you can't hear me out the back door."

As the girls' summer-bare feet slapped up the stairs, Juba's mistress gestured at the old woman and said, "This is . . ." and strung together a series of unpronounceable Indian syllables that Juba assumed was a name. "I think the three of us should have a cup of tea."

As Juba busied herself swinging the kettle in over the fire and crumbling tea leaves into the pot, she watched out of the corner of her eye as the old witch squatted down on the floor. She sloughed off her blanket, disclosing that the huge hump on her back was in fact a basket strapped to her shoulders. Molly settled onto the floor as well, in that demure Indian woman's posture of resting the weight on one hip and drawing both feet up against the other.

Once Juba had poured out three cups of tea and handed out two, she was faced with the problem of whether to sit in a chair or squat down on the floor. She found a compromise in the low stone ledge fronting the hearth. Molly began to talk to the witch in Mohawk. The old woman nodded and hummed and swayed back and forth, then fished through her basket and handed Molly a pouch while rasping out a stream of Mohawk. Molly handed the pouch to Juba, saying: "Huckleberries, for his liver."

Several pouches came out next. "This is sarsaparilla, choke-cherry bark, and yarrow. If he gets the shivering sickness again—pneumonia—we boil a bit of each together.

"This goldenrod is for the pain in his side. . . ."

When the witch was gone, Juba watched Molly slump into a chair and run her hands through her beautiful black hair while she stared at the pile of pouches on the table. "Am I a fool, Juba, to listen to old wives' tales when we have so many learned doctors to call on?"

"It seems to me, Mizt'ess Molly, that at the least we'll be putting something back into him for what the doctors bleed out."

Mistress Molly laughed a bitter little laugh and began to pick through the pouches, reciting: "Huckleberries for his liver, goldenrod for the pain in his side . . . and then there is my own prescription, for which she had no better cure."

"What's that, Mizt'ess Molly?"

"When the pain gets so bad he can't even roll over in bed, I sit with his head in my lap and sing: 'Will you come to my arms, Billy boy, Billy boy, will you come to my arms, darling Billy. . . ?"

Juba knew she couldn't say it aloud, but she shook her head

slowly and said in her mind: Oh, child, you know he's bound to die long before you.

Molly watched her husband turn into a caged bear, and there was nothing she could do about it. For two years, after the French took the fort he'd built on Lake George and butchered the garrison, Fort Johnson was the north and west frontier of the British Empire.

One winter evening as the war moved into its third year, she was sitting on the hearth rug in the music room embroidering a warrior's kilt for her brother, while her husband sat in a chair on the other side of the hearth, reading through yet another set of dispatches. He snorted: "Every time I think I've learned what demmed fools these demmed fools are, they show me I ain't even begun to plumb their depths."

"Whose depths?"

"Whose else? Demmed North American Command of His British Majesty's pitiful excuse for a bleedin' army. They've come up with the idea of givin' captain's commissions to some Iroquois warriors, to dazzle the poor benighted savages into the illusion that they're part of a military force to be reckoned with. The commandin' general'd like me to furnish 'im with some names."

"Binds Two."

"Joseph? He ain't even shavin' yet. Oh. Well, ye catch me drift. . . ."

"You said yourself he has a talent for war."

"Wish I could say the same of His Majesty's bleedin' professional soldiers. Very well, as of now yer little brother's Captain Brant—for all the good it'll do to 'im, or any of the rest of us."

But then came the glorious year of 1759, when England's lucky star finally pushed out from behind the shadow of the moon. A general named Wolfe died taking Quebec, but he took it. A general named Clive drove the French out of India. A king named Frederick won the war in Europe for his English allies. And at Onondaga, the League of Peace dug up their hatchets to follow Gets Business Done in a British expedition to Thundergate, where the waters of the west roared down toward the French fort Niagara.

While Sir William Johnson was gone from Fort Johnson,

Catty Weisenberg finally went down the long road she'd been threatening to step onto for so long. Molly did her best to condole Ann and Mary, but she had no reason to mourn their mother and had the best of reasons to be self-absorbed.

After four years of wondering whether her pigheadedness had not only killed her and William's first child, but destroyed any chance of having another, she was pregnant again. The baby passed the stage where she'd lost the first one, and still kept on growing. The only marring factor was that she was afraid Gets Business Done wouldn't be back from Thundergate when the child was ready to be born. She couldn't for the life of her say what he could do to help, only that she'd feel safer with him there.

She had grown so protuberant, she understood what loons felt like walking, when her mother came to say a runner had arrived at Canajoharie from Thundergate. Molly clutched her hand and said: "What's happened?"

"First, Gets Business Done is safe. So are Binds Two and Carrying News. The English general in command was killed early in the fighting, so Gets Business Done became the war chief. The French sent reinforcements to save the fort, and our men trapped and defeated them, so the French had no choice but to surrender the fort. The English have a new toast now: 'Johnson forever.' "

Molly leaned back in her chair as a wave of something washed over her—she couldn't say whether it was pride or relief. Her eyes drifted to the window—where she should've been able to see the two black walnut trees William had planted in her first autumn with him—and encountered once again nothing but the bricks that had forced them to live by candlelight in the downstairs rooms for four years. She made a military decision and summoned the overseer. The war was over.

She was sitting in the music room noticing that the leaves on Billy tree were yellowing faster than Molly when her ballooned womb suddenly tautened into a boulder. It had happened before, so she knew what to do: grip the arms of her chair or anything else within reach and try to keep breathing until it passed. When it did, Molly was able to fill her lungs again, and was just beginning to enjoy doing so when another spasm seized her. When that one passed, she used her first lungful of air to bellow: "Juba!" Juba came hurtling out of the cellar hatchway. Molly gasped out: "Maybe it's just another—"

"Maybe, but I don't think so. . . . Jemmy!"

Juba and Jemmy helped her up the stairs, with Juba rattling out an unbroken string of words—sometimes to her, sometimes to the footmen who came running to help. "That's all right, Mizt'ess Molly, we'll just rest on this stair till it passes. Go fetch the doctor! One more stair now. Go fetch the midwife! Go fetch Mizt'ess Molly's mother!"

By the time they laid her down on the bed, there were surges of something not exactly pain but just as intense passing down between her hips. Juba and Jemmy stripped her clothes off piece by piece between the surges and covered her upper body with a sheet. She felt quite ridiculous in the lulls between the waves—perfectly lucid and normal until the next one hit. In one of those between times she said: "I think I would like a glass of water, please."

Jemmy jumped up with: "I'll fetch it."

"No," Juba said. "Bring a tin cup, case'n her teeth clamps down."

The midwife arrived, then her mother, then the doctor. The doctor put his hands on her and said: "Ahem, everything seems perfectly healthy to me. If you ladies need me, I shall be downstairs."

By then the waves were almost constant and felt like they were tearing her apart. A warm hand brushed the sweat out of her eyes, and Juba's voice said from far away: "That's the worst part almost over, honey." Molly became aware that she'd been grunting and screaming loud enough to crack the rafters.

A long time later, when the rolling waves had been replaced by a burning feeling and the windows had become black mirrors reflecting candle flames, only Juba was there; the midwife and Molly's mother were in a corner hissing at each other. When they came back, Mother said in Canienga: "We are going to lift you up and set you on the floor. Are you ready?"

"Yes—uh—yes . . ."

They almost dropped her as Juba reached back to snag the sheet and throw it down before Molly's feet hit the floor. The midwife on one side and Molly's mother on the other held her upright in a squat by her hands and armpits as something impossibly big forced its way out of her. Her mother said: "Breathe hard—stop pushing now."

There was a squirting feeling and the midwife muttered: "Well, I'm buggered."

As Molly was being lifted back onto the bed, the doctor reappeared to make a slapping sound that engendered a hellish squalling. A squealing, hot, red thing was settled down between her breasts. Her mother said: "A boy." Molly wrapped her arms around her son, heaved herself up into a sitting position and swung her legs off the bed.

The doctor protested: "You cannot—"

"She can and she will," her mother rudely cut him off.

Molly said: "A blanket . . ." They draped a blanket over her shoulders and she stumbled downstairs and outside.

Moongleam rippled on the river of the Caniengas. She sat down in the water and mingled her own blood on the skin of Peter Warren Johnson into the river. Before Sir William Johnson set off on the war road, they had decided that a male child would be named after Sir Peter Warren, Sir William's uncle, the admiral who had brought a certain Anglo-Irish by-blow across the ocean to manage the land he'd bought in the Mohawk Valley.

Molly's mother and grandmother had both warned her that all firstborns came hard. In this case it was worth it, because even by moonlight Peter Warren Johnson was obviously the most beautiful and healthy baby the world had ever seen.

CHAPTER 28

In the spring of 1763 a British officer came cantering up the Mohawk Valley. He'd last been in the valley fifteen years before, as a lowly subaltern in the little garrison at Fort

Hunter. Since then he'd risen to major, lost an arm in the service of his country, and had had the good sense and connections to get himself a staff appointment while he still had limbs to save.

A lot had changed in fifteen years. Schenectady was by way of becoming a full-sized town. The lower reaches of the valley were more farmland than forest. The road passed by several estates with immense stone houses and carriage drives.

The home of Sir William Johnson had more fortifications around it than the major remembered. The gate was open and there was no sign of a gatekeeper.

The major wasn't sure what kind of reception to expect. He expected nothing but ease and informality from the jovial fellow who used to host carousals for the officers of Fort Hunter, but that had been long before a certain eccentric backwoodsman became Sir William Johnson, the "Heaven-Taught General."

There were no footmen in evidence on the steps of Sir William Johnson's house, so the major hitched his horse to the post, clamped the dispatch case under his stump and plied the door knocker. The door was opened by a liveried Negro who intoned: "Good afternoon, suh."

"I have dispatches for Sir William Johnson."

"I am devastated to have to be the conduit of disappointment, suh, but I must perforce inform you with regret that Sir William Johnson no longer resides here. Perhaps you would care to speak with Mr. Guy Johnson, Sir William's nephew."

"I suppose I'd best."

The major was ushered into the parlor, where he introduced himself and explained his business. "My uncle's built himself a new house," Guy Johnson informed him, "a few miles upriver. I'll take you there."

"There's no need to interrupt your afternoon. If you simply give me directions—"

"Not at all. Theopholis, have someone saddle me a horse."

"It shall be done with the utmost of dispatch, suh."

The new road they followed ran along the creek behind Fort Johnson and plunged into the woods. "I am not a colonial," Guy Johnson remarked. "My uncle, you see, brought me over from Ireland to be Deputy Superintendent of Northern Indian Affairs. Rather a family tradition, uncles helping nephews get a leg up in the world. In this case I helped myself as well. My bride's Sir William's daughter, Mary. Saved her the trouble of changing her name."

After that, Guy Johnson said nothing. He seemed not the least bit curious, or even interested, about the major's mission, or anything else not directly pertaining to Guy Johnson. They rode for miles, deeper and deeper into a forest so tall and thick that the summer sun never shone on the vines tangled around the ancient trunks and roots.

Just when the major was beginning to suspect Guy Johnson might be a lunatic, he heard the sounds of human activity ahead. There was a half-built town of log cabins and clapboard buildings. The major looked around in vain for signs of a mine or some other advantage to the location, then said to Guy Johnson: "Seems an odd place to build a town."

"'Tisn't a town. Just servants' and trademen's quarters for Johnson Hall."

The road continued along a stream with a half-built mill, and then opened up into a swath of cleared land several hundred acres broad. A few old forest giants had been left standing here and there, but the rest was all burnt-off stubble or new-laid lawn or new-ploughed fields or sprouting gardens. The forest walls resounded with the din of mallets and axes and the jingle of draft horses' chains. In the center of it all stood a mountainous, pink, dressed-stone manor house that could have been transplanted from any country estate in England.

As he followed Guy Johnson up the carriage circle, the major saw that the house wasn't dressed stone after all. There was a scaffolding along one wall and workmen were painting slabs of wood to look like dressed stone.

The painters began jumping down off the scaffolding and running around to the back of the house. Guy Johnson yelled at the nearest one: "You there, fellow! Your work's not done yet!"

"William and Joseph are at it again!"

"Oh. You may find this amusing, Major."

The major twitched his horse's reins to follow Guy Johnson's around the scaffolding. The back of the house was a mirror image of the front, with the same large windows and imposing entranceway. One corner of the lawn was covered by a yelling ring of workmen, farmhands, liveried house servants, and Mohawks. Inside the ring were two young Mohawks stripped down to loincloths, leggings, and moccasins. They were wrestling Indian fashion, gripping each others' biceps and pushing back and forth, trying to trip each other up or find an advantage. One of them was tallish and quite slender; the other was built like a bull and had green eyes.

They went at each other for some time, twisting and flipping and bouncing on the ground and springing up again as the crowd roared encouragement. The major wasn't exactly an aficionado of Indian wrestling, but it seemed to him that the slender one was the trickier, constantly feinting and twisting and trying to use the green-eyed one's weight against him.

The major's eyes drifted away from the wrestlers and onto the newly laid-out garden behind them. There was a round marble fountain with a pink flamingo daintily stalking through the dancing waters. There was a long lilac hedge with a tunnel cut through the middle of it to a cupolaed outhouse.

An eruption from the wide ring of watchers drew the major's attention back to the wrestlers. Inevitably, the slender one had made one feint too many and was pinned. Guy Johnson said disgustedly, "No bloody point laying wagers anymore. Must be two hundred times now and he hasn't won once. Think he'd learn his bloody lesson," and clucked his horse through the dissipating crowd.

The two wrestlers were on their feet again, puffing and blowing and wiping the sweat off their faces with their shirts. The slender one was leaning on the shoulder of a striking-looking young Indian woman wearing gold earrings and what would've been a typical Mohawk dress if it weren't wine purple shot silk. She was rubbing his chest and bantering in Mohawk. He was nuzzling her hair with his nose and laughing breathlessly. The major had often labored in vain to convince fellow staff officers who talked of the stone-faced red Indians that Indian husbands and wives could be quite surprisingly openly affectionate in informal settings.

Guy Johnson stopped his horse in front of the three Mohawks and said: "This is Joseph and Molly Brant. The major has some dispatches for my uncle."

Molly Brant said: "He's at Canajoharie having words with Little Abraham. He is expected back soon."

Guy Johnson shrugged at the major, and said, "I suppose you'll just have to wait for him, then," and turned his horse, adding over his shoulder, "Oh, and this is my uncle's natural son, William of Canajoharie. Good day." The major opened his mouth to thank him for showing the way, but he was already out of earshot.

Molly Brant surprised the major by calling out to a passing ostler: "Caleb, would you see to the major's horse for him, please?" The ostler surprised him even further by stepping forward obediently and holding the bridle while the major dismounted.

Molly Brant topped that by saying, "I believe you're just in time for tea, Major," and escorting him and Brant and Sir William's bastard son into the house as though she owned it.

She did appear to have an extraordinarily regal way about her. On the way to the house she said something offhanded to another Mohawk woman lounging on the lawn, who immediately leaped up and bustled off as purposely as a corporal given marching orders.

The ground floor of the house was laid out the same as the major remembered Mount Johnson, only on a much grander scale. There was a large open hallway running from back to front, with two rooms on either side. The hallway was large enough to host a dance in, and had an immense stone fireplace on one wall. Perched on the mantel was a green parrot, which squawked a greeting that would have cost him a fine in the officers' mess. Stretched out on the floor were a white-haired Indian and an Irish wolfhound snoring together. The Brants stepped over them as though they were a lump in the carpet. On a chair by the hearth was a blind man tuning an Irish harp. He cocked his head in their direction and said: "Would you care for a bit of an ode with your tea?"

Molly Brant replied, "Not today, thank you, Mr. Kain," and carried on into a white-walled parlor where a very substantial afternoon meal had already been laid out at one end of a long mahogany dining table. A straw-haired bumpkin in rumpled livery was unpacking bright-colored Indian curios from a straw-filled barrel in one corner. Molly Brant said to him: "Do you know where the Bartholomews are?"

"Down in the cellar, I 'spect. Want me to fetch 'em?"

"Please. And I suspect the major could do with a flagon of ale to wash the dust out of his throat. Do sit down, Major."

The major sat, trying to work out some sort of explanation for why the servants didn't seem perturbed at three Indians escorting a stranger into Sir William's house and preparing to tuck into his victuals.

The voice of the straw-haired bumpkin bellowed from the back of the house: "Bartholomew!" A moment later two liveried dwarfs appeared in the parlor doorway, one bearing a teapot and the other a flagon of ale.

Molly Brant said: "The ale is for the major, Bartholomew. Just set the tea down here, Bartholomew—I'll pour."

Both Bartholomews said: "Yes, Miss Molly."

"Miss" Molly's husband—or perhaps not her husband after all—said with a strange twinkle: "I suppose, Major, I should call you 'sir,' since you outrank me. I'm only a captain."

"I must say, Captain Brant, I'm astounded at your facility with the English language. I only wish I could boast of an equal grasp of Mohawk."

"Any credit is due to the Reverend Wheelock's school in Connecticut. Although, the Reverend's son received an education of his own when he told William to—"

The woman cut him off with something that made the major certain Joseph and Molly Brant were man and wife: "You're not going to tell *that* story again?"

"It's a good story, and a true one, and the major hasn't heard it before. Not long after William and I arrived at the Reverend Wheelock's school, the reverend's son told William to saddle his horse for him. William told him that the son of a gentleman didn't take orders. The reverend's son sniffed: 'Obviously you do not know what a gentleman is.' And William replied: 'I most certainly do. A gentleman is a person who keeps racehorses and drinks Madeira wine, which neither you nor your father do.' "

William of Canajoharie slitted his green eyes and pushed his heavy shoulders up around his ears, as though embarrassed at being singled out for attention, but not exactly displeased. Joseph Brant added: "But I wouldn't want to give you the impression, Major, that we don't appreciate what the Reverend Wheelock did for us. He taught me to be a Christian, and had it not been for my secular education at his school, I would not hold my present position as Sir William's interpreter."

Molly Brant put the seal on the major's assumptions by putting in: "So *you* can do the job that Guy gets paid for." The major had yet to meet a wife who didn't know of some man somewhere who was taking undue credit for the sweat of her husband's brow.

William of Canajoharie said archly to Joseph Brant: "And had it not been for your religious education, you would not hold your present position as son-in-law of a very pious Indian indeed." One corner of Molly Brant's mouth quirked up, as though the joke—whatever it was—had no reflection on her.

The important thing as far as the major was concerned was that Joseph Brant's position in the Indian Department explained why these three were allowed to make so free with Sir William's victuals and servants. No doubt Sir William had given instructions that his interpreter was to have the run of the house.

The major was congratulating himself for accurately spying out the lay of the land, when a knee-high boy and shorter girl toddled into the doorway and the boy said: "We've had our lay-down, Mama, can we go out now? Magdalen's still sleeping."

Molly Brant replied: "Of course you may, but stay away from the scaffolding where the men are working."

"Yes, Mama."

Joseph Brant stood up and announced: "Well, I have a wife waiting for me at home. . . ."

William of Canajoharie said: "I'll ride along with you." The Brants kissed each other good-bye, William and Joseph bade the major adieu, and he was left alone with a woman he didn't know how to address.

Fortunately it was only a few minutes before the front door crashed open and a bull-moose roar shook the rafters with: "Horace! Bartholomew! Any-bleedin'-body!"

Sir William Johnson stomped into the white parlor in thigh-high riding boots with deer-hide patches where the English leather had worn through. Sir William didn't look markedly older than the major's memory of him, but then, when the major had been a subaltern, he'd been of an age when everyone looked old to him.

The major stood up, and Molly Brant said: "The major brought dispatches for you."

"We've met before, Sir William—though so long ago I'm sure you don't recall. I stood a posting at Fort Hunter in 'forty-eight."

"Ye had two arms then."

"That I did, sir."

"Well, look on the bright side—at least it was yer left."

"I was left-handed, sir."

"Oh." The straw-haired, liveried bumpkin reappeared with a mug of ale for his master. "And bring another for the major. Demmed dusty ridin' for a spring day," he added, and turning to "Miss" Molly Brant: "And ye, m'dear . . . ?"

"No, thank you, sir." She put a strange inflection on the "sir," as though it were a nickname rather than a title. The major didn't have more than an instant to ponder on it, though, because she went on to say, "I have a feeling Magdalen's about to wake up hungry," and left them alone.

The major handed the dispatch case to Sir William, who growled at it: "Just let me catch m'breath before I go rootin' through the swamp of military cant hopin' for truffles." He flung open one of the cupboard doors flanking the mantelpiece, showing the major a glimpse of a wallpapered passage that the Heaven-Taught General disappeared into. There was the sound of another door banging open, the thump of a laden dispatch case hitting a bed, and Sir William reappeared, shrugging: "Demmed Froggy bullet twinges when I climb too many stairs, so Molly confined me to the first floor except for music nights. They must be up to the nostrils in commissioned officers at New York Town to be sendin' majors deliverin' dispatches."

"It was rather a plum, sir, to carry dispatches to the Mohawk baronet. And this particular dispatch case is more along the lines of a diplomatic pouch. France and England have signed a treaty setting out the terms for the conclusion of the recent war."

" 'Recent'? Took 'em more time to write their bleedin' treaty than it did for us to win the bleedin' war."

"Headquarters was of the opinion that you would want to be apprised as soon as possible of what the diplomats decided."

"Not much to decide, was there? We gave the Froggies a

sound thrashin', and that's the end of 'em in North America. Which—treasonous or not—is all I care a bleedin' dem about."

The rumpled bumpkin appeared again, bearing a fresh flagon of ale and a silver cup upon a silver salver. He set the flagon down in front of the major and turned to his master. "Ahem. Sir William—Miss Molly says it's time."

"Oh dem." Sir William accepted the silver cup and looked into it disgustedly, swirling it around like a child facing a dose of castor oil. "Don't know what she puts in this bleedin' concoction. Probably better off not knowin'. Steeped old stockin's and poison ivy, by the taste. But I haven't had a trace of gout since she started forcin' this swill down m'throat. Oh well— here's a health to yer enemies' enemies."

Sir William held his nose and tossed it back, immediately clanging the cup back onto its waiting salver and snatching up a quaff of ale to wash the taste out of his mouth. Straw-haired Horace peered suspiciously into the cup. "Yes, I bleedin' drank the whole bleedin' thing! Ye can go and tell yer mistress that. And while ye're about it, ask her which room she wants the major in," and turning to the major, "I take it ye'll want to stay the night before startin' back."

"That would be very kind of you, sir."

"I'm afraid we're still a bit rough-camped in the new place, but ye'll find we set a tolerable table nonetheless."

"I had no idea you had relocated. I went first to Mount Johnson."

"Well, the old place was gettin' crampish, what with all the wee beggars and me nephew and all. And, as Molly pointed out, there ain't any call to live in a fortification, bein' as how the Froggies have been thrashed and the wild Mohawks are me relations. And, quite frankly, what with one thing and another, I'm growin' rich as a lord—at least on paper—might as well live like one. And it didn't cost so much as ye might think to carve an estate out of the forest. Along with their rents, all me tenants have to pay me every year, 'one fat fowl and one full day's work,' and these frontier bumpkins know how to work. So I decided— Ha! What the divil am I sayin'?—*Molly* decided ... So here we are at Johnson Hall.

"If ye take a stroll through County Meath someday, ye might find yerself feelin' a twinge of what the Froggies call déjà vu when ye come across a certain manor house. The Warrens used to call it charity to let me in the back door, and now I *own* the bleedin' place—or its twin."

"I take it . . . I take it, then, that Miss Molly is . . . your mistress?"

"Ha! She's *every*body's bleedin' mistress, in case ye ain't noticed. What she is is Lady Johnson in all but name. Ah, there ye are, Horace. Did ye *crawl* back and forth across the bleedin' hall?"

"That would have scuffed up the knees of my breeches, sir."

"Well, show the major to his room. I expect he'll want to freshen 'imself up before dinner."

The major left Sir William heaving out of his chair to go peruse his copy of the Peace of Paris, and followed Horace up the toll-road-wide staircase. At the top of the stairs was another vast hallway, this one with a harpsichord in one corner and a broad bank of tall, arched windows at either end to let in the sun. In fact, now that the major had a moment to reflect upon it, the profusion of glass panes in every wall was one of the pleasantest aspects of the house. The place was filled with light, gleaming on the fresh-painted wood paneling and a flocked wallpaper garish enough to grace a Parisian brothel.

Horace said, "Mind the floor, sir, she's just got her first coat of wax," and opened one of the four doors leading off the hallway. There were three beds in the room, one of them with a trundle bed underneath it, and one wall was still only half papered. The major's saddlebags were draped over a chair beside a washstand.

Horace said: "Sir William likes to have plenty of accommodations, for company-like. I'd say the comfortablest bed's the big one with the buffalo hide on her. There's hot water in the pitcher, case'n you'd care to shave. Miss Molly keeps a formal table."

"Thank you, Horace."

But the major had only got halfway through the tricky business of plying a straight razor with a hand that ten years still hadn't made adept when he began to hear the thump of riding boots beneath him and the bull-like grumbling of Sir William in a passion, interspersed with bellows.

A pair of shoes came castanetting up the stairs and skittered to a halt, followed by a thump and a grunt. There was a pause, and then a discreet tap on the door. The major said: "Come in."

A straw-haired head poked in. "You'd best come quick, sir. Something in them papers has reared him up on his hind legs, and I ain't joshing."

The major wiped the remaining lather off his face. Horace held his coat for him, which saved the major the embarrassment of demonstrating what he could do with one hand and his teeth. Instead of leading him into the white parlor, Horace turned at the foot of the stairs toward the doorway of the room behind it. The major registered a fleeting impression of coppery green walls, a canopied bed with a bearskin flung across it, and a desk Sir William was pacing in front of, slapping the rolled up Peace of Paris against his booted thigh. Then Sir William rounded on the doorway, roaring: "Where the divil's Claus?"

Horace said: "I don't know, sir."

"Well bleedin' *find* 'im! What's the use of havin' a bleedin' resident secretary for a son-in-law if nobody can find 'im when I need 'im? And *ye*," pointing the crumpled treaty at the major like a blunderbuss, "d'ye have any notion in hell what's in this blessed document?"

"I can't quote you chapter and verse, Sir William. But I did read through several copies as they were made, to make certain of their accuracy."

"Well what about the bleedin' Ohio, then?"

"Pardon me, sir? What about the Ohio?"

"The French have ceded the Ohio country to His British bleedin' Majesty!"

The major blinked at him. "I should think they would, sir. You did say yourself that the French would have to cede their rights to any part of North America. And with the exception of those little fishing islands—"

"*Rights*? The French *have* no demmed rights to the Ohio country, and never did have! It's Indian huntin' grounds."

"Well, sir, if I might point out: so was Johnson Hall, and New York Town for that matter, until—"

"Until what? I'll *tell* ye until what—until white colonists started comin' in and buildin' farms and paid the Indians for the right to live there. There's never *been* any whites—French or English—along the Ohio, exceptin' fur traders and missionaries. What d'ye think the Iroquois are goin' to do—and the Delawares, and Ottawas, and Shawnees, and Mingoes—when they find out about this? What d'ye think *ye'd* do if ye found out that a treaty had been signed wherein the King of Prussia ceded Devonshire to the King of Spain?"

"Uh . . ."

"Yes, 'uh'! 'Tain't bad enough that blessed genius Amherst has to cut off all presents to the Indians the instant we don't need 'em to fight for us anymore, now *this*!"

Molly Brant appeared in the doorway, saying: "Who are you yelling for this time, sir?"

"Claus!"

"Daniel and Ann went to scout out a location for their house, just as you suggested."

"Well how the divil am I supposed to send off a letter when me bleedin' secretary's off moonin' over honeymoon cottages and these blasted idiots have put me in such a state I'd only blotch up the paper with ink blots?"

"I'll write it for you." She headed for his desk.

"That's a kind darlin'. I'm sorry, Major, but ye won't have the comfort of a feather bed tonight As soon as Molly's done the clerkin' for me; ye'll be gallopin' back for New York Town. If yer horse is all in, ye can borrow one of mine.

"Ahem. 'Dear blasted idiots . . .' "

CHAPTER 29

Molly kissed her two warriors good-bye on the steps of Johnson Hall. Sir had been right about the Peace of Paris being the last straw for True People already enraged that the English Governor General, whose victories they'd helped make, had been treating them like expendable vermin ever since the war was won. An Ottawa chief named Pontiac had roused a great alliance of the western nations to show the white men who the Ohio and Erie country belonged to. Many British forts had been burned and their soldiers massacred. So General Johnson and Captain Brant were leading a column of redcoat regulars and colonial militia and Canienga warriors to try to relieve the siege of Fort Detroit and make a peace.

The Clan Mothers had debated long and hard whether the Canienga should help the British in this war. Senecas were rumored to be among Pontiac's warriors, and it would shake the Tree of Peace to its roots if the Keepers of the Dawn and the Keepers of the Sunset should have each other's blood on their war clubs. From the dispatches Molly was privy to at Johnson Hall, it was clear that Pontiac had already proven to the king's ministers that the True People of Turtle Island had to be treated with respect, even when they were no longer needed as allies against the French. But if the war went on much longer, the British would become convinced that none of the True People could ever be trusted to live with them in peace.

As soon as the column marched away, Molly had Sir's portrait brought down from the attic to hang in the bedroom. He'd had it done by a fashionable painter in New York Town in the days when she had still been running bare-legged along the Ohio, and he loathed it. "Look at those demmed, elegant, narrow, hangin' shoulders. *Mine* are very thick and square. And that bleedin', prissy, simperin', droopy, spaniel-eyed expression. Do I look like a fawnin' demmed little spaniel dog to ye?"

But it did bear a vague general resemblance to him, at least when her eyes were still gummed with sleep. And the painter had managed to capture that odd trick of Sir's eyes. The pupils were slightly misaligned, so you could never look him directly in both eyes.

All that Molly could do while her men were on the war road was to perform the tasks necessary to make sure they had homes worth coming home to, and pray that they would. Sometimes she even prayed to the white god, just in case. Her prayers were punctuated by the clang of tools and workmen's curses from outside. After all the assurances that there was no need to live in a fort anymore, there were two stone blockhouses going up at the corners of Johnson Hall, with tunnels connecting them to the cellar.

A runner brought wampum strings from the west to Canajoharie, and from there to Johnson Hall. There had been no battle yet, and Gets Business Done and Binds Two were smoking tobacco with various western chiefs around campfires or in the council room at Fort Niagara.

Molly emerged from hearing the message to find a full moon coming up before the sun went down. Peter Warren and Elizabeth and Magdalen were splashing naked in the fountain, with Juba watching from one side to see that Peter didn't drown his little sisters, and the flamingo watching from the other to see that the squealing creatures stayed on their half of the pool.

Molly wrapped her children in a towel and sat them down in her lap—a tight squeeze with their burgeoning little brother or sister narrowing the territory. She was six months gone with her fourth child. Since the end of the French war, she and Gets Business Done had been getting down to business.

She said: "Can you see the woman in the moon?"

Peter Warren said: "Da says is *man* in moon."

"You tell your da when he gets home not to fill your heads with English superstitions. There is a woman in the moon, weaving, with her dog lying at her feet. She weaves and weaves, and once a month, when she steps away from her loom and the light goes out, her dog jumps up and rips apart her weaving. Which is very lucky for all of us; we should thank that dog. Because if she ever finishes what she is weaving, Turtle Island will sink back into the sea."

Elizabeth said: "I see her!"

Magdalen snuffled and snored.

Peter Warren said: "Is dinner yet?"

When the leaves turned red and danced away with the wind, General Johnson and Captain Brant led their forces back to the Mohawk Valley. Molly stood on the steps of Johnson Hall wondering if there was anything she'd forgotten. The broad lawn within the circle of the carriageway was covered with trestle tables laden with hams, sausages, potatoes, bread, corn, and onions. Between the tables stood barrels of sauerkraut and the products of Johnson Hall's brew master's art. Whole pigs and oxen turned on spits over open fires. There was a milling crowd of the returning warriors' immediate families, distant relatives, and any stranger who'd happened to be passing by and heard the fiddles tuning up.

From down the road through the woods came the sound of several hundred male voices singing "The Girl I Left Behind Me," accompanied by a fife and drum and the relatively rhythmic tramp of booted feet. A cheer broke out when the Union Jack came fluttering out of the forest, with Sir William Johnson in his bright red major general's coat riding along beside the flag bearer.

The ranks behind him broke immediately into a rush for wives and sweethearts and ale. Sir called after them, "Dismissed!" and urged Old Knobby into a trot toward the house.

Molly felt a funny little rolling-over sensation inside her rib cage at the sight of that beefy, ruddy-brown face and silly, hand-on-one-hip military riding posture bearing down on her. He reined in in front of the steps and saluted: "General Johnson reportin' for duty, Miss Molly."

"Oh, get down off there before I pull you down."

"That is one order it'll be a pleasure to obey." He grunted as his weight settled onto his left leg to heave down off the saddle. Once his boots were on the ground, he stooped to put his arms around her, bowing his back to clear the encumbrances of his belly and hers, and whispered desperately into her ear: "How long?"

"Another month."

"Sufferin' Judas . . . and then another month for ye to recover. . . ."

"Maybe not that long. And there are other ways . . ."

"Ahem." He straightened back up, actually blushing. She wouldn't have imagined it possible to get any more red into that complexion. He settled his hand on her shoulder and looked out over the feast on his greensward. "Well, Molly m'gel, ye've done me proud."

"You've done us all proud."

"Didn't win no battles—just spent the summer gassin' around a council fire."

"Far better to win a war with words than bullets."

"'Tain't necessarily won yet. We'll see next summer. What

say we go put somethin' in our bellies before all the bounty of
our table's been bleedin' decimated?"

"You already have."

"Have what?"

"Put something in my belly."

He blushed again. She could learn to enjoy this game.

They wandered through the celebration. Her brother was
there, and her stepfather, and so many white men who'd made
themselves part of her family by marching with her husband to
Lake George or Thundergate.

She tugged on Joseph's ear and said: "Do you like being a
peacemaker better than a warrior?"

"Our father would be terribly disappointed in me—all the
way to Thundergate and back and not one scalp. And the Reverend Wheelock would be even more disappointed that I might
be a little disappointed, too."

She tickled him under the armpit and said: "You're not as
bloodthirsty as that."

"Not near so much as my sister." He turned somber. "I do
wonder, though, why it is that all those soldiers and warriors—
maybe even Pontiac himself—should have to be sacrificed so
that those of us who live can have peace."

"Wonder tomorrow. Today is for dancing."

It was a glorious homecoming of white and Indian neighbors, made even more glorious by the fact that every one of
the men who'd marched out of the Mohawk Valley had
marched back. But when the bounty of Johnson Hall had been
decimated and the last farm wife had heaved her snoring hero
onto the back of the wagon, Molly lay beside hers, watching
the pictures the magic lantern of her mind cast on the canopy.
In Canajoharie tonight there would be a Thanks Giving dance
around the painted pole, with the capering shadows of Binds
Two and the other young men stretched long across the walls
of the longhouse, and the sounds of drums and rattles, lilting
yells and stamping feet.

But that was the bargain she'd made. She couldn't very well
live in the manor house and the longhouse at the same time.

CHAPTER 30

The farm that King Hendrick had willed Brant's Joseph was at German Flats on the south bank of the Mohawk, halfway between Canajoharie and the twin bluffs called the Noses. After spending most of the day translating for a Seneca delegation come to formalize the peace made in the west last summer, Joseph was using the remaining hours of sunlight to replace the storm-battered shakes on the roof of his chicken coop. Even with the hired girl to tend the garden and milk the cow and help keep the house in order when his wife was confined to her bed, he always seemed to be at least eight chores behind.

An adventurous red pullet came plummeting down out of the sycamore beside the henhouse, flapping and squawking and shedding feathers up Joseph's nose. He shooed her off the roof, almost falling off himself, then regained his purchase and sat for a moment sucking the iron taste off the blacksmith's penny-a-pound squareheads nestled in the corner of his mouth, gazing down at his home and family.

The lawn in front of the house was rich green and clipped smooth, courtesy of the cow. There was a cornfield on one side and a wheat field on the other and a field of barley on the island that was part of the property. Behind the barn was a fenced pasture for his growing collection of horses, and beyond it the wood lot to provide all that was needed in the way of cooking fuel and fence posts and to keep the fireplace humming through even the longest of winters.

Twenty-two years old was very young for a Hodenosaune to consider himself capable of taking on a wife and family. But not every Hodenosaune had a handsome salary from the Department of Northern Indian Affairs, or had inherited a handsome piece of farmland. Joseph had a sudden twinge of wondering if there weren't some truth to the Senecas' whispering that the Caniengas had become more white than Hodenosaune. The very notion of "his" farm was alien to the longhouse.

He brushed the twinge away and focused his eyes on Margaret nursing Isaac on the riverbank. She shone in the sunset. But then, she always had in any light, from the time they'd first shared a desk at the white school at Fort Hunter. As she'd grown into a woman, it had become clear that the ethereal glow in her skin was partly due to the only white man's gift that killed more True People than smallpox or rum: tuberculosis. But Joseph was determined that if Margaret were delicately cared for, she would live her full three score and ten.

Unfortunately, Isaac had come hard. After a year, Margaret still shivered with terror whenever Joseph's hand touched her in the night. Among unchristianized Hodenosaune, a year's wait after childbirth was the norm, but the husband wasn't expected to cleave to his wife and to her only. The Reverend Wheelock, though, had taught Joseph that patience was a virtue. And long before the Reverend Wheelock, his Teacher had dinned it into his *onikonhra* that patience was the difference between a hunter with fat children and starving ones.

Out of the red-and-green-bronzed world of sunset on the trees and river came a silhouetted horse and rider, with a musket propped across the pommel. The gun belied the fact that the rider appeared to be a woman.

As the silhouette grew closer, Joseph recognized Juanita's trick of kicking her heels up as she trotted. He took the nails out of his mouth, slid along the slope of the roof and jumped down. Molly had reined in beside the chicken coop and was climbing down off the saddle, still holding the gun. One side of the barrel was split open, with ragged edges like a torn cloth cast in metal.

She didn't kiss him hello or even say "I greet thee," just spat out, "Look!" and thrust the musket at him.

He looked, unsure of what he was supposed to be looking for. On either side of the split in the gun barrel there were matte-black splotches, with a red tinge. He said: "Blood?"

"A man can lose a lot of blood with three fingers. One of

the Canajoharie women brought that to me after it blew up in her husband's hands."

He could understand her being appalled by such a terrible accident, but that didn't explain her anger. Before he could ask, his wife said: "Why to you?"

Joseph kept his eyes on the gun barrel and his mouth shut. It was always handy to have something else to devote his attention to whenever Margaret and his sister were in the same place.

His sister ignored his wife's question and told him: "Scratch your fingernail along the crack in the gun barrel. No—inside the lip there . . ." He did what he was told. Impossibly, he could feel his fingernail scratch through the surface of the steel. Molly shouted: "Lead! It's lead!"

Joseph said uncertainly: "Well, if he was foolish enough to load the ball before the powder, I suppose a bit of lead might—"

"He didn't. He loaded it just like he should've, but at the first shot it blew up. He bought it from a trader named Ebenezer Cox. I nosed around and found out Ebenezer Cox and his partners bought up a stock of worn-out old army muskets. The quartermaster assumed Cox meant to try to sell them to gunsmiths to melt down. But what Cox did was fill up the barrel cracks with lead to sell them to Indians."

Joseph ceased to wonder at her rage, as his *onikonhra* instantaneously became one with his sister's again. He felt that sudden stiffening at the roots of his neck, pulling his head erect, and the tingling in his hands, which he'd first felt the day he saw the bigger boy using his baggataway stick on the little green-eyed boy. He said: "Where is this Ebenezer Cox?"

Molly put her hand on his on the gun barrel and shook her head. "That is not the way to go about it. If you kill Cox, his friends will come looking for revenge and the whole valley will go up in flames. But if you can prove this to a judge, the governor will take away Cox's trading license. We need to have one of these guns for proof."

Margaret said: "Looks to me like you have one already."

"If it was hard for me to convince Binds Two that this gun wasn't just clumsily loaded, how much chance would there be with a white judge? We need to have a gun that isn't burst yet.

Someone has to go to Cox's trading store and buy a 'new' one from him."

Joseph said: "I will do it."

In the morning, he put on his greasiest old hunting shirt, smeared a few streaks of vermilioned bear grease under his eyes, and rode over to Cox & Company's trading store. There were more white men lounging about inside than he would've expected of an establishment that did most of its business with Hodenosaune. The man behind the counter said in English: "What can I do for you, brother?"

"Want gun."

One of the loungers said: "Say, ain't you old Johnson's interpreter?"

Joseph turned stiffly toward him and repeated: "Want gun."

The man behind the counter said: "Can't tell one from the other with their faces painted up and their heads shaved bald. You want gun?"

Joseph turned back toward the counter and nodded.

The counterman said, "Furs? You got furs?" and lifted up an ermine pelt by way of illustration.

Joseph shook his head, "Got money," and opened his hand to display a collection of the most battered old coins he'd been able to find about the house.

The counterman looked at the coins skeptically, plucked one up, tried it with his teeth and said: "Well now . . . Sure, we'll take your money. A fine British army musket will cost you this one, and that one . . . and these two." He lifted them out of Joseph's palm. "Here you go, brother—finest military firearm ever made."

Joseph weighed the gun in his hands, hoping his expression didn't say that a guinea, eight shillings, and fourpence was several times the going rate for an aged Long Land Pattern musket. The trader snatched up the coin Joseph had put on the counter to free his hand for the musket. "You want powder and shot, too, brother? Boom, boom?" Joseph nodded, and the coin disappeared into the waistcoat pocket.

As Joseph went out the door with his "new" musket, six musket balls, and a paper twist of gunpowder, he heard laughter behind him, and: "Wait'll old Coxy finds out you sold another one!"

Instead of heading back to his farm, Joseph rode straight to

Schenectady and laid a complaint that Ebenezer Cox's license to trade with Indians should be revoked. By the time he got home, the sun had set and Margaret and Isaac were both asleep. He padded about the kitchen as noiselessly as his Teacher had managed to train him, rummaging out some cheese, bread, and an onion, and sat munching by candlelight while he peered over every inch of the musket.

For the life of him, he couldn't find anything that looked even remotely like a hairline crack or abscess that had been filled in with lead. Either Ebenezer Cox's gun doctors were very good at their jobs, or Joseph Brant was about to make a fool of himself.

On the day the circuit court was due to sit in Schenectady, Joseph set out early in the morning with William of Canajoharie and John Deseronto, another alumnus of the Reverend Wheelock's school and the French war. William was generally referred to now as Big William, since his filling-out had left not the remotest doubt that he was William Johnson's son. Even Joseph found it hard to believe he'd ever had to break a baggataway stick across someone's nose to protect the same green-eyed boy who now boxed the ears of any white man who looked down his nose at an Indian. Joseph wouldn't have considered going into a potentially difficult situation without Big William any more than without his loincloth and leggings.

The arms of the elms and oaks arced over the road like the buttresses in the Reverend Wheelock's illustrated book of the cathedrals of England. Deseronto and Big William bantered and sang and gossiped and leaned down off their horses to scoop up acorns to throw at each other. Joseph did his best to make it a trio of young bucks, but he couldn't quite drag his *onikonhra* from the blanket-wrapped brace of Cox muskets— the one he'd bought and the one Molly had left with him— propped across his horse's shoulders.

Deseronto and Big William stayed outside the courthouse to prepare the linchpin of the case Joseph planned to present. Joseph sat in the back of the courtroom with his pieces of evidence propped between his knees, listening to the docket drag on through disputes over farm boundary lines and carriage drivers accused of running the tollgate near the Big Nose.

The light through the casement windows was turning honey-colored when the bailiff announced: "A complaint brought against Mr. Ebenezer Cox by Captain Joseph Brant, sometimes known as Brant's Joseph or as Thigh-und-a... They-and-a ... by an Indian name."

A man in a brown broadcloth suit sitting next to Ebenezer Cox stood up and said in a honeyed voice: "M'lud, I have been engaged by Mr. Cox to represent him in this matter. Mr. Cox is insulted and wounded to the quick that such a calumnious accusation should ever come to court. But he graciously swallows his pride because he understands that the only bridge to our peaceful but half-civilized neighbors is to show them that British justice dispenses itself equally and impartially to all British subjects, whatever their color or superstitions."

Joseph picked up his bundle of muskets and walked down the aisle toward the judge's bench, trying to hold onto the one piece of advice King Hendrick had given him about speaking in public.

Joseph presented his complaint, and presented his two muskets to the bailiff to present to the judge. The judge looked over the unburst one and said: "It might be that the light has grown too dim as we've wound our way through this *very* long docket, but I can discern no trace of lead filling."

Joseph said: "Nor can I." There was laughter from behind him, particularly from the place where Ebenezer Cox sat with his lawyer. "The musket has never been fired since it was purchased from Mr. Cox's store. If my lord would come outside with me, where it can be done in safety, we will fire the gun and discover what happens. The bailiff can do the loading, so we'll know it's done right."

The judge elevated his eyebrows and pursed his mouth, then pronounced: "It is a highly irregular way to proceed, Captain Brant, but the court is appreciative of any suggestion that will resolve the matter quickly at this late point in the day—pardon me, *evening.*

"Mr. Cox, are you amenable?" Ebenezer Cox and his hired voice were whispering to each other. "Mr. Cox ... ?"

The hired speaker dragged his ear away from his employer's mouth and turned back to the judge. "M'lud, it would be irregular—"

"Didn't I say that? Didn't I just say that? Clerk of the Court! What did I just say?"

The clerk stopped his frazzled scribbling for an instant. "You said, m'lud—ahem, 'It is a highly irregular way to—' "

"Thought I'd said that," the judge said, turning back to Cox and his spokesman. "Well? Are you amenable to Captain Brant's suggestion or are we going to sit here swapping tall tales till the sun goes down?"

Cox's spokesman said: "Mr. Cox has nothing to fear from Captain Brant's demonstration."

The courtroom—judge, bailiff, clerk, and all—trooped outside with the air of a school let out for playtime. On the lawn in front of the courthouse, Deseronto and Big William had planted two forked sticks lined up in front of a wide old oak tree. They had been sitting by their sticks and waiting for Joseph all afternoon, but they'd learned patience in the same schools as he.

The bailiff loaded the musket. Joseph propped it across the forks of the sticks and tied it in place with thongs, then tied a loop in the end of a long string, worked it carefully over the trigger and stepped back, waving the crowd to do the same. He looked again to make sure there was no one between the muzzle and the tree, then yanked the string.

There was a crash and a spray of sparks and a cloud of smoke. When the cloud cleared, there was a smoking hole in the skin of the old oak tree and the musket was lying on the ground with the forks of the broken sticks still tied to it. Outside of a few grass stains, close inspection revealed it to be utterly unaltered from the moment when Cox's storekeeper had handed it across the counter.

Cox's spokesman said loudly: "I just hope I can persuade Mr. Cox to still pay my hire after Captain Brant's gone and done my job for me."

Joseph raised his voice to try to be heard over the laughter: "The fact that it had one shot in it doesn't mean it's sound. The next shot might—"

"M'lud, are we to stand here all night while Captain Brant fires ball after ball into that poor old oak tree? *Any* barrel will burst if it's been fired till it's red hot."

"Only one more shot," Joseph pleaded. "If the barrel remains intact after one more shot, I take my oath that I will argue this no further, that I will pay the fees for Mr. Cox's lawyer, and I will pay any fine my lord determines for taking up the court's time with a false suit."

The judge looked interested—a portion of every fine levied went into the pockets of the presiding magistrate. Cox was impossible to read—perhaps he was weighing his chances that the gun might have one more shot in it, or perhaps Molly had been wrong all along.

Joseph added: "And so we don't have to wait the time it would take to cut and plant two new sticks, once the bailiff has reloaded, Mr. Cox can give us a demonstration of his marksmanship."

The judge's eyebrow went up and he looked at Joseph closer than before, then turned to Cox and his spokesman. "Well?"

Cox's mouth stayed shut and his eyes bored into the air. His lawyer looked at him, seemed startled at what he saw, and blustered: "I would like to consult with my client, m'lud. . . ."

"I don't propose to keep on sitting on this case till the crack of doom. Captain Brant has proposed a way to put an end to it immediately. Captain Brant is willing to put his money where his mouth is. The question is—is Mr. Cox willing to put his fingers where his mouth is? Mr. Cox . . . ?"

"M'lud, Mr. Cox would like to consult with—"

"I'm not talking to you, I'm talking to Mr. Cox. Well, Mr. Cox . . . ?" Cox said nothing. "Mr. Cox, I'm warning you—if you refuse to take up one of your own muskets and pull the trigger, and if you can't give me a good reason why not, I'm bound to assume that the reason is that Captain Brant's charge is well-founded. Mr. Cox?" Cox said nothing. "Bailiff, herd them back inside. Let's get this over with."

The court decided that the charges had been proven beyond a reasonable doubt, and would strongly recommend to the governor that Cox & Company's license to engage in the Indian trade be immediately revoked before he started an Indian war. The judge's last words were to Ebenezer Cox: "Captain Brant probably just saved your scalp. Your affidavit says you were about to set off on a trading expedition to the western tribes. I hear they don't go in much for the niceties of civil suits out Alleghany way; and they draw out the execution of their justice for a long, long time."

By the time Joseph came out of the courthouse, the sun was

painting a pretty blush on an ugly mound of storm clouds. He and Big William and Deseronto decided to stay at an inn on the edge of town and head home in the morning.

After a few slices off the chop in the public room, Deseronto and William began to drink. Whether because of the Reverend Wheelock's lectures or because he'd seen too many Caniengas turn into fools for the night, Joseph never drank much. He knew it made him seem standoffish, but there always came a point—usually just when the warmth in his belly started tempting him to make it warmer—that he saw his father losing his dignity.

Joseph got up and went out to the little shed behind the inn, pulled open its door, changed his mind and relieved himself in the clean rain instead. When he came back in, he found his way blocked by the legs of a red-bearded man who'd stretched himself out into a rather awkward-looking position in order to get his feet onto the bench at the next table. Joseph had the feeling that he'd seen him somewhere before, but there were a lot more red beards around these days, and brown and yellow, than even a few years ago.

Joseph considered simply stepping over the legs. But there was something in the white man's expression—as though he were only pretending to listen to the conversation of the other men around the table—that made Joseph hesitate to put himself in such a vulnerable position. So instead he tapped the obstruction on the shoulder, saying: "I beg your pardon, but—"

The red-bearded man sprang to his feet, bellowed, "Push me, would you?" and then doubled over as though he'd been walloped in the stomach. Before Joseph could ask him if he'd lost his mind or was having some kind of fit, the white man leaped backward and came out with a long, thick-bladed knife. "Fair enough, Injun—you started it, but I'm a-goin' to finish it."

Too late, Joseph realized where he'd seen the man before. He was the lounger in Cox's store who'd asked wasn't he "old Johnson's" interpreter. Joseph hadn't thought to bring a knife to court.

"Binds Two!" Big William's knife came sailing hilt first. Joseph snatched it out of the air. The rest of the men were snatching up their drinks, forming a ring and clearing the benches and tables out of the way. The innkeeper was bleating

resignedly: "Outside, gentlemen, outside!" Big William and
Deseronto were sidling around the outside of the ring to keep
an eye on the other men who'd been at the red-bearded one's
table. The red-bearded man was coming on in a half crouch,
weaving his knife in a slow figure eight. It obviously wasn't
his first tavern knife fight, and he was obviously certain that it
wouldn't be his last.

Joseph found himself smiling, rolling the pommel of Big
William's knife between his caressing fingers—it was heavier
than his own, but it would do—and saying to the advancing
redbeard: "So you want to match knives with Thayendenegea?
Tell me first if you have a wife and children, so I will know
whether I should kill you without remorse or just slice off what
you've already used."

Joseph stayed standing straight-spined until the white man
got within stabbing range, then snapped down into a crouch,
yelling: "Saa!"

The white man jumped back and away. Someone in the ring
of watchers laughed. Joseph stalked forward with his eyes focused on the blue ones under the red tufts of eyebrows, reacted
to the peripheral flash of firelit steel, felt and heard the blades
clang against each other, used the momentum of the clash to
drive a thrust at the receding red beard and then jumped back
himself.

Redbeard was a slicer—coming back at Joseph with long
sweeps of his knife meant to drive him backward step by step
until he lost his equilibrium and left an opening for a stab. But
Joseph's arms were a good handsbreadth longer. As another
sweep of the knife went by, Joseph cocked his right arm across
his chest, leaned forward and sprung his arm out full length,
whacking the blade of his knife—not the point—into the side
of the red head.

Redbeard dropped his knife and fell to his knees, flinging
his hand up to his red-gushing head. Half his left ear lay beside
his left knee. Joseph kicked him sprawling on his back, leaped
on his chest with both knees, grabbed a fistful of hair and
jerked his head up, brandishing his knife with a scalp yell. Before the gasps of horror in the ring of watchers could turn into
action, he let the red head fall back to the floor, said, "My old
enemies would be ashamed to have their scalps in the same
bag as this one," and rose to his feet.

Joseph flopped back down at the table with Deseronto and Big William and got drunk. Big William said: "I don't know why you should feel knotted up—he was a puppy in your hands."

"Puppy or not, even puppies have teeth, and this one had a knife."

CHAPTER 31

Molly had decided it was high time her brother had a mat among the circle of Royaners, and a voice in the Great Council at Onondaga. He had already been accepted as a man to follow on the war road. And in his position as intermediary with the Superintendent of Northern Indian Affairs, he was already doing a great deal to maintain the *orenda* of all Six Nations. Any Hodenosaune who hadn't been aware of that before, knew so after the incident of Ebenezer Cox and his hunter-maiming muskets. If Joseph had to be the instrument of the Royaners' decisions—both on the war road and in the back rooms of the Indian Department—the least they could do was let him have a voice in the making of those decisions.

The problem was that he hadn't been born into any of the families that owned Royaners' names. Even if he had, it was unlikely that he would've been chosen to fill the place of one of the Founders. He was too much the warrior. It was one thing for an eloquent speaker like King Hendrick to come in off the war road and don the antlers of a Royaner, but Joseph was no Hendrick. He could speak well and clearly, and would do even better with a little judicious coaching, but his *onikonhra* was too direct. He didn't have it in him to weave those elegant, multishaded tapestries of words and gestures that the Royaners loved so well, which, without offending, could seed doubts in those who thought they'd been convinced by the previous speaker. He did have a wit that could make people laugh, which was an essential ingredient for a Royaner, but his was more like a knife than a tickle.

But the Founders of the league had foreseen, as they had foreseen all things necessary for their children to keep the Tree of Peace alive, that there would be men whose voices should be heard around the Fire That Never Dies, but who for one reason or another could never be Royaners. So the Founders had allowed for the creation of Pine Tree Chiefs, who were said to stand alone like a pine tree on a mountaintop, because their voice was not inherited and would die with them. Joseph was going to be a Pine Tree Chief. This particular Pine Tree Chief wasn't necessarily going to speak only for himself, but also perhaps occasionally for two people at Johnson Hall who could never be Royaners either. But no one need be made too aware of that.

The first step was convincing the women of the Wolf Clan at Canajoharie and then the Clan Mothers of all the Canienga. That wasn't too difficult. By the time the Canienga delegation was preparing to embark for Onondaga, all the Canienga Oyanders—and hence their Royaners—believed that Binds Two should be made a Pine Tree Chief. But all the nations of the confederacy had to agree on adding a new voice to the council fire, and some of them were of the opinion that the Canienga had too many voices there already.

So Molly slung Peggy's cradle board over her shoulder and left Peter Warren, Elizabeth, and Magdalen in the charge of their Canienga nursemaid for the last month of the summer. If Peggy happened to grow hungry in the middle of some sparkling flow of oratory around the Fire That Never Dies, Molly could simply unbutton her overdress and carry on listening.

As the carriage waited in front of Johnson Hall to carry her down to the river and the Canienga delegation's canoes, Molly lingered on the front steps with her husband. He said: "How long d'ye guess on bein' gone?"

"A month, perhaps six weeks, depending on the weather. I must've told you that a dozen times already."

"Thought maybe the weather might've changed since the last time." He grumbled: "Goin' to be demmed lonely here without ye. Lonely and unruly. P'r'aps I'll chain the progeny in the root cellar till ye get home."

"Horace has been given strict instructions that you are to be given nothing else to drink of an evening until you've drunk your tonic."

"*I'm* the one what pays his demmed wages!"

"If you want to carry on eating two oxen for breakfast and washing them down with black ale, you have to take something to keep your blood clear. I don't wish to come home and find you laid up with a bad liver."

"P'r'aps ye'll come home and find me laid up with somethin' else. Ha! Fancy that? The new nursemaid's demmed comely...."

"I could make her a good deal less comely before I go. Wouldn't take but a moment. Just so you won't have to suffer temptation."

"Well ... God and little fishes bring ye back safe to me."

"May God and Horace keep you well till I return."

Juba stood by the outside cellar door under the front steps watching her mistress ride away from her master. She understood that Molly had responsibilities to the people she'd been born into, and ambitions for her brother, but it also seemed to Juba that a man and woman who had as much together as Molly and Sir William shouldn't allow themselves to be dragged away from it except by the direst necessities. The winds of the world didn't blow balmy so often that anyone could afford to throw away the days. Juba also found herself wondering at times whether little Sissy hadn't become just a bit too fond of telling the winds which way to blow.

The mistress of the house had barely been gone a week when the master took poorly again. Doctors came and went. Juba and Horace argued over the exact way Mistress Molly used to mix the ingredients for his tonic, or whether the charm had been in the Mohawk words she murmured as she mixed it. Nothing seemed to make much difference.

If Juba had been more thoroughly civilized, she might've said it was a judgment when Molly came home in the bright autumn, jubilant from getting her way yet again, to find her man prostrate on their bed as helpless and gasping as a beached sea monster.

Mistress Molly seemed to take it as her own doing, even if no one else did. Flocks of old Indian women joined the parade of doctors in and out of Johnson Hall. The only times Molly left the master bedroom were when she came down to the kitchen for yet another fiercely whispered consultation with yet another clutch of witches, ending in brewing up yet another tea or poultice that hadn't been tried yet.

Molly sat on the edge of the bed holding Sir's limp, massive hand, listening to the breath wheeze in and out of him. She wasn't certain whether he was awake or asleep, or whether there was much difference at this point. Her eyes strayed around the room: the fireplace set into the wall of books he loved so well, the writing desk piled high with documents he hadn't read, the silver-filagreed eagle-feather headdress in its glass case . . .

His hand twitched. She looked at his face to see his eyes were still closed. He had been up and down so long since she'd got back from Onondaga that she couldn't remember a time she didn't look at him anxiously. One day he would look ruddy and full of sap, the next gray and parchmenty. The doctors bled him and fed him sulfur and arsenic. Their diagnoses varied from "imbalance of the nervous ether" to "overfathering." Molly's uneducated opinion was that he'd lived too hard for too many years and needed a rest. Her terror was that the rest he was going to get was the one down the long road where the strawberries are always growing.

She squeezed his hand and whispered: "Sir . . . ?"

"Hm?"

She hesitated, then blurted out: "I must go across the river to Canajoharie." She'd been hesitating for some time, afraid that if she let go of his hand and left the room, he would die; afraid that if she didn't go to Canajoharie, she would lose the only chance of keeping him alive. "It won't be more than overnight. Maybe not that long."

His eyelids fluttered and he breathed out: "If ye must, ye must."

She galloped Juanita down the forest road to the ferry and rode straight from the ferry to the farm of Nickus Brant. Her mother was out back slopping the pigs. Someone Lends Her a Flower was now the Elder Sister of the Clan Mothers of

Canajoharie. Molly said: "I ask you to call a council of the Clan Mothers. Now."

"For what cause?"

"I have heard tell of a pool of medicine water in the forest east of Albany, a hot spring that our grandfathers enclosed in a house of logs and clay. I want my husband to be taken there."

"No white man may go there."

"Gets Business Done is a Canienga. Have I not heard the Clan Mothers crying: 'What will become of us and the English the day Gets Business Done is eating strawberries?' "

"Are thee that afraid for him, my daughter?"

"I am."

The Clan Mothers eventually agreed, but the final decision rested with the men's council, most of whom weren't too happy about being dragged out to the ceremonial longhouse in the middle of the night. But with the new Pine Tree Chief Binds Two and the Royaner Carrying News supporting the women, Little Abraham and the rest of the council were persuaded to allow what had never been allowed before.

Molly could only go with him as far as Albany, because the forest pool was warriors' medicine. The citizens of Albany turned out to watch Sir William Johnson being lifted out of a canoe onto a bier shouldered by the first of many relays of Canienga warriors and disappearing into the forest. Molly went home to attend to his children and estate—and to wait.

She waited a month with no news of him. There was snow on the ground when the back door of Johnson Hall crashed open and a voice like boulders rolling down a hill roared: "Someone fetch me a mug of ale to wash the taste of bleedin' brimstone out of me throat! Molly! Horace! Molly! Everybody go bleedin' deef while I was off bein' percolated in bleedin' pickle juice?"

CHAPTER 32

On an autumn day in 1768, Joseph saddled up his roan stallion, tied a sack of provisions and camp gear behind the saddle, and went into his house to kiss his family goodbye. Margaret was finally pregnant again, so there was no question of her traveling. And Joseph suspected she wasn't all that brokenhearted at she and Isaac being left in untrammeled possession of the enclosed little kingdom of wood lot, gardens, farmyard, and the island out on the river.

Margaret was sitting in the kitchen with Isaac on her lap, playing cat's cradle. Her sister Susanna, who'd come from Oquaga to help out, was stirring something on the hearth. Joseph stooped to kiss Margaret and said: "I wouldn't be going if I didn't have to."

"I know. Don't worry, Susanna will take good care of us."

Susanna said shyly: "I'll try." She said everything shyly. She hadn't inherited the same fine features as Margaret, but she had inherited the same ethereal skin glow of the coughing sickness.

Joseph said to Isaac: "Would you like me to bring you something when I come home?"

"Bring me a . . . scalp!"

Joseph laughed. "It's a *peace* conference. But if it turns ugly, yes, I'll bring you a scalp."

Big William and Deseronto were waiting for him in the yard. Although Deseronto lived too far upriver to be as constant a companion as Joseph and Big William, whenever some occasion brought Caniengas from all the valley together, the three of them always made a unit. The combination of the

Reverend Wheelock's school and the war road set them a little apart from those who only knew one or the other.

They were traveling to Fort Stanwix, which the British had built after the French war showed them the importance of the Carrying Place, where a short portage could move boats between the headwaters of the Mohawk and the Great Lakes. A lot of people were traveling to Fort Stanwix. A very ugly, desultory warfare had been going on between the northwestern nations and the Big Knives—as the True People had christened the whites who were drawn toward the frontier, for their habit of wearing knives the size of Big William's forearm. So Gets Business Done was going to sit down at Fort Stanwix with the king's hat on his head and draw a line across the continent, to mark for all time the border between the English colonies and the True People of Turtle Island.

Joseph could have traveled by canoe, either in the flotilla bearing the Canajoharie delegation or in the one transporting the Department of Northern Indian Affairs. But he had a feeling it was better he not arrive as a member of either party. It was complex at times, being both Binds Two and Joseph Brant, but it had its uses.

By the time he, Big William, and Deseronto reached Fort Stanwix, Joseph was feeling loose and limber. It was pleasant to have a farm and a family and a salary, but it wasn't right that a man should forget what it was to smoke a pipe beside a campfire, listening to deep, male voices joking lazily about who'd caught the biggest fish.

The palisades of Fort Stanwix were surrounded by a kaleidoscopic flood. Red-coated soldiers moved among a swirl of Cayuga and Seneca turkey-feather bonnets, Canienga neck bibs, and painted warriors wearing the pelts of wolves or panthers so that their faces appeared to be staring out of the beasts' yawning mouths. There were Oyanders in overdresses of calico or velvet or fringed deer hide, all of them beaded and embroidered and decked with appliquéd silk ribbon, silver broaches, and beadworked belts and necklaces.

Above the flood waved a forest of tail feathers set in spinners on the tops of skullcaps, so they could bob and weave with the wind or the wearer's movements but still stand upright. A Canienga wore three feathers, an Onondaga two, and a Seneca, Cayuga, Oneida, or Tuscarora only one. There were other nations there besides the Six: Delawares, Shawnees, Wyandots, mongrel Mingoes, and some whose identifying signs Joseph didn't know.

A whoop went up from the riverbank as an employee of the Department of Northern Indian Affairs knocked in the head of a barrel of rum. Big William smacked his lips and turned his horse in that direction. Joseph said: "I have to tell Gets Business Done I'm here."

"You tell my father I'm here, too, but got other business to take care of."

Deseronto said: "We came here to make a treaty, not get drunk."

Big William said: "The counciling don't start until tomorrow. Well?"

Deseronto shrugged. "All right." He clucked his horse to fall in beside Big William's. "But if you start pawing other men's women again, I'm heading for higher ground."

"I don't start pawing *them*, they start pawing me."

"That's even worse."

Gets Business Done and Joseph's sister weren't hard to find. A crisp new Union Jack fluttered over General Johnson's palatial campaign tent. The corporal guarding the door flap said: "Sir William ain't seeing anyone till tomorrow."

"I am Captain Brant. See to my horse."

"Yes, sir."

Inside, Sir William was standing in front of an easel with a map pinned to it, and Molly was sitting on the carpet nursing baby George. Sir William said: "*There* ye are, Joseph. Demmed glad I won't have to fumble through me own translatin' tomorrow. Take a pew. Horace, fetch another glass."

Joseph crouched down to kiss his sister hello and brush his fingertips along his suckling nephew's downy head, then sat in one of the ingenius folding chairs ranged around the staff table. Horace ladled out another tumbler of limed rum punch, and the Superintendent of Northern Indian Affairs raised his with: "Here's that we may always have a clean shirt, a clean conscience, and a guinea in the pocket.

"This is big doin's, Joseph. As big as any I ever set me hand to. . . ." As the bouldery voice rumbled on and the pick handle of a forefinger stabbed at the map, Joseph was inexorably drawn in to see that if the delegations gathered at Fort Stanwix could agree on a boundary line, the True People and the new people could live together as good neighbors with a good fence between them. If not, his wife and son and all the other innocents of Turtle Island were sooner or later going to find themselves living in a Boiling Kettle of blood.

Not for the first time since he'd become a conduit between the Six Nations and the Indian Department, Joseph found he had to concentrate on the matter at hand so as not to be overawed that this was *Sir William Johnson* asking him to be an ally.

Molly put George back in his cradleboard and sat at the table. She let her husband and brother do all the talking, but it seemed obvious to Joseph that the opinions Sir William was expressing had already been tinged with hers.

It also seemed to him that there was something evasive about Sir William's manner when it came to certain areas on the map. Joseph told himself he was carrying healthy suspicion too far. Was this not the same William Johnson who'd inaugurated the practice of treating the True People as lawful owners of the land, to be bought out through deed and title and value received, just as though they were Englishmen? Was that not Sir William's own son hanging in a Canienga cradle board, with a charm bell dangling from the face hoop?

The morning began with the annual distribution of presents from the king, to repolish the Covenant Chain. One of the many things William Johnson understood about the True People that other white men couldn't seem to grasp was that no words meant anything unless accompanied by a gift. The chiefs and Royaners in turn presented the king's representative with furs and wampum that Joseph highly doubted would ever find their way to the king.

With the niceties out of the way, Gets Business Done got down to business in the huge, open-air arbor that an army of carpenters had erected for the occasion. And Joseph got down to work translating English and several dialects of Hodenosaune and Delaware. Starting life as a Mingo had accustomed him to a stew of languages, but after the first few hours, his *onikonhra* grew numb with words.

Not so numb, though, that he didn't notice at an impasse point a Cayuga Oyander with a Wolf Clan headband leaning forward to whisper something to her Royaner. When the wampum was passed to that Royaner, he suggested a certain large sum of English money would compensate the Hodenosaune for certain rights they were being asked to give up. Molly had been busy.

On the fifth of November in the Year of Our Lord 1768, the True People of Turtle Island and the British Empire signed a treaty for all time. To replace the old, hopelessly confusing Proclamation Line, a line was drawn southwest from Fort Stanwix, following the natural courses of mountain ranges and watersheds to the Muskingum and Ohio rivers. Everything northwest of the Stanwix Line was Indian Territory. The Mohawk River valley fell in the undefined area before the start of the line, but the Keepers of the Dawn had been living with the English for so long, they didn't need a formal treaty.

When Joseph passed the pen on from signing "Joseph Brant—Thayendenegea," his sister flung her arms around him, splashing his shirt with champagne, and squealed: "We did it!"

"Until the next time."

"There won't *be* a next time."

"You think not? After the English have filled up all the country on their side of the line, you think there won't be white farms sprouting up like mushrooms on the Hodenosaune side?"

"Of course there will—and they'll last as long as mushrooms. The soldiers of the king won't defend anyone breaking a treaty with the king's name on it. Once the Big Knives realize that anyone crossing the Stanwix Line without permission is handing himself over to Hodenosaune justice, they'll learn to stay at home.

"Don't you understand what we've done here? With the French driven out, the only reason for another war was if the True People and the English couldn't get along. We've made a peace that will last as long as there's a king in England. Come on, smile . . ."

She tried to tickle him under the armpit, which always hurt more than it tickled. "Smile!"

CHAPTER 33

The consumption finally took Margaret Brant. Molly couldn't truly say that she was sorry, except for what it did to Joseph. He couldn't seem to abide being near the house he'd lived in with Margaret. He handed Isaac and baby Christina over to Margaret's sister Susanna, hired laborers to look after the farm, and took up residence with a theologian at Fort Hunter, to devote himself to translating the Acts of the Apostles and the Catechism into Canienga.

Molly couldn't understand why he would turn for comfort to the English religion instead of the ways they'd both learned in childhood. She could understand that the Christian heaven and hell were a much more concrete vision than the strawberry road, but that was exactly why the old ways made more sense to her. Perhaps he didn't want to have to hear: "Now *be* thou condoled." Or perhaps immersing himself in the gospels was just a way of hiding himself away from the world.

She had never been able to make him see that white religions weren't like those of the True People, who didn't separate the sacred from even the most mundane parts of life. But then, Joseph hadn't had the early advantage of seeing the difference between what the white people in the school in Schenectady said on Sunday and how they treated Juba. Perhaps the Reverend Wheelock had actually practiced what he preached.

Sir said to her: "There's demmed little I would presume to teach ye or tell ye, Molly m'gel. But I will say this, and ye can take it as coin of the realm. Don't ever set yerself between a man and his religion. Ye'll get crushed. Joseph wasn't made to spend 'is days scribblin' at a desk and singin' psalms. Leave 'im to it and he'll weary of it eventually."

"Just as John will of Clarissa Putnam?" It was a low blow, and she knew it. John Johnson, now *Sir* John Johnson, had refused to marry any woman but Clarissa Putnam, the daughter of an innkeeper at Tribes Hill. His father had declared that the day Clarissa Putnam became Lady Johnson was the day Sir John Johnson's name was blotted out of his will. Both Sir William and Sir John had declared there was no compromising on the matter. The compromise Molly had worked out was that Clarissa and John took up housekeeping without benefit of clergy at Fort Johnson. Guy and Mary Johnson had been relocated to a monumental estate christened Guy Park, which Sir had caused to be erected to show his son the difference between a father's smiles and frowns.

Sir was more than big enough to take low blows without squealing. He merely growled: "Mark m'words—John'll rid 'imself of that demmed woman before m'will gets read." After three years and two children, Molly doubted it, but she held her peace.

Joseph was still Sir's interpreter, so despite his cloistering, she still saw him at Johnson Hall from time to time. He came looking for his employer on an afternoon in April which happened to be a special occasion for the children, the day the peacocks and the monkeys were set free from their cramped winter cubicles.

Joseph kissed her hello, and she told him Sir was still at Fish House, "But he's due back this afternoon." Rumor had it that fishing wasn't the only activity that drew Sir William Johnson to his lodge on Vlaie Creek, but Molly had learned not to listen to rumors. If the Wormwood sisters truly could draw a little extra strenuous exercise out of him at this stage in his life, good luck to them.

Joseph said jauntily: "Then I'll lend you a hand with the menagerie." She looked at him again. His eyes were gleaming and he actually seemed part of the world again. "Elizabeth, if you and Magdalen can lift that end of the cage, I'll take this one."

Magdalen said: "They bite my fingers, Uncle Joseph."

"You don't have to put your fingers through the bars, just

slide your palms under the bottom, like I'm doing. Peggy, hold on to George so I don't back over him."

"Yes, Uncle Joseph."

"All right, girls—lift!"

Molly followed them out with the smaller carrying cage for the little monkey the Royal Governor had sent Sir William for some favor or other. Joseph backed across the lawn toward the big, permanent cage set in the garden, amusing the girls by imitating the cries of the peacocks happily stretching their legs.

Peggy said: "Mother, wouldn't the monkeys be happier free like the peacocks?"

"I'm sure they would, my dear, for a short while. They'd scamper right off into the forest and we'd never see them again. Those that didn't starve—because the food in our forests isn't the same as theirs—would freeze to death when winter came."

"Wouldn't they come home?"

"Not all creatures do what's good for them."

Once the monkeys were happily scampering about their summer home, Molly's brother turned to her and said: "I have something to tell you. . . ."

"Girls, take George to the kitchen and tell Juba I said to give you each a cherry tart. But only one each." It had taken her some time to get accustomed to rationing children's food, but in the longhouse they didn't have to be hungry for set mealtimes.

As the girls were organizing themselves into who would hold which of George's hands, and moving off at toddling speed, Joseph looked toward the fountain and said: "I do miss the flamingo. But as the Reverend Wheelock used to say, all flesh is mortal. Did I ever thank you for the feathers?"

"Yes."

He glanced around to see if anyone was in earshot, and then fixed his glistening brown eyes on hers and grinned. "I have a blood brother."

Among the Hodenosaune, a warrior's blood brother was closer than his wife. A Hodenosaune war party was made up of pairs of warriors who watched each other's backs in battle and shared their blankets on frosty nights. In times of peace they shared each other's secrets and served as each other's mirrors; a blood brother could advise a man that he was starting down a path that was foolish or dishonorable when no one else could. It had seemed strange to a lot of people that Binds Two was approaching thirty years and still had no blood brother. Molly suspected it was because Margaret would have been jealous.

Molly snatched hold of his hands and said, "Who is it? Tell me," wondering whether he'd say William of Canajoharie or John Deseronto. She hoped he'd have enough sense to choose Big William, who loved him dearly and whose *onikonhra* was of a simpler grain than Deseronto's. But either way, the important thing was that it meant Joseph was finally emerging from his white-ways mourning closet and becoming a living Canienga again.

"Lieutenant Augustine Prevost."

"Who?"

"You remember Lieutenant Prevost. You remarked upon the splendor of his uniform when they paraded the garrison at Fort Hunter."

She remembered, but she couldn't believe it. "There was nothing else *to* remark upon. He was a corn-silk-haired husk doll in a gold-braided coat!"

"You don't know him as I do."

"How long have you known this paragon of warriors?"

"A man doesn't need a lot of time to recognize a noble heart in another man."

"Doesn't he now? After twenty years of knowing Big William, you haven't recognized the nose on your face, or you wouldn't do this to him."

"Do what to him?"

"Pass him by in favor of some prancing white parade-ground hero you hardly know."

He stepped back, wrapping himself in his dignity, and said: "I am told, One Against Two, that you speak with great wisdom in the councils of the women." He turned and headed for the paddock, leaving her with nothing to flail at but the bars of the monkey cage.

Sir came home not long after, stumping into the white parlor with the cane he had to use more often than not these days. "There ye are, Molly m'gel. I handed Juba a creelful of trout on m'way in. Had a divil of a time paddlin' back up the creek this mornin'. It was easy enough to get down there—they just loaded me and a feather mattress in the canoe and let me drift down to Fish House. Creek's high—I caught our dinner off the front porch. Why the divil was Joseph standin' about in the muck of the stableyard instead of waitin' for me in here?"

She told him. But instead of joining her in railing about her brother's idiocy, he said: "It seems to me, Molly m'dear, that what I said about settin' yerself between a man and his religion holds just as true for a man and his blood brother."

"What would you know about blood brothers?"

"Demmit, Molly, I may not be a Mohawk by birth, but I've spent the best part of me life among 'em. By far the best part. And this blood brother business ain't somethin' unique to the Iroquois. Seems to me them demmed old Greeks and Trojans and such had somethin' along the same lines. Sufferin' Judas, I'm beginnin' to think I should've advised m'*self* not to get between a man and his sister."

"Forgive me, Gets Business Done, I should not be shooting the arrows at you I meant for Binds Two."

"Ye may well be right that Joseph's makin' a mistake, but it seems to me the best way to learn is to make as many bleedin' idiot mistakes as y'can while ye're still young and limber enough to bounce back. Seems no need to make things any harder on Joseph than he does 'imself. I don't have to tell ye yer brother's got a terrible serious streak in 'im. Things that'd roll off ye or me like water off a duck strike him to the quick and fester.

"Besides, this Prevost ain't a bad sort. Ye might even get to likin' 'im."

He plunked himself down at his desk to read the correspondence that had come in while he was gone. Partway through the first, he began to snort and huff like an irritated bull. She said: "What's wrong?"

"What else? Demmed Bostonian rabble-rousers and their precious Boston Massacre. 'Massacre' me arse. If they were ruled by any other power than His British Majesty, and a mob started playfully throwin' snowballs with rocks in 'em at a troop of soldiers, there'd be a dem sight more'n four rioters dead."

After that day, Molly saw even less of her brother. When he had to come to Johnson Hall on business, he would politely kiss her hello—as though she had mortally offended him but was still his sister—and then hie himself back to Fort Hunter and the Reverend Dr. Stuart and the gospels.

She saw him at the Green Corn Festival. Through the crowd of women dancing with cornstalks and roasting the year's first ears, men unwrapping the bear and deer meat they'd baked in the forest, Keepers of the Faith bringing out the peach stones for the men and women to gamble against each other, came flamingo-feathered Joseph with his blond blood brother in tow. The lieutenant was decked out like an extravagantly wealthy Canienga warrior, except that he wore breeches and silk stockings under his warrior's kilt.

Behind the two blood brothers came dead Margaret's sister Susanna, with baby Christina in her arms and Isaac stomping along sulkily beside her. When Molly greeted her, Susanna flickered a grateful smile and then lowered her eyes again to their permanent focus on the ground—except when she felt it safe to steal a worshipful glance at Joseph.

At the Thanks Giving Festival, a council of the Clan Mothers was convened. Molly's mother sat on the mat at the head of the circle, as she had ever since Little Abraham's wife relinquished it.

Someone Lends Her a Flower began the council with: "Sisters—I am no longer a living part of our *orenda*. As our grandmothers did before me, it is time for me to step back from the council fire, to stand behind a woman whose blood still flows through the unborn who will have to live with our decisions. It is time for me to stand in the shadows and give what advice an old woman can to one who is still bound fully to this life.

"Sisters—since the Strawberry Festival, we have talked long and fully among ourselves as to who should take my place on this mat and who should wear the name Someone Lends Her a Flower. I thought they both should be the same woman, but I kept as quiet as I could, knowing that my *onikonhra* might not see clearly on this matter. But it seems yours saw the same as mine, for now we are all agreed that our new Elder Sister and the new Someone Lends Her a Flower will both be my daughter, One Against Two."

Molly was dazed. She'd had a dream long ago that she'd

never told anyone—that she and her brother were sitting on either wing of the eagle at the crown of the Tree of Peace.

They raised her to her feet and led her over to the mat her mother was standing away from. Her mother whispered in her ear: "Don't be afraid—I'll tell you what to do. Until you get sick of being told."

Molly looked around at the expectant faces of the Clan Mothers. They looked different from this end of the circle. "Sisters . . . Ahem, sisters . . ." She always broke out in a bit of a sweat under her overdress whenever she had to address a council, but now she was positively dripping. "If I am to be the one that speaks first over every string of wampum, how do the rest of you expect to ever say a word?"

The laughter was such that Molly suspected that the men and children and younger women feasting under the stars must be wondering which of the venerable Oyanders inside the ceremonial longhouse had tripped on her skirt and fallen into the soup pot.

The blue parlor at Johnson Hall became a meeting place for any Canienga Oyander with an opinion to express on any subject, or any woman of the Wolf Clan from any of the Six Nations. Sir growled at Molly, "I can't walk into me own demmed house anymore without dodgin' some tobacco-chewin' harridan or trippin' over their caterwaulin' progeny," but she knew he was proud of her.

She was sitting with some of those harridans, trading guesses on what might come of the fact that the Virginians had fought a battle against the Shawnee to make them stay on their side of the Stanwix Line, when Horace shuffled in and announced, "Um, Mistress Molly . . . I don't mean to come barging in like the dog what smelt the bitch, but . . . It's your brother, you see, he—" and Joseph moped in and sat on the floor. Horace shrugged helplessly and went on about his business.

Joseph didn't say a word, just sat there looking as though his favorite horse had broken its leg. Molly attempted to carry on with her conversation, but it was stilted at best. When the Oyanders had gone, she said: "What has happened?"

"Augustine!" he wailed. "They are sending him to join his regiment in the West Indies! What am I to do?"

"You must have known something like that would happen eventually. White soldiers have to go where they're told."

"What am I to do?"

"I suppose you will have to find yourself another blood brother. You have plenty of good friends who—"

"That is exactly what the Reverend Dr. Stuart said. He even offered to stand in himself." Molly tried to picture the reverend at a scalp dance. "Neither of you understands. A man can't choose another Friend while the first still lives."

"I try to understand, Binds Two. If I could take away thy sorrow, I would."

"Why does everyone I love get taken away from me?"

"Not everyone, I hope."

"Maybe I'll go get drunk."

"You don't need to go anywhere to do that. There is a decanter of Madeira on the table, and several taverns' worth of barrels and bottles in the cellar."

In the end, he drank two small glasses of Madeira, which at least put a little blood back in his cheeks. He stood up and said: "Perhaps the best thing for me would be to go back to Fort Hunter and to work. We've almost finished the catechism." He kissed her softly and murmured: "I thank thee, Someone Lends Her a Flower."

"For what?"

"For being my sister, I suppose."

CHAPTER 34

Joseph married again, but not for long. The doctors and the medicine societies had reached the same conclusion for a change: the same disease that had taken Margaret would kill her sister before the spring. Joseph had a notion that it would give Susanna some happiness to have had a home, children, and a husband she could call her own for at least a few months of her life. And the notion was far from entirely charity on his part. She bloomed again and outlived all the wise prognostications: spring was ripening into summer when she coughed her last.

The week after Susanna's funeral, Joseph took his children to Canajoharie for the Strawberry Festival. As soon as they were inside the stockade, he set Christina down, and Isaac took her hand to help her toddle along. Isaac could be such an affectionate boy. It was only the missing of his mother that tied him up in knots sometimes.

Joseph let them wander off among the dancers and the drummers and the hordes of other children milling around the women handing out strawberry cakes. Virtually everyone in the crowd was a relative of Isaac and Christina's and would look out for them.

"Binds Two." Joseph turned to see Big William leaning against the painted post. Over the last two years, he'd seen more of the Reverend Dr. Stuart than Big William. "What's a good Christian doing at a pagan festival?"

"What's a good pagan doing leaning against the painted post?"

"It won't fall over."

"Not if a man of normal human proportions leaned against it."

A boy and a girl approached, bearing a birchbark basket between them. A Keeper of the Faith hovered along behind them. Joseph knew what was in the basket without looking. The first ripe strawberries found in the forest were mixed with water and maple syrup to make a spring medicine for body and soul.

Big William raised the basket to his mouth and drank, wiped the juice off his chin with the back of his hand and said to Joseph: "Would a Christian drink?"

"This Christian can use any medicine he can get."

As Joseph raised the basket, he smelled the pine gum used to seal the seams, then smelled strawberries. The taste of strawberries and maple sugar sweetening clear water put him back with his father and mother keeping Canienga customs among the Mingoes. He heard his father saying: "This Ohio water is well enough with berries in it, but someday you will taste *our* river."

The taste of the strawberry wine did something else as well. Despite the Reverend Wheelock and the Reverend Dr. Stuart, Joseph found himself feeling more at peace about Margaret and Susanna than any gospel readings had made him—as much at peace as one could feel about dead lovers. There was something mysteriously right about the idea that the first fruits of life returning from the winter should be the same that grew along the path of death.

As Joseph looked around at the other celebrants, it also seemed particularly fitting that not all of them were Caniengas, or even Hodenosaune. William Johnson's wasn't the only white face that appeared at Canajoharie festivals. It added to Joseph's feeling of peace to be reminded that the varying strains of humanity in the Mohawk Valley had grown into good neighbors, the kind that tend their own gardens but attend each other's celebrations. The Herkimer brothers were there, as was the ferryman whose yellow beard was growing paler with time, and the Scottish midwife who'd helped deliver all of Joseph's nieces and nephews, and—

"Look at that one, Lemuel, with the leaves on his head!"

"Maybe someday I'll buy you a hat like that."

"Cain't be much good for keepin' the rain off."

"But real good for jumpin' up and down and goin' 'Woo-woo-woo-woo!' "

They were a group of whites Joseph had never seen before. From their flat accents, they were immigrants from one of the other colonies, apparently one where there were few True People left to learn manners from.

Joseph could feel Big William swelling up even bigger with anger. He put his hand on William's forearm and shook his head. "They are guests in our castle. We mustn't harm them."

"I wasn't going to harm them, just take them by the wrists and ankles and toss them out over the stockade."

The white group were mimicking the dancers and laughing and talking loudly among themselves, as though part of the crowd at a circus:

"They pray to them leaves, you know—think there's gods inside 'em."

"Stop joshin' me."

"I ain't. They'll get right down on their knees and pray to a tree. Or an old lump of rock or a pile of pigeon droppin's. Hell, they'll pray to anything."

"Well what'd you expect? Ignorant savages is ignorant savages."

"Land sakes—look at that old ugly one with the tattoos all over her face."

"If'n you had a face like that, wouldn't you tattoo it, too?"

Joseph could see the Caniengas within earshot having a difficult time ignoring the rudeness and carrying on with the festival. But it would've been extremely ill-mannered to point out to ill-mannered people that they were being ill-mannered. So the products of a higher civilization were allowed to carry on braying and mocking, blithely unaware that the only reason they could have their circus was that the menagerie were all well-brought-up Caniengas.

All except, of course, Miss Molly Brant. Joseph saw her stalking toward the gawkers with steam coming out of her ears, and decided it might be best if he followed her. He'd almost caught up with her when she planted herself in front of the circus-goers and said: "Are you aware of the fact that virtually every one of these ignorant savages knows the English language well enough to understand every word you've said?"

"Land sakes, Lemuel—she speaks English better'n you!"

"I would hardly call that an accomplishment to boast of."

"I believe what my sister is trying to impart to you is that we do have eyes and ears."

"Watch out, Lemuel—he's wearin' a knife!"

"Oh, hell, these are tame Injuns. They'd no more brace a white man than—"

"That particular tame Injun," Gets Business Done's voice rumbled over Joseph's shoulder, "could eviscerate ye before y'could pronounce 'Please, Jesus.' Once saw 'im do exactly that to a Frenchman outside Fort Niagara. And his sister's the mean one in the family.

"So it's for yer own good that I'm advisin' ye that if y'don't either start conductin' yerselves like proper guests or vacate the premises forthwith, I'll have ye up on charges for trespass."

"Ya cain't go chargin' trespassin' in Injun huts! 'Tain't private property!"

"I can and I will."

"Come along, Lemuel. That's Sir William Johnson. He can do what he likes."

"Just 'cause'n you got a 'Sir' in front of your name," Lemuel barked as he backed away, "you think you can lord it over all creation. When the day comes that the Sons of Liberty rise up, you'll larn just what that German king on the English throne is worth. And so'll your Injun friends."

" 'Sons of Liberty,' " Sir William snorted as the Big Knives disappeared toward the gate. "After all their tub-thumpin' about tyranny and taxes, they ain't been able to rouse out a ring of dancers around their demmed Liberty Bushes lately except by servin' out free rum.

"Well, Molly m'gel, shall we go sample the good ladies' strawberry puddin' again, just to see if we guessed right about the taste of brandy?"

"I'll follow you in a moment. Binds Two—I thank thee."

"For what?"

"For being my brother, I suppose."

"It is a councillor's duty to step in between two parties quarreling in the longhouse. And someone had to do the Christian thing and stand between you and those poor fools."

She kissed him on the cheek and followed after her husband. Joseph turned and was surprised to find Big William standing not an arm's length behind him, instead of leaning against the painted post where he'd left him, then was surprised at himself for being surprised; of course Big William would've drifted along behind him to watch his back.

It seemed to Joseph he was seeing William clearly for the first time in a long time: the wide, green eyes that pretended to be less sharp than they were, the fierce loyalties and the love of a good fight, the never-to-be-resolved confusion of being not entirely the son of King Hendrick or of Sir William Johnson. . . .

Joseph said: "William of Canajoharie, it seems to me that you have many half brothers and stepbrothers. But neither thou nor I have a Brother."

"I thought I did since the day someone smashed a baggata-way stick on someone's nose."

CHAPTER 35

Although Juba felt a touch disloyal about it, she did look forward to the times when Sir William went away to Fish House, or—as now—to Albany on business. When Sir William wasn't at home, Mistress Molly would come down to the kitchen for a cup of tea before going to bed. Not that it was treated as an expected thing. Mistress Molly would just appear on the cellar stairs and say something like: "Oh, Juba, are you still awake? I'm not quite sleepy myself. Perhaps we should have a cup of tea, if you don't have things to do."

So whenever Sir William was gone, Juba would rush the kitchen girls to finish up the supper dishes, and rush herself to make sure everything she would need to cook breakfast was in order, all the while accidentally leaving the kettle full of water on the hearth.

Juba was just hanging up the last scoured skillet when she heard the voice from the stairs; "Oh, Juba, are you still awake. . . ?" While the tea was steeping, Mistress Molly said: "I had a letter from Peter Warren today. It sounds as though he's outgrowing the school in Montreal as quickly as the one in Albany. Sir William was talking last week about a school in Philadelphia where Peter Warren could learn business. 'Not business like some bleedin' shopkeeper, but the business a gentleman needs to know to manage 'is estates.' "

"He sure is one smart boy, Mistah Peter Warren. A lot smarter'n Sir John."

"So is the average fence post."

They both giggled like kitchen girls sneaking jokes about the butler. As Mistress Molly sipped her tea, Juba leaned back and took a look at her. It seemed to Juba that at thirty-five or thereabouts, Molly was just growing into herself. The big names and responsibilities that her own people had given her, and the authority of being queen of Johnson Hall, seemed to sit easy and natural on her now. The fine lines around the up-turned corners of the mouth and nose only made her look more human. But Juba doubted that those black eyes would ever look completely civilized. Perhaps it was their odd, blown-dewdrop shape, but Juba suspected it was the glint of mischief that no amount of years seemed likely to put out.

Mistress Molly leaned across the table and whispered: "Juba, I'm pregnant again."

"That can't be. You still feeding little Mistah Frederick."

"I thought the same. My mother tells me it is unusual for a nursing mother to conceive, not impossible."

"I never heard the like."

"It must be true. I'm more than two moons late."

"Won't Sir William be pleased when he get home!"

"I wonder," Molly said dubiously. "The house is overflowing with progeny already."

"There ain't nothing he like more, no matter how he grumble about it."

"Perhaps. But it does make for a lot of children to provide inheritances for."

"He don't mind that. Ain't nothing Sir William like more than giving things away—so long as he got no use for them no more." Mistress Molly smiled at the joke, but the smile looked forced, so Juba added quickly: "Besides, the way you looking after him, there'll be ten children more before anyone inherit anything."

Mistress Molly finished her cup of tea, and Juba raised the pot to offer another. Molly put her hand over her cup and said, "It's past time for Freddy's feeding. Then again, I would've heard him if he'd wakened. He's usually so punctual. . . . Well, let sleeping infants lie, as Sir William says," and she moved her hand off the cup.

Halfway through the second cup, Molly began to yawn luxuriously, and sighed: "I suppose I'd best be lighting myself to bed while I can still climb stairs. Thank you for the tea."

"It's your tea, Mizt'ess Molly."

"It's your kitchen, Juba. Good night."

"Good night, Mizt'ess Molly."

As the light of Molly's candle moved away through the gloom between the kitchen table and the cellar stairs, Juba busied herself putting away the tea things, humming under her breath. She was just hanging up the rinsed teacups when she heard a sound from overhead: a muted, high-pitched groan that sounded not exactly human. She snatched the candle off the table and hurried up the stairs.

The only light showing in the hall was from under the door of the master bedroom. Juba was about to knock when she heard a stifled whimpering beyond the door. She turned the knob and opened it.

Mistress Molly was on the floor with her back against the bed frame and both hands over her mouth, her streaming eyes staring at the cradle in front of her. Juba started toward the cradle, but her mistress let out an emphatic "Mm!" through her muffling hands and shook her head, then took her hands away just long enough to gasp: "He's dead."

"You can't be sure—"

"I . . . know . . ." The words came out in an uneven whisper, as though her lungs were stammering. "It's the same . . ."

Juba understood. It had happened once before, to the baby girl born between Master George and Miss Martha. Juba also understood why Mistress Molly wasn't shrieking aloud. The younger children were sleeping just across the hallway, and the older ones just above.

Juba crouched down and put her arms around her. Just now, Mistress Molly wasn't Mistress Molly, or an Iroquois chief, only a woman who'd come upstairs to nurse her baby and found him dead.

CHAPTER 36

Sir Big Billy Johnson sat ruminating in his hip bath in front of his blazing bedroom hearth. It had been "his" bedroom for eight months now, ever since little Susanna took up residence in the new cradle. Molly had burned the one Freddy had died in, just in case it housed some lingering infection.

Susanna wasn't yet able to sleep a night through, which meant her father couldn't when they were in the same room. Once he was awake, he was awake, no matter what time of night. So Molly had relocated to what had been her sewing room. She still paid the occasional visit to his bed—one of which had conceived the probability that the same sleeping arrangements would continue indefinitely. Time was when he could snore on undisturbed with half a dozen infants caterwauling around his bed, and had, but those days were gone.

The day had come up blustery and cool, so he'd taken it as a sign that he should spend the morning giving himself a good scrub and soaking his hip and drinking hot punch and letting his mind drift through the steam, while Horace fed the fire and shuttled the kettle up and down the back stairs.

His mind drifted to his still-unconsummated eighty thousand acres. Tucked away somewhere among his papers was a yellowing deed for eighty thousand acres of Mohawk land, which would round out the last corner of his estates just nicely. But the long-done deal still needed royal approval. Every London agent he'd employed to procure it eventually wrote back a variation on: "If you could only represent the matter in person . . ."

The notion wasn't without its charms. He hadn't strode the streets of London for thirty years: the spangled playgoing mob in Drury Lane, the beaux and belles of Marleybone . . . particularly the belles. They'd entertained him well enough in his youth, but what a swath he would've cut if he'd been the wealthy, titled military hero he was today. Oh well, in his time he'd cut enough of a swath on this side of the ocean to satisfy any man—if "man" and "satisfy" weren't fundamentally incompatible.

A trip to London would give him an opportunity to have a few face-to-face words with the gentlemen in the Colonial Office about the danger of getting too complacent. Although a few wise reversals in Parliament had made the North American colonies placid enough in general, people like that demmed yokel at the Strawberry Festival had gotten into the habit of running riot to get their way. It would take more than a couple of years of relatively inoffensive government to wean them of the habit.

But the thought of going to London and securing his eighty thousand acres had a bitter undertaste to it. Their only purpose was to bequeath a principality to his son's sons in an unbroken line of Mohawk Valley Johnsons marching on to the crack of doom. But his son had no sons, at least no legitimate ones, and showed no signs of getting any. So where was the joy in the eighty thousand acres?

Not even Molly seemed able to understand why he would rather see John disinherited than married to that tavern wench Clarissa Putnam. Perhaps no one could understand who hadn't been born to Anne Warren Johnson of County Meath. Anne Warren had been born in the manor house, but had made herself a love match with a tenant of the Earl of Fingal. Anne and her husband would still be lying under paupers' stones if their oversized lout of a son hadn't made himself rich enough to commission a marble monument. And Big Billy hadn't spent his life crawling out of the bog to see his heirs slide back into it.

The bedroom door swung wide open and Horace stepped across it with no visible kettle. "Sorry to disjointify your comforts, Sir William, but your son's here to see you."

"Which son?"

"Beg pardon, Sir William—sometimes it gets hard to remember you got more'n one. Sir John."

"Well, fetch 'im in, and give me a hand out of this demmed

contraption, and hand me a towel, and close that demmed door
before I freeze off what's left of me manhood."

"Which shall I do first, Sir William?"

"All of 'em! Ye're supposed to be a bleedin' gentleman's
gentleman, ain't ye? Doin' four things at once ought to be yer
stock-in-bleedin'-trade."

By the time Horace fetched Sir John in, Sir William was
more or less dried off, and in his dressing gown and furry
house moccasins. John said: "Good morning, Pater."

"Don't see what's so bleedin' good about it. The minute I
decide a mild chill in the air means I should order up a bath,
Fahrenheit's bleedin' thermo-meter drops ten bleedin' degrees.
How're things at Fort Johnson?"

"In a state of flux, Pater."

"In a bloody flux? What the divil is that supposed to
mean?"

"I have decided to be married—pending your approval, of
course."

Big Billy felt his bile rising dangerously. "We've had this
out before, John."

"The lady in question is Miss Mary Watts, or 'Polly,' as she
is known to her intimate friends. She is the daughter of the
Honorable John Watts, President of the Council of New York
and—"

"I know who bleedin' Johnny Watts is. Come to me, arms,
y'rascal." John stepped forward stiffly and stood at attention
while his father threw his arms around him and slapped his
back. But Big Billy was too transported to be thrown off by
anything. "How long has this been goin' on? Ye subtle little
rascal. This calls for champagne. Horace—fetch a bottle and
two glasses. No, three—bring one along for yerself. No, make
it four—fetch yer mistress as well.

"Well? What are ye standin' around lookin' cow-faced for?
When yer master barks, ye're meant to jump."

"Maybe you don't recolleck, Sir William—Mistress Molly is
at Canajoharie for the day."

"Well obviously I don't bleedin' recolleck, do I—or I
wouldn't have said to fetch her. We'll make do with just the
three of us. And see that a measure of rum is served out to all
the servants and field hands, so they can toast the marriage of
the heir." He turned back to his son. "Well, John. Well, John.

Well . . ." He sucked in a big enough lungful of air to make a start at expressing what he had to say, but all that came out was: ". . . John."

A month after Sir John and Lady Johnson took up residence in Fort Johnson and Clarissa Putnam and her children departed with the reverse dowry Sir William had settled on them, Molly's brother came to Johnson Hall on business and remarked to her with an odd smirk: "You seem to have been legitimized, or elevated in a way."

"How is that?"

"The existence of a Lady Johnson has necessitated the coining of a new phrase in the lexicon of the Mohawk Valley—or anywhere else Sir William Johnson is spoken of, I suspect. There is 'Lady Johnson' and there is 'the Brown Lady Johnson.' "

"Where did you hear that?"

"Everywhere. The seamstress says: 'I've been hired to make a new gown for the Brown Lady Johnson'; the new ensign at Fort Hunter says, 'So you're the brother of the Brown Lady Johnson. . . .' "

"I'm not sure I like that."

"If they didn't like *you*, Mistress Molly, they wouldn't have coined the title."

It was arranged for Sir William Johnson to sail for England in July. Not long before he was due to leave, Molly found him out in the garden feeding the peacocks and sniffing at the sassafras in the air. He said: "Demmit, Molly, if I have to spend a few months kickin' around dirty old London town on me own, it might just as well be in the winter when it's gray everywhere, though I'd love ye to see Hyde Park in high summer. . . ."

"If the ladies of New York disapprove of me—"

"Who did? Who said they did? If any of them pursemouthed, dried-up old bitches has been cruel to ye, by God and little fishes I'll—"

"No one has been cruel to me. But it would have been uncomfortable, would it not, if I'd gone to John's wedding? How much more so would it be in London?"

" 'Tain't the same demmed thing at all. They'd be climbin'

over each other's shoulders to invite ye to tea. London society's a far cry from these pious demmed colonials. Ha! After forty years I suppose I'm a demmed colonial m'self—but at least I ain't pious. Won't y'come to London with me, Molly?"

"I'll be here when you get back."

He made arrangements to sail in September, but when the leaves turned the valley red and gold, he decided it would be a pity to leave before they fell. On a gray October day he climbed into the carriage and propped his left boot up on his traveling trunk. By now Molly was so thoroughly pregnant again, there was no question of her accompanying him. She called Horace to fetch a stirrup cup of Madeira and a glass for herself. She raised hers to her husband and did her best to imitate his broguey English: "May the road rise to meet you; may the wind be always at your back; the sun shine warm upon your face; the rain fall soft upon your fields; and until we meet again may God hold you in the hollow of his hand."

He sniffed and croaked, "Demmit, Molly . . ." then raised his own glass and bellowed: "May the Lord keep ye in his hand—and never close his fist too tight on ye." The carriage wheels ground the smashed glass into the gravel.

She'd had to live without him for months at a time before, but this was going to be more like a year. Fortunately, in December someone came to Johnson Hall to help fill the gap in her life and in her heart. She was having a back-easing lie-down in the master bedroom that was hers again while the master was gone, when she heard the back door open and close, followed by a cacophony of children squealing and cascading down the stairs. What they were squealing was: "Peter!"

It was almost worth missing her husband to steal a chance to get to know her son again. At fourteen, Peter Warren was tall and elegant, with a fencer's grace and black Canienga eyes which, for all his quick intelligence, seemed to be perpetually perplexed. Although George was almost six years old now, Peter Warren had been her only son for so long, she'd probably never lose the habit of thinking of him that way.

His brother and sisters seemed just as delighted to have him home as she was. He would take them on candlelight explorations of the tunnels between the cellar and the blockhouses, and sit them down in the eerie dark to tell them ghost stories.

Just before Christmas, several of the Oyanders from
Canajoharie and the Lower Castle came to trade guesses on
what might come of the fact that a bunch of white men dis-
guised as "Mohawks" had dumped a shipload of tea into Boston harbor. The colony governors and the military officers
seemed to be very angry about it.

The informal council of Clan Mothers sat in a semicircle on
the floor in front of the hall fireplace. All except Someone
Lends Her a Flower, whose any-day-now pumpkin belly relegated her to a chair.

The matter of the Boston Tea Party finally resolved itself
around the fact that the "Mohawk" disguises didn't appear to
have fooled very many people. Therefore any retribution from
the crown would come down on the Bostonians, where it belonged. If and when the king showed any signs of thinking the
real Mohawks had anything to do with it, then the Canienga
would send a message to open his eyes.

The Oyanders were just on their way out when Horace
herded the children in from skating on the pond. Peter Warren
had a black eye and his coat was torn. He said stiffly by way
of explanation: "Ezra Fonda called me a dirty Tory."

"What does that mean?"

"I don't know."

The other Clan Mothers were trying to look severe, and not
doing any better job of it than the Bostonians trying to look
like Caniengas. Molly turned to Horace. "Do you know what
it means?"

"Well, Miss Molly, there's some folks—some of the ruder
sort—they're startin' to use 'Tory' for to mean someone who's
loyal to the king."

"That seems hardly an insult."

"Some folks think it is—like I said, miss, the ruder sort."

"Did you get there in time to stop it?"

"Well, ahem . . . by the time I got there, Mistress Molly,
Master Peter seemed to have the sitty-ation well in hand, as
you can see by the state of his'n. I sure hope Ezra Fonda's
ma's a dab hand with the sticking plaster."

Molly took Peter Warren down to the kitchen to bathe his
skinned knuckles. Juba cut off a piece of beefsteak for his eye,
saying: "I wouldn't give a pinch of snuff for no boy what

didn't come home with a black eye oncet or twice. Did you wallop him good, Mistah Peter?"

"I would've walloped him a good deal better if he hadn't run."

Molly said sternly: "The next time someone calls you a Tory, you tell him you are and proud of it."

"Yes, Mother. But what if that just eggs him on to persecute me further?"

"Then you wallop him good."

Nancy Johnson was born on one of the last days of 1773. After Frederick's death, Molly was in the same anxious panic for the first few weeks of Nancy's life as she'd been with Susanna, spending day and night in the nursery.

Molly finally emerged to discover that everyone else on Turtle Island was in a state of anxious panic. It wasn't so much the Tea Party itself as what the Massachusetts Assembly had done in response—namely, nothing. All the colonies were worried about how the king would respond. In the Mohawk Valley people were worse than worried. They were worrying whether they *should* be worried, and wanted Sir William Johnson home to tell them.

Molly was soon presented with another reason why her people wanted her husband home. She was sitting in the blue parlor nursing Nancy when she heard a horse and cutter coming up the drive. She couldn't look out to see who it was because on brutally cold days like this the downstairs windows were always shuttered tight.

A footman went to the door. Molly lowered her overdress over Nancy against the coming gust of winter air. There was a murmuring in the hallway and the thump of feet stomping snow off—feet in moccasins, not boots—and then Molly's mother and Carrying News came into the parlor. Molly didn't see them very often these days; they had their own crop of children to attend to, just as she had hers.

Molly dispatched the footman to have Juba send up a tea tray and to fetch the nursemaid to take charge of Nancy. She gestured her mother and Carrying News into chairs by the fire. It was obvious they'd come to say something in particular, but it would've been bad manners for them to broach it immediately, and she was too well-brought-up to ask them directly. So the three of them chatted about her children and theirs, and the state of the ice on the river, and Little Abraham's rheumatism.

Then Molly's mother spidered her liver-spotted fingers around the arms of her chair and said: "That meadow by Schoharie Creek, where the Canienga let Gets Business Done pasture his bull when it was bad-tempered . . . He sold that meadow to the Herkimer brothers."

"I know. I witnessed the deed."

Carrying News said: "It wasn't his to sell."

"It wasn't?"

Both pairs of eyes looked down at the floor and both gray heads shook slowly from side to side. Molly's mother raised her eyes again and said: "And those eighty thousand acres Hendrick sold so long ago, that Gets Business Done has gone to get the king's approval of . . . Hendrick never sold them. I remember him telling me he'd signed a paper giving Gets Business Done the right to rent out pieces of that land to white farmers and share the money with the owners: the Canienga Nation."

"That isn't what the deed says."

"Hendrick was never much for reading when there was someone there to tell him what he was signing and save him the trouble."

Carrying News said: "Binds Two is caught in the middle of a fight between a white farmer at Fort Hunter and the council of the Lower Castle. The farmer has a piece of paper saying Sir William Johnson sold him a piece of land the council had given to Sir William Johnson. Only the council never gave it. It was just one Royaner who didn't even have the right to call himself that after the Clan Mothers had stripped away his name for getting drunk too often."

"My brother has said nothing to me of this."

"No one knows whether to speak to you of these things or not. People think, since you are Gets Business Done's wife, that perhaps you are part of all these things."

Molly felt a prickling at the back of her neck. She said with deliberate precision: "So what you have come to tell me is that the chattering little bird Tskleleli has been flitting about singing evil stories about the best friend the Caniengas ever had, and about me, and no one has had the courtesy to come and ask us whether there is any truth to his twitterings."

"That is why we came—to say that the only way to stop the poison spreading is for the Canienga to sit down with Gets Business Done in the open, and discover what is true and what is not."

That mollified her to a certain extent. They hadn't come to accuse, only to find a way to deal with the accusations. She said: "As soon as he comes home, we will set a day for that to happen. But you may find that those who are eager to whisper rumors behind Gets Business Done's back will melt away when it comes to lying to his face."

But when she began to look back carefully through the sheafs of deeds and transfer papers in his strongbox, she began to notice places where two and two seemed to somehow add up to five. She was at his desk all afternoon, feeding Nancy abstractedly whenever she woke up, lighting candles from the guttering stubs of the last ones. She was there late into the night, and still came up with nothing but myriad pieces of a puzzle that wouldn't fit together. She grew so dazed and exhausted that she began to hear laughter—the laughter of King Hendrick and Gets Business Done at the great joke of the Stevens Purchase.

He came home much earlier than predicted. Peter Warren had barely headed back to Philadelphia when the hired cutter bearing his father came jingling up the road through the woods. She wanted desperately to take him aside immediately and confront him with the rumors, so he could tell her they had no grounds. But that would have been stealing his homecoming from the children.

After the distribution of presents and the cooing introduction to Nancy, after the demolishment of Juba's splendid turkey and the shooing of the last overexcited daughter off to bed, she prepared herself to get down to business with Gets Business Done. But before she could begin, he heaved himself out of his chair, went to the window and said: "Can't see a demmed thing—what with the candles in here and the belly of night beyond the glass." Not to mention that the shutters were still fastened outside. "But I can see every snowed-in flower bed in m'mind's eye as clear as day.

"Demmed odd—there I was in the capital of the world, with all its wonders me oyster, and all I could think about was: Is the old sycamore still standin'? Did the new slates on the roof hold? Did Molly have a boy or a gel, and did she come through it safe . . . ?

"They were on at me again in London to be the next Royal Governor of New York. I could no more live in New York Town than the moon. Not while there's a Mohawk Valley to come home to. D'ye think, Molly m'darlin', a man could get to lovin' a piece of country too much?"

"No. But he could get to loving too much of it."

He turned to her with his broad forehead furled quizzically. She told him what her mother and Carrying News had come to tell her. He said: "Ah, that's it."

"That's what?"

"Ye've been holdin' somethin' back since I came through the door."

"I . . . looked through your old deeds and papers. There were things in them I couldn't understand."

"Not surprisin'. That's forty years of accumulated hodge-podge done by different clerks and secretaries and scrawled on scraps of paper usin' a horse rump for a desk."

"But you could explain them to me?"

"I doubt I could explain 'em to *m'self*, not without wadin' through the whole rats' nest to refresh me memory."

"I think," she said carefully, "that you should do that, then."

"Demmit, Molly—after twenty years of livin' with me, d'ye think me a thief just because the little bird that sings stories has been flittin' about?"

She didn't know what to say. It was the last thing she wanted to believe, but she'd seen too many times that it was precisely what she didn't want to believe which was true.

"Molly . . . ?"

"The only way to quiet that bird is to take it by the throat and face it."

"I do have a few other matters on me plate just at present. I don't doubt the Department of Northern Indian Affairs has put off a year's worth of decisions with no superintendent for four months."

"What could be more important to the Department of Indian Affairs than the superintendent's good name among the Indians?"

"Even once I get the time, it'll take me a divil of a time to sort through it all."

"How long?"

"Demmed if I can say. To be sure, what say ye tell yer fellow councillors we'll kindle a fire here come autumn and I'll answer all their questions then."

"That's too long. The longer you wait, the worse it will fester. Besides, autumn is the time for the Great Council at Onondaga."

"Summer, then. Sometime in August."

"July."

"Ye drive a hard bargain."

"There's nothing wrong with an honest hard bargain."

She looked at him staring out the window no one could see through. She got up and went to him and raised her hand to his shoulder. "Gets Business Done—thou and I are now done with the business that had to be done. I shall not speak of it or think of it again until the day I see thee stand beside the council fire and choke that little bird to death." To prove it, she moved on cheerily to: "In between bearing daughters and all, I still managed to finish the inventory."

"Inventory . . . ?"

"You asked me to make an inventory of everything in the house, so you could make out your will now that John's settled down to producing legitimate heirs."

His hawk-browed eyes shifted off her to her reflection in the window, then slid off even that to a blank spot on the glass. He murmured, "Ah yes, me will . . ." and raised his hand to scratch at the blank spot. Then he suddenly looked directly at her. "Y'do know, Molly, that ye're the great love of my life and always have been, don't ye? Despite whatever may be said or written or interpreted slantwise . . . y'do *know* that, don't ye?"

CHAPTER 37

The rest of the world appeared to have taken leave of their senses while Big Billy'd been away from Johnson Hall. The demmed Bostonians' Tea Party hadn't just been an annoying prank; it had cost the East India Company *money*. Parliament had reacted in equally lunatic fashion, by closing the port of Boston until the tea was paid for, and performing drastic surgery on the government of Massachusetts with a few strokes of a pen.

There was more lunacy in the west. Despite the Stanwix Line, another bloody little war had bubbled up along the Ohio, with back-country militia massacring whole Indian villages whenever a horse was stolen—usually villages of a tribe other than the horse thief's.

Things weren't much saner in the Mohawk Valley. The Royaners and Oyanders were determined that Gets Business Done answer all the grumblings about his land dealings. It really was a bit much, after forty years of standing by the Mohawks, to have them suddenly turn around and demand an accounting. All right, so maybe he had smudged the occasional number on a deed, or served out a bit more rum than usual if there happened to be a particularly pretty piece of property on the table, but since when was that a hanging matter? He'd always stuck religiously within the form of British law, which was a good deal more than could be said for any of the colonization companies or frontier farmers.

The date fixed for having it out with the Mohawks turned out to be the day the new courthouse in Johnstown was to open. The Mohawk Valley was becoming so densely settled that it had been declared a separate county, with Johnstown as the county seat. One couldn't very well have a seat of government without a courthouse and a jail. The local magistrate would be, of course, Sir William Johnson.

The night before, he was at his desk poring through his files of yellowing deeds, trying to concentrate through the rain and thunder battering at the window, when Horace announced he had visitors. It was seven concerned gentlemen from Albany and New York Town. They did have an exquisite sense of timing.

Six of them were men Sir William knew from doing business with their shipping companies or banking houses. The seventh was a tall, gaunt personage he hadn't met before. All seven of them looked not unlike drowned rats. Fortunately, Molly was busy with the children, where she couldn't see the boots making puddles on the fresh-waxed floor. "Good evenin', gentlemen. 'Tain't a fit night for man nor beast. Bartholomew—I believe a round of hot buttered rum would be in order. Oh, but I'm afraid it is Jamaica rum. . . ."

"There is no longer any need to forego imported spirits, now that all the tariffs have been removed. Except, of course—"

"I ain't bleedin' likely to offer a man a cup of *tea* on a night like this. Speakin' of which, what brings ye out so far from home in weather when all sane ducks are battenin' down the hatches?"

The eldest one began: "The storm caught us by surprise—"

"But we would have come anyway," the tall, gaunt one cut him off. "These are not days for Patriots to be hiding in their beds."

"At any rate, Sir William, you are aware that there is to be a meeting in Philadelphia of elected representatives of all the colonies? The First Continental Congress . . . ?"

"It'll be the bleedin' *last* if ye get up to any shenanigans like yer friends in Boston."

"Heavens no, Sir William. All that the congress intends is to compose a petition to the Crown that we can all stand behind. It is well known that as you go, so goes Tryon County and the Six Nations' Confederacy. The representatives from the other colonies are bound to ask us where you stand."

"Where I stand on what?"

"On the Intolerable Acts."

"Which acts would those be?"

"The laws punishing the Commonwealth of Massachusetts," which was about what he'd expected to hear, "and the Quebec Act."

"The Quebec Act? What the bleedin' hell's intolerable about it?"

"By extending the borders of the Province of Quebec to the Ohio, the Crown has delivered the virgin heartland of North America into the hands of the Pope."

"If y'can't abide Catholics, there's a hundred and fifty Catholic ex-Highland soldiers settled just downstream of here, I suggest ye go tell 'em so to their faces. For that matter, I was born Catholic m'self."

"We all believe in religious tolerance, Sir William. These colonies were founded on the principle that all men have a right to their religious beliefs. But under the jurisdiction of Quebec, Catholics can hold public office—"

"*If* they sign a bleedin' oath that in temporal matters they recognize no higher authority than the king! What say we have done with all this religious flummery and admit that what's got yer backs up about the Quebec Act is the Governor of Quebec might actually respect the Stanwix Line and keep ye from stealin' the Indian Territories for yerselves."

"What say we have done with *all* flummery," the cadaverous stranger said, "and speak of what we came to speak of. Many Patriots fear we dare not go too far, because we cannot hope to prevail against professional soldiers. But you and your ragtag militia and Iroquois did precisely that at Lake George— and it shocked the world—and again at Niagara."

An awful stillness took possession of the room, broken only by a creaking that Big Billy identified after the fact as his own chair responding to his back going taut.

"What he means to say," the eldest gentleman put in quickly, "is that if the military authorities knew that Sir William Johnson and the Iroquois were in sympathy with us, they'd be more inclined to recommend that our protests be listened to."

Big Billy sipped his toddy and said softly: "Oh, is *that* what he was sayin'? I'm demmed relieved to hear that. And so should ye be. Because I *am* a magistrate of the Crown, and it sounded to me like what he was speakin' of was armed rebellion and treason."

"If this be treason," the gaunt Patriot proclaimed, "make the most of it!"—although his six companions looked like they'd be just as happy if Sir William made as little of it as possible, thank you very much.

"Sufferin' Judas, gentlemen, I understand how it galls ye to be at the mercy of every shift of the wind in London—"

"With all respect, Sir William, you were not born here, so how can you understand—"

"I was born in *Ireland*, laddy-buck. If y'think Massachusetts is bein' bleedin' punished, ye should someday spend a pleasure tour followin' Cromwell's trail across the green hills of Erin."

The skeletal gentleman opened his mouth to reply and then abruptly closed it again as Molly wandered in, glittering with gold earrings and bracelets and bangles. She raised an eyebrow at the rain drips on the floor, poured herself a glass of Madeira and settled onto a chair by the hearth.

There was a round of how-do-you-do's and a few general remarks on the suddenness of the thunderstorm that was still rattling the shutters, then nothing more. Sir William looked around at the mute delegation and said: "Well, is that all ye galloped miles through the deluge to say?"

"Begging your pardon, ma'am . . ." the firebrand muttered in Molly's general direction, then turned to Sir William, "but I'm not accustomed to discussing politics with women."

"Ye'd better get bleedin' used to it if y'come to this house to discuss 'em. And if ye hope to know where the Six Nations stand on anythin', ye're a demmed sight better off askin' Molly than me."

One of the gentlemen said earnestly: "Miss Molly, we all of us have some dealings with the Iroquois. I'm sure your people can understand that all we wish to do is erect a Tree of Peace of our own—"

"Ye already live under the biggest Tree of bleedin' Peace in the whole demmed world—the British Empire! Oh, excuse me, ye were addressin' m'wife."

Molly wove her fingers around the stem of her glass and said: "I have not heard what you've said to my husband this evening, but I know who you are, and what you and your brothers have been saying in other places, and *oh yes* . . ." She tracked her eyes around the delegation like a stag's Guardian eyeing a pack of hounds. "I know what you want from him.

"I think you do not understand how the League of Peace came to be. The original Five Nations did not join together all at once. Only when all five nations had decided for themselves, and agreed amongst each other, could the Tree of Peace grow."

"Well, that is exactly what our twelve colonies hope to—"

"No." She didn't raise her voice, but the black blaze of her eyes raising off her firelit glass was more than enough to silence the interrupter. "No, you are not. We Hodenosaune, you see, do not decide matters by force of vote as you English do. You are not speaking of each colony reaching an agreement in its own longhouse and then taking that agreement to a Great Council. What you are speaking of is elected spokesmen going to a council and then bringing home an agreement made by men who might well have been voted *against* by half the people they claimed to speak for.

"If the Peacemaker and Hiawatha had tried to build their league that way, every longhouse would have been torn to pieces by war clubs dug up to be used by brother against brother and father against son. Is that your notion of a Tree of Peace?"

Watching his flare-bright Molly tightened a band around Big Billy's chest. It took a few tries for him to say: "I know that most of yer Patriot laddies are simply good men pushed to distraction. And some are demmed bitter-bellied rascals who'd burn their own house to make a change.

"The bloody-minded among ye might think they can make fools of the wiser ones. But I know I'll never live to see the day when His Majesty's colonies raise their hand in open war against 'im."

The gaunt gentleman said with some disgust: "So your answer is that you remain loyal to the king, regardless what he or his ministers may do to us?"

"I'll *tell* ye what I remain bleedin' loyal to—" There was that demmed fist around his heart again. Perhaps he could fob it off as a dramatic pause. "I remain loyal to the blood of British soldiers and Iroquois warriors, that ye put yer foot on with every step y'take across yer precious America. They went down defendin' ye in the name of His British Majesty. Not because they believed the king walks on the water, but because the king means British law and British government. If ye cut down that Tree, where d'ye hope to take shelter?"

When the gentlemen from Albany and points east had bidden their adieus, Molly came to his chair and kissed his forehead and murmured: "You should get to sleep; you will have a long day tomorrow."

But when he went to his room, the stack of deeds and transfer papers and affidavits was still waiting on his desk. He sat down to pick up where he'd left off, just to clarify a couple of details. It certainly was a hellish tangle. How the divil was he supposed to remember what some long-dead chief or other had remarked before making his mark on a piece of paper in the small hours of a rum-fuzzed night a quarter century ago?

He was still sitting there when Horace came to wake him. It was a clear, bright morning, but by the time he got back from inaugurating the courthouse, the day had turned demmed hot. Horace had laid out his general's uniform in preparation for a formal council. The lace stock fit demmed tight around his throat, and the day wasn't made for red wool and gold braid, but he wanted to leave no doubt in anyone's mind that Gets Business Done spoke for the king.

He left his cane behind and limped out the door that faced his gardens. Molly and Joseph were waiting on the steps. He walked with them to the arbor and council house that had been built at the end of the gardens the same year the blockhouses went up. Given the blaze of the sun, he would've preferred today's council fire to be kindled under the Council House roof, but the Iroquois preferred to do this kind of business in the open, where there was room for everyone who cared to see and hear.

There were several hundred Mohawks gathered in the arbor. It stung his eyes to see the faces of the Royaners and Oyanders frozen into that impenetrable mask they put on for councils with any white man other than Billy Johnson.

The servants of the Department of Northern Indian Affairs served out a measure of rum. The superintendent raised his with: "May ye have warm words on a cold evening, a full moon on a dark night, and the road downhill all the way to yer door."

Joseph translated that as much as possible. The faces around the circle remained stony, but they drank politely. Sir William nodded and another measure was served out. "I give ye—His Majesty King George the Third of England, Ireland, Scotland, Wales, and all British colonies and possessions girdlin' this whirlin' globe!"

Once the second toast was drunk, Big Billy waved his interpreter away and proceeded to speak for himself in as fluent Mohawk as he'd been able to grasp over the course of forty years. It felt like he talked for a long time, but there was so much that had to be said before things got down to grubbing over details of land deeds. He talked of the Covenant Chain, of the Bloody Morning Scout and all the other occasions when the soldiers of the king and the League of Peace had been blood brothers to one another, and of the many gifts the True People of Turtle Island and the English of the Mohawk Valley had given each other.

The old bullet in his hip began to burn like billy-o. His belly and his wig-capped head and wool-cloaked shoulders sizzled. His throat begged to croak for a mug of good ale. But there still was more that had to be said. The faces swimming in the heat waves looked confused. He told them: "In the days to come there will be men comin' among ye—p'r'aps they already have—tellin' ye that the advisers of yer Father across the water have filled 'is head with snakes and that his children must break free of 'im. Ye must not be shaken out of yer shoes."

It was high time he sat back down on his mat. He had just turned to do so, rehearsing in his mind the words he'd decided to remember Hendrick saying about those eighty thousand acres, when a fishhook from some troller in the clouds snagged his heart and yanked.

CHAPTER 38

Joseph saw Sir William slump sideways, and leaped up to catch him before he fell. He caught him well enough, but he was too heavy to hold upright. Just before they both toppled over, a thick pair of hands took hold and Big William shifted his shoulder in under his father's arm.

Sir William slurred: "I think I must be helped inside." They walked him across the garden toward the house. Sir William did his best to stumble along with them, but his left leg was dragging and his right boot kept catching its toe in the ground. Joseph could hear Molly shouting orders to fetch the doctor from Johnstown and John from Fort Johnson. Sir William's lolling head turned toward Joseph. The gray eyes with their strangely misaligned pupils squinted with confusion.

The confusion cleared for an instant just as they got him to the steps. He whispered thickly: "Joseph . . . control your people . . . I am going away."

They sat him down in the armchair beside his desk. Molly loosened his neck band, mixed some wine into a glass of water and held it to his lips. Joseph went out onto the steps to wait for John and the doctor. The doctor came almost immediately, but Fort Johnson was a lot farther off.

Soon, there seemed to be more Caniengas on the lawn than had come for the council. More drifted out of the paths through the woods and sat down beside their brothers and sisters, until the silent circle ringing the house was three deep.

Finally Sir John appeared, running down the road in his English riding boots. He was hatless and clutching a riding crop in one hand, pumping it up and down like a relay runner's baton.

Joseph moved down the steps to meet him. John fell against him and gasped out: "I've killed my horse. Is he . . . ?"

"He's in his room, with Molly and—" But there was no point adding "the doctor and Horace" at the boot heels disappearing up the steps and through the door.

A moment later came a woman's howl from inside the house. Outside, the voice of Little Abraham began to sing, "Hai! Gets Business Done . . ." but his "Hai hai!" was drowned out by a chorus of a thousand other voices as the Canienga Nation rose slowly to its feet.

Joseph watched the toes of his moccasins climb the steps to the door of Johnson Hall and carry him inside. Sir William Johnson was stretched out across his great four-poster bed, still in his general's uniform. Sir John Johnson was sitting on the edge of the bed with his head in his hands. Joseph's sister was kneeling by the other side of the bed, with her hands clutched around one big, limp paw and her forehead pressed against its knuckles. When Joseph put his hand on her shoulder she sprang upright and away from him, slicing her arm through the air. Her eyes were wild through the tears. She shrieked: "They murdered him!"

"Who did?"

"I don't know . . . those 'Patriots' . . . or those Caniengas who were so proud to call him friend until this year! The juice of the yew berry in a drink can stop a man's heart."

He tried to make his voice as soft and reasonable as possible. "Someone Lends Her a Flower, no one poured for him but you or his servants. You've said many times to me that he had trouble with his heart. He was no young man, and he lived hard."

"He was well! He was better! Somebody murdered him!"

He stepped toward her. She flailed at him. He pinned her arms and pressed her to him. She struggled for a moment, but he wrapped his arms around her tighter and shouted in unison with the voices encircling the house: "Hai! Gets Business Done!"

She sobbed into his shoulder: "Hai, hai . . ."

PART THREE

SOMEONE LENDS HER A FLOWER AND CAPTAIN BRANT

This is no time to fill the joyous cup,
The mammoth comes—the foe, the monster Brant,
With all his howling, desolating band . . .

—THOMAS CAMPBELL
"Gertrude of Wyoming"

Chapter 39

On a glorious April day the year after Sir William Johnson was interred in the church at Johnstown, a column of redcoat infantry were ordered to march from their garrison in Boston to confiscate the weapons hidden in the town of Concord. In the village of Lexington, and then again at Concord Bridge, several madmen pulled their triggers. By the time the soldiers of the king marched back into Boston, one hundred redder coats lay in the ditches of the road to Concord.

Molly heard the news at Fort Johnson. Sir's will had left both Johnson Hall and Fort Johnson to John, but John believed that his father's intention was that Molly should have the smaller house for her lifetime. Molly was just as glad to make the move; the memories in Fort Johnson were more distant.

The will had only referred to her as "my housekeeper, Molly Brant," and had expressed Sir William's wish that "my beloved wife, Catherine Weisenberg" be disinterred and laid to rest beside him. Joseph had been furious, but Molly remembered what Sir had said to her when she told him she'd done the inventory, and knew that the will was just Gets Business Done taking care of business. There had always been some question whether he and Catty Weisenberg had ever been married. If John were only another of many illegitimate sons, he would only have a dubious right to inherit his father's baronetcy and the bulk of his estates and establish the dynasty of Mohawk Valley Johnsons that Sir had dreamed of.

And Molly had no cause to complain about the material aspects of the will. She was a wealthy woman, and her children had all been given enough land to build their own nests when they left hers. Sir had made a point of willing her Juba and Juba's sister Jemmy and Abraham, the field hand Jemmy had been keeping steady company with. There was one other servant who seemed unlikely to fit into the household of Sir John and Lady Polly that she'd brought with her from Johnson Hall. Horace was now the overseer of Fort Johnson farm.

The news of Lexington and Concord brought Peter Warren galloping home before his school term was done. After a riotous reunion supper, the family retired to the parlor to jabber about everything except revolutions. Whenever one of the other children tried to bring the subject up, Peter brushed it aside. Finally the younger girls and George grew tired enough to take their overexcitedness up to bed. A few minutes later, Elizabeth and Magdalen surprised Molly by saying they would make an early night of it.

Peter Warren walked his two oldest sisters to the parlor door with an arm around each of their waists, then stood leaning against the doorframe and waving them up the stairs. When their footsteps ceased to echo in the hall, he said offhandedly over his shoulder: "Mother, do you still have Father's old militia uniform?"

"I believe it's in the attic somewhere. The coat, at least. Why?"

He turned back toward the room. "Do you think it could be cut down to fit me?"

"Why?"

"You know which side Father would want me to fight on."

"No side! You're only a boy!"

"I will be sixteen in September. Uncle Joseph was thirteen at Lake George."

"That was completely different."

"Why?"

"Because . . . your uncle Joseph had already been trained to be a warrior. And everyone who could carry a musket had to try to stop the French."

"Do you think everyone who can carry a musket doesn't have to try to stop the rebels? I would not presume to call myself a Canienga warrior, only to join the loyalist militia. All up and down the colonies, boys younger than I are shouldering muskets to help the rebels tear down everything Father built."

For the first time in her life, Molly found herself unable to argue. Peter had always been a good chess player, and she couldn't outmaneuver him when all she could think of was that British military coats were red so blood wouldn't show. She said: "There will be a council at Canajoharie, to determine what the Canienga should do. You are still a Canienga. After the council renders its decision, we will speak of this again."

Molly had been to a lot of councils where people were distraught about looming events, but never like this. Canajoharie was a Boiling Kettle in more than name. If the war that had started on the other side of the Adirondacks made its way into the Mohawk Valley, the Caniengas wouldn't be able to defend themselves, because the rebel Safety Committee had intercepted the annual shipment of gunpowder through the Indian Department. Little Abraham declared: "But we have no need to defend ourselves against either side. The Covenant Chain between us and the king's men has not been broken. And the Continental Congress has sent wampum to all six nations, promising to leave us in peace if we remain neutral, and swearing that if they do win their freedom from the king, they will still respect the Stanwix Line for all time."

When the wampum belt was passed to Someone Lends Her a Flower, Molly stood weighing it in her hands for a long time, thinking of Peter Warren and a lot of other things. When finally she spoke, it was to say: "Who are these men of Congress who make us such fine promises? Is the most fervent Patriot in our valley not that same Ebenezer Cox who would happily have gone on crippling our warriors for money if Binds Two had not brought him up before the king's law? Is not the war chief Congress elected to lead them the Town Destroyer?" which was the name the True People had given Washington for his innovative way of dealing with Pontiac's warriors: burn their towns and fields and food stores, so that the warriors will be too busy keeping their families alive in the forest to fight.

"Was it Congress who kept the Big Knives from trying to take our land with guns, or was it not—" She couldn't say "Gets Business Done" without starting to cry, so she just said, ". . . our friends among the king's men who made them abide by the king's law? We have two choices: we can stand beside the king to fight the rebels now, or we can stand alone to fight the rebels if they win the war."

There were many murmurings of "Yo!" throughout her speech, but when it was done, she still hadn't solved the question of how they were to fight anybody with no gunpowder and no hope of getting any as long as the Safety Committee controlled the roads.

Then blunt Binds Two stood up to take the wampum. "The officers of the Department of Northern Indian Affairs mean to flee north to Canada before the Safety Committee comes to arrest them. Any Caniengas who go with them will be fed and housed and armed by the King until the war is over. Once the rebellion has been put down, we can return to our valley as before. I know it sounds like madness—to leave our homes to save them—but it is the only way I see."

Molly looked at the faces around the circle. Some of them looked like what her brother had said *was* madness; some of them looked like it would be madness to stay.

Molly needed Horace's help to ferret out which of the trunks stacked in the attic had Sir's old major's coat in it. It was in the bottom one, of course. She had to pick the threads out of most of the gold braid to make it not too showy for a green volunteer, and bring in all the seams considerably.

Peter Warren grinned at his uniformed reflection, but his grin crumpled when he turned away from the mirror: "What are you crying for, Mother?"

"Oh . . . oh . . . because . . . Look at that shoulder seam, it's all crooked!"

As she sat altering her alterations, Peter Warren poured himself a glass of Madeira and stood toying with the pieces on the chess table, as he always had when there was something he wanted to say, ever since he'd grown tall enough to reach them. He threw back the last swallow of his Madeira, clapped the glass down decisively among the pawns and kings and said gravely: "Won't you reconsider?"

"You should never waste your breath, Peter, arguing over what's already been decided. There is nothing for me to fear by staying here. The rebels aren't going to concern themselves with a harmless old widow."

Peter Warren stood away from the chess table and cocked

his right fist on his hip, just as his father used to do when he'd ceased tallyfobblin' about and got down to business. "In the first place, Mother, you're a long way from old. In the second place, you're about as harmless as Big William when his blood is up. And thirdly—and perhaps most germane of all—the Whigs hereabouts know that. Some of them are of the mean and petty sort. The worse things go for their Revolutionary Army, the more they're bound to resent a Tory in their midst."

"I wasn't married to the richest man in the valley for twenty years without being resented once or twice before, and I'm still here. There are three dozen good British regulars at Fort Hunter, which is more than enough to suppress anything of the mean and petty sort. If there were any danger, John wouldn't be staying on at Johnson Hall."

"If you'll forgive me, Mother, John couldn't be pried loose from his palace by anything short of the Beast of the Apocalypse. He and his private army would be a lot more useful going where the fighting is."

"There, you said it yourself: there is no fighting going on around here. While you're busy beating the rebel army, I'll be busy here seeing to it that your land is tilled and that the cattle of Fort Johnson produce enough spare progeny for you to start a herd with. Now try this on again and we'll see what . . . Well, it's *better*. . . . If only your shoulders weren't so square. . . ."

Her fine-tuning was interrupted by the arrival of her brother and his children and new wife—so new, in fact, that they'd had no time to arrange a church wedding and were only man and wife by pagan Hodenosaune rites. The girl called Trembling Earth was statuesque enough to appear a full-grown woman, but Molly suspected that Joseph would have waited another year or two except for the guns at Concord Bridge. Molly also suspected that Joseph's attraction to Trembling Earth wasn't just that she was striking to look at. Although her father was one of the many Irishmen Gets Business Done had brought over to staff the Indian Department, her mother was the sister of Tekarihoga, the only name on the roll call of Royaners that came before Hiawatha. A son of Trembling Earth might someday be Tekarihoga.

Joseph said: "The Indian Department has promised that all who go north with them will be accommodated at Fort Niagara or Montreal, but I have no idea what conditions will be like there. I do know that for the first while I will have to be traveling back and forth to Oswego, and to Quebec to speak with the governor. I don't know when it will be possible for me to make living arrangements for my family. Might they stay with you until I can do so?"

Molly turned to Trembling Earth, who sat looking down at her hands folded meekly in her lap. How had it ever come to pass that tall young women could be timid of little Si-isha? Molly said: "That would help keep me from feeling lonely when so many others of the family are so far away."

Trembling Earth whispered: "Thank you, Oyander."

"Not 'Oyander'—'sister.' " Molly turned back to Joseph. "Why will you have to speak with the governor in Quebec?"

"If we are going to fight for the king—"

"*If?*"

He shrugged uncomfortably. "Many Hodenosaune are asking a question, and there is no Gets Business Done to provide an answer they can trust: will the king remember how much he loves us when he no longer needs us to help fight his war? Many people remember that as soon as the French were defeated, the English stopped the distribution of presents and stopped trying to make the Big Knives obey the law—until Pontiac had to start another war to remind them of the Covenant Chain. I don't know if I can convince everyone to believe a promise from even the king's governor-in-chief."

"Then go to the king himself." He goggled at her. "Carrying News's father and Hendrick went to England when the English had less reason than now to court the Hodenosaune. If the king gives you his word to your face, no minister or governor can take it back."

At dawn the next day, Sir John Johnson marched his little private army of tenants and retainers down to Canajoharie to stand guard in case the Safety Committee tried to interfere with the exodus. The sky over Canajoharie Castle was raked with the wailing and screaming of families the whites perceived as stone-faced Mohawks. Molly looked at her mother and Carrying News bidding good-bye to their two warrior-aged sons and eldest daughter, then at balloon-wombed Mary Johnson looking pale and terrified, waiting for Guy to join her on the wagon seat, then at Little Abraham clasping the shoulders of those Royaners who had elected to go north, one of whom carried a pot of coals from the Fire That Never Dies.

Molly stretched her hands up to her son's red-coated shoulders and said, "May the road rise to meet you, may the sun be always at your back—" then couldn't say any more.

Another pair of hands settled on her shoulders from behind, and her brother's voice growled: "Ye needn't weep tears for us, Molly m'gel—save 'em for them demmed Bostonian heretics."

But the demmed heretics seemed to do rather well for themselves. The Town Destroyer besieged Boston while another rebel army invaded Quebec. Worst of all, the Oneidas attended the autumn council only long enough to throw a wampum belt into the fire and declare that they had made a new Covenant Chain with the Continental Congress.

The lieutenant in command of the little garrison at Fort Hunter came to Fort Johnson rimed with frost. "Why, thank you, Miss Molly, a cup of rum punch would be very welcome. I have news I wished to be the first to tell you. The arch rebel Ethan Allen and a force he was leading toward Montreal were taken by surprise and taken prisoner. The man that captured Ethan Allen was a certain Peter Warren Johnson."

Molly's hands fluttered up to her mouth. All she could say was: "Oh my."

" 'Oh my' indeed, Miss Molly. In consequence, Peter Warren Johnson is on his way to England with Captain Brant and other officers of the Indian Department—with Ethan Allen and his chains as ballast—where Peter Warren Johnson is to be added to the rolls of the Twenty-sixth Regiment of Foot as an ensign. I am told that when Governor Tryon was informed, his response was: 'Ensign? They should have made him a general!' "

"Oh my."

"I am afraid, though, Miss Molly . . ." The lieutenant cleared his throat and moistened it with punch. "I am afraid that . . ." His throat didn't sound any less dry, and his eyes stayed trained down at his cup. "That wasn't all the news in the dispatches. We have been ordered to vacate Fort Hunter and proceed with all due haste to Staten Island. The High Command has decided to concentrate our forces so as to drub the rebel army once for all. Consequently, all outlying, nonstrategic districts—such as the Mohawk Valley—are to be abandoned."

"We will still be here."

He looked up at her. "Excuse me, Miss Molly, perhaps I've not made myself clear, military lingo and all—"

"I know what 'abandoned' means."

CHAPTER 40

When Molly heard the wagons jingling and grinding up the road, she bounced out into the bright spring sun, only to discover that the wagons were still loaded down with their sacks of cornmeal and flour from the Fort Johnson mill. And there was no sign of any of the articles she'd listed for Horace to pick up at the hardware and dry goods stores.

Horace climbed down slowly and stood fisting and unfisting his hands. "I'm sorry, Miss Molly, but they say they won't do business with Tories."

"Who says?"

"Everybody. They won't buy from us or sell to us and they won't shoe Tory horses nor brew Tory barley nor spin Tory wool. They say they'd rather go all the way to Schenectady than pay mill fees to a Tory. Some of 'em felt bad about it, and some whispered to me, on the sly-like, that they don't want to go along with this but they're afeared of the Safety Committee. I tried everything I could think of, from callin' 'em names to even offerin' to sell cheap, but that pump just won't prime. I'm sorry, Miss Molly."

"It's hardly your fault, Horace."

"I don't know what we're a-goin' to do."

"I'll tell you what we're going to do: we're going to get

along just fine without them. When Sir William built this place, there were no markets or hardware stores to go to. We have beef and mutton on the hoof and fish in the river, and the spring isn't so far along that we can't widen the garden to grow all the vegetables we'll need. They taught me how to spin wool in Schenectady, and I was sewing my own clothes before I was as tall as your elbow. You can shoe a horse as good as any blacksmith, and the old brew kettle and barrels are still stacked in the shed. We'll still be sitting here fat and warm when the king's armies march back from squashing the Town Destroyer for good. And then the Tryon County Committee of Safety is going to wish to God they'd never threatened anybody.

"When you have unloaded the wagons, I'd like you to take Isaac to Little Abraham at Canajoharie." Joseph's son had been making himself so unpleasant that she'd decided it was high time he had a Teacher. "In the evening, if the wind stays calm, you can marshal the field hands and footmen to burn off the undergrowth on what used to be the side garden, so we can start hoeing in the morning."

She went back into the house and found Isaac sitting alone in the music room with his pack basket beside him. She said: "I expect Little Abraham will want you to stay with him a few days to begin with, to get you accustomed to having a Teacher. After that, you will be back here, and he will come to fetch you when he has another task for you." Isaac said nothing. "I know it isn't easy to be shunted about like—"

"I'm used to it." He picked up his pack basket and went out to sit on the steps and wait for Horace. Molly tried to remind herself that Joseph had gone through a surly couple of years at the same age, and come out the other side. But she couldn't help but wonder why she'd been blessed with Peter Warren and Joseph cursed with Isaac.

She had other children to concern herself with, though. She assembled them and Trembling Earth and Juba and Jemmy in the dining room and explained to them why Fort Johnson would have to become self-sufficient again. "You will all have to help—well, not the babies *yet*, and I'm sure this will all be over before they're big enough. Tomorrow morning we'll start hoeing out a new garden. Trembling Earth, perhaps you and

Elizabeth could go out into the woods this afternoon and find some tickleweed."

Elizabeth said: "Why tickleweed?"

Trembling Earth said: "If the water the seed corn gets soaked in to soften up has some tickleweed in it, the first crow to steal a seed out of the garden will flap around in crazy circles and scare all his brothers away."

Juba laughed: "You ignorant savages sure could learn a lot from white folks about building scarecrows and squatting out in the fields with a shotgun all day."

Molly said nothing, just blushed at the fact that Elizabeth was the same age as Trembling Earth and still hadn't been taught by her mother about tickleweed and seed corn.

George said: "I can help hoe."

Molly said: "No, dear."

"I'm big enough."

"You are, but it is not for men and boys to work among the Three Sisters. I'm sure Horace will be glad to have your help in clearing out the undergrowth."

In the morning, she debated whether to go out to the garden in just her skirt, as her grandmothers had before her, and then decided that not all customs could last forever. With the inundation of white settlers and missionaries, it had been years since the women of Canajoharie or the Lower Castle took off their overdresses before taking up their hoes. Her daughters would be working in English gardening dresses anyway; the only Canienga clothes they owned were ceremonial.

Out in the soot-blackened field, still smoldering in places, Horace and Abraham and a few other field hands were chopping at the bases of the trees that had grown up in the years since Fort Johnson had had to grow enough vegetables to feed the army of servants and employees kept by William Johnson. Molly called to Horace: "There is no need to make work for yourself. Simply girdle the trees—cut off a strip of bark all around—and they will die. Next year they will be easy enough to pull down or burn down."

"Well, that'd be a smarter way of goin' about it, wouldn't it, Miss Molly?"

She arranged her hoe-armed troops in a line to her left and her right: Elizabeth, Magdalen, Peggy, Trembling Earth, Christina, Juba, and Jemmy. Peggy and Christina weren't big enough yet to be of much help, but they could learn while they were doing what they could. Martha and Susanna hovered around the edge of the garden, keeping an eye on Nancy to make sure she didn't eat more dirt than was good for her.

Molly bit her hoe into the earth and began a song for breaking a new field. Trembling Earth joined in. The girls all spoke Canienga, but had never had occasion to learn the song. They began to pick it up after a while. The only Canienga words Juba could pronounce were names of food concoctions, but she la-laed along lustily.

Molly found it hard to keep up the song and the hoeing at the same time. She'd underestimated how soft she'd grown in twenty-odd years of issuing orders to field hands while she puttered in her flower beds or sat adding up household accounts. She'd forgotten that hoeing a garden of vegetables to stock up for the winter was somewhat different from hoeing a decorative border of rosebushes. She had the distinct impression that Trembling Earth was working at half speed so as not to get ahead of her.

By the time Molly got to the other end of the burnt-off plot, she was puffing and blowing and her soft palms were already feeling blistered. Her nostrils were filled with the smells of soot and fresh-turned earth and her own sweat. She leaned on her hoe and looked back at her line of daughters and sisters. Magdalen was lagging behind even Peggy and Christina, red-faced and hacking fiercely but getting nowhere. Molly went to her. Magdalen looked up and wailed: "I'm *trying*, Mother."

"I know you are, dear. Let me see your hoe. I thought so. It's dull."

"Dull?"

Molly felt herself blushing again, at realizing she'd raised a daughter who was budding breasts but still didn't know that a hoe whose blade hadn't been sharpened was about as useful as a blunt knife. "Yes. Run and find Horace and ask him for the ax file and I'll show you how to sharpen it." Magdalen loped away with her red hair flying, and Molly went back to pace out the next set of rows.

As the spring advanced, there were fewer and fewer servants to lend a hand, as more and more denizens of Tryon County discovered strict Republican principles—sometimes with the help of a midnight visit from the Safety Committee. But Molly grew stronger with the work, and the older children did their share when they weren't at school, and Trembling Earth was a big, strapping girl who seemed to blossom now that there were so many useful things for her to do.

It was a kind of gift to have Fort Johnson forced to become more of a longhouse. Somehow the years at Johnson Hall had snuck by without Molly noticing how much like an English family her family was becoming: with the children compartmentalized into schooltime and playtime while the adults attended to business, and with work and socializing separated. But there were times, when she crawled up the stairs with her candle after the nightly strategy session with Horace, Juba, and Trembling Earth, that she would have gladly traded this feeling of being a closer-knit family for a few bits of wool that someone else had carded, spun, and knitted.

If feeding and clothing her household weren't enough to keep her from getting fat, she was still the Elder Sister of the Wolf Clan and the Canienga Clan Mothers. Far too many Hodenosaune were waiting to see which way the wind was going to blow in this war, or had already decided that the wind was blowing against the king. It took a lot of maneuvering for her to see to it that the wampum runners who went west from Canajoharie all bore essentially the same message: the early successes of the Continental Army were only a weasel drawing blood from a hibernating bear and waking it.

One May morning, Molly carried her hoe out into the garden and discovered that—wonder of wonders—all the hills of the Three Sisters were hoed and sprouting, and there were no weeds worth worrying about for the nonce. She yoked the hoe across her shoulders, cocked her wrists over the haft and turned in a circle. Since the day she'd first led her hoeing troop out to open the soil, she hadn't seen anything when she stepped outside the house except what was within the boundaries of the garden. Now she saw that the slope of Mount Johnson was rouged with wildflowers, the chestnut trees were hung with candelabra, and the river was running high and clear with the last of the melt-off from the mountain streams. She couldn't help but feel sorry for her brother and her son—stuck in England when spring came to the Valley of the Caniengas.

She put away her hoe, pulled a bouquet of succulent-looking vetch, and went looking for Juanita. After twenty foals and thousands of miles, it had been decided that poor old Juanita should be put out to pasture. Before Molly reached the fence, Juanita saw her coming and came prancing through the other horses for her carrot or chunk of maple sugar or, were it a banner day, the chance to lap the head off a mug of the latest batch of Fort Johnson Brewery's brown ale.

Horace was over by the barn showing a couple of the field hands how to mend a wagon wheel properly, while George looked on intently. Molly called Horace over. "Don't you think, Horace, that she looks years younger?"

"A bit of rest from time to time can do a body a power of good, Miss Molly."

"She looks more than strong enough to take me in the saddle again."

"Well . . . it'd be your decision to make, of course, Miss Molly. But me, I were always of the opinion that oncet a horse has been told she's earned her day in the sun, it's best not to take it back."

"I suspect you're right, Horace. Would you saddle me the bay gelding, then? It's a glorious day, and I can't remember the last time I went riding."

"Ahem, um . . ." He crinkled up his eyes and forehead like a winter apple doll. "Where . . . where was it you was reckonin' on goin' ridin' to, miss?"

"I don't know. Upriver or down, wherever the flowers look brightest."

He tugged on the nearest fence post and mumbled at it: "I wish you wouldn't."

"Whyever not?"

"Well, you see, miss . . . them Patriots and sech, they was willin' to be no more'n a nuisance so long as the war was goin' their way. But since they got chased back out of Canada, they been turnin' pretty sour. And they're goin' to get a dang sight sourer if'n they get chased out of New York Town as well. If'n they see you out ridin' around alone . . . I don't mean to say they'd do you any harm, but a lady like you shouldn't oughta have to suffer name-callin' and the throwin' of mud clods and sech. And if somethin' like that was to happen, you just might go and lose your temper. . . ."

"Then I won't go riding alone. When was the last time you

took half a morning to go out riding and get a bit of rest from carrying Fort Johnson around on your shoulders?"

"That's mighty kind of you to offer, Miss Molly, but that might prove even worser'n you goin' ridin' alone. You see, I got a temper of my own. . . ." After twenty years and more, she'd yet to see it, but she was willing to take his word for it. "I'd be bound to lose it if'n someone was to . . . I'm gettin' a tech old to be holdin' up my end in a roadside scuffle."

"I would not care to be the man that raised your ire, Horace."

"Well . . . you see there jest ain't no winnin' in that there kind of sitty-ation, miss. Them Patriots what went and started the set-to with Big William in the tavern last year sure regretted it, but he's the one had to clear out of the country afore the funeral turned into a hanging mob. I'm sure they'll let you be, so long as you stay on your own place—"

"Stay? Do you mean to tell me I'm in jail?"

"A jail with guards."

"Guards? You mean the watchers in the woods?"

"You've seen 'em?"

"Most white men aren't very good at hiding themselves."

"Well, I'm danged sure there's some others we don't see. Oneidas, most likely."

"What would Oneidas want here?"

"Well, I ain't called out to ask 'em, but I suspicion they want the same thing as the Safety Committee. I'd guess they're waitin' for Master Peter Warren or your brother, so as to welcome 'em home like." He raised his head and gazed around at the fields, gardens, and buildings enclosed by the river and Mount Johnson and the forest walls. "You may call it a jail, but she's a big, airy cell. And it ain't forever."

"Just until the king's armies win the war."

"Well, to tell the truth, Miss Molly . . . I know Sir William'd beller me out of my shoes for sayin' so, but I don't really care a hang one way or t'other who wins this war. I'm still goin' to have to scythe the same barley whether it's the king or some congress puts the taxes on it. I just wish they'd get it over with so's I could stop havin' to wonder whether I should patch the roof or not 'cause next month the armies might be meetin' hereabouts and droppin' cannonballs through 'er. It'd sure put my mind at ease if'n you'd promise me you won't go jauntin' up and down the valley till this is over."

"I have to go to Canajoharie for councils."

"They can come here, cain't they? No one minds Little Abraham and them other neutral Mohawks comin' and goin' where they please. But everybody knows you ain't never been neutral on anythin' in your life. It'd sure put my mind at ease, Miss Molly, if'n you'd promise."

What she felt more inclined to do was put on her gaudiest dress, saddle up and trot up and down every road in the valley. But Horace wasn't exactly given to needless alarms, and she'd lived long enough to know she wasn't invulnerable. "All right, Horace. I promise."

"Thank you, Miss Molly."

But she was moved to break her promise almost immediately. The mother of the Canienga girl who cleaned the militia headquarters in Schenectady came to tell her that the rebels were planning to descend on Johnson Hall in sufficient force to overawe John's private army and take mass hostages. Horace had to stretch his powers of persuasion to convince her that sending a messenger to warn John would be just as effective as going herself.

By the time the Safety Committee and militia got to Johnson Hall, Sir John Johnson and his loyalist tenants were long gone on the trail to Canada. Lady Polly and her children were still there, though, since she was in no condition to travel and it was assumed that even Patriots wouldn't harm a pregnant woman. They didn't, but they took her and her children back to Schenectady as hostages. As had happened at Guy Park, as soon as Johnson Hall was empty, a horde of Patriots took up residence without as much as a nod at the laws of trespass, and proceeded to make free with the wine cellar and food stores. Molly was determined that the same would never happen at Fort Johnson. She and her children were the only evidence left in the Mohawk Valley that Sir William Johnson had ever existed.

Juba poured tea a little nervously for Mistress Molly and Miss Trembling Earth, then went to the barrel in the corner to tap out Horace's evening mug of ale. She heard over her shoulder: "Oh, this is wonderful, Juba."

"You like it, Mizt'ess Molly? I could see we was coming to the bottom of the boughten tea, so I asked Miss Christina and Miss Peggy to pick as many different kinds of wild mint as they could find. . . ."

"It's been so long since I lived in the longhouse, I'd forgotten the taste of wild tea. Young raspberry twigs are very good, too. There's different teas for every season. I don't know if I can remember them all." She turned to Trembling Earth. "You'll have to help jog my memory before you go."

Juba said: " 'Go,' Mizt'ess Molly?"

"Yes. Trembling Earth and I have been talking, and we decided it would be best for her to take Isaac and Christina to their grandfather at Oquaga, out of reach of the rebels. It can't be much longer before my brother comes back and joins in the fighting. If the rebels think they can keep Sir John out of the war by taking his wife and children hostage, they might be tempted to try the same on Joseph."

Horace said: "What about you and your children, Miss Molly? Like you said—you got a brother who'll be fightin' against the rebels soon. And a son."

"I did think of that, Horace. But then I looked around and realized that if they imprisoned everyone who had a loyalist son or brother or cousin, the whole valley would be in jail. No, if they do take any more hostages, it will only be wives and children."

The conversation moved on to farm matters and then to Mistress Molly and Trembling Earth trying to come up with a list of all the different tea plants that grew at different times of year, laughing at the memories that went with the remembered tastes. It seemed to Juba that her mistress had grown years younger since the spring. Her body looked tauter and all the outside work had turned her skin the same glowing olive-brown as it had been at the start of every school year after a summer of running free. Her hands and face always sported some healing, unheeded scratch or insect bite now, like any healthy child's. Juba had never thought to see her happy again after Sir William died. Well, perhaps she wasn't exactly happy, but she was too busy to be lonely.

When Mistress Molly bade her good-nights and started up the steps to the dining room hatchway, Juba naturally stood up to start clearing the table. But when she reached for Horace's cup, she saw he was showing no signs of moving from his chair, and neither was Trembling Earth. Horace said: "I wouldn't say no to another half a mugful, Juba, if'n we can spare it."

"The way you and Abraham keep cooking up new batches, we could spare half a *barrel*ful." She filled his mug, then poured out the dregs of the tea for herself and Trembling Earth. It was obvious Horace wanted to say something— everything was obvious with Horace—but he just sat sipping his ale and studying the ceiling beams.

Finally, Trembling Earth said: "Horace, whatever it is you want to say to Juba, you can say in front of me. I live here, too—at least for a little while longer." Something of Mistress Molly was definitely rubbing off on her.

Horace blushed and said to Trembling Earth: "It ain't like I was wantin' to push you out of the way, miss, just I didn't know as you'd be partial to feelin' like a third ear." He turned to Juba. "She'll listen to you when she won't listen to no one else."

" 'She'?"

"Who else? Miss Molly."

"Huh. Maybe a little. But there ain't been nobody could say anything she'd listen to less'n it was something she wanted to hear since Sir William died. 'Cepting maybe Captain Joseph, and he's a long ways away."

"Well maybe you could at least give 'er a try."

"Give what a try?"

"Tryin' to talk Miss Molly into all of us clearin' out of here to Canada where it's safe."

"It's safe here."

"That's what Sir John and Lady Polly thought."

"That ain't the same and you know it. Them rebels was afraid Sir John and his tenants'd fight against them. Why'd anybody be afraid of us? So long as we just stick to our property, like you said we should, and don't get mixed up in what's going on outside, nobody got any reason to think twice about us."

"And just what do you figure the odds are on Miss Molly not gettin' mixed up in what's goin' on outside? You think the Safety Committee don't suspicion how Sir John got warned they was comin'? And the spies in the woods see the Mohawk councillors comin' and goin' from here. It won't take 'em a lot of brain work to figure out what kinds of things she's sayin'."

"Lord Jesus, Horace, you turning into an old woman. Miss Trembling Earth—was it you that worried maybe you and Captain Joseph's children ain't safe here?"

"Well, I did start to wonder, after what happened at Johnson Hall. But it was Molly who brought it up."

"There, you see, Horace? You think Mizt'ess Molly wouldn't rather have a good, strong worker like Miss Trembling Earth to help out here? But so soon as she sees it maybe ain't safe here no more for Captain Joseph's wife and children, she says: you got to go to a safe place. Mizt'ess Molly ain't walking around with horse blinds on. She wouldn't keep her own children here if it ain't safe."

But after Horace and Trembling Earth had gone up to their beds, Juba sat remembering all the times she'd seen Mistress Molly's slanted eyes get that hard fire that meant she had made up her mind what she was going to do and wasn't going to think about it anymore. It was a trait that served her well, and everyone around her, when she was right.

CHAPTER 41

The lion of London's latest social season, the Mohawk Captain Brant, came downstairs into the public room of the Swan with Two Necks and found the landlord's wife weeping. She crushed him to her ample bosoms and wailed in her cockney twang: "Aow, you been so kind to us!"

"Not at all. It's you who've been kind to me, and to Chief Deseronto."

"That's our *business*. But you—you and your friend

could've been lodging in any fancy place in London, but you wouldn't leave us."

"What would we do in some polite club where the only sound is the butler yawning? Here in dear old Lad Lane we could go to sleep to the sounds of bellowing and clattering and singing and fistfights and laughter. It was almost like being back home in a longhouse."

"Well . . . don't you go letting any of them bloody rebels come sneaking up behind you."

"I fully intend to live to come back to you someday. If I do, I'll bring you a rebel scalp to hang over the door."

"Ooh—wouldn't that bring in the custom!"

The party from the Department of Northern Indian Affairs arrived in Falmouth a few days before they were due to sail, to stock up on provisions for the voyage. Besides potted salmon and French wines, Joseph and Deseronto bought a few more suits of clothes and stacks of presents for the folks back home, all at the king's expense. Joseph didn't feel the least twinge of guilt. The English taxpayers weren't going to be the ones running through the woods of Turtle Island with rebel musket balls whistling around them.

Their ship was a squat little merchantman called the *Lord Hyde*, newly equipped with twelve three-pounders in case of rebel privateers. She would be sailing in a convoy guarded by three warships of the Royal Navy. The convoy's embarkation would hardly be a secret, as one of the London gazettes had paid a messenger to go to Falmouth, so they could be the first to inform their readers of the departure of the celebrated Captain Brant.

All the attention made Joseph a little uneasy, wondering if Deseronto wasn't getting a trifle annoyed at the constant "Captain Brant and his companion." It was a tenet of the Hodenosaune that it was dangerous to become "too great a man." But it was also a tenet of the Hodenosaune that ambassadors should be sent out in pairs—one to speak and one to advise. If Deseronto didn't like the custom, he could take it up with the Founders.

Early in Joseph's career as the conduit between the Department of Northern Indian Affairs and northern Indians, Gets Business Done had given him a prescription to be used whenever he found himself wondering whether the people he was making decisions for were harboring resentments or disapproval: "If it don't gall 'em enough to make 'em say it to yer face, it don't exist." Nonetheless, for many reasons, Joseph had found himself wishing that it could have been Big William who'd accompanied him to England. But it was hard to argue with the council's opinion that subtle diplomacy wasn't exactly Big William's strong suit.

The morning the *Lord Hyde* was due to sail, a pale-haired, dark-eyed, fresh-minted officer of His Majesty's 26th Regiment of Foot came running down the dock, with a panting porter trundling a trunk-laden barrow along behind. "Uncle Joseph!"

"Ensign Peter Warren Johnson. Had enough of army life already?"

"Not at all. Well, not until we've won the war, at any rate. I got leave to come see you off. And I thought," gesturing at the trunk, "I bought some presents, you see, for Mother and all. I thought perhaps I might prevail upon you to take them with you. You see, I don't know whether the Twenty-sixth will get sent to New York or the Carolinas or Quebec or—"

"I will be more than glad to carry your presents with me." Joseph reached up and playfully tugged on the lapel of Sir William Johnson's old, altered major's coat. "I would've thought the Twenty-sixth Regiment of Foot would provide you with a uniform."

"They did. But I prefer this one."

"So you would." Joseph moved his hand off the threadbare lapel to cup his nephew's neck, and said in Canienga: "May thy Guardian watch over thee, son of Someone Lends Her a Flower and Gets Business Done."

"And over thee, Binds Two. *Thine* over thee, that is."

Joseph kept his hand on his nephew's shoulder and tried to think of some way to convey to him that it wasn't necessary to fumble so painfully hard to do the right things or say the right things. Joseph knew himself to be only a minor cog in the war machinery of the British Empire and the Six Nations, but looking at Peter Warren made him feel like the most casehardened old war chief on the planet. "Peter Warren, it is a good thing to pay heed and respect to those who carry more battle scars, but never forget that you, too, are a warrior." It was hopelessly inadequate, but maybe its very inadequacy would help Peter Warren see that everyone else was fumbling along, too.

"But I'm not a warrior, Uncle Joseph. I'm a soldier."

"Captain Brant! We're rolling up the gangplank!"

Joseph got Peter Warren's trunk on board just before the *Lord Hyde* cast off. The little cabin in the stern that he and Deseronto were to share had grown even littler once they'd loaded in their personal supplements to the galley stores, and the presents they meant to give and the ones they'd received—among which were a pair of pistols the king had presented to Captain Brant, saying: "We trust that you will never shoot these at our loyal subjects."

There were also two beautiful English hunting rifles that had been presented to Joseph and Deseronto on the Falmouth dock. It was frustrating to take them out of their cases and admire them and wonder what their range was and whether they shot straight, but have no targets to try them out on except the endlessly undulating waves.

But that was a fleabite to the frustration of being confined to this stubby wooden island crawling across the ocean when the time had finally come to act. The rifle Joseph's fingers itched to try out was nothing to the real weapon he and Deseronto carried with them. The king and the prime minister had taken them by the hand and promised that the Empire would stand by its Indian allies whatever the outcome of the war.

The convoy sailed south to catch the prevailing westerlies, keeping as close together as possible but not too close together. At night or in fog, trumpets blew from every ship to keep from colliding. The warships fired off their guns at the stroke of every daylight hour to bring up stragglers.

But with all those precautions, somewhere off Bermuda the *Lord Hyde* found she was the only blot in a blue universe of sea and sky. The captain tacked in all directions, and finally another sail appeared. Just as everyone was congratulating the captain for finding the convoy again, the lookout bellowed: "Privateer!"

Joseph and Deseronto found a place by the stern rail to stand out of the way while everyone else ran around shouting. The guns were finally run out—one of them running out a bit too far, smashing through its port in a hail of wood chips and plunging into the sea. As the privateer came swooping down on them, it became far too apparent that she was a hawk to the lumbering duck of the *Lord Hyde*.

The *Lord Hyde* fired a broadside, sending up a pretty file of fountains, about half a day's ride from the privateer's nose. There were several puffs of smoke from the privateer's gun ports, then a distant booming sound that was immediately drowned out by rending, tearing, and screaming overhead as the topsail came down. The *Lord Hyde*'s amateur gun crews were yelling orders at each other and kicking at their guns. The captain was kicking at his sailors and ordering them up the mast to cut away the shattered rigging.

Joseph stood digging his fingers into the railing, fighting the urge to crouch down behind it. There was no shelter from the cannons, no forest to run through—either toward the enemy or away.

Deseronto leaned close to his ear and said calmly: "You know those lovely London rifles . . . .?"

"It does seem like the perfect opportunity."

Deseronto disappeared and came back up the gangway carrying both rifles and their shot pouches and powder flasks. By the time they were loaded, another broadside from the privateer had carried away a few more of the *Lord Hyde*'s sails and sailors. Deseronto pointed at a tall man on the privateer's deck extending his arm toward the gunners. "That's their captain."

Joseph nodded, knelt beside the railing and waited for the next wave to raise the *Lord Hyde* and lower the privateer. With any other gun he'd ever fired before, he would've aimed high at that distance to arc his shot. But he decided to take the English gunsmiths at their word and put his sights straight on the tall man's chest. When the waves coincided, he squeezed the trigger. When the smoke cleared, there was no more tall man on the privateer's deck.

Deseronto exchanged his loaded rifle for Joseph's spent one, bellowed over the cacophony, "The one in the blue hat!" and went to work reloading. Joseph squinted through the cannon smoke and flying splinters and saw what Deseronto meant. A man in a blue hat had taken the place of the tall man, striding up and down behind the privateer's guns. He set his sights on the blue hat, dropped the barrel a hair's breadth, and dropped the privateer's new captain.

Deseronto took a couple of shots of his own, then grunted and went back to loading for Joseph, a little slower and clumsier than before. Any man on the privateer's deck who made the mistake of assuming command was brought down as soon as anyone started following his orders.

A cheer went up from the sailors of the *Lord Hyde* as the privateer sheered off and sailed away. Joseph stood up and discovered two things: there was blood seeping down into his right eye, and Deseronto had a foot-long sliver of good English oak through the fleshy part of his arm. Joseph wiped the blood out of his eye and pulled the splinter out of Deseronto's arm. Then the *Lord Hyde*'s captain was in front of him, sputtering: "I confess to you, Captain Brant, that I pshawed when I was told Mohawks got no more nerves than a stone, but now I believe it!"

Joseph couldn't fathom how to reply to a man who'd managed to grow a gray beard without learning that fear and pain were the only enemies no warrior ever killed. So he just slapped his hand against the barrel of his rifle and grunted: "Heap damn good English gun, ugh."

It was ten more days before the *Lord Hyde* stumbled into New York harbor—or Staten Island, rather. New York Town and the mainland were still in the Town Destroyer's hands. Staten Island was a city of tents and temporary armories, waiting for the troopships bringing reinforcements. The Royal and rebel armies sat staring at each other across the east mouth of the Hudson River, waiting.

There was a small Canienga contingent among the tents on Staten Island. Joseph looked in vain for Big William, but he was still in the north with the troops guarding Canada. But there was a young man who'd come recently from home, looking for Joseph. "I bring a message from your sister, the Oyander."

"I wouldn't've thought the rebels would be letting people come and go through their lines."

"Ha! White sentries—I could have stolen the shot out of their pouches as I went by. I told the Oyander I could bring a letter to you, but she thought it safest that I not carry a piece of writing. Her message to you is that you must not try to see her. Fort Johnson is being watched by men hoping to kill you."

"I have no more fear than you that white watchers will see me passing."

"Not only white men. Oneidas watch the house as well."

"Ah. And my wife and children—are they safe?"

"Yes, but not at Fort Johnson. The Oyander sent them to Old Isaac at Oquaga, since the rebels in our valley started taking hostage the wives and children of men who fight for the king."

It was almost the end of summer by the time the last of the reinforcements arrived from England, among them the 26th Regiment of Foot and Ensign Peter Warren Johnson. Joseph didn't get much chance to get reacquainted with his nephew, because Staten Island changed overnight from an aimless mass of shirtsleeved barracks loungers to a red anthill forming ranks, folding tents, and distributing ammunition. There was no attempt to disguise the activity from the sentries across the river. The soldiers of the Continental Congress had known all summer long they would be coming at them sooner or later; the soldiers of the king knew that they knew.

Joseph sat with his back against a tulip tree honing his hatchet, with quick-marching boot heels pounding the ground around him on their way down to the boats, and drums and bugles pounding blood through his ears. It seemed as though he'd spent the last year fumbling and mumbling his way through cotton wool. Now, finally, the air was clear.

CHAPTER 42

Molly jerked awake in the middle of the night to find a man standing at the foot of her bed. Since the first frost, she'd been building up the fire in her room every night before going to bed, but it had sunk down so low there was only a faint glow on the man looking down on her.

She forced her body to stay in the same curled position and held her eyes to slits. She was thankful at least that the nights weren't cold enough yet to have Nancy and Susanna in with her as mutual warming pans. Peering through the eyelash-veined, tear-blurred embrasures of her eyelids, she saw that the man wore a scalp lock, then that he was her brother. She threw the covers back, vaulted out of bed and leaped on him.

He seemed strangely reluctant to be kissed and embraced. Once she'd touched him enough to convince herself that he was really there, she stepped back and said: "I sent a message, warning you to stay away."

"I got it."

"But the Oneidas—"

"There was only one tonight. Do you still remember how to make a hoop to dry a scalp? I'm afraid I won't have time to do it properly while I'm traveling."

"You couldn't know there'd be only one of them tonight. You shouldn't take such chances." But she was more than glad he had and got away with it.

"I had no choice. It seems the Royal Mail coaches are finding it difficult these days to service all of His Majesty's North American colonies, so *some*one had to deliver," he reached inside his shirt, "a letter posted by Ensign Peter Warren Johnson."

She snatched it out of his hand, ran to the hearth, threw a few sticks of kindling on the coals and squatted on the hearth rug to rip the letter open. Her eyes dove into Peter Warren's penmanship-prize handwriting and her ears heard the sound of his voice:

My dearest mother,

I know that not one word of this will register unless I first assure you that the close of this year's campaign finds me with not a scratch on me—although it does feel odd to be able to say so, after seeing so many good fellows fall on either hand.

We have driven Washington out of New York Town and so we shall spend a pleasant winter getting fat under warm roofs. It appears now that we could have cut off the rebels' retreat and ended the revolution with one stroke. But Uncle Joseph tells me that is always the way in war—if one always knew the situation of one's enemy, one would never lose a battle.

The letter went on to talk of Captain This or Ensign That, names that meant nothing to her but had obviously come to mean a great deal to him. He ended with:

> May I see you gray and combing your children's hair.
> Yr evr affcte son,
> Ensign Peter Warren Johnson,
> 26th Rgmt of Foot

The hand holding the letter went limp and settled into her lap. Molly looked up at Joseph through hazy eyes. She couldn't say whether the tears were more of joy at having the letter or gratitude to him for chancing his life to bring it to her. She stood up, wiping her eyes, put the letter on the mantel and said: "Come downstairs and I'll get you something to eat."

Juba and Horace were in the cellar kitchen in their nightclothes, feeding beef and pickled onions to Joseph's traveling companion, who used to run a tavern in the valley until there was no more William Johnson to keep him in business. Joseph reached into his traveling pack and brought out a present from Peter Warren to his little brother—a huge, brass-bound horse pistol. Molly said: "For *George*? He's only nine years old!"

"When he's big enough to lift it, he'll be big enough to fire it. Horace can show him how to load and aim. Peter Warren brought back a trunkload of presents for all of you, but I had to travel light. The only reason I weighted myself down with this one is it's not just any pistol. It was surrendered to Peter Warren by the rebel Ethan Allen."

As Joseph stuffed himself with a very late supper, Molly plied him with enough questions to discover that the two of them were trying to get to Fort Niagara at Thundergate, where Joseph could start to organize the Canienga refugees into a fighting force for next summer's campaign. And he plied her with enough questions to discover that the Caniengas who remained at Canajoharie and the Lower Castle weren't likely to follow him. Little Abraham had convinced them that their wisest course was to stay neutral.

Then he asked her a question she was a little afraid to answer: "What's happened to my farm?" It had been unceremoniously taken over by a German farmer and erstwhile Indian trader with Ebenezer Cox & Company.

It seemed they'd had only a moment to exchange stories of home and exile before he stood up and said: "If we are to be safely away before daylight, we must go."

"Stay here. You can spend the day inside the house and be rested for a start tomorrow night."

He shook his head. "They will find the Oneida who sought to find me. They may have already." Juba put a ham and a few other bits of food in a sack. At the door, he put his hand on Molly's shoulder with the same strange hesitancy she'd noticed in the bedroom and said: "It shall not be so long this time, my sister, before I lay these eyes on thee again."

She went back up into her room, built up the fire and read Peter Warren's letter some more. The riot of the children waking up brought her attention to the fact that she'd been reading by the light coming through the window. As she dressed herself, she debated whether to tell them that their uncle had been there. She decided that the less they knew, the better, at least until the uproar over the scalped Oneida had died down.

CHAPTER 43

When night came down again, Joseph and his traveling companion crawled out of their bed of fallen leaves in a ravine a half mile north of Fort Johnson and borrowed a canoe that someone had carelessly left moored in plain sight. They paddled upstream through the maze of islands until they came to one that Joseph knew well, since it had been an outfield of his farm for fifteen years.

There were still a few hours of darkness left, but not enough for what Joseph wanted to accomplish. They could lay up safely on the island for the day. Even if the German squatter were to choose that particular day to ferry his plough and team across to do his autumn tilling, it was unlikely that he'd take it in mind to explore the willow copse to see if anyone might be napping there. And if he did . . .

Once the sun had traveled across the valley once more, they paddled across to German Flats and beached the canoe on the spot where Joseph used to launch summer picnics with Margaret and Isaac. The dogs came baying and snarling as they snuck into the stableyard, then changed to fawning and whining when they smelled who it was.

As Joseph's dogs licked his hands and jumped up against him and batted his leggings with their tails, he held himself rigid and tried not to think of the German farmer and his wife snoring in the bed he'd shared with Margaret, and Susanna, and Trembling Earth. He tried instead to listen to the voice of his Canienga Teacher: "Are you a war chief of the Hodenosaune, or an undisciplined boy who would throw away his war mission for the sake of revenge? The only way you will ever get your home back is to win this war."

He had no difficulty finding his way into the darkened tack room; he'd set the doorposts in himself. He would've thought all tack rooms smelled the same, but this quite clearly smelled like *his* tack room. Isaac and Christina used to perch on the workbench while he mended harness, and ask him what this buckle or that strap ring was for. But there was a new tinge in the odor now, of coarse tobacco and gin.

The new proprietor had gone and rearranged everything, so it took a while for Joseph's fumbling hands to find two saddles and two bridles. His horses came trotting when he whistled softly in the pasture. He picked out his two favorites, promised the others he would come back to claim them someday, and started up a deer path that wound from behind his farm to the top of the valley.

By morning they were clear of the Mohawk Valley. They were pursued, though. As soon as the sky grew gray enough to discern anything but sparse-leafed treetops against the stars, Joseph discovered that one of his dogs was loping along behind—the floppy-eared yellow bitch he'd hunted with for years.

The route they were taking to Thundergate was exceedingly roundabout. It was partly because the journey was also a recruiting expedition, and partly because Joseph wanted to see his family at Oquaga.

Once away from parts where people might recognize Joseph Brant on sight, he and his traveling companion became an Oneida and a New Jersey militiaman on leave from Washington's army, and traveled by day. As they forged farther south into New Jersey, they became two hunters. The floppy-eared bitch contributed to the disguise.

They were almost at the place where the trail along the Delaware divided, forking across country to the Susquehanna and Oquaga, when they met an old man hauling logs out of his wood lot with a team of horses. "How do, strangers? We don't get many strangers down around these parts these days, what with the war and all."

Joseph's companion said: "We have to go farther and farther afield these days. Whole damned country's getting hunted out."

"Hunters, be you?" The old man spat a contemplative stream of tobacco juice, with his eyes lingering on the king's brace of pistols thrust into Joseph's sash. "First time I ever seen hunters so loaded down with guns what ain't good for nothing but man-killing."

Joseph didn't have to look across at his traveling companion to know that the same thought was passing through his mind: they couldn't leave the old man alive to alert the countryside to a pair of suspicious travelers pretending to be hunters. Joseph drew one of his pistols and looked at it, then looked at the old man and said somberly: "I lost a brother a couple of years back to a bear that someone else had shot but hadn't killed. It was so mad with pain, two rifle balls couldn't stop its charge. I managed to kill it with an ax while it was busy eating my brother's head. Ever since then, I don't go out in the woods without . . . Excuse me, I always get a bit choked up when I think of poor Theopholis."

The old man looked down and shook his head sadly and spat again. "Dang shame there's so many fools with guns roaming about the woods these days what don't know enough or care enough to chase down what they've gut-shot. Oughta be a law. Bet you shillings to sheep shit it were some damned Tory or redcoat out playing 'sportsman' for a day. Don't you worry, though, good old George'll have 'em run out of the country by next year, mark my words. Well, good luck to you."

"Thank you."

"Sorry about your brother, mister."

Little Isaac came running to launch himself up at his father as they rode into Old Isaac's yard. "Little" Isaac wasn't so little anymore. All of Joseph's family had grown taller since he'd left them, including his wife. He hoped she wasn't planning to grow much taller, or he'd have to start looking up to her. Although in a way, he already had to. Perhaps it was something in the bloodline of Tekarihoga, but she already carried herself with the grandeur of a born Oyander. Or perhaps it had more to do with spending a year in close company with the Brown Lady Johnson. She even flicked her hair back when she laughed, like Molly did.

Grandeur or no, Trembling Earth was still a lithe and growing girl with the kind of shoulders that held breasts high and made a long-lost husband long to acquaint himself with what had changed inside her overdress and skirt while he'd been gone.

By the end of the week Joseph allowed himself at Oquaga, the winter had set in. The rest of the journey would be a rough trek on snowshoes. He had no choice but to leave Trembling Earth and the children behind, promising to come back for them in the spring. Old Isaac and a few other trail-hard Oquaga men elected to go with him to do some trading with the British at Thundergate.

When Joseph stood up from tying on his snowshoes to kiss Trembling Earth good-bye, she surprised him. She didn't cling to him or wail, nor was she cold at being deserted yet again. She stood tall and regal, brought her hands up to frame his jaw and neck and said softly: "Come thee back safe to me, my man."

Now that they were traveling under the Tree of Peace, there was no longer any need for Joseph Brant to pretend he was anyone but who he was. There was also no need to carry much in the way of provisions, or to sleep in the snow. Everywhere they stopped, whether a stockaded castle of longhouses or a lone hunter's bark wigwam or a whitewashed farmhouse that wouldn't've looked out of place in Albany, whatever food was in the house was naturally shared out with the travelers, and sleeping space cleared around the fire. At every place they stopped, Joseph repeated the same message: dig up your hatchets and carry them to the fort at Thundergate, or to Oquaga in the spring.

As the Union Jack over Fort Niagara appeared through the trees, Joseph found himself jogging along a path where clumps of scenery leaped out on either hand with crystal-sharp images writhing around them: that old cloven pine tree was the one the French officer fell back against when Joseph's bullet took him in the jaw, that snow-dusted rock had been green with moss when Little Abraham's son turned it red-black with his blood. . . . At the time, it had all seemed like a whirling riot of flaring colors and screams, which couldn't possibly have registered on his mind with any separate clarity.

The fort had been improved somewhat since William Johnson and his benighted savages took it from the French. But the cluster of elm-bark hovels huddled among the drifts against the stone bastions weren't Joseph's idea of an improvement. The sentry on the wall called down: "Who goes there?"

"Captain Brant and friends." As they paused inside the gate to take their snowshoes off, he asked the gatekeeper: "What date is it?"

"Twenty-eighth of December."

"Ah. I thought I'd lost count."

The heart of Fort Niagara was a gargantuan stone building with batteries of cannons among the forest of chimneys on top, and floors of barracks rooms and offices below. Joseph asked the Officer of the Day to show him in to the Officer Commanding. "I can, but it won't do you much good. He took a chill last week and died. We got him propped up in the icehouse till the ground thaws."

"Ah. Who's in charge, then?"

" 'Colonel' Butler seems to think he is. 'Though it's beyond me how a commission in the Mohawk Valley Militia gives a man the right to lord it over—"

"Perhaps because he's also His Majesty's representative for Indian Affairs for Niagara and environs. If you don't think that gives him some authority, try counting up the number of red skins versus red coats around here. Where is his office?"

John Butler had aged more than a year since Joseph had shaken his hand good-bye to embark for London, and he had developed an underlying air of permanent bewilderment. He'd lived most of his forty-some years as the heir-presumptive and then lord of the only estate in the Mohawk Valley older than William Johnson's. Now, in the wink of an eye, John Butler was a landless man with no income but what the Crown doled out for taking orders from Guy Johnson, who'd inherited the post of Superintendent of Northern Indian Affairs when Sir John Johnson made it clear that it was the one thing he had no wish to inherit.

After he and John Butler had shaken hands again, Joseph settled into a chair and said: "I thought I'd best prepare you in advance for a large draw upon your stores of provisions and arms when the warriors start coming in."

"What warriors?"

"I've been spreading the word throughout the Six Nations—or four, I suppose, if the Oneidas and Tuscaroras stay stubborn—that the king has given his hand to stand beside us if we stand beside him in this war."

"I have no orders regarding Indian allies."

"Small wonder—there have been none to speak of, until now. Once the commander-in-chief is informed that the Iroquois are digging up their hatchets to fight for the king, I'm sure you'll see some orders."

"I don't know, Joseph . . . General Carleton's none too sure that setting Indians loose is the way to fight a war."

"Then why the hell did I abandon my home and cross the ocean and spend the last two months risking my neck to get here?"

"Easy, Joseph . . . I didn't say the general was against it, just that he's none too sure. I'll send the message to him. In the meanwhile we'd best find you a billet and get you settled in."

When Joseph stepped into the corridor outside John Butler's office, the crook of an elbow hooked around his throat from behind, a thick forearm viced against the back of his neck and a guttural voice growled in his ear: "Got you now, you Tory bastard!"

Joseph squirmed his torso to the left and drove his right elbow back. He could almost hear the pleasantly sonorous drum thump. He did hear a surprised grunt in his ear, and felt the clamp around his throat loosening. He slipped free, skipped across the corridor to put his back against the wall, and said: "I greet thee, Big William."

"Huh. Some greeting. Let's go get drunk."

They didn't exactly get drunk, just shared a cup of watered rum in the cubicle that was Big William's quarters. Big William said: "It ain't much of a home, but it beats spending the winter in a knocked-together wigwam. Seems there's always room inside Fort Niagara for a son of Sir William Johnson—at least an acknowledged one. Feels funny being in here while everyone else is outside the walls or in the woods. But it wouldn't do them any good to have me out there with them eating their food and taking up five children's sleeping space."

"The king promised we'd be provided for if we left the valley."

Big William shook his head. "*Guy Johnson* promised. Ain't the same thing. They give us food and blankets, but not much else."

"They'll give us a lot more soon enough. The king himself has promised to stand beside us as his allies. That is the message I came to bring here, and Deseronto to those Hodenosaune camped outside Montreal. Once the Hodenosaune help the king's men win a few battles, they'll give us anything we ask for."

Big William rolled his lips together and slitted his green eyes down at the floor, as he always did when he had something to say he'd rather not. "While you been gone to England, and your sister holed up in Fort Johnson, a lot of Hodenosaune have been listening to the old song sung by others: let the whites kill each other while we sit back and take the presents both sides give us to keep us from joining the other side.

"And those that *do* want to fight mean to do it in the old way: each war chief with a dozen or two dozen warriors who choose to follow him will decide when and where and if they're going to fight."

"We can't fight this war that way."

"*You* don't think so. And I don't think so. But it ain't going to be easy convincing other people."

"When has it ever been easy?"

Joseph went about the business of getting settled at Fort Niagara, insisting that his quarters be large enough to house Trembling Earth and the children as well. But as the winter wore on, he grew more and more unsettled. No files of eager warriors came trotting down the ancient Forbidden Path to Thundergate. And then there was the matter of his salaries as interpreter for the Indian Department and a captain in the British army. The paymaster had no listing for him under either heading. So Joseph went to Colonel Butler again.

"The difficulty, Joseph, is that our superiors in Montreal and Quebec have yet to determine whether you should be paid through the Indian Department or the War Department."

"Suffering Judas, there's a *war* on—how do they expect to win it if they can't even make up their minds which department pays which junior officer?"

"As you say, Joseph, there is a war on. The High Command has other matters to contend with than your salary. I've given orders that you be allowed to draw anything you want from the fort stores."

"On *credit*? I'm not a beggar! I have a family to provide for. And nothing I say to the warriors I'm trying to convince to fight for the king will mean anything unless a present goes along with it."

"Easy, Joseph. As I said—you can draw anything you need, for yourself or for presents. And I'm sure long before you bring your family here, I'll have received orders regarding your salary."

Joseph told himself it wasn't fair to take out his frustrations on John Butler. He said: "Speaking of orders, has the High Command given you any inkling of what role they would like the Hodenosaune to play in this year's campaign?"

"I believe the commanding general is still debating how best to employ Indian allies."

Joseph looked into John Butler's kindly, guileless visage and suddenly suspected that it wasn't the commanding general who was squeamish about unleashing the savages, it was John Butler. But he could only communicate to the commanding general through John Butler.

The instant the rivers and creeks ceased to be maelstroms of swirling ice, Joseph set off back along the Forbidden Path, with only Big William and a paltry dozen other warriors loping behind. They picked up a few more warriors from the castles along the way, but not many. Joseph grew desperate enough to try to take his message within the borders of Oneida country, but it soon became apparent that with the Oneidas—as with the Senecas, Onondagas, Tuscaroras, Cayugas, and three-quarters of the Caniengas—Captain Brant was just pissing into the wind.

At Oquaga he ran up the Union Jack and waited. It was mostly a matter of form: by now he didn't expect much to come from the waiting. Trembling Earth did her best to cheer him with the fact that there were fifty warriors camped around the house instead of the dozen he'd started out with, but he knew she was only trying to put a good face on it.

After a week of fruitless waiting for new warriors to materialize, Joseph muttered to Trembling Earth: "It serves me right. . . . All those months in England, I was perfectly content to let the news sheets brag that I would put three thousand warriors in the field . . . to let the king shake me by the hand and think me head chief of the Iroquois—as though there were any such thing. . . ."

"You were only letting the English believe what they could understand, so that the king would give his promise. You've already done more than any other Hodenosaune in this war."

"You don't understand. This is a *war*. It means nothing which warrior did more than another, it only matters which side wins the war."

And then a remarkable thing happened. Joseph was sitting with Isaac on his knee, looking at the engravings in Old Isaac's Bible, when Trembling Earth came in and said: "There are some men outside to see you."

There were about forty of them, all Big Knives, squatting in the shafts of spring sun through the trees or leaning on their head-tall Pennsylvania rifles, puffing pipes or spitting tobacco juice and murmuring to each other through their beards. One of them came forward, an odd-looking man somewhat shorter than Joseph but with arms at least as long. He had red hair and a red, splotchy face that looked like it had been put together out of plates like a turtle's back. "You Cap'n Brant?"

"I am."

"My name's Ezra Hawkins. Me and the rest of the boys is
what they call damned Tories. There's a lot more of us back
along the Delaware, but most stayed home to wait and hear
what you said to us'ns. You see, we figure it's about dang time
we got tore-in in this war, but there ain't no dang way we're
going to put on red coats and march in circles while some
powder-wigged Macaroni with a ramrod stuck up his farthole
calls the tune. But we ain't none of us perzackly military ge-
niuses. So we figured, if'n it were all right with you, we figured as how we'd enlist in this here regiment we hear you're
putting together. Like I say, we cain't march in time worth spit,
but most of these here boys been shooting the eyes out of
squirrels at a hundred yards since twelve years old. Some was
slow starters."

Joseph said: "It'll be hard traveling and hard fighting."

"That's what we figured. We also figured, uh, if'n it were
all right with you ... we figured as how we'd call ourselves
Brant's Volunteers."

"I think, gentlemen, that that would be just danged fine."

Chapter 44

There were two Herkimer brothers Molly knew well
from the days when every major celebration in the Mohawk Valley was hosted by Sir William Johnson. One of the
brothers had fled to Canada, but Nicholas Herkimer was now
the general of the militia of Montgomery County, as the rebels
had taken it upon themselves to rechristen Tryon County. He
lived in a big brick house a half day's ride upriver from Fort
Johnson, with the Oneida girl he'd taken up with after his wife
died.

When it became known in the valley that Captain Brant was putting together a Tory regiment at Oquaga, General Herkimer sent a proposal for a peace conference on neutral ground at Unadilla. According to the Caniengas who visited Fort Johnson, the preparations going on suggested that General Herkimer was planning to take every militiaman who could march and every cannon he could muster to the peace conference.

Molly didn't like it. It would be just like Joseph to take an invitation from an old comrade-in-arms at face value. Over Horace's protests, she loaded Sir's old campaign tent onto a wagon and set off for Unadilla, with Fort Johnson's last remaining footman to drive the wagon, Juba to do the camp cooking, and George, who was big enough to help with the tent and was suffering the confinement at Fort Johnson worse than his sisters.

As the wagon rolled southwest under the blue sky and fresh green canopy of treetops, Molly began to feel a little guilty about escaping from jail and leaving her daughters behind. It was strawberry time, and every campsite meant a pleasant ramble through the woods for after-supper and breakfast sweets.

It wasn't all pleasant, though. The mood of the country had changed. Now people stared suspiciously when they passed each other on the road. The road went past several farms where the houses had been burned, and one place where someone had nailed a dead cat to the gatepost.

There was no sign of Joseph at Unadilla, so Molly kept on going toward Oquaga. About halfway there she encountered something she hadn't seen for two years—a Union Jack flapping brazenly out in the open. It was being carried by a man on horseback in front of a long line of men coming along the road. At a guess, Molly figured there were about two hundred of them: Big Knives, Caniengas, Cayugas, and even a few Senecas. Some were on horseback and some were on foot, but all of them were armed to the teeth. Beside the standard bearer rode her brother, with his rifle crooked in his arm, his shot pouch and powder horn slung over his shoulder, his waist sash weighted down with a brace of pistols, a tomahawk, and a knife, and the sun gleaming off the gold ring in his ear. He jumped down off his horse and she jumped down from her wagon and they met on the road in between.

He sputtered: "What are you doing here? Has something happened at Fort Johnson? Where are the rest of the children?"

"They're back safe at Fort Johnson. I came to take my part in your council with General Herkimer."

"It isn't safe for you to be traveling."

"You don't seem to be too concerned who sees your flag passing by."

"There's a lot more of us than there is of you. And anywhere east of Unadilla we'd have to take to the woods."

"Well, I'm here, so it must've been safe for me to travel."

He grunted and looked at the sun and said: "We still have an hour or two before making camp. We'll talk then."

Juba hung a pot over the campfire and set to work making a stew while the footman finished putting up the tent and Master George went scavenging for more firewood. Mistress Molly paced and fidgeted, waiting for her brother. All around them were the sounds of male laughter and male voices singing or shouting or murmuring low. Juba felt a bit like a spy in the midst of this camp of men easy with each other's company. She also felt utterly safe for the first time since the war began.

When Juba started slicing up salt beef and onions, Mistress Molly knelt down beside her to lend a hand, but Juba could see that her attention wasn't on it. Some trick of the slanting, evening sunlight also made her see that Molly's face had grown heavier around the jawline while she wasn't looking. Not jowly by any means, just that the once sharp-honed half oval of jaws and chin—like the small end of an egg—had grown a little blurred around the edges. To Juba it was still obviously a face that would make any man suck in his stomach, but she was aware she wasn't entirely unprejudiced where Mistress Molly was concerned.

Captain Joseph and Big William came ambling out of the woods. It seemed to Juba there was something different about Captain Joseph. He wasn't swaggering, but there was a certainty about him, as though anything that was going to get decided hereabouts was going to get decided by him.

Captain Joseph and Big William sprawled down beside the fire and lit their pipes and began to talk with Mistress Molly. Juba hummed to herself. She was certain that this exact same aura of wild domesticity—perfectly at home with just a cook fire under the trees and family members gathered around it—was how she would've lived her life in Africa.

After twenty-odd years in a household filled with Mohawk-speakers, Juba had picked up enough of the language to follow the gist of the conversation. It helped that these three also slipped in English as fancy suited. They traded news of the outside world and the Mohawk Valley. Master George came back with an armload of wood and snuggled against his half brother's immense knee to listen in as an accepted part of the circle, just as Juba was doing. It was all very cozy until Mistress Molly said to her brother: "I thought at first you were being foolish, wasting your time coming to talk to Herkimer. And then I realized it will be easier to urge the Royaners to dig up the hatchets if we can say we tried our best to make peace with the rebels."

Juba saw Captain Joseph and Big William look to each other as though they heard footsteps at the threshold of their secret. Then Captain Joseph looked into the fire with hooded eyes and said: "Who knows—we may do more than try. If the congress will guarantee to respect the Stanwix Line, we have no reason to fight them."

Mistress Molly looked like she'd been hit on the back of the head with a skillet. "No reason? What about our promise to the king?"

"The Hodenosaune only promised not to fight *against* the English. And are not the rebels English as well?"

Mistress Molly opened her mouth to jump in, but her brother held up his hand to show he wasn't done speaking. "What purpose comes before all others to a Pine Tree Chief or the Elder Sister of the Wolf Clan? Preserving the Tree of Peace, is it not? The roots of the Tree are rotting. The Fire That Never Dies has been snuffed out—by the Oneidas and Tuscaroras drawing away from it, and the Onondagas grown too weak from smallpox to keep it burning on their own. All that remains of it are the embers we sent to safety in Canada. If the Town Destroyer and the congress sign a pact to leave us in peace, we can rekindle the fire at Onondaga and the Tree can grow whole and strong again."

"You just spent two years getting ready to fight!"

"And they will be two years well spent, if our show of strength has frightened the Americans into making peace with us. The purpose of the Eagle is to keep evil away from the Tree, not to go looking for it."

Juba couldn't say for sure whether Mistress Molly looked more angry or bewildered, but she definitely looked more lost than since the days just after Sir William closed his eyes. She practically shouted at her brother: "The Americans can make us any promises they want, and then take them back if they win the war!"

"So can the English."

"When have they ever done that before?"

"Not often. At least not while Gets Business Done was alive. But there is no more Gets Business Done to keep them honest. And no more Gets Business Done for us to be loyal to." And then Captain Joseph leaned across to put his hand on his sister's, and he said something that made Juba almost drop her stirring spoon into the pot. It was as much the ruthless directness in his voice as what he said. "I would ask thee, Someone Lends Her a Flower: is thy *onikonhra* more dedicated to the *orenda* of the Hodenosaune or to the ghost of Sir William Johnson?"

After Captain Joseph and Big William had gone, Mistress Molly just sat there with her mouth open and her uptilted eyes wide, muttering: "Of all people . . . of all people . . ."

Juba tried to think of something leavening to say, but the best she could come up with was: "I don't know about all this talk of eagles and roots, Mizt'ess Molly, but I'ze sure Captain Joseph knows what he's doing."

"Do you think so? Well, it makes little difference, because whatever he chooses to do, he's going to do it regardless. You would think, Juba, that after all these years, I would've seen my little brother in every mood or character there was to him. But until today I had never seen the war chief on the war road."

Except for functional remarks, Molly and her brother didn't speak again until the day their column passed by Unadilla and Big William came jogging out of the woods to announce: "Herkimer's there, all right. With two or three hundred of his militia. They're camped on the flats on the north side of the Susquehanna, with cannons pointing south. There's a big old beaver meadow on the south bank they've put up a long sort of shed in the middle of—guess that's where they plan to hold the council."

Joseph said: "There's a plateau on the west side of that meadow, isn't there?"

"Well, there's a little sort of hill. . . ."

"That's where we'll camp. Tell Herkimer that neither he nor any of his men are to approach that hill. And tell him we won't be doing any conversing inside any enclosed pavilion, but out in the open where everyone can see us. Oh—and you might ask him what the object of his visit is."

It was hard to find an open space on the wooded hill that was large enough and flat enough to accommodate Sir's palatial, patched, once-white campaign tent, but Molly managed eventually. As the footman busied himself erecting and anchoring it, and Juba went about the business of making its interior comfortable, Molly and George went down to the border of the meadow and peered out through the leaves. In place of the lodge that had stood in the middle when it was a beaver pond, there was the shed Big William had described. It was more of an arbor, actually, with poles stuck in the ground to hold up a roof of spruce boughs. She supposed it was supposed to look something like a longhouse, but it looked more like an overgrown rat trap.

She saw Big William loading his white flag into a canoe in front of the militia camp, and went back to her tent. She and Joseph, Big William, a Seneca war chief named Cornplanter, and the spokesman for the Big Knife volunteers squatted down under the same roof General Johnson and King Hendrick had sat down under on the night before Lake George. The Big Knife, who was introduced to her as Sergeant Ezra Hawkins, had twined a feather in his red hair and smeared a couple of streaks of ocher under his eyes. He said: "No offense, ma'am, but it do feel funny holdin' a military powwow with a woman."

"It feels rather funny doing it with a white man. I suppose we'll both get used to it."

Joseph asked what Herkimer had said. Big William said: "Unless you tell him different, he says him and a couple of his officers will start out unarmed from their side of the meadow in the morning and meet you in the middle, along with whoever you want to bring along as advisers. When I asked him why he'd come, he said he'd just come to have a friendly conversation with his brother Captain Brant. So I asked him if all those other men and their cannons had come to talk to their brother, too."

"And what did he say to that?"

"Not much—just got a little redder in the face."

Molly said: "Why would he come all this way, and propose a council in the first place, if he has nothing in particular to say?"

Ezra Hawkins said: "Less'n he was just hopin' there wouldn't be enough of us to handle his militia, and he could finish off Cap'n Brant's regiment afore it even got tore-in in this war." Molly wondered if he had any idea that Cap'n Brant was seriously considering sitting out this war if the Continental Congress guaranteed to leave the League of Peace alone.

When Cornplanter spoke, the tiny silver bell pierced through his nose to dangle above his upper lip tinkled softly. He looked the perfect picture of a white man's notion of a misty-minded savage—besides the bell in his nose, his ears were pierced and weighted in several places to make pendulous flaps of skin—but he was anything but. He said: "Herkimer must've come empowered by the congress to offer us *something*. Perhaps he is just holding back in hopes that we will ask for something smaller first."

Molly said: "If we let him think we have any doubts whether the league is strong enough to defend itself, he won't offer us anything."

In the morning the whole camp, with the exception of Juba and the footman and a few sentries, armed themselves to go down to the edge of the meadow. Molly was shocked to see George coming out of the tent toting Ethan Allen's pistol in both hands. "What do you think you're doing with that?"

"Horace showed me how to load and aim—"

"He *what*? Teaching a ten-year-old boy to . . .?"

George put on his stubborn face and hugged the pistol to him. Joseph *had* said that when George grew big enough to lift it . . . But Joseph wasn't George's mother, and George had always been big beyond his years. On the other hand, if the council did turn into a battle, the Montgomery County Militia weren't going to stop to ask birth dates. She said: "Stay close to me. And don't you *dare* pull back the cock on that thing until I say you may."

"Yes, Mother."

They joined the stream of Brant's Volunteers flowing down to the base of the hill. At the woods' edge Molly put her hand on George's shoulder to stop him, and stood looking out through the leaves at the old beaver meadow. General Herkimer and about fifty of his militia had already taken possession of the arbor. They appeared to be unarmed, but at that distance they could all be carrying guns and swords under their coats.

Molly looked over at Joseph and said archly: " 'And a couple of his officers' . . .?"

Joseph said, "Nicholas Herkimer wouldn't stoop to treachery if he was selling a horse to a stranger," and began to strip off his weapons and pile them up in front of George.

"Nicholas Herkimer isn't the only one out there."

"So I noticed." He raised his voice to call out in Canienga and then in English: "I need a few dozen men to walk out with me. Leave your weapons behind." The red-haired Big Knife propped his rifle against a tree and began to unsheath his big knife, but Joseph shook his head. "No, Ezra—they came expecting to meet only us Iroquois."

"I'd feel a dang sight better about this, Cap'n, if'n me and the boys was out there with you."

"So would I. But not today." He turned to Molly. "Well, you came to council—let's go council."

Molly, Joseph, Big William, and Cornplanter stepped out into the naked sunlight and started across the meadow, with about forty painted warriors following behind. General Herkimer and a couple of his officers came a little ways forward from the shed and then stopped and waited. One of the officers was Ebenezer Cox of the exploding rifles. When the two parties met, General Herkimer stuck out his hand and said: "Well, Joseph . . ."

"Well, Nicholas."

"Well . . . I understand you prefer to talk in the open air, Captain Brant."

"It doesn't look like rain, General Herkimer."

"No . . . no, it doesn't at that. I brought a spade out here this morning and cut a circle in the grass just over there. I thought that you and I and one or two of our officers could go inside that circle to talk and everyone else stays outside."

"That sounds perfectly amenable to me." Joseph gestured his warriors to wait and moved with General Herkimer and his two colonels inside the circle. Molly followed them across the rut that General Herkimer had cut, as did Big William and Cornplanter.

As Joseph squatted down among the pasture grass and wild-flowers, Molly settled down onto her knees and hip behind him. General Herkimer nodded at her and mumbled, "Miss Molly," as though he wasn't quite sure whether to be sociable or not, and waited for her to be seated before he sat down. Captain Brant's forty warriors and General Herkimer's fifty took up positions on opposite rims of the circle, although some of the militiamen didn't look all that comfortable sitting on the ground.

There were no longhouse niceties—no presentation of wampum, no council fire, no tobacco ceremony. The general tried to pass a few remarks about the weather, and Joseph cut him off with: "What is the reason of my being thus honored by a visit from the general of the Tryon County Militia?"

Ebenezer Cox said: "*Montgomery* County."

"That remains to be seen."

Nicholas Herkimer waved Cox to be quiet and said: "There is no need, Captain Brant, to look at this meeting so formally. I just thought it high time I paid a friendly visit to my neighbors of the longhouse."

"And these . . .?" Joseph gestured at the militiamen hunkered in the grass beyond the circle, and the unseen ones across the river and in the woods. "They have come to pay a friendly visit? All these men want to see the poor Indians? It is very kind."

"After our visit with you, we were planning to carry on to see the chiefs at Unadilla—"

"No. You have come far enough."

"Well, perhaps you can make them understand at Unadilla that we Americans only want the same thing you do: to be free." The general went on into a long, rambling description of all the intolerable evils that the king's evil ministers—though not the king himself, of course—had loaded onto the backs of the Great Father's American children. Among his apparent ramblings, he salted in little probing questions: Didn't Captain Brant agree that this or that tax or arbitrarily imposed law would try the patience of the saints? Hadn't the Iroquois themselves always deposed chiefs who grew too high-handed?

Captain Brant invariably replied without actually replying. In fact, Molly was surprised at how adroitly Joseph parried the requests for agreement while still holding out the prospect that he might agree at bottom. But she wondered when he was going to get tired of General Herkimer talking about the hand he was holding and demand that he lay a few cards on the table.

Joseph finally did so by laying down a few of his own: "The king's wampum belts still lodge with the Six Nations. We intend to keep faith with him as our fathers did before us. We were not afraid to fight the whites when you were all united. Now that you are divided against each other, why should we be afraid?"

Ebenezer Cox shouted: "You impudent little bastard! If you're all damned dyed-in-the-blood Tories, there's no use in talking! If you want to do the same as your fathers, we'll send you down to join them in their graves!"

Joseph threw his hand up, and suddenly the militiamen were the only ones sitting outside the rim of the circle; the forty warriors were running back toward their weapons in the woods. It cost Molly a great effort to stay sitting where she was. A devil's symphony of war whoops went up behind her, accompanied by a smattering of gun cracks. The militiamen bobbed back and forth like children with overfilled bladders, unsure of whether to run back to the river or listen to the general roaring: "No! No! No! Captain Brant! Colonel Cox is just carried away! This is a truce!"

Joseph stood up and turned to face his warriors, raised his arms over his head and brought them down past his shoulders in an arc. The whooping and shooting stopped. He turned back toward the general, who was wiping his face with a checkered handkerchief and trying to light his pipe. Molly sat surreptitiously squeezing her skirt in her hands to sponge off the sweat, trying not to look like a lamb just snatched back from the threshold of a slaughterhouse, and trying not to gawk at her little brother.

There wasn't much more said that day. Outside of a few

more aphorisms, all that General Herkimer came out with was: "It's known that among your Volunteers there are several notorious Tories, a certain Ezra Hawkins for one. They should be surrendered to us to take back for trial."

"No."

"These men have broken the law and committed—"

"No."

But Joseph did agree to meet with the general again the next morning. When Ezra Hawkins had been filled in, he said: "This child don't see much point in wastin' another day jawin' about bull feathers."

Molly said: "It may be that Herkimer has just used today to see if he could wheedle us into an agreement without giving anything away. Now that he sees he can't, he can spend tonight thinking over how to present what the congress authorized him to say."

"Still don't see much point. The lines was drawn from the first shot at Concord Bridge."

Before the sky had turned from red to purple, it was already night in the forest. There was a scratching at Molly's tent flap, and a male voice said: "Oyander . . .?"

"Yes."

One of the Canienga warriors who'd cast his lot with Binds Two brushed past the door flap, with his hand clamped around the arm of General Herkimer's Oneida girl. "I caught her sneaking around and spying, and she said—"

"I wasn't spying!"

"She said she'd come to see you."

"Please, Oyander—I have to tell you—" The Oneida girl cut herself off and darted her rabbit eyes up at the warrior with the snare grip on her arm.

Molly's head shook itself in disbelief that there could ever have been a time when she had been that young. She said to the Canienga: "Wait outside."

When he was gone, the girl started blubbering: "Please . . . I don't know—I don't know what to do! I can't betray my man, but I can't let him—"

"Ssh. Sit, child, dry your eyes. Take a breath while Juba pours you a glass of wine. Now—you can't let him do what?"

"Tomorrow morning, four of his men are to climb up into trees on the east side of the meadow and take aim at you four—Binds Two, William of Canajoharie, Cornplanter, and you. If Binds Two won't make the promises Nicholas wants him to make, Nicholas will step out of the circle and . . . they will kill you!"

"Are you sure of this?"

"I heard Ebenezer Cox begging he be allowed to be the one to shoot your brother."

Molly found her brother curled up beside a campfire with his elbow propping up his head, exchanging sleepy murmurings with Big William. Joseph sat up when he saw her coming.

She'd expected him to react with anger or outrage at what she'd come to tell him. Instead, his features grew steadily more impassive as she told it, and his soft brown eyes grew cold and murky. When she was done, he said blandly: "*Nicholas Herkimer* would take me by the hand under a white flag just to twist my back toward an assassin's bullet . . .? And his Oneida woman told you this?"

"Yes!"

"Why would she do that?"

"She may be an Oneida, and Herkimer's bed warmer, but she is still Hodenosaune."

"How noble of her. And what a strange coincidence that she should come to *you*, and tell her story to you alone before vanishing back into thin air—when you have all along been trying to sway me against trusting the Americans."

Molly could feel tears starting, and hardened her eyes to stop them. She could have told him that George and Juba had heard the story as well, and that the Oneida girl had had to scuttle back to Herkimer's camp before she was missed. But the notion that she would have to present evidence to make him believe her choked her off.

William of Canajoharie twisted his massive shoulders around to face his friend and said: "Binds Two, that thought wasn't worthy of you, much less your sister."

Joseph lowered his eyes. "You're right. Forgive me."

Molly said: "I do."

The brown eyes came up again. "I still find it difficult to believe that Nicholas Herkimer would do such a thing."

"These days everyone is doing things that would be difficult to believe two years ago."

"The question is . . ." Joseph tugged on his lower lip, "what to do tomorrow?"

"You're not thinking of going out there again?"

"I must. Herkimer has yet to tell me what the congress has sent him here to offer. If it's an offer that can be accepted, the League of Peace might be spared a war that is tearing us apart."

"Then I'll go out with you."

Big William intoned: "And so will I."

"No. No one will."

Molly said: "You're not Tekarihoga, Binds Two. And not even Tekarihoga can tell one of the Clan Mothers where she can or cannot go."

"In the face of the enemy, even Tekarihoga does what the war chief tells him. If I have only myself to worry about, I can keep my eyes open and see that Cox doesn't get a chance at me if the council starts going badly. Besides," he got a funny little glitter in his eyes, "think on the brighter side of this."

"Which side is that?"

"Ebenezer Cox may try to shoot me with one of his own guns."

In the morning, Joseph appeared in a mottled old deerskin hunting shirt instead of the bright calico longshirt he'd worn yesterday, and he'd left aside the silver officer's gorget the king had given him. Once again, everyone but a few sentries and Molly's servants trooped down through the woods to the edge of the meadow. But this time only Joseph stripped off his weapons. He said to Big William, "If they are fool enough to start a fight and I can't get back, let Cornplanter be your war chief," then turned to Molly. "Well, my sister . . ."

He bent to kiss her cheek. She clamped her arms around his neck and whispered into his ear: "Don't go."

"I must."

He straightened up again and stepped out onto the meadow. Molly watched his back grow smaller as he walked toward the clump of men around the spruce-roofed pavilion. There appeared to be a lot fewer of them out there today than there had been yesterday. When he moved into the council circle, General Herkimer did as well, but this time with only one of his colonels. She called up to a warrior who had climbed a nearby tree: "Is it Ebenezer Cox?"

"No—I don't see Cox anywhere."

Molly reached down and picked up one of her brother's pistols and his knife, then stood squinting at the three doll-sized figures. Joseph and the other two stayed standing instead of settling down on the grass. It seemed to Molly that the general and the colonel kept shifting from side to side, and that her brother kept shifting with them, in a strange dance that kept one or the other of the blue-coated backs between him and the woods on the east side of the meadow at all times.

Suddenly he stabbed his arm straight up at the sun and let out a war yell that pierced the sky. An instant later the woods on the west side of the meadow were fronted with a quarter-mile-wide line of feathered, ululating demons waving their weapons in the air. Molly jumped out and howled with the best of them, brandishing Joseph's knife and pistol over her head.

He stayed standing in the circle a moment longer, then turned and walked back calmly to his company of warriors. He waved his arm and they all melted back into the woods. As soon as they were safely under the shadows of the trees, she grabbed his arm and said: "What happened?"

"The Oneida girl spoke the truth. Herkimer was very nervous. I don't think the congress sent him here with anything to offer us at all, except a few head of beef by way of hospitality. I thanked him for his civility in coming so far to see me, and advised him he should go back home now. We'll stay here a little longer to see if he follows my advice."

They had a fine feast on the general's beef. Halfway through it, though, the sky blackened and the clouds opened up. They all ran laughing through the pelting rain, carrying dripping hunks of steaming beef back to their tents or lean-tos or sheltering pine trees.

Not long after the storm was over, Joseph came to her tent and said: "General Herkimer took my advice, so we might as well head back to Oquaga and see if the High Command has sent us any orders. What do you intend to do?"

"Go home as well. Heaven knows what's been happening to my bean vines while I've been playing diplomatist."

"Maybe it's time you started thinking about packing up the children and going to Niagara."

"I don't see why I should. General Herkimer has no reason to shoot me now that this is over."

"Well . . . wait a day or two here before you start back, so you don't catch up with the militia on the road. I fear for you, staying at Fort Johnson."

"I fear for you."

"I fear you have less cause. I don't know when I shall see thee again. You saved my life."

"The Oneida girl did."

He shook his head. "She would never have betrayed her man's secrets for my sake. Promise me you'll wait one day at least before you start back."

"You don't trust me without a promise?"

"Not when it comes to being brazen."

Within a week of her return to Fort Johnson, she was so immersed in all the summer things that had to be done to provide her family's needs for the winter that Unadilla seemed a year ago. Summer was also the season for war, and hence fresh crops of war rumors sprouting in all directions.

The eldest of the Three Sisters was just beginning to show her silky hair when there came a piece of war news that was too close to home to be a rumor. A British army had marched down from Oswego to besiege the rebels who had taken over Fort Stanwix. Accompanying the redcoat regulars were Sir John Johnson's regiment of white exiles from the Mohawk Valley, and Brant's Volunteers.

In the middle of the night, Horace rapped on Molly's bedroom door. "Miss Molly, there's a young fella here from Canajoharie what won't take 'tomorrow' for an answer."

"I'll be down directly." She threw on her dressing gown and hurried downstairs.

Horace had tapped out a mug of beer for the "young fella" squatted on the parlor hearth rug. "Oyander—we were nightfishing and saw there were lights burning in Nicholas Herkimer's windows far later than there should be, and many horses coming and going. When the lights went out at last, we think it meant Herkimer is gone."

"Gone where?"

"No one knows. But there were a lot of other lights and noises up and down the river, like the militia were digging up their hatchets."

Molly could think of one logical place where General

Herkimer might be taking his militia: Fort Stanwix. She could clearly see her brother and all the others shooting at the enemy behind the fort walls, and another force of rebels descending on their undefended backs. She said briskly: "How did you come here?"

"By canoe."

"Good. Are there other paddlers with you?"

"No, Oyander. The rest stayed fishing."

"How many will your canoe hold?"

"Three. Four if they're not too big."

"Horace, would you wake up George, please."

"What for?"

"What for? Because I asked you to. Going back upriver won't be as easy as coming down, and George is a better paddler than anyone else in the house, including me."

Horace pursed his lips together, shook his head glumly at the floor and murmured: "What're you fixin' to do, Miss Molly?"

"I'm going to pay a call on our sweet little Oneida neighbor upriver."

"Damn it, Molly! I mean . . . hang it, Miss Molly . . . Why don't you just put a knife to yer throat and pull the trigger?"

"It's pitch-dark, Horace—no one will see us going. And there's a lot of islands we can skirt between on the way back. And even if some eager farmer gets up early enough to catch a glimpse of us, what's the harm in me going for a morning boat ride with my son and a friend? Now will you please go wake George, or do I have to do it myself while I'm trying to put some clothes on at the same time?"

By the time they got as far upriver as Canajoharie, Molly's shoulders were knotted from paddling double time. She and George waited at the foot of the Boiling Kettle while the canoe's owner ran to fetch the fastest runner left in Canajoharie Castle. A moderately well trained Hodenosaune runner could cover forty miles in a day.

Even though George was a long way from his full growth, the canoe wallowed a little with four. The sun was up by the time the big brick mansion came in sight. Molly left the other three leaning on their paddles, panting, and urged her stiff legs up the bank, hoping she wasn't too late for what she had in mind.

Nicholas Herkimer had got himself a new wife, but his Oneida girl was still part of the household, officially a chambermaid or kitchen maid or some such. But it did complicate matters. If Molly had got there in time, though, there would be no need to deal with complications.

The little house at a remove from the Herkimer mansion wasn't nearly as elegant as the one at Fort Johnson, but it did have a surrounding wisteria arbor. Molly watched through the curtain of trellis and vines as the household trooped out one by one for the first call of the morning. After the new Mrs. Herkimer had come and gone, and her new stepchildren and several servants, Molly began to fear she'd have to force her way into the house. But then the Oneida girl came out and headed across the back lawn walking briskly and tightly, crossing one foot over the other.

Molly considered letting her do what she had to do and accost her after, but decided the more pressure, the better. Just as the Oneida girl was reaching for the outhouse latch string, Molly stepped out from behind the hedge.

"Oh! Oyander, I—" The rabbit eyes flicked back over her shoulders. "What are you—"

"Where has he gone?"

"Where has who gone?"

"Don't play stupid with me. Your white man and his militia. Where did they march off to?"

"I don't know."

"You know."

"I can't tell you."

"You told me when he had plans to murder me and my brother and Big William."

"That was different," she whimpered, twisting her hands between her thighs, "and even then, I felt bad after. . . ."

"You don't know what feeling bad is. I can make a corn dolly with your face on it and cut out its womb. I can put fishhooks in your father's bread. I can scatter smallpox dust along the road to this house. I can—"

"*Please*, Oyander! I can't betray—"

"Betray who? Your own people? Your own clan?" The little slut's sobbing maybe should have made her feel some sympathy, but it didn't. "Are you a Hodenosaune woman of the Wolf Clan or just a Dutchman's whore? Where has he gone?"

"To Fort Stanwix to sneak up behind the king's soldiers!"
"By which road—the south bank or the north?"
She blubbered: "I don't know."
"By which road?"
"The military road, through Oriskany Ravine!"

CHAPTER 45

Oriskany Ravine. Joseph knew it well. Muskingum had hunted turtles along its banks, and once on a moonless night, his Teacher had sent him to find his way from one end of Oriskany Creek to the other without getting his moccasins wet.

As soon as the runner delivered Molly's message, Joseph knew that Oriskany Ravine was the place to meet General Herkimer. At this time of year the creek was more of a swamp that the road crossed over on a narrow, log causeway. On either side of the marsh was a snaking maze of slopes and gulleys covered with woods thick enough to hide an army. Which was exactly what Joseph proposed to do.

His commanding officer, Colonel St. Leger, called a staff meeting in response to the news about Herkimer's militia, and began with: "I don't mind telling you, gentlemen, that this puts us in a bit of a pickle. If we abandon the siege to take on the rebel relief force, we'll be leaving our rear open to a sortie from Fort Stanwix. And as yet we have no knowledge of how strong General Herkimer's—"

"Eight hundred to a thousand." Joseph's schooling and travels had cured him of his primitive reluctance to interrupt, even when it came to commanding officers. "Mostly Provincials, some from as far away as Albany, with a few Oneidas. They're marching straight along the open road, without flankers or even an advance guard. We can lay for them in Oriskany Ravine. All I need is a couple of hundred other men to add to mine, which will leave you more than enough men to keep up the siege."

"That sounds to me, Captain Brant, like an excellent plan. Let's see now . . . that sounds like the kind of fighting that regular soldiers aren't exactly made for. And holding up a siege isn't exactly what Indian braves and irregulars were made for. So, what say . . . Colonel Butler, will you add your Rangers to Captain Brant's force?"

"Gladly, sir."

"And—Sir John, fifty of your Royal Greens should flesh out the numbers nicely."

"Certainly, sir. I'll put them under the command of Major Watts and I'll remain here with the bulk of my regiment to support you."

In the night, one of Joseph's Canienga scouts came to where he and Big William were sleeping. "Binds Two, there are three white men from Herkimer's camp blundering around in the woods in circles. It looks like maybe they're trying to sneak their way to the fort. Should we kill them?"

Joseph thought about it for a moment. "No. Herkimer will want the fort to know he's coming. If he doesn't get a signal that his message got through, he might wait. If it looks like the three white men can't find their way, make a few noises behind them to scare them in the right direction."

Joseph lay back down again and closed his eyes, but didn't exactly sleep. The morning dawned hot and sultry, with a low-hanging canopy of cloud. The whole summer had been hotter than usual, but today the air felt and tasted like boiled wool, with storm clouds pressing down on it. Joseph wondered what it was about him and Nicholas Herkimer that made a storm rise every time they met.

The plan was simple, like the best plans always were. Brant's Volunteers, Butler's Rangers, and Major Watts's Royal Greens would spread themselves out through the woods on either side of the road through Oriskany Ravine, like a pouch that opened at both ends. Once Herkimer's army was inside the pouch, the drawstrings would close.

Joseph and Big William found themselves a nice big oak tree with a deep hollow between its roots and a clear view of the last stretch of the road where it rose up out of Oriskany Ravine toward Fort Stanwix. Joseph's first shot would be the signal for everyone else to let fly.

Big William leaned his rifle and war club against the oak tree and took out his pipe. Joseph clucked at him: "Look at you—half white and still more primitive than any pure-blood Indian. Hasn't anyone told you that the hatchet has replaced the war club, just as the gun has the bow?"

"This isn't just a war club, this is the power of my second father." Joseph knew that, and he'd heard the explanation several dozen times before. But the purpose of the moment was to not think too much about what was coming. "When I was a boy, King Hendrick took me out into the woods and we picked out an ironwood sapling and he showed me how to tie the living sapling into a knot just above the roots. By the time I was old enough to travel the war road, and Hendrick long since was traveling the strawberry road, my little sapling had grown into *this*," and he brandished his seamless length of ironwood with a knotted end the size of a baby's head.

Joseph puffed on his own pipe, which was also his tomahawk, and said: "That is all well and good, but old things are not always the best things. Out of all the inventions that the white man brought to Turtle Island, what could be more salubrious than a hatchet like mine, with a pipe bowl on the butt end of the blade? All I needed to do was take out the pith of a handle-sized branch, and I can sit here sanctifying my war weapon with tobacco. And it means I have one less article to find a place for in my war bag or to remember to pick up every time camp moves on."

"If your *onikonhra* had come equipped with a memory, you wouldn't have to worry about forgetting your pipe."

They slipped into silence for a while, sitting smoking what might be their last pipe, waiting. Joseph remembered the times when Little Abraham would stand him poised with a throwing hatchet in front of a target and leave him in that position while he sat whittling or braiding a fishnet for what seemed like hours, then suddenly shout: "Now!" But now still hadn't come. Joseph sighed: "I tell thee truthfully, my brother, I would that there weren't Oneidas coming with the militia. Before this day is out, I might well find myself with the blood of my children's uncles on my war hatchet."

"Better that than the other way around."

They smoked their pipes out with still no sign of the militia. Big William said: "Maybe they decided to wait for reinforcements."

"Let's hope not."

The thick air suddenly cracked with a gunshot that made them both jump and then laugh at each other as they realized it was a cannon miles away. Two other cannon booms followed in quick succession, all from the direction of Fort Stanwix. Big William said: "You think maybe they saw us sneaking away and figured now'd be a good time to try a sortie?"

Joseph shook his head. "That was the signal that Herkimer's messengers got there. Took them long enough. I wouldn't be surprised if part of Herkimer's plan is for the fort to launch a sortie at the same time he's advancing, but Colonel St. Leger has more than enough men to handle any breakout from the fort."

"Huh. If the redcoats and Hessians ain't all buck naked in the river to get away from the heat." William had always had a knack for rooting out the positive.

They sat waiting. Joseph began to wonder if he hadn't been wrong about the three cannon shots being a signal to General Herkimer. And then the warrior whose hiding place was nearest to his and Big William's turned toward them and sliced his hand upward through the air in a signal that had been passed along the line faster than any messenger could gallop.

Joseph stretched himself out prone with the barrel of his fine English rifle sloped across an oak root and checked the powder in the priming pan one more time. One of his scouts came sprinting and dodging through the undergrowth and flopped down beside their tree to pant out: "They're coming on fast—more like running than marching. Their baggage wagons are getting left behind."

"Do they have an advance guard?"

"Some. Three horsemen are far out in front."

"Do they have any scouts in the woods?"

"A few Oneidas. But they're not far enough out from the road to see us." He got his breath back and grinned: "Many scalps today, Binds Two."

Big William grunted: "Maybe ours."

Then there was no more sound but the sighing of the trees, the chatter and skitter of the squirrels, and the sweet notes of a warbler overhead. Into the timeless summer music of Oriskany Ravine came a thudding of booted feet and shod hooves. Joseph wiped the sweat out of his eyes and off his trigger hand.

Big William leaned over from where he was lining up his own rifle, to put his hand on Joseph's shoulder and whisper: "May thy brother the wolf be with thee on this day, Binds Two."

"And the redbird with thee, William of Canajoharie."

Three horsemen came into view on the twisting aisle of road cut through the trees. The one in the middle on the big white horse was Ebenezer Cox.

Joseph centered his sights on the bridge of Ebenezer Cox's pointy nose. His finger twitched against the trigger but he held it steady, debating whether to fire or let them pass. It was up to him to gauge whether to let the advance guard go by to make sure all of Herkimer's column was inside the pouch of Oriskany Ravine before the drawstrings closed. But if the scout was right that the baggage train was getting left behind, the column was too stretched out to trap them all in the ravine regardless.

The three horsemen were almost past the oak tree when the front rank of the jogging militia rounded the bend in the road behind them. Joseph pulled the trigger. The forest on either side of the road exploded, as did Ebenezer Cox's face. Big William's shot took the horseman on Cox's left—no one had needed to tell Big William which one Joseph would be aiming at. The one who'd been riding on Cox's right wheeled his horse and galloped back, straight into a hatchet in the chest. The remnants of the front ranks of the militia were running back over the bodies of their friends, unaware that there were more enemies behind them than in front of them.

Joseph reloaded his rifle, slipped his hand through the wrist thong of his tomahawk and jumped up. With Big William whooping along beside him, he charged down through the tangle of brush on the side of the road toward the marsh and causeway in the center of the trap. One of the militiamen was sitting with his shoulder propped against a tree, weeping and trying to reload his musket with one hand. Joseph's hatchet hacked through the back of his neck as he went by.

Out of the corners of his eyes Joseph saw the end of a musket snaking up from behind a deadfall. He flung his arm up in front of Big William and they both took cover, William flinging himself down behind a convenient boulder and Joseph pressing his back against a walnut tree.

Joseph leaned out to fire his rifle at the deadfall and then skipped back behind his tree. As the militiaman's return shot sprayed his cheek with bark chips, Joseph was already dropping his rifle and flipping the haft of his hatchet into his hand as he bounded toward the deadfall. The militiaman seemed surprised to be interrupted in his reloading. He looked even more surprised when the blade of Joseph's pipe bit into the place where the side of his neck joined his shoulder.

Then it was Joseph's turn to be surprised. Behind the deadfall was a little hollow where lay two wounded militiamen the dead one had been trying to protect. One raised a pistol to point at Joseph's chest. But before the pistol went off, a war club with a knotted end the size of a skull came down on top of the militiaman's head.

As Big William whipped his club back up as easily as though it were a willow wand, the other wounded militiaman screamed: "Please! Joseph—don't you know me?" Maybe he did or maybe he didn't. The face seemed vaguely familiar, but he couldn't place the name. So he cut the throat as gently as possible.

Joseph went back to get his rifle and reload. Then he and Big William ran zigzagging down the wooded slope ringing with gun cracks and war whoops and the clanging of steel against steel. Where the slope leveled out and the woods thinned, Joseph grabbed a passing oak branch to keep his momentum from carrying him headlong into the marsh. The end of the bough broke off in his hand, but it served to slow him enough to regain his balance and look to see what was in front of him before he came crashing out of the woods. He looked and stopped dead.

The front ranks of the militia fleeing back from the ambush had run into the rear ranks running forward from the ambush behind them. They were all milled together along the causeway and among the cattails and willow hummocks rising from the marsh. The Rangers and Royal Greens had come at them with bayonets, and it had turned into a hand-to-hand melee. Joseph had seen that happen in many battles before, but never like this.

They were snarling and rolling about in the mud like dogs, stabbing and grappling and biting at each other. On a grassy knoll, a Royal Green kept slamming a rock down on the remnants of a dead militiaman's head until a militia bayonet took him in the back. Two men up to their knees in bog were slashing at each other with knives, even though they were both already cut to pieces and so covered with mud and blood it was impossible to tell what color uniforms they wore.

Then Joseph saw the German who had taken his farm, and understood. Before Joseph had time to think, he had already thrown his fine English rifle up to his cheek and pulled the trigger so quickly that he missed cleanly at thirty yards. It was all he could do to keep himself from throwing down his rifle and charging at the German with his tomahawk, even though there were a hundred militiamen between them.

Butler's Rangers and Brant's Volunteers were fighting men they'd hunted with and barn-raised with for years—all their lives in some cases. And then those same men had driven them and their families out of their homes and taken them for their own.

Joseph's eyes latched onto the distance-diminished figure of Nicholas Herkimer. On a piece of high ground in the middle of the militia's ragged defensive circle—already littered with the bodies of men and horses—General Herkimer sat with one leg covered in blood and stuck out at an odd angle. They'd stripped the saddle off his dead horse and propped it against the base of a tree to give him something to sit on. He was puffing on his pipe, mingling tobacco smoke with the clouds of powder smoke hovering over the battle.

The sight of Herkimer calmly puffing away and directing his officers reminded Joseph that his own job wasn't just to fling himself into the fight. The first thought was that he didn't know whether all of the militia column had been caught inside the trap.

With Big William trailing after him, Joseph bulled his way through the sucking marsh, skirting around the battle, and climbed the south slope of the ravine, backtracking along the road the rebel militia had followed down into Oriskany Creek. As the din of the fighting at the bottom of the ravine faded behind him, the sounds of another battle came from above: men and horses screaming, crackles of gunfire. . . . When he crested the slope, he saw Herkimer's rearguard and ammunition wagons frantically trying to turn themselves around to run from the arrows and musket balls coming at them from the woods on either side of the road.

Joseph turned back toward the ravine and raised an ululating shout that brought a few dozen of his warriors charging up the slope. With Joseph leading half of them on one side of the road, and Big William on the other, they set off weaving through the thickets, spurring the militia's flight with sniping.

The rebels weren't easy to keep up with. Even though the baggage wagons were weighed down with militiamen clinging to their sides, the teamsters kept whipping the foam off the backs of their horses to make them gallop with the load. Some of the militiamen who couldn't find a place on the wagons were throwing away their guns and shot bags to run faster. Finally, Joseph threw down his own rifle, leaped out into the middle of the road and ran after them, with his tomahawk in one hand and knife in the other. Big William and the others followed suit. The occasional militiaman stopped and turned to fight, but most of them kept running until they were cut down or speared through the back.

Joseph's arm grew weary from swinging his hatchet, and his lungs started to hurt from running and hacking at the same time. He remembered that the real fight was still going on far behind him in the ravine. He stopped and flung out his arms to tell the rest of his warriors to stop, then leaned his hands on his knees and breathed himself out. A few warriors ignored his signal and kept on chasing the militia—they would serve to make sure the rebel rearguard didn't find their courage again soon.

Once Joseph had caught his breath, he turned and loped back down a road dotted with dead men, and with wounded ones trying to crawl into the bush. A few of Brant's Volunteers stopped to do a little scalping, but Joseph and Big William kept on moving toward the sound of gunfire.

Standing on the lip of Oriskany Ravine seemed to Joseph what it must be like to stand in the Sky World looking down on a lightning storm. The heavy, sultry air kept the powder smoke from rising, so it had been pressed down into a thick, ground-hugging cloud lit by crashing flares of musketry.

He gestured to the warriors who'd followed him back, and started down the wooded slope. As he descended into the cloud, his eyes and nostrils began to sting. He slitted his eyes and breathed through his teeth, taking shallow breaths so as not to trigger a cough and draw a bullet. As it was, it was more like chewing the air than breathing.

Big William took hold of his shoulder to stop him, shook his head and murmured into his ear: "Slow. Listen. Where's our front line?"

Joseph stopped and listened. The sounds of screams and roars of rage, clanging steel, and gunfire came from up ahead and either side. It was no longer the sound of two armies clashing, but of several hundred scattered conflicts—men sniping at each other's musket flashes or hacking and bludgeoning at each other with whatever came to hand.

Joseph nodded at Big William and moved forward more cautiously. Up ahead he could make out the back of one of his Cayuga warriors taking cover behind a tree. The Cayuga performed the old trick of baiting a hidden enemy into shooting and missing, and then running forward to tomahawk him before he could reload. Only this time the instant the Cayuga bounded out with his tomahawk raised, another shot from behind the same deadfall as the first took him in the belly.

Joseph beckoned two of his warriors. "You to the left, you to the right. Tell everyone that Herkimer has given orders for *two* militiamen to hide themselves behind each piece of cover."

That was the last captain's thought Captain Brant had for some time. From then on he became just another warrior, thinking only of whether the vague form flitting toward him through the smoke was an enemy or friend.

He was crouched in a stand of bulrushes reloading his pistols when the clouds that had been heating up all day finally burst. The rain came in wind-driven sheets that bent hundred-foot oak trees like saplings and washed him clean of sweat and blood in an instant, and also washed the powder out of his priming pans. It was impossible to fire a gun in this kind of tempest, or even keep a reliable grip on the handle of a hatchet. Shielding his eyes with his arm, he sent Big William off to the left and he moved to the right, spreading the word to fall back and find shelter to wait out the storm.

John Butler had had the same thought. He and Joseph and Big William hunkered down under a pine tree with the captain who was now in command of the contingent of Royal Greens. It was eerie to hear only the roaring of the rain, the crack of branches torn away, and the occasional muted wail of a wounded soldier.

Colonel Butler shouted to make himself heard over the wind: "How are your losses, Captain Brant?"

"Impossible to know exactly in this mess, but heavy." Certainly a lot heavier than was customary in wars of the True People of Turtle Island.

"High casualties among my Rangers, too, and the Royal Greens. Nothing compared to the slaughter done among the rebels, though. But General Herkimer still has a few hundred effectives left. As soon as the storm has blown itself out, we must be at them again—until he sees he has no choice but to surrender."

Joseph knew John Butler was lying, although perhaps to himself as well. The rebel militia would never run up a white flag to a force made up largely of Indians. They'd heard too many stories of torture stakes.

The rain started to let up. It had cleared away the smoke. Oriskany Creek was running like a spring stream again, except that it flowed red from the blood washing out of the marsh. The unscathed and the walking wounded crawled out from under their bushes and cutbanks and went back to killing each other.

Joseph and Big William were working their way along the bank of the reborn torrent of Oriskany Creek when three Oneidas sprang out of the woods at them. Joseph dropped his half-cocked rifle and threw up his hatchet to lock against the one coming down at him. He snaked one of the king's pistols out of his waist sash and fired point-blank, then whirled around to defend himself from the other two.

Big William had already dispatched one of them and was swinging his war club down at the other. The Oneida was too smart to raise his own war club to try to block a blow from Big William. Instead, he arced it downward against William's shin. There was a sickening cracking sound and Big William went down like a felled oak tree. The Oneida cocked back his war club, howling with glee, and Joseph's second pistol put a bullet in his gaping mouth.

Joseph crouched down beside William of Canajoharie. Big William's Teacher had done his job well. William just said in a level voice: "It's broke. Finish fighting and then we'll set it."

"This isn't a safe place to leave you."

"I'll crawl up the slope a ways—"

"Don't be ridiculous—you've got a broken leg. I'll carry you."

"Don't be ridiculous—you couldn't lift me even when we were wrestling."

"Then I'll drag you. Sit up a bit more. . . ." Joseph passed his arms under Big William's armpits from behind, just managing to girdle his chest, locked his hands together and started dragging. William helped as much as he could by pushing along with his good leg, but when his other leg bumped over a tree root or a rock he'd let out a little gasp and go limp.

In a shaded little run-off gulley was a moss-covered boulder. There were a couple of dead militiamen, or perhaps Rangers, sprawled nearby, but there was no place in Oriskany Ravine today where there weren't dead men lying nearby. Joseph wrestled William's shoulders up against the boulder and sat back gasping. Big William said: "Even with a broke leg, you're the one that has to call a halt to wrestling with me."

"Just catching my breath . . . Here, I'll leave you my pistols just in case—"

"Don't be ridiculous—they ain't loaded."

"Well, I'll load them, then, won't I?"

He did so and handed them to Big William. William said: "You can use my war club if you like."

"I can't lift it."

"Well, go kill some more white men with your little ax, then. But don't get *yourself* killed—no one'd know where to find me."

Joseph started back down the slope toward where he'd left his rifle. But he hadn't gone ten steps when he got a funny little tingling feeling at the back of his neck, as though there were something he should've done but hadn't. He turned around. One of the dead white men behind and above Big William's boulder was up on his knees with a bayonet raised in both hands over his head. Joseph's hands flew to his waist sash for the pistols that weren't there as he screamed, "William!" too late.

Big William jerked once as the bayonet buried itself in his chest. Joseph scrambled back up the slope, tugging out his tomahawk. The white man stayed hunched over Big William, straining frantically at the haft of the bayonet, but it was planted firmly and slippery with William's blood. He looked up at Joseph as the tomahawk swept down. Joseph's eyes registered an image of chalky white skin framing gaping blue eyes, then it was gone. He knelt beside Big William and put his hand to the tree trunk of a neck. It might as well have been wood, for all the life left in it.

Joseph hacked at the body of Big William's killer until it was red pulp, then helter-skeltered down the hill, leaving his pistols behind. The only thought left in his mind was that there were plenty more of Big William's killers left to kill.

There was a red-rimmed time that might've been minutes or hours, and then someone was tugging at his shoulder and yelling in his ear: "Joseph! Captain Brant!"

Joseph became aware that he was kneeling on a patch of amber moss and engaged in the act of scalping a brown-haired corpse. He looked back at the hand yanking on his shoulder and then up into the shouting features of John Butler. "Joseph! We must abandon the battle and make haste back to camp!"

"Why?"

"The rebels in Fort Stanwix are making a sortie against our camp!"

"Colonel St. Leger has more than enough men to handle any—"

"No—our camp was taken by surprise!"

"How could they be surprised by—"

"There's no time to argue! We must hasten to the rescue!"

Joseph moved farther back into the woods and raised the cry for Brant's Volunteers to gather around him. He detailed a few scouts to stay behind and keep him informed, and then set off at a lope leading Brant's Volunteers back toward Fort Stanwix, with the Rangers and Royal Greens following at a quick march.

By the time they reached the camp in front of Fort Stanwix, there was no rescuing left to be done. The rebel sortie party was safely back behind their palisades, leaving a shambles behind. Sir John Johnson was wandering around the ruins in his shirtsleeves, muttering dazedly: "Deuced villains! All my papers, my tent, my sword . . . They even took my deuced coat!"

Joseph asked him: "What happened?"

"The heat was enough to stifle a salamander, and the rain only succeeded in making it muggier, so I retired to my tent and took my coat off—"

"You *what?*" Joseph could hear the echo of Big William's voice: "If the redcoats and Hessians ain't all buck naked in the river . . ."

Fortunately, before Joseph's hands could rise up to deprive Sir William Johnson's bloodline of another son, a voice behind him called: "Binds Two!" It was one of the scouts he'd left behind in Oriskany Ravine, panting from sprinting several miles. "Binds Two—Herkimer's militia—what's left of them— they're heading back the way they came, as fast as they can hobble, leaving their dead behind."

Joseph rummaged a spade out of the wreckage of the camp and plodded back down the road to Oriskany Ravine. When he got there, the sun was turning red and the crows and wolves were taking their first tentative nibbles at the banquet laid out for them. All up and down the creek banks, across the causeway and the marsh, along the road and the fringes of the forest, the bodies of men lay tangled together. In some places where the fighting had been thickest they were piled three and four deep, in long mounds like erratic foundation walls. They couldn't live together in the Mohawk Valley, so now they were entwined forever in Oriskany Ravine.

The Oneidas and militia mustn't have found Big William's body, because he still had his scalp lock, which would please him. The shallow depression he was lying in was relatively clear of rock veins or tree roots, so Joseph would only have to widen it and deepen it a little. He lifted his unfired pistols out of his Brother's lap, wrestled Big William up out of the hollow, and went to work with the spade. Then he went down to the marsh and stripped off his hunting shirt to use it as a sack for rocks dug up out of the creek bed. He could easily have had help, but he didn't want any. As he worked, he sang to himself:

"Hai!
Big William
Hai hai!
Was there ever a wrestler like you?"

He dragged Big William into the grave and folded the ham-sized hands around the haft of his war club. Joseph only had one small string of black wampum with him, so he added in all the scalps he had taken that day. It took a lot of rocks to cover him. Once it was done, it was getting almost too dark to see.

Joseph cut a few patches of moss to make a vague approximation of a blanket over the grave, still singing "Hai hai . . ." At the end he switched into English, "Unto thy mercy, O Lord, we commend the spirit of our brother. Ashes to ashes, dust to dust . . ." then couldn't remember the rest, so he settled for: "May ye have food and raiment, a soft pillow for yer head, may ye be forty years in heaven before the devil knows ye're dead."

The siege of Fort Stanwix went on, with Colonel St. Leger's troops diligently digging trenches and tunnels to safely bring their cannons within range. Joseph spent his days alternately coaxing and threatening his own warriors. The tradition of Turtle Island warfare was to take to the war road once the weather was good for traveling, fight one battle and then come home. They had definitely fought a battle at Oriskany Ravine, so why shouldn't they go home? Joseph managed to convince them that it was a different kind of war they were in this time, but it took some doing.

Joseph wasn't quite sure whether he felt all that good about convincing them. He had no doubt his sister would congratulate him for accomplishing it, and Sir William Johnson would've, too. But he did wonder whether the ruthless attrition of civilized warfare was much of a gift to the benighted savages of Turtle Island. On the other hand, if the Six Nations fought this war by the old lackadaisical methods, they'd be ground down under the Town Destroyer's reprisals as Pontiac had. It was all very confusing.

The artillery moles had almost dug close enough to the fort walls when the little bird Tskleleli came singing of a rebel army of three thousand coming to relieve the siege. Joseph and most of the other officers whose homes were in the Mohawk Valley were of the opinion that they should at least *see* this rumored army before fleeing from it. But Colonel St. Leger believed his duty was to get his troops back safely to winter quarters in Oswego.

Joseph sat on a hill watching and listening to Sir John Johnson and Colonel St. Leger in the camp's parade square shrieking their opposing opinions at each other. Although Joseph's opinion was the same as Sir John's for a change, it seemed to Joseph that making the wrong decision wasn't as harmful as the spectacle of two war chiefs throwing tantrums. That wasn't what Big William had died for.

The argument was resolved by a Seneca with a brutal sense of humor, who called out from the top of the hill: "They're coming!" His British Majesty's Mohawk Valley expedition lit out up the Oswego road, spurred on by English-speaking Hodenosaune shouting "They're coming!" whenever they could stop laughing long enough to get the words out.

Long before Oswego, Captain Brant and those of his Volunteers who still had the stomach for it split off across the Adirondacks. Joseph was looking to find the army of General "Gentleman Johnny" Burgoyne, who was supposedly marching down the Hudson Valley to Albany while Colonel St. Leger was marching down the Mohawk Valley to link up with him. There must be *someone* in all the king's men who'd gone to war with the intention of fighting.

CHAPTER 46

Molly was carrying her candle up to bed when she heard a horse's scream slicing through the stone walls of the house as though they were cheesecloth. It didn't stop. She ran downstairs and toward the back door, guttering out her candle. But there was another light coming from the narrow back room where Horace had taken up residence since Fort Johnson became a jail. He was carrying a dark lantern and shrugging the strap of his fowling piece on over the coat he'd clapped on over his nightshirt. She yelled over the screams from outside: "What is it?"

"Well I don't know exackly, do I, miss? Else'n I wouldn't be goin' outside to have a look-see." Although his voice was matter-of-fact, she could tell that the screams dug into the roots of his teeth as much as they did hers.

George came pelting down the stairs carrying the pistol Peter Warren had sent him, wearing nothing but a pair of hastily buttoned breeches. Horace said: "Why don't you give that to me, Master George—I'll put 'er in my pocket and you carry the lantern and we'll each pick up one of the gardening hoes on our way out the door. Close the gate on the lantern when I open the door, and don't open 'er again till I say so—and then keep 'er held out away from you."

Molly started to follow them out. Horace put his arm out. "You'd make a fine target in your white nightgown, Miss Molly."

"You don't think anyone would—"

"I don't rightly know. But there ain't no sense in leadin' 'em into temptation. Me and Master George'll be safe enough out in the dark. But please stay inside till we've had ourselves a look-see. Would you do that for me, please?"

She went into the dining room, pulled out a chair and sat down stiffly with her hands folded obediently on the table. Horace nodded approvingly and went out the door with George.

The girls snuck downstairs in their nightgowns, the littler ones whimpering and covering their ears against the horrible shrilling from outside. Juba, Jemmy, Abraham, and the last of the hired field hands came down from their quarters in the attic. They all sat wincing around the table where they sat down to dinner every night.

Molly tugged little Nancy up onto her lap. Juba did the same with Susanna. The other four girls sat in a rigid row, clutching each other's hands fiercely. Abraham snugged his chair up next to Jemmy's and draped his black roof beam of an arm across her shoulders.

There was a boom of a shotgun from outside that made them all jump. When its echoes faded, the torture-stake shrieks were still there. A little while later—although it didn't seem like a little while—there was another gunshot and the screams were gone.

All the sounds that Molly hadn't been able to hear since the screaming started seemed unnaturally loud: the ticking of the parlor clock, her own heartbeat, the seeming seashell roar of eleven people breathing with their lips clamped shut. She heard George's voice getting louder, whining, "Bastards!" and other words his mother wasn't supposed to know he knew. The back door opened and closed, but no one got up from the table. When Horace and George appeared in the dining room doorway, George looked like he wanted to strangle someone, and Horace looked like someone had strangled him.

Horace shuffled over to her chair at the head of the table and snuffled: "It were Juanita, Miss Molly. They put her eyes out."

"They . . . ? Eyes . . . ?"

"Well, they . . . they brought sewin' needles with 'em, you see, and they . . . stuck 'em in her eyes. If'n I'd had any notion I'da loaded up this old gun with more'n rock salt. From what I could see of the side of her stall, though, Juanita spattered a bit of blood that weren't hers. I didn't . . . I didn't know what else I could do, miss," and he tossed George's pistol onto the table.

She looked down at the pistol and heard herself saying coldly: "I always wondered why they called them horse pistols." It was odd how cold she felt. All she wanted to do was to coldly proceed with the business of finding out who "they" were and then coldly informing the warriors at Canajoharie—if any of the Canienga men who'd stayed in the valley could still be called warriors.

Horace said: "Don't you think, miss, the children ought be up in their beds by this time of night?"

She realized the girls were all crying. She kissed them good-night once more, wiped their eyes and assured them that Horace had seen to it that Juanita wouldn't suffer anymore, then sent them back upstairs, telling Nancy and Susanna they could sleep in her bed tonight. George hung back and didn't want to go. She said: "If you stay, Elizabeth will want to come back downstairs, and then Magdalen will want to come with her, and then Peggy and Martha, and the next thing you know even Susanna and Nancy will be pattering down the hall."

When they were alone, Horace said: "'Who do you think's goin' to be next, Miss Molly? One of the other horses? Or Miss Elizabeth? Or maybe Miss Nancy?"

"They wouldn't harm the children!"

Juba said: "Mizt'ess Molly, anyone who'd do that to a poor old horse'd do anything."

Molly looked at Juba in dismay. Throughout all of Horace's glum predictions and urging that they had to leave the valley, Juba had simply gotten on with her life at Fort Johnson unconcernedly. But now Juba's yellowing, muddy eyes looked directly into hers and she said: "Mizt'ess Molly, we gots to get away from here while we still can."

Horace said: "Juanita were just a warnin'."

Molly said distantly: "I know that." She felt herself drowning. A piece of flotsam bobbed up in front of her and she clutched it. Even as straws go, it wasn't much. "I'll go to the new magistrate in Johnstown tomorrow. He's an old friend of mine." Perhaps "old friend" was a bit of an exaggeration, but the man had been a guest at Sir William Johnson's table more than once.

Horace said: "After Oriskany Ravine, I don't know as you got any friends in Johnstown."

It had been a long time since Molly had had to squeeze herself into the constricting livery that white women saddled themselves with. But since the Mohawk Valley had grown so civilized, she suspected she'd be more likely to be listened to if she weren't dressed like an Indian.

It turned out not to be difficult to squeeze into the green dress after all—it was impossible. All the servants' work she'd had to do lately couldn't alter the fact that she was ten years older than the day Sir had mentioned offhandedly that he suspected she'd look demmed fetchin' in green.

While Jemmy was letting out the waistband of the green dress as far as it would go, Molly went outside to tell Horace he needn't hitch up the carriage just yet. There was the sound of a gunshot from the forest on the far side of the stables. Gun-shots in the forest in daylight weren't unusual: even the most dedicated of farmers got a yen for wild game from time to time. But something made her hitch up her skirts and start running, through the creek and toward the farmyard on the other side.

As she rounded the barn she saw that Abraham and the last of the hired hands were crouched behind a corn rick and a fence post. The hired hand hollered, "Get down, miss!" but she kept on running for the dark lump disfiguring the barley field.

Horace was lying curled up on his side. When she rolled him over, a paste of blood speckled with half-chewed grains of barley dribbled out of the corner of his mouth.

She could feel a howl welling up through her throat, and then pictured the glee of the watchers in the woods. So she dug her hands into the dirt between the rows and lifted them over her head, sifting earth out through her fingers and singing: "Hai! Horace! Hai hai!" But she couldn't find any other words.

The black silk dress that had been made for Sir's funeral still fit her. The carriage horse made it clear that he knew it wasn't Horace's hands on the ribbons, but the hired hand still managed to keep them on the road. When they stopped in front of the undertaker's in the town Horace's master had built, she took out her handkerchief and pocket mirror to wipe her cheeks dry before accepting the field hand's proffered hand and stepping down.

The undertaker practically jumped out of his chair when she came in. He glanced nervously at the clerks and workmen taking a pause for tea and said: "Miss Molly! I—"

"I know. You're not supposed to do business with Tories. I'm sure no one will object to you making coffins for them."

"Coffins? For who?"

"Horace."

"Old Horace? What—?"

"They shot him down from hiding while he was standing out in his golden field of barley."

"Oh God. What did poor old Horace ever do to anyone? I think it's a damned, dirty, stinking coward's crime, Miss Molly, and anyone what don't like me saying so can go hang—as well they should. Don't you worry, miss, I'll do Horace up right. I don't even have to measure him—I can see him standing there clear as day."

"So could his murderers."

The new magistrate had plumped up a good deal since Molly saw him last, but he still looked undersized in the desk chair built to fit Sir William Johnson. He heard her out with many sympathetic clucks and head-shakings and then said sadly: "It's a terrible shame. The number of times I've urged the Assembly to pass laws against hunters firing within range of cleared fields—"

"It wasn't hunters! They murdered him!"

"Now, now—I understand how you're distraught. Who wouldn't be? Many bereaved or injured people have sat in that same chair for the very same reason: because they feel that some intentional crime, no matter how horrendous, would be easier to bear than accidental—"

"Was it accidental that they stuck needles in Juanita's eyes?"

"Who's Juanita?"

"My horse!"

"I thought Horace was—"

"My *horse*! The one Horace had to shoot, before they shot him."

"Who shot him?"

"The watchers in the woods. The same ones that put out Juanita's eyes."

"Ah. That was a terrible crime, of course. I'll certainly inform the sheriff of it. And I can see how, in your distraught state of mind, you'd naturally tend to connect the horse with Horace—"

"Would you be so good as to write down on a piece of paper your full name and where you are residing these days?"

"Pardon me? Why?"

"So I can hand it to the officers of the king when they march in here."

He turned purple and pointed his finger at her. "The day you see another redcoat in the Mohawk Valley is the day they go skating in Hell! Peel your stinking Tory cunt off that chair and march it out of here. And if you know what's good for you, you'll keep on marching it as fast as it'll go straightway to London. Bailiff! See that the seat of this chair is scrubbed down with lye before anyone else has to sit in it."

She paused in the doorway just long enough to say: "Were you at Oriskany Ravine, Your Honor, or huddled safe at home? Ah—I'd thought not. Ask the ones who were there what to expect."

Horace used to go to the Lutheran church. The minister said dubiously: "I'm not certain whether he still considered himself part of our congregation, ma'am, any more than you do. I can't recall the last time I saw him in church. . . ."

"More than a year ago, I should expect. I believe he missed it, but he didn't want to be the cause of trouble. That would have been the Christian thing to do, would it not?"

He sucked his lips thoughtfully and said: "He didn't have much family, did he?"

"He had a sister in Schenectady, but she stopped writing him letters when he refused to stop working for a dirty Tory."

"So it would be a . . . small funeral?"

"A very small funeral. Small and unobtrusive. So unobtrusive that I doubt it would cause even the most stringent member of the Safety Committee to suspect you of harboring loyalist sympathies."

On the way back to Fort Johnson, the road wound past a farm where the farmer and his two sons were out harvesting. When they saw the carriage approach, they put down their scythes and reaping hooks, stooped to pick up clods of earth, or perhaps stones, and started toward the road. A ruddy-faced woman stepped out of the cabin door and shouted: "Ephram! You and the boys go on about your work now!" Ephram looked from his wife to the carriage and back again, then dropped what he held in his hands and returned to his scythe. The woman didn't leave the doorway until the carriage was safely past, but neither did she call out any greeting to Molly nor look directly at her.

Molly kept her eyes on the woman, craning her neck around as the farm dropped behind the carriage, expecting at least some flicker of recognition from a fellow human being. None came. The woman certainly knew her. She was the Scottish midwife who'd assisted at the births of Peter Warren and Nancy and all the others in between.

After supper Molly flopped down on a chair in the parlor to dip into the last of Fort Johnson's stock of brandy before going upstairs to change into less binding, Canienga clothes. After the first glass she decided she might just as well stay where she was and finish off the bottle and then change straight into her nightdress.

She was staring into the last tincture of firelit red-gold at the bottom of the glass when the front door crashed open and a dozen Oneidas burst in whooping.

Molly charged toward the parlor doorway, yelling at them in Canienga to get out of her house, then repeating it in English when she saw that half of the "Oneidas" were white men in very rudimentary disguises. One of them—recognizable under the clumsy daubs of paint as a militia colonel whose name she remembered as something like Stacey—yelled back at her: "This isn't your house, Tory bitch. The property of traitors belongs to the congress. We're here to start the confiscation before you get the chance to bury all your money. And maybe we'll take a little something else besides, if you and your pretty little daughters don't have the sense to run and hide."

Molly knew the last threat was idle, even if he didn't. The Oneidas might have broken away from the league for now, but they'd been brought up Hodenosaune, and among the Hodenosaune there were few taboos stronger than the one against rape, even of women captured in war.

But there was no taboo against killing boys who suddenly appeared with cocked pistols in their hands, such as George did now at the top of the stairs. As the rifles came up, Molly shrieked: "No! George—put it down!" George did what he was told. One of the Oneidas sprang up the stairs to confiscate the pistol.

Colonel Stacey started to push his way past her into the parlor. She pushed back, and he swung the back of his hand against her jaw, spinning her around. She turned a full circle, but managed to keep her feet. Colonel Stacey had taken another step forward and was standing in front of her with his legs braced wide and his arm drawn back to backhand her again as he called over his shoulder: "Come on, braves, heap good plunder in—" He cut himself off in midsyllable with a squawk of surprise that bugged his eyes out. There was one thing that stiff-soled, pointy-toed, white women's shoes were better for than moccasins.

As Stacey doubled over, suddenly knock-kneed, one of his

"braves" swung a rifle butt at the side of her neck and another swung an ax handle. The last thing she saw was shriveled little black Juba erupting out of the kitchen hatchway brandishing a meat cleaver.

Molly woke up in what had to be the dreamworld. She was lying on a cloud and her brother was suspended above her. The blacksmith hammering her head flat made it difficult to focus her eyes, but the face hovering over her was unquestionably Joseph's—although a good deal altered from when she'd seen it last. The sleek, clean-lined look of him had been honed down to a razor. Even his lips looked thinner. The only part of him that didn't look leaner and harder was his eyes, which appeared to have grown larger and darker and softer.

The hallucination of her brother said worriedly: "Can you sit up?"

"I can . . ." Her tongue and lips seemed to have grown thicker while he was growing thinner. "But I don't want to."

It seemed that she was still lying on the floor of the parlor in Fort Johnson after all. But someone had put a pillow under her head and shoulders and loosened her dress. She said to Joseph: "It can't be safe for you traveling through the valley. You can't fight the whole county."

"We won't have to, if we move quickly. After Oriskany, none of the militia companies is strong enough to fight us. By the time several companies can assemble together, we'll be halfway to Onondaga. I've sent a message to our mother and Carrying News to be ready to travel by morning. Are you well enough to do the same?"

She nodded gingerly and asked George to assemble his sisters together, composing herself to tell her children they would have to leave their home. The littles ones cried, stiffening the resolve of the older ones.

When she went upstairs to try to select one sackful out of all her possessions, she found the job had been made easy for her. Most of her clothes had been ripped apart and strewn about the room. The floor was ankle-deep in feathers from her mattress and pillows. All of her silk dresses were gone, along with the mahogany box with all her gold earrings and all the other jewelry Sir had given her over the years.

It was a full wagon, what with all the children and Juba, Jemmy, Abraham, and Horace in the oak box the undertaker had tailored to him without having to measure. The last of the hired field hands, who'd spent the last three years agreeing with Horace that he didn't care a hang who won this war, marched alongside with the rest of Brant's Volunteers.

Molly looked back over her shoulder at Fort Johnson. The two black walnut saplings Sir had planted and christened Billy and Molly were taller than the house now, dappled with gold and heavy with fruit that someone else would eat. She whispered in Canienga: "Gets Business Done, I *will* see thy grandchildren swinging from those trees, and a few brave Patriots as well."

Two other wagons were waiting at the Lutheran cemetery. One of them held Molly's mother and stepfather and their children. Little Abraham held the reins of the second wagon. Behind him sat those other Royaners and Oyanders who still believed the Canienga could stay neutral, and a few young men who still believed them.

The Lutheran minister spoke briefly before Horace was lowered into the ground. The shovelfuls of earth from Little Abraham and his helpers were still drumming onto oak when Molly climbed back on her wagon.

None of the Patriot farmers came out of their cabins to jeer or throw stones as they went by. In fact, through the whole length of the Mohawk Valley, Molly saw not one human soul except her fellow refugees on the two wagons and the double file of painted warriors loping along on either side.

There was plenty to talk about when they camped that night. Molly was desperate for news of Peter Warren. Joseph had none, except that the 26th Regiment of Foot had been one of the ones dispatched to help take Philadelphia.

Joseph did manage to make the whole family laugh when he told of his first meeting with the king. The king had graciously extended his hand to be kissed, and Joseph had said: "I do not kiss men's hands, but I will be glad to kiss the queen's if she will allow me."

When there was no one left awake around their campfire except she and Joseph and their mother, and no signs of life in the rest of the camp except the sentries and a low murmuring from the next campfire over, Joseph looked around as though to make certain no one would overhear what he was going to say. He opened his mouth, then abruptly closed it again and looked into the fire, with his mouth and eyes drooping at the corners.

Molly was confused for an instant, then understood. There had been one person among Brant's Volunteers who could hear Joseph talk out moments of doubt and indecision without getting alarmed that Captain Brant might not know all there was to know. But that person was no longer there. Molly leaned across to put her hand on her brother's shoulder and whispered: "Hai, Big William."

He rasped out "Hai," then wiped his nose, cleared his throat, and said in a low voice, still staring into the fire: "I begin to fear that this war will not be over quickly. When I told the *London Chronicle*, after a parade drill put on to impress me and Deseronto, 'This may do here, but it won't do in America,' they thought I was being witty."

He shook his head and then went on: "And what I saw in Burgoyne's camp bodes even worse. It was the same thing you see in a man who stands up to fight in a tavern because he's supposed to, not because his *onikonhra* is on fire.

"If this war were lost, the British generals will only go off to another war on the other side of the world, or back to their estates in England. I don't know how much good we can do fighting under men who only want to march about with bands playing and stand ranks of red coats up in front of ranks of other-colored coats."

Molly said: "Then don't. Don't fight for the British, fight for the Hodenosaune."

He squinted at her.

"How did the Town Destroyer defeat the Shawnees and Miamis?" she asked. "He burnt their crops and their homes and their food stores, didn't he? Until a warrior had not even a handful of parched cornmeal to keep him on his feet, nor spare moccasins to put between his feet and the war road when the old ones wore out.

"Our valley and the ones around it are the larder for most of New York Colony, and half the other colonies. Burn the white men's farms and crops. Take their cattle and horses. Kill their pigs and chickens and anyone who tries to stop you. Make them know that their lives aren't worth a farthing if they stay within the country of the Hodenosaune. How long can the soldiers of the Town Destroyer keep on fighting if you drive the white farmers back to the sea?"

Then the mother of Muskingham and Si-isha said: "Maybe the True People of Turtle Island should have done so long before you were born."

CHAPTER 47

The frost brocade on the windows of Captain Brant's quarters in Fort Niagara had receded somewhat, but not enough to see more than a few crescents of gray sky. So Joseph swung the casement open and stood looking out at the snow melting off the battlements. The window faced east, toward the western mouth of the Forbidden Path and the land of the Keepers of the Sunset, and beyond them the land of the Cayugas, where his mother and his sister and their families were eking out the winter. Beyond the land of the Cayugas, the path arced south to Oquaga. From Oquaga he would launch his war.

Trembling Earth called from behind him: "Come back to bed. And won't you *please* close the window? Don't you feel the cold at all?"

He laughed. "I think my body still remembers when my mother dipped me in the Muskingum between the ice floes. After that, nothing seems cold." He pulled the window closed and went back to bed, but only to perch on its edge while he tugged on his moccasins and shirt. Trembling Earth shrieked when he put his cold hand on the taut pumpkin of her belly. He said: "If you dip him in the river near the foot of the falls, he will have a big, roaring voice for giving orders."

"He might be a she."

"Females have been known to give orders. I am afraid I won't be here when she comes, or he."

"I think you will. All the grandmothers are agreed that he or she's coming soon."

"I have to be gone soon. The snow's almost gone."

"Why do you have to start out so early? No one else will get started till the summer."

"If *someone* doesn't get this campaign launched quickly, maybe no one will get started at all." The surrender of Gentleman Johnny Burgoyne's entire army to the rebels had stunned a lot of loyalists into second thoughts. Joseph was stunned himself. Perhaps if the army sent to take Fort Stanwix had done so and carried on to Albany, Burgoyne wouldn't have given up.

Regardless, it had happened, and now all those loyalists who'd expected the king's soldiers to sweep the rabble aside had to be shown there was another way to win this war. So with the ground still hard between the last diehard patches of snow, Brant's Volunteers loped out of the old gate with PORTE DES CINQ NATIONS carved in the lintel and set off on the war road.

At the foot of Cayuga Lake was a town of old longhouses and white-style frame farmhouses, including the Wolf Clan longhouse that had taken in Joseph's mother and sister and their families. His reunion with them was dampened by the revelation that his mother and Carrying News had both turned into frail, gray-faced old people overnight. The first chance Molly had to take him aside, she said: "They won't last another winter here. I'm going to take them to Niagara."

"People are living in bark huts at Niagara. There's enough room in my quarters for the two of them, and you, but all the children . . ."

"I'm going to take my children to Montreal."

"Montreal?"

"There are schools in Montreal. When the war is over, I don't want my children left with knowing nothing but how to skin a rabbit and spell their names. One of the times when . . . Gets Business Done was deathly ill, he made me promise that the children would get more school education than he had."

Molly hadn't wasted the winter. There were fifty Cayuga warriors waiting to join Brant's Volunteers, and she'd arranged a council of war chiefs and Royaners from the other Cayuga castles and the Senecas and Onondagas. Among them was the Seneca Old Smoke. Old Smoke had grown into his name: what was left of his hair looked like wisps trailing out of a pipe bowl, and like Hendrick before him, he could only take the war road on horseback. But if anyone could be called the war chief of all the Hodenosaune, it was Old Smoke.

Old Smoke stood with the red-painted wampum in his hands and said: "When this war began, it seemed to me that the men of Boston and their allies were unruly children who needed rebuking. Now I begin to have regrets. How many Hodenosaune died on both sides in Oriskany Ravine, and in the camp outside Fort Stanwix? And to what end? To please a king we have never seen? To destroy our own longhouse for the sake of a quarrel in the one next door?

"Hodenosaune hatchets have been drinking Hodenosaune blood. I begin to believe that if we sent white wampum to our brothers the Oneidas and told them we would not fight them in the white man's war, they would bury their hatchets, too, and the longhouse would be whole again."

It strained all the lessons in self-discipline Joseph's Teacher had taught him not to reply to Old Smoke's speech, especially when some of his own warriors muttered "Yo" as the most famous warrior living preached peace. But if he turned the matter into a contest between himself and Old Smoke, it would be no contest.

The Elder Sister of the Wolf Clan took the wampum and spoke directly to Old Smoke. "Thy grandfather was one of the four 'Indian kings' who crossed the water. With her own hands, Queen Anne put a coronet upon his head—the only Hodenosaune to ever be thus honored. When many Senecas felt closer to the French at Thundergate than to the English in the Valley of the Caniengas, thee marched with . . . Gets Business Done . . . to Lake George. . . ."

Joseph wondered if she would ever be able to speak of Sir William without weeping. This time she just let the tears flow and kept on speaking through them. "When the western nations begged the English to rid them of the French, thy warriors stood beside Gets Business Done in front of Fort Niagara, and he beside thee. I remember him saying: 'So long as Old

Smoke lives, we need never fear the Senecas will break the Covenant Chain.' *What would he say now?*"

Old Smoke was weeping, too. He said: "Someone Lends Her a Flower, I stand rebuked. With my old friend gone, I thought the world had changed. But thy husband's voice shall never die so long as thou hast breath."

It was decided that it would only be fitting for Binds Two and the Keepers of the Dawn to wage their war around the eastern gate, while Old Smoke gathered together the Keepers of the Sunset to deal with the rebels south of the western gate. Joseph kissed his mother and sister good-bye, and Brant's Volunteers headed down the Forbidden Path toward the upper reaches of the Susquehanna. The last words Molly said to him were: "If you hear word of Peter Warren . . ."

"I will send a runner to find you, whether you are at Niagara or Montreal or on the other side of the world."

There were a few dozen other Hodenosaune warriors waiting for him at Oquaga, and more at Unadilla. There were even a few Oneidas and Tuscaroras among them. Just because their councillors had decided against fighting for the king didn't mean the occasional warrior couldn't go his own way.

Also waiting at Unadilla were those of the Big Knife contingent of Brant's Volunteers whose homes were far enough in the backwoods that they hadn't had to winter at Fort Niagara for safety. Ezra Hawkins seemed disappointed that the plan was to stay put at Unadilla for now. He went back out to where his fellow Big Knives were camped, and came back with: "The boys is itchin' to get movin', but they allow as how they're willin' to wait a little longer if'n that's Cap'n Brant's say-so."

"Cap'n Brant" knew damn well he couldn't afford to wait much longer than a little. The parched corn in his warriors' pouches was all gone. Fortunately, a few loyalist farmers donated steers and flour. He assured them that very soon his pocket army would be providing its own provisions. One advantage to making war by destroying the enemy's supplies was that you could destroy them just as well by eating them as burning them.

On an apple-blossomed morning in May, Captain Brant sat on a hillside looking down at the fat farms studded along

Cobbleskill Creek. It hadn't been difficult to bring three hundred armed men from Unadilla to that hillside without being seen. The intervening country was all towering rock ridges covered with virgin forest, seamed by a maze of interconnecting valleys and embroidered with deer trails.

Joseph stood up and turned to give his Volunteers the simple Orders of the Day: "We will burst out of the woods making as much noise as our throats can stand. Kill no one who doesn't try to kill you. Bring all prisoners to me in the big house with the yellow roof. Burn all the other buildings."

An Onondaga said: "I came to take scalps, not prisoners."

"I am not one of those who admires a man who wears the scalps of women and children on his belt."

Ezra Hawkins said: "No disrespect, Cap'n, but if one of them farm women shoots at me, I'll scalp her sure."

Joseph smiled. "So will I. But I doubt if even many of their men will stop running long enough to pull a trigger."

He was proved right: the only prisoners were those who were too surprised or too slow to make it across the creek and into the woods before the howling wave of warriors crossed the fields. Joseph stepped out onto the porch of the big house with the yellow roof, into a vision of the Reverend Wheelock's sermons on the Day of Judgment. Through the fire-bright billows of smoke came the sounds of cattle bawling, pigs squealing, flames crackling, the crash of roof beams falling in, and laughing voices making bets on who could set a house ablaze the fastest. Some of Brant's Volunteers were breaking eggs over their mouths, some were herding cattle toward the road, some were wringing chicken's necks for tonight's supper, some were prancing about in farm wives' Sunday hats.

Joseph had the odd feeling that he was someone other than who he was, someone familiar since childhood, someone known of but not known. Then he placed who it was. For today at least, his *onikonhra* had been replaced by that of the Left-Handed Twin, the crooked-minded—the Destroyer.

Back at Oquaga, while his Volunteers put some meat back on their bones with rebel beef, Joseph busied himself signing up new recruits and employing the little bird Tskleleli to keep the rebel militias charging about from Cherry Valley to Schoharie Crossing to German Flats and back again. A message came to Oquaga from the west. Butler's Rangers and Old Smoke's Senecas were planning to descend on the Wyoming Valley of the Susquehanna and destroy the rebel fort and farms there. John Butler wanted Brant's Volunteers to come with them. Joseph and Old Smoke managed to persuade Colonel Butler that the Rangers and Senecas were more than enough men to do the job, and that it was best to stick by the agreement Old Smoke and Joseph had made in the spring.

Brant's Volunteers went back to doing the work of the Left-Handed Twin in the valleys around the Dawn Gate. They burned Andrewstown and Springfield and several places without names. On many of the farms that the Destroyer didn't get around to visiting, the crops rotted in the fields because the farmers had fled east for fear of him.

A flock of Tsklelelis began to sing songs of what had happened at Wyoming: Butler's Rangers and a horde of Iroquois had massacred all the inhabitants, tomahawking women and impaling babies on bayonets. Joseph didn't pay the songs much heed, especially since a recurring refrain was that the Iroquois at Wyoming had been led by Captain Brant.

Then someone arrived at Oquaga who knew firsthand what had happened at Wyoming: a Ranger captain come to take charge of the new recruits for Butler's Rangers. Invariably, a number of the men Joseph recruited for the king's cause ended up going to Butler's Rangers instead of Brant's Volunteers, since Colonel Butler was authorized by the War Department to pay wages. Brant's Volunteers fought for nothing but lean rations and the hope of winning back their homes.

Joseph asked the Ranger captain about the stories of the Wyoming Massacre. The Captain snorted: "Grossly exaggerated."

" 'Exaggerated'?" That wasn't quite the same thing as saying "lies."

The captain became a bit evasive. "Well, there were some . . . unfortunate incidents with prisoners. . . . We took two hundred and thirty-two prisoners—all of them rebel militia or officers, of course, no women and children. But, unfortunately . . . couldn't be helped . . ."

"What couldn't be helped?" There was a tentacle of bile working its way up Joseph's throat.

"Well, it was a long, rough trail back to Fort Niagara. Some of the prisoners had difficulty keeping up, and there were several escape attempts, and several . . . other incidents, before we could deliver them safely into the hands of His Majesty's—"

"How many?"

"Five."

"*Five?* You sat back and let them kill five prisoners?"

"No, um . . . five arrived at Niagara. Well damn it, Brant, what could we do? The Indians—the Senecas—were set on taking scalps to appease the spirits of their brothers killed at Oriskany. Once they get their blood up, it's impossible to control them. You know that."

"No, as a matter of fact I don't know that." He also highly doubted that it had only been Indians who'd done the killing.

Joseph was determined that before the summer was out he would carry the war into the heart of the Mohawk Valley. He knew several alternate back routes into German Flats—after all, it had been his home for fifteen years. Somehow, though, German Flats knew they were coming. By the time Brant's Volunteers burst out of the woods, all the inhabitants were sealed within Fort Herkimer or its sister fort across the river— all except two foolish white men who thought they could outrun Caniengas.

Joseph wasn't too perturbed that the surprise had been spoiled. With all the farmers and their families huddled safely in their forts, it was easier to go about the Destroyer's business among their fields and farms.

It wasn't the best day for burning. A hard rain came with the sunrise and didn't leave all day. But once the houses and barns had been coaxed into flame, enough moisture sizzled off the edges of the fields to get the crops going.

One of Joseph's Caniengas came to where he was standing on the riverbank contemplating the gray smoke rising from the flames to merge with the gray clouds the rain was falling from. "Binds Two—there is one farm . . . The farmer is fled into the fort with his family like all the others . . . but we don't know what to do."

"What to do about what?"

"Binds Two—it is your farm."

Joseph looked out over the gun-metal surface of the River of the Caniengas, with lead pellets of rain spattering pockmarks.

On days like this, he and Margaret and Isaac would just batten the doors and windows and curl up in front of the fireplace to roast chestnuts. "Burn it."

After German Flats, Brant's Volunteers burned the village of Peenpeck on the Neversink River and then headed back toward Oquaga through the blazing autumn forest. As they approached Unadilla they came across a farm that was nothing but a swath of soot and charred beam ends. The Canienga farmer was sitting slackly on a stump while his wife and children picked through the ashes of a cornfield, hoping to find a cob or two that hadn't burned entirely.

The farmer looked up at Joseph and said dazedly: "Binds Two . . . why weren't you here?"

"What happened?"

"What you were away doing to them, they came and did to us. All of Unadilla is like this, and Oquaga. And another troop of rebels burned down some Seneca towns."

Joseph blinked his eyes looking around at the devastation. He was the one, after all, who'd unlocked the door that set the Destroyer loose, but hadn't protected his own people. He said through the knot in his throat: "Were there many killed?"

"No. They got a few prisoners, but the rest of us ran safe into the woods."

That news freed Joseph's *onikonhra* to look at other facets. If the Continental Congress thought the best way to hurt him was to do exactly what he was doing to them, he must be hurting them badly. And now that the rebels had struck at the homes of Hodenosaune who were trying to stay out of the war, Little Abraham and the other Royaners still preaching neutrality were going to find it difficult. But those thoughts did make him wonder if he wasn't growing as crooked-minded as the Left-Handed Twin. He said: "We were lucky indeed that no one was killed."

" 'Lucky'? We have no home."

"None of us will until we win this war. Take your family to Thundergate—the king's men at Fort Niagara will give you food and shelter. And they will see that your family is taken care of when you come out on the war road with me next spring."

Joseph had intended to disband Brant's Volunteers for the winter when they got back to Oquaga, but he couldn't let the last stroke of the campaign be the enemy's. So he turned his back on the ruins of Unadilla and started back east.

A day out from Unadilla, he sat with his back to a beech tree, munching jerked beef and bean bread, watching Brant's Volunteers settling in for the night—shadowy figures moving through the sunset-tinted smoke of campfires. He was proud of his Big Knives. A year ago his Caniengas had to hold themselves to a crawl so the white men wouldn't break their ankles or their toes on tree roots. Now the bearded contingent loped along with their toes pointed inward, bounding like deer through tangled forests that other white men called impenetrable. Even the two escaped black slaves who'd bought their freedom by offering to fight for the king now moved like men instead of broken draft horses.

His reverie was interrupted by a bedraggled Cayuga runner bearing a dispatch from Fort Niagara. The dispatch turned out to be a sodden mass of gray pulp. The runner shrugged: "The Genesee was higher than I thought it'd be this time of year. But I made them tell me what the paper said, just in case, and send wampum with the paper so I'd remember." He held up the string of wampum. "Captain Butler is bringing his Rangers and Old Smoke's warriors to meet up with you at the foot of the Forbidden Path, where the Chemung meets the Susquehanna."

"You must have it wrong. You mean *Colonel* Butler."

The Cayuga looked miffed. "I have a memory, Binds Two, and so does the wampum. *Captain* Walter Butler—John Butler's son."

"The men of the congress hanged Walter Butler for a spy after Oriskany."

"So thought we all. But that General Arnold showed him mercy and only locked him in a dungeon. Walter Butler fed the guard some rum and got away."

"Why does Walter Butler want to meet up with me?"

"They didn't tell me that—just that the king's war chiefs want you to."

So Brant's Volunteers turned around again and headed west along the frost-hardening deer paths and through the Chemung River, sparkling prettily with ice crystals. At the first campfire on the edge of Walter Butler's camp, Joseph saw the skull-taut face of Red Jacket, the astoundingly eloquent young Seneca

Royaner. Joseph hadn't seen Red Jacket since Oriskany. At the first crackle of gunfire in Oriskany Ravine, Red Jacket and three of his friends had started running, and hadn't stopped until they reached the Genesee.

Joseph held up his palm and said: "I greet thee, Cow Killer." The only eyes around the campfire that didn't twinkle in response were Red Jacket's. When Red Jacket had got home from Oriskany, he'd promptly hosted a victory feast and roasted a cow that belonged to a neighbor who was still out on the war road. The Hodenosaune had no criminal code for any act short of murder. Red Jacket would only have to drag the name Cow Killer around until they laid him in his grave.

Walter Butler had changed since Joseph had seen him last. He now looked like a tallow candle with an impacted wick—pasty-faced and burning for revenge against those who'd dared to clap him in chains and perch him on the lip of a gallows. Joseph said pleasantly: "Good to see you safe, Walter."

"Good to see you *at last*, Captain Brant. Were you traveling on Indian time?"

" 'Indian time' . . . ? If you mean the kind of time that's affected by sheltering in the woods for an hour instead of trying to march through freezing rain, or pausing to net a few fish so we don't starve to death before we get here—yes, I suppose that is the brand of time we traveled on."

"Well, now that you're here, we can set off for Cherry Valley tomorrow."

"Back the way I just came . . . ?"

"It seems the best route."

Joseph swallowed his annoyance. "Actually, there are several alternative routes, if Cherry Valley seems the best objective, as I believe it is at the present—"

"What you believe or don't believe means not a pinch of coon shit, Captain Brant, no more than do your 'alternative routes.' I've mapped out the campaign and I am in command here."

"You?" Joseph started to laugh. "Half the men here were fighting in wars of one sort or another while you were in swaddling clothes. Why should they take orders from you?"

"Because my father said so. If you want to see his signature on the order placing me in overall command, I'll show it you."

That evening, Ezra Hawkins spat into the campfire and said:

"I don't like the smell of this, Cap'n. Is it true this here Cap'n Butler's never even been blooded?"

"He fought at the siege of Fort Stanwix."

"I don't recolleck him there."

"Well, he was. And he did lead the patrol from there to German Flats."

"Huh. The one what ended up with all of 'em in irons."

"They were caught by surprise. It could've happened to anyone."

"I don't recolleck it happenin' to you very often. I hates to have to say this, Cap'n . . . but the boys've been sayin' it's gettin' late in the year for campaignin'. They been sayin' maybe it's time we started seein' to our families and gettin' hunkered in for the winter."

Joseph was perfectly aware that Old Smoke, puffing his pipe on the other side of the campfire, had suddenly let his shoulders slump into a more relaxed posture, like a cat who is emphatically not hearing the skittering sound along the doorjamb.

Joseph affected to puff his own pipe serenely, and said: "You and the boys, Ezra, are volunteers, of course, so you're free to call it a campaign when you see fit."

"Maybe it wouldn't be such a bad idea, Cap'n, if'n you was thinkin' of doin' the same."

Old Smoke said dourly: "It was always Binds Two's voice that was the first to say the Hodenosaune must fight for the king. If Binds Two were to turn his back on this war party, it would seem like a very bad sign."

Joseph stared into the crumbling, bright embers, feeling Old Smoke's hazy, dark eyes and Ezra's sharp blue ones enfilading him across the campfire. He didn't like the idea of taking orders from Walter Butler any more than they did, but he remembered Peter Warren on the Falmouth dock: "I'm not a warrior, Uncle Joseph, I'm a soldier." *Someone* had to serve as the bridge between the British and Hodenosaune ideas of military discipline if they were going to fight this war together.

And, after all, who was Joseph Brant to put himself above the High Command that had authorized this expedition? Leading a few raids and ambushes hardly qualified him as a Heaven-Taught General.

Along with all that went the fact that the Hodenosaune

women and children and old men at Fort Niagara and Montreal were being fed and clothed because their warriors were fighting for the king.

Joseph took his pipe out of his mouth and said: "Then I suppose I mustn't turn my back on this war party." It came out sounding a little more dolorous than he'd intended, so he tacked on: "Besides, if I expect them to eventually pay me like a British officer, I suppose I'll have to learn to take orders like one."

"Well, watch your topknot, Cap'n."

"Keep your powder dry, Ezra. I'll send word of where to meet me in the spring."

"I hope so."

Walter Butler had a ferocious temper, and Joseph fully expected him to lose it at the pulling out of a third of Brant's Volunteers. But he merely said: "I must commend you, Captain Brant, on the fine sense of loyalty you've inspired in your troops."

The farther the raiding party progressed toward Cherry Valley, the further the autumn progressed toward winter. Red Jacket got up from yet another shivering camp and announced that he hadn't taken the war road to die of pneumonia. Several Cayugas and Senecas turned back with him. Several others followed after them the next night.

Joseph managed to put a stop to it for a while by referring to the deserters as the Cow Killer's war party, but Walter Butler had a genius for coming up with new ways to encourage men to not come back from a stroll in the woods. His aesthetic sensibilities were offended by the bit of yellow lace that Brant's Volunteers had taken to wearing on their hats or scalp locks, and he threatened to withhold provisions from any man who didn't remove the offending badge and sign on with Butler's Rangers. He didn't mention that there had to be a certain number of names on a regimental list for its officers to qualify for a colonel's or a captain's pay. None of Brant's Volunteers added their names to the Rangers' list, but by the time the expedition got within striking distance of Cherry Valley, Joseph had barely twenty men left under his command.

There weren't enough leaves left on the trees to make the forest wall anything more than a sparse curtain, so the camp on the lip of Cherry Valley was fireless. Joseph stood in the dark, looking down on the lights of the fort and the farms around it. Unlike Cobbleskill, where the houses had been stretched out along the creek bank, Cherry Valley was loosely scattered farms sprinkled about the valley bottom and its arms. Despite the fort and its garrison of the Continental Army, Joseph hadn't been lying when he'd agreed with Walter Butler that Cherry Valley was ripe for the plucking. After an entire summer of Tskleleli singing that Captain Brant was going to descend on Cherry Valley tomorrow, they were hardly likely to believe it on this particular night.

Joseph knew the valley well enough to easily pick out the lights of the Wells farm. The Wellses made no bones about their preference for Parliament over Congress, but they were so inoffensive and highly thought of that not even the local Safety Committee objected to them. Robert Wells had spent a summer canoeing to Oswego with Joseph and Margaret and baby Isaac, floating down the rivers in the golden afternoons.

Some of the farm lights far below Joseph's moccasins moved: the minuscule, bobbing firefly of a farmer carrying a lantern back from securing his animals for the night. One by one the lights of Cherry Valley went out.

No one in the camp of raiders slept that night. Joseph sat up with a blanket across his shoulders, listening to the murmurs and chuckles all around him and the honing of hatchets. There was a quality in the sounds he'd never heard in all the nights he'd spent in camps of men whetting weapons for the morning. There was the same kind of anticipation and working up of fury as the night before Oriskany or the Bloody Morning Scout, but none of that tempering feeling of bolstering each other's courage to face death. It wasn't the sound of men preparing for a battle, it was the sound of men getting ready for a hog slaughtering.

Walter Butler and several of his lieutenants wandered by, grinning at the blade sharpeners. Joseph stood up and said: "Captain Butler, might I have a word with you?"

"Certainly, Captain Brant," he replied, but showed no inclination of moving out of earshot of the others or lowering his voice to a confidential tone.

"A private word."

"Captain Brant, I have nothing to say that I'd be ashamed to say in full hearing of these brave men. Do you?"

Joseph could think of a great many things he'd be glad to say to Walter Butler in front of these brave men, but he remembered Sir John Johnson and Colonel St. Leger yelling at each other in the middle of the camp outside Fort Stanwix, and what an uplifting effect it had had on their troops. There was another Covenant Chain: the chain of command that was the *orenda* of an army. So Joseph just turned away from Walter Butler and walked farther into the woods, flexing his hands.

It was a miserable morning. Countless generations of Hodenosaune hunters had handed down various ways to keep warm when it snowed or to keep dry when it rained, but when both of them came together . . . Captain Butler delivered the Orders of the Day, translated by Old Smoke and Joseph. "Captain Brant and his small party shall proceed southwest through the woods in an encircling motion to cut off any escape. The rest of us shall quick-march straight down the road directly to the fort, to forestall any attempt at a sortie and to prevent the people of the outlying farms from fleeing to its safety. With the enemy's arms thus checkmated, I shall remain in command of however many men may be necessary to keep up the siege, while the rest spread out and put the place to the torch and the sword."

"Captain Butler?"

"Yes, Captain Brant? I assume you must have some good reason for interrupting the Orders of the Day . . . ?"

"Perhaps you would prefer that someone else command the besieging party, so that you could oversee the business of determining which of the farmers to take prisoner and which are loyalists."

"A rebel is a rebel, Captain Brant. I'm sure your people can smell them as well as I can. Now, as to our order of march . . ."

Joseph turned and sat down on the ground with his hand over his eyes, only vaguely aware of Walter Butler's voice brazening on and Old Smoke's translating. Joseph knew of a shorter route into the heart of Cherry Valley—down the hill, across the stream, and over the fields—but he didn't say so. He knew the back path from traveling it many times to sit in the Wells' kitchen smoking tobacco with Robert while the Wells' girls and their mother filled the room with the smells of baking bread.

One of the few remaining of Brant's Volunteers shook Joseph's shoulder. "Binds Two, it is time."

He stood up and waited as Butler's Rangers and the rest set off down the road. He had not the remotest intention of proceeding in any encircling motion. As soon as the tail end of the main column disappeared into the sleet, he started to run: down the hill, across the stream, and over the fields.

He slipped and fell a few times, but still left his warriors calling they couldn't keep up. Both his elbows were burning and his leggings and moccasins were as much ice as leather. On the far side of the fields he could see the roof peak of the Wells house on an encroaching tongue of the valley's walls.

The field had just been ploughed for winter wheat, and the sleet that hadn't frozen onto its surface had soaked into it knee-deep. His shortcut had turned into a quagmire. He floundered, let the mud take his moccasins and then threw his rifle aside—the powder was too soaked-through to fire anyway. It seemed impossible that Walter Butler's column wouldn't get there by the longer road before he'd fought his way through this swamp, but it was too late to turn back now. He dropped his belt and pistols and kept on popping his bare feet out of the sucking mud, as much falling forward as running.

He could hear gunshots and whoops and screams from up ahead. By the time he'd scrambled up the slant at the far end of the field and fell against one of the trees in the windbreak, he was covered in freezing mud, shivering and gasping. He pushed off from the tree and broke through the brambles.

There was something sprawled across the back threshold of the Wells house, another in the garden, and another by the barn. Joseph stumbled through the house, up the stairs, and then out the front door to sink down on the porch swing. He'd counted twelve of them in all, or it might have been thirteen. Some of them had been wearing dresses or would have been no taller than his elbow if they'd been able to stand up. But one of the others might've been Robert, it was impossible to tell.

Smoke was rising from the east and west. There was a sound of gunfire from the direction of the fort. His warriors appeared at the porch rail, caked with mud and sheened with sleet. One of them had his rifle and another his pistols. "Binds Two—what should we do?"

"Take as many prisoners as you can and hold them for me. For *me*—you understand?"

"Yes, Binds Two."

Joseph pushed himself to his feet and started down the road. The first house he passed, Rangers and warriors were running in and out of the doors and smashing the windows. But from the next house came, impossibly, the sound of a woman singing. Joseph went inside.

There were several children huddled in a corner watching their mother smooth a tablecloth with flatirons heated in the hearth. "Are you mad, woman, to be thus engaged while your neighbors are being massacred around you?"

"We have nothing to fear. It's well known that we are loyal to the king."

"So were the Wellses." Cackles and war whoops were approaching. "Quick—get into your bed. Moan a little, as though you are ill."

A moment later two Senecas and one of the Caniengas who'd elected to follow Old Smoke instead of Binds Two crashed through the door. Joseph said: "The woman of this house is ill. I think it may be the smallpox."

They peered through the doorway at her. She gave out a convincing little moan and they got out quickly, tossing over their shoulders: "You should not stay here, Binds Two."

As soon as they were gone, he stepped outside and emitted the high-pitched yell meant to assemble Brant's Volunteers. Two of his Caniengas heard through the bedlam and came running. He said, "Paint my mark on this woman and her children," although it was an open question whether even the sign of two parallel lines looped together, marking them as Binds Two's prisoners, would guarantee their safety today.

It took two days to raze Cherry Valley. The garrison that had been posted to defend it did nothing but fire the occasional potshot at the figures capering about the flames. Joseph could hardly blame the bluecoats for huddling behind their walls: they were heavily outnumbered and had lost their officers before the siege began. Their colonel had been cut down running from the Wells house, where he'd been billeted. Their second-in-command had stepped out of his own billet to see what all the noise was about and promptly found himself a prisoner. He was a certain Lieutenant Colonel Staccia, although most people gave up trying to pronounce his name and just made it "Stacey."

Despite the initial butchery, there were a lot of prisoners. At dawn on the third day, Walter Butler's expedition set out herding their prisoners northwestward. When sunset found them barely a few miles from Cherry Valley, Captain Butler gave in to Captain Brant's suggestion of letting the women and children and old men go. As Captains Butler and Brant watched the freed prisoners straggle back down the road toward the remnants of their homes, Colonel Stacey said nervously: "What do you intend to do with me?"

Walter Butler mumbled: "You are a prisoner of war." Over the last three days, Captain Butler's habitually brassy and commanding tone of voice had sunk to a mumble.

Stacey brayed: "Just like the prisoners of war from Wyoming? Have a care, you will be held to account when we win the war! Now that the French have come in on our side—"

"I've fought the French before," Joseph cut him off. "They die just as easily as Patriots. And were I you, Colonel Stacey, I would not encourage Captain Butler to meditate on what accidents can happen to prisoners of war. Because after tomorrow you will not have me along to discourage him."

Walter Butler said: "How not?"

"There are a few isolated clumps of farms in easy reach along the Mohawk. It won't take many men to—"

"You will not have one man from my command! And you have not approached me for permission to embark on any further—"

"Your father's letter ran out the instant we turned our backs on Cherry Valley. And I have not the least desire to encumber myself with even one of your Rangers. As for Brant's Volunteers, they ask permission of no one but me."

"Good God, Brant," Walter Butler muttered, "haven't you had enough for one year?"

"I've had enough of *you*." But Joseph couldn't resist adding to Colonel Stacey: "It might be better, though, for you, if some accident *did* befall you along the road back to Fort Niagara. My sister is only a few weeks' sail from there in Montreal, and she is bound to hear you are a prisoner."

Colonel Stacey tried to bluff. "Your sister's got no reason to care a damn one way or t'other."

"Do you really think the Mohawk Valley has so many people in it that anyone could stick a couple of feathers in his hair and go unrecognized? You and I may have met only once or twice in passing, but we remember each other. We came within a hairsbreadth of meeting again last autumn at Fort Johnson. If we had, you'd not be standing here today."

Joseph's intention to toss an acidic squib at Colonel Stacey and leave it at that was crumbling quickly under his memories of the bruises on Molly's face. His hand went up toward Stacey's throat. Stacey flinched, but Joseph just straightened the gilt collar on the blue coat, whispered, "Pray God you don't live to meet me again," and turned and walked into the dark.

Before the snow set in, Joseph and seven diehards managed to burn four more Mohawk Valley farms, take three prisoners, and kill no one. But as the Forbidden Path wound toward hearing range of Thundergate and the end of this year's war road, Joseph began to worry about his three prisoners and the gauntlet. The three were all oak-muscled farmers who kept amazing him with their helplessness; they even had to be told that if camp-roasted beef were difficult to choke down with no salt, the white ashes at the edge of the campfire would do just as well.

The last miles of the trail would wind through two villages of refugee Hodenosaune—or perhaps three or four by now. Any male prisoner would have to run the gauntlet between two lines of warriors and women and children whacking at him with sticks, whips, and tomahawks and trying to trip him up. It wasn't all that dangerous if the runner knew the rules. The people in the lines hoped to see a man run bravely through to the painted post in the middle of the village. Even if a man who ran bravely happened to stumble and fall partway, only the blunt ends of the hatchets would be used, to spur him back to his feet. But any man who faltered or showed fear would be chopped to pieces. These three big babes in the woods seemed just the type to panic at the sight of a few dozen painted Indians clacking sticks together and practicing their wolf howls.

Two days out from Niagara, Joseph sent a runner ahead with a note to the fort commander, suggesting that the day after tomorrow might be a good time to take a barrel of rum to Nine Mile Landing and knock its head in for the benefit of His Majesty's loyal Iroquois—debited to Captain Brant's account, of course. When the path to Thundergate opened up into a clearing filled with bark huts, there was no one there except a few old people and a waiting escort of British soldiers—and a black-haired, slant-eyed woman wearing the mink cape Sir William Johnson had given her.

Joseph enveloped his sister in his arms as she enveloped him in her cape. He croaked into her ear: "I thought you were gone to Montreal?"

"The war mucks up a lot of plans." She stepped away from him and took him by the shoulders. "Our mother, and Carrying News, they are both eating strawberries."

He looked down at the snow and whispered: "Hai ..."

"And Trembling Earth—put your hands in mine, Binds Two ... Trembling Earth lives, but her child and thine was born dead."

After a while he said: "Perhaps this is not a time to be among the living on Turtle Island."

CHAPTER 48

"Molly Brant wishes to see you, Colonel."

John Butler wanted to reply, "Well, I don't particularly wish to see her," but he couldn't. Sir John Johnson and his meddling little squarehead functionary of a brother-in-law, Daniel Claus, had put it into the governor's head that she had more influence over the Indians than the entire Indian Department. Claus had even written in an official dispatch: "One word from her goes farther than a thousand from any white man without exception." Consequently, the governor had handed down orders that she was to be given anything she wanted, and she always wanted something.

The devil of it was, Sir John and Claus weren't all that far from right. So Colonel Butler leaned back from his desk and sighed: "Very well, Sergeant—send her in."

She was wearing the gold earrings he'd finally managed to procure for her, and her dress and moccasins and leggings were practically covered over with bead work, embroidery and lace, and appliquéd silk ribbon. Draped over her shoulders was a plain blue wool blanket, but it was amazing how the Iroquois women could make a blanket swirl and whirl and fold as though it were the most elegant of opera capes.

She took a chair without being asked and occupied it like a throne. Butler had been in Indian Affairs long enough now to know that it wouldn't be polite for her to come right out and tell him what she wanted. He had to make at least a few stabs at guessing, in hopes that he might offer it to her before she had to ask. He said: "I'm afraid I still have no news of your son, beyond that general information on the Twenty-sixth Foot's movements during last year's campaign."

"I hadn't expected you would."

"Ah. Well, the earrings look splendid on you. Would you like me to see if I can order up another pair?"

"I only have two ears. But another pair or two would be good for presents, if you should come across them—of earrings, not ears. One can never have too many presents on hand."

He cast about for some other possible reason for her visit, and had just hit upon asking her whether her people had enough provisions—although his own stores were nigh on empty—when she offered: "I had a dream last night."

"A dream?" This was even worse. Traditionally he would now have to start guessing what she'd dreamed, and then guess what the dream might mean she wanted.

Fortunately, she wasn't entirely traditional. "Yes. A dream of Stacey."

"Colonel Stacey?"

She nodded. "In my dream we had his head outside the fort and we were kicking it around like a football."

Colonel Butler choked and sputtered: *"We?"* It came out rather like a squeak.

"We Hodenosaune. When I told them of my dream, they said it sounded like a very powerful one."

"Well ... Ahem ... It is certainly a dream which ... bears much careful meditation. I would like to think about your dream awhile, to try to divine what it might mean. What say you come back again another time and we'll talk about it further. Perhaps tomorrow, or the day after—"

"I will be back in one hour."

When she was gone, Colonel Butler sat chewing on his fingernails. Butler didn't know how much Molly Brant did or didn't believe in all that superstitious nonsense about dreams, but there were a great many Iroquois camped around Niagara who certainly did believe, and they didn't take kindly to harm or insults offered to their Clan Mothers. Not to mention the fact that a certain John Butler's salary from Northern Indian Affairs was based entirely on keeping the Iroquois happy.

After a half hour of pondering, interspersed with variations on "Why does this always have to happen to *me*?" Butler called the sergeant to fetch a keg of rum and some sign paint from the quartermaster's stores. Butler never claimed to be an artist, but he managed a credible cartoon of eyes, mouth, and nose on the face of the keg. With the sergeant toting the keg along behind him, he went outside and across the acres of parade square.

There was the usual collection of Mohawks, Senecas, and Cayugas loitering around the gates. Butler found one who could understand English and said: "The Oyander told me of her dream. Some people call a keg a hogshead, and the Oyander seems to feel that Colonel Stacey is a pig ripe for butchering, so I think this will fit her dream."

He went back to his office for another hour or so of inspecting ledgers, and then took a stroll along the parapet. Two teams of somewhat erratic Iroquois were footing a hollow keg across the snowy river flats. Among the most enthusiastic of the footballers was the Elder Sister of the Mohawk Clan Mothers, running full-tilt with her skirts hiked halfway up her thighs.

Two days later the sergeant announced that Molly Brant had come to have another word with him. This time, as soon as she was settled in her chair she said straight out: "I had a dream last night."

"'Again?'"

"This was a different dream than the last one."

"Oh!" He brightened considerably.

"This time Stacey's hat was still on his head. The funny thing was, no matter how high we kicked it, his hat still stayed on."

Colonel Butler was just about ready to start taking bites out of his own hat. He managed to locate a Continental officer's tricorne among the souvenirs from last year's campaign. It was difficult to nail it on securely without splitting the barrel head. He would leave it up to the Iroquois to figure out a way to break open the top of the keg without dislodging the hat and spoiling the dream.

Leaning back with his paintbrush in his hand, Butler had to admit he'd done a better job on the eyes this time. And, in all modesty, he'd truly captured the line of Colonel Stacey's nose.

Three days after the second foot keg game, the sergeant announced: "Colonel, Molly Brant is here to—"

"Shitting hell!"

"Pardon me, sir?"

"Nothing. You may as well send her in."

Butler waited while she took her chair and smoothed her skirts. She folded her hands in her lap and said primly: "I had another dream."

"Colonel Stacey is a prisoner of war! He does not belong to me, but to His Majesty King George the Third! If you want someone to make your dream real, you will have to tell it to the king."

"Hm." She looked as though she might be considering it. "Does Stacey know how you have come to save his head twice this week?"

"I don't know. One of the guards might've told him. . . ."

"If you make certain Stacey knows, I think perhaps I will dream of him no more. Oh—and do tell him he's damned lucky he let those Oneidas move into Fort Johnson instead of taking it himself."

CHAPTER 49

It took months longer than Molly had expected to make arrangements to take her children to Montreal. Several sets of letters had to go back and forth between Niagara and the East before the government agreed to pay the school fees for Martha, George, and Peggy and find suitable accommodations for her and the children too old or young to go to school. Once she had all that in writing, there was still the question of transportation. The shallow-drafted little ships that spent their lives on Lake Ontario were finding it difficult enough to squeeze on all the troops and matériel that had to be ferried from fort to fort, much less a woman traveling with seven children, three household servants, and a quantity of luggage.

She finally managed to arrange passage on a supply ship returning from Niagara with nothing in its hold but the sparse fruits of a wartime trapping season. But when she informed John Butler, he said: "You can't! I've been ordered to lead the Rangers east to block the rebels from invading through the Indian Territories. Someone has to stay here to keep your people under control."

"They seem perfectly well controlled to me."

"You know as well as I do that if left to their own devices, half the men would drift off into the woods to hunt food for their families instead of going on the warpath, and the women will start making more and more outrageous demands if there isn't someone here to remind them that the Indian Department's stores aren't bottomless. Why do you think the Indian Department's been subsidizing you so handsomely to stay here?"

"To do the job the Indian Department pays you to do." Her

404

voice didn't taste acidic as much as alkaline. "Don't worry, Colonel Butler—while you're away, I'll see the children don't run riot."

As soon as Butler's Rangers had marched off with their drum rattling and fife twittering, Molly called an immediate council of all the Clan Mothers around Niagara. "Sisters— sometimes the king's men here forget that the food and clothing they give to us are not the generosity of a good gardener to a poor one. They forget sometimes that the only reason we need the king's charity is because we chose not to abandon the king and so had to abandon our homes for a while.

"But sometimes *we* forget that the king's men here can only give what they have to give, and that though their corn ricks might look filled to overflowing in the autumn, there will be no more corn until the lake boats can come again in the spring. I ask you to remember that. But I also have a little feeling that they will never give you enough unless you ask for too much.

"In all the wars the Hodenosaune have fought since the planting of the Tree of Peace, we have never fought a war like this one. Even the young men weary of it. When you look at the empty places by your hearth fires, when you look at your children growing up in bark huts, eating flour paste and thin soup, remember that we cannot go back to Canajoharie again, or Unadilla or Schoharie, until this war is won.

"The last thing I have to say to you is to beg you not to play too rough with Colonel Butler. He is *so* afraid that as soon as I step out of the longhouse to relieve myself you will be swinging from the roof poles and spilling your soup in the fire." After they were done laughing, she touched their hands good-bye and just managed to make it up the gangplank before the ship with her children on it sailed off without her.

They had fair winds all across the length of Lake Ontario. The ship's last port of call before turning around and starting back again was Carleton Island, where the lake narrowed into the St. Lawrence River. A big new fort had sprung up there, with thick, log-and-earthwork walls and cannons poking through the ports. Looking at the massed white tents of soldiers overflowing the fort, the sprawl of bark huts housing Hodenosaune warriors, and the gunships floating in the harbor, Molly found it inconceivable that a power that could instantaneously transform a few tumbledown sheds into an island for-tress could ever be defeated by a batch of farmers and bank clerks and barrel makers.

The rest of the journey was accomplished in flat-bottomed bateaux. The Canadian boatmen sang as they rowed, and laughed when they came out at the bottom of rapids in one piece.

Molly and her children and servants spent their first night in Montreal at the home of Daniel Claus and Ann Johnson Claus. Daniel made Molly laugh by still saying "dachshunds of eggs" despite all his facility for languages. And Ann made her sad by reminiscing about "Papa," and how she and her sister had thought of him as the giant in "Jack and the Beanstalk" until Molly came and made him human.

Molly said: "If there's one thing your father always was, it was human. He just didn't know what to do with daughters. He thought they should be locked safely in a dovecote and visited once a day to eat out of his hand and coo. Which is why," she added, turning to Ann's husband, "he grew so angry when he found out a fox had snuck in."

Daniel Claus blushed all the way up to the sparse roots at the crown of his head and protested earnestly: "Sir William was entirely mistaken if he thought that anything untoward had—"

"Of course he was." Molly laughed. "He just naturally assumed the worst—which was that all men were the same as him." She laughed some more and dried her eyes and went up to her empty bed.

In the morning she took possession of the house the Indian Department had leased for her. It wasn't exactly Johnson Hall, or even Fort Johnson, but it had a walled rose garden, a cherrywood dining table, and a coach house with a carriage and a trained trotter. Molly had a great deal of use for a carriage, what with inspecting prospective schools and provisioning the house and buying new wardrobes for the children. But a coachman hadn't been provided, and a lady couldn't very well go about driving her own carriage.

Abraham surprised her by saying: "I can do it, Miz Molly."

She had her doubts about a field hand turned house servant guiding a skittish carriage horse through the streets of Montreal. But he did look splendid sitting up front with one of Sir's old lace-trimmed tricornes on his head. And once he and the horse had got used to each other, they navigated the cobble-stoned cul-de-sacs like a Hodenosaune paddler with a good Ojibway canoe. Molly said: "You must've been born to it, Abraham—you certainly had no opportunity to learn by practice."

"I has to confess, Miz Molly, there was times I oughta been pitchin' hay or splittin' rails, when I was loafin' around the stables with Mistah Horace."

They got lost a few times, and the people of old Montreal looked more than twice at a lace-hatted black man driving a carriage for an Indian woman in full Mohawk regalia, but that was half the fun. One of the first places she visited was the wartime home of Sir John Johnson. John had aged a good deal in two years, and he wore the perpetually perplexed expression of those who can't fathom what they did to make life turn out different from what they'd been led to expect. But John had a half brother she was more concerned about. The first thing she said to John after their greetings was: "Peter Warren . . . ?"

She didn't have to say any more. John looked down at the floor and said: "I'm sorry, Molly—I've inquired at every deuced government office even vaguely connected with the War Department, and at every regimental headquarters in Quebec. No one can give me any news of Peter Warren, beyond the fact that the Twenty-sixth Foot is still taking part in the Carolina campaign."

"In three years he must have written at least one letter."

"He may have written dozens. What with privateers and all the other hurly-burly of the war, it's a tinker's chance if even official dispatches get through. He may well have never received any of your letters. But were I you, I'd keep on writing them. I'm sure they're a great comfort to him if . . . if even only the occasional one gets through."

She stiffened her mouth. "You meant to say 'if he's still alive.' "

"What can we do in these times, Molly, but hope for the best?"

"We can do our damnedest to make sure the best happens. To that end, I brought along a letter I've written to my brother, to give him some idea of how things stand with those Caniengas who followed Deseronto to Montreal. As you said, the mails aren't terribly reliable these days, so if you could hand it to Joseph when you see him—"

"I expect you'll see him long before I do."

"No. I expect to be in this end of the country for the next year at least. You'll be seeing Joseph in a few weeks, when you lead your Royal Greens west with the army sent to stop the rebels attacking the Six Nations."

"I won't be going west—or not that far west. The new governor has received intelligence that the Americans may be planning to attempt another invasion of Quebec. So the regulars garrisoned here will remain here, and my regiment will be posted to Oswego in case of—"

"What kind of fucking loyalty is this? We spend three years fighting to help the English, and when our country is invaded, the English stay home because of *rumors*?"

"Now, Molly, it isn't up to us to decide what—"

"You must arrange for me to see this governor."

"I can't do that. For one thing, he's in Quebec City—"

"Then I'll go to Quebec City."

"People wait weeks, or months, to see the governor. And even then ... He does have a war to manage, don't you know."

"You write that governor a letter and tell him that if the king wants the Iroquois to help him win this war, his governor had better talk to me. I'll have Daniel Claus do the same."

"I don't know what that will accomplish."

"The one thing you should've learned from your father, John, is that no one knows what anything will accomplish until they do it."

The carriage trip to Quebec City took three days, by which time the dispatch riders bearing Daniel's and John's letters should have reached the governor. Neither Molly nor Abraham spoke French, but a jingling purse sounded the same in any language, and they never stopped any longer than to snatch a meal or a few hours' sleep.

The brick-paved streets of Quebec were even narrower and more contorted than those of Montreal, and there was even more of a feeling of age, with the stone-walled citadel brooding on the cliffs above. At the inn where they stayed in the Lower Town, Molly discovered that the only ways to reach the Upper Town from there were by climbing a long series of stone steps or by a very circuitous road. She was inclined to choose the direct route of the steps, but then decided that a lady should arrive in a carriage.

Very early in the morning, she dressed herself in an overdress, skirt, and leggings made of black silk and white doeskin, and arranged her hair so the gold earrings showed. When Abraham handed her into the carriage, he said: "My my, Miz Molly—was I that governor, I'd give you anything your heart desired."

"He doesn't have the power to do that, Abraham. But I'll settle for what he can give."

The governor's vast anteroom was filled with men: redcoated officers offering snuff to each other, periwigged personages tapping their toes impatiently, wooden-shoed farmers clutching petitions. . . . Every one of them turned and looked at her as she came through the door. She couldn't see through them to the far end of the room, but she assumed that was the direction the governor was in, so she headed that way. Most of the men in her path stepped aside, some of them with a bemused gesture toward their hat brims, some of them looking down their noses at the crown of her head.

At the end of the room was an immense set of doors flanked by two mitered soldiers standing with their muskets grounded. In front of the doors was a long table with three harried-looking officers shuffling through petitions. The one in the middle looked the eldest and had the most gold braid on his coat, so Molly planted herself in front of him and said: "I would like to see the governor."

"As would everyone else here, madame."

"Miss. Tell the governor that Miss Molly Brant, the widow of Sir William Johnson, the sister of Captain Joseph Brant, and the chief woman of the Wolf Clan of the Iroquois, is here to see him."

"That's a lot of women for him to see at one time, madame."

She said, "It certainly is," but she could feel the embarrassment creeping up her cheeks.

"I'll put you on the list."

There were carved oak benches ranged along the walls. A farmer and a priest squeezed sideways to give her a place to perch her hips, which she was suddenly aware were somewhat

broader than either of theirs. As the wait drew on, she began
to doubt her wisdom in not dressing like a white woman for
the occasion. It was one thing to amuse herself with the second
glances of the people on the streets of Montreal, and quite another to sit waiting in this roomful of white men intent on
business, feeling like a doe in a bullpen.

Men were called and ushered in and out of the big doors,
emerging looking smug or smoldering. There didn't appear to
be any rhyme or reason to who was called and who wasn't.
Some who'd arrived long after Molly were ushered in while
she still waited; some who'd been there when she'd arrived
still languished uncalled.

A tall man came in from outside who didn't fit in with any
of the others: although he was dressed in broadcloth and brocade, he had the sun-cured look of the peasant farmers and
some of the less resplendent officers. His hawk-sharp eyes and
nose were softened around the edges by the signs of a man
who enjoyed a butt of malmsey and a barrel of oysters and
made no bones about it. There seemed to be something
vaguely familiar about him, but Molly knew she was at the
stage where she was willing to half recognize anybody.

The tall man chivied his way through the crowd, caught her
in the corner of his eye, swung his head around with a start,
stepped toward her and swept his hat off with: "Bless my pitiful excuse for a soul—Miss Molly! I never expected to see you
here!"

"Nor I you . . ." which allowed her just enough time to race
her mind over the "Mr. MacTavish" she'd heard as he'd
worked his way through the crowd, and come up with "Simon."

Simon MacTavish had come from Scotland as an apprentice
clerk when William Johnson was still in the fur trade business.
When Fort Johnson ceased to be a trading post, young Simon
had set up for himself at Albany. Molly had a vague memory
of someone mentioning that Simon MacTavish had shifted
north the year after Sir died.

"You look to have done well for yourself, Simon."

"Not near so well as I hope to. We have a plan afoot to
amalgamate all the traders in Montreal into one North West
Fur Trading Company. Wouldn't care to invest, would you?"

"I'm afraid I'm a little short of capital just at present."

"Ain't everyone? This blasted revolution's playing hell with business. But if no one carries on doing business, there won't be any exchequer to pay these soldier boys to march around and keep the Empire intact."

Molly found herself smirking. "Who is she, Simon?"

"*She?*"

"I remember you always used to say you were like a fish out of water when not in love. You seem to be swimming boisterously these days."

Simon blushed and smirked back. "The devil of it is, Miss Molly, had I been near so lucky an angler as Sir William, I wouldn't have to go toting my pole from pond to pond."

The senior officer behind the table called out: "Mr. Simon MacTavish."

Simon shrugged, said, "Business calls . . ." and excused his way toward the big double doors.

A few more hours that perhaps were only a few minutes passed with the assembled gentlemen talking over and around her. The doors opened again and Simon MacTavish emerged jauntily. He tipped his hat in her direction as the officer called out. "Miss Molly Brant!"

A fussy-looking little man waiting just beyond the doors said: "I am the governor's interpreter."

"I speak English relatively well."

"The governor doesn't. He can manage to make himself understood, if you can get past the Swiss-French accent and only need to know when to fix bayonets, but otherwise . . ."

His British Majesty's new Governor of the Province of Quebec, and commander-in-chief of all His Majesty's forces within that province and along its frontiers, wore the apologetic look of a plain old war chief who suddenly finds himself wearing one of the names in the roll call of Royaners. He clicked his heels together as he stood up from behind his desk. "Mademoiselle Molly—so much I have about you hear . . ."

The governor's interpreter sniffed: "What the governor means to say is—"

"I can understand the governor perfectly clearly. You may leave us. That is, if the governor finds *my* English comprehensible without translation . . ."

The governor shrugged, said, "So much like any other's," then blinked at the interpreter and fluttered his hand at the door. "*Comprenez-vous? Allez, allez!* Please to be sit, Mademoiselle Molly—if I am not too *familiaretez* . . ."

"Thank you."

"I Sir William did know. When he Niagara took, I commanded the reserve force at Oswego."

"I know. He always said that Fort Niagara would have fallen to us sooner if you'd been able to be there to take command instead of him."

"Ah, mademoiselle," he waggled his finger at her, "either you make flattering or he did. I know of many field officers who make anger that an *amateur* like your husband did make such victories, but to me a victory is a victory. I am a good professional soldier, but I have not the genius—the chance-taking that seem like so much madness until of a sudden the enemy take to his heel.

"In my times, I have serve with two men who did have this thing: General Wolfe when we did take Quebec, and Sir William Johnson. I think if they were with us still, this revolution would never this far have come.

"But now, tell me what it can be that bring you so very, very far from your forest home?"

She told him. When she was done, he sighed and ran his hand across the wisps of snow crowning his scalp, wisps very much like Old Smoke's. "Ah, mademoiselle . . . so much of war is . . . how you say—*rheumer* . . . ?"

"Tskleleli."

"*Excusez-moi?*"

"The little bird that flits from place to place singing stories."

"Ah. Just so. 'Tskell . . .'?"

"Tskleleli."

"Just so. I must remember . . . So, here I am sitting, with a very, very wide frontier and very, very little troop at my command, and that little bird he sing to me so many different story. I must ask to myself: *Is* there an army of rebel make advances up La Susquehanna for Niagara? Or is it an army of rebel to come at Oswego for Montreal? Or is it both? I hope there is not one or other, but . . . in the end I must decide to keep those troop I have here to guard, and hope those troop at Fort Niagara can hold that place."

"What about the places between the rebels and Fort Niagara?"

"If those troop in Fort Niagara go to La Susquehanna to intercept the enemy, and the enemy skirt around and take Niagara, we are finish in the west—just as Sir William finish the French when he take Niagara in 'fifty-nine. I must think of strategy before tactic. You did live so long yourself, mademoiselle, with a man who was himself a general. You must know how it is."

"I am beginning to. I suspect that the king's loyal Indian allies between the Susquehanna and Niagara will learn much more quickly."

"We all have so much to learn. Here I am the governor of *un pays* I have learn so little of—but for where is this fort or that depot. I am hear that even the name I know for this whole vastness of place is not the name your people know. What name is it you called this land of North America before we men white came to name it?"

"Ours."

Chapter 50

𝔚𝔚 Joseph sat behind a barricade outside the Delaware town of Chuknut, with his legs stretched out so he could surreptitiously flex a little of the pain out of his right foot. He'd taken a bullet fragment in the heel a month ago in a skirmish with the Mohawk Valley militia. Perhaps it would have healed more quickly if he'd stayed off it, but now was not the time to be lying abed with his foot propped up, nor for giving any of the meager six hundred other men behind the barricade any reason to feel less than perfectly confident in their war chiefs.

He didn't want to be sitting behind any barricade waiting to spring a standing fight on an army of four or five thousand. It seemed to him their best chance was hit-and-run, hoping to whittle the Americans down without losing men they couldn't afford to lose. But the chief of the Chuknut Delawares had declared that if the Hodenosaune and white loyalists let the rebels raze his town like they had the ones downriver, the Delawares might just as well sue for peace and let the invaders march unimpeded into Seneca country and on toward Niagara.

It was an ancient tradition among the True People that when different nations fought as allies, the chief whose people were in the most immediate danger determined where and how they would fight. Joseph and Old Smoke had managed to persuade John Butler that even if it seemed a primitive custom, when it was broken, people started to ponder on the difference between allies and dupes.

So here they sat behind their barricade beside the Chemung River: Brant's Volunteers on the right, where the Americans' line of march would strike first, Butler's Rangers in the center with the paltry fourteen redcoat regulars John Butler had been able to pry out of the commandant of Fort Niagara, then Old Smoke's and Cornplanter's Senecas, and finally the Delawares on the far left, where a steep hill rising out of a marsh anchored the line.

They sat behind the barricade all day, baking in the hot, dry sun and listening to their stomachs growl. Rations had recently been reduced to seven ears of corn per man a day. Near sunset on the second day, a scout brought word that the rebel army was moving very slowly. Ezra Hawkins spat: "I coulda told you that."

That evening, Colonel Butler sought out Joseph. "You have to do something about the Delawares! They came down off the hill today and say they won't go up again tomorrow."

Joseph went looking for the Delaware chief. The chief shrugged: "What can I do? My warriors say they would rather fight from beside the hill than on top of it."

"If the bluecoats can get up the other side of that hill, they'll be behind us."

"If we see them trying that, we'll get up top before them."

"You wouldn't have to outrace them if you were on the hill to begin with."

"That is how you see it, Binds Two, and maybe the way I see it. But it is not the way my warriors see it."

Joseph was moved to say: Can't you get your own troops to obey your orders? But there were no words to say that in Delaware—or Canienga, for that matter—just as it would've been impossible to explain in English how a warrior could sing at the torture stake.

After another thirsty morning behind the barricade, Joseph began to hear a rumbling louder than his stomach: boots and hooves and the wheels of baggage wagons and artillery caissons. There was a smattering of distant gunshots, and a brace of Canienga scouts came running out of the woods bordering the plain beside the river.

"Binds Two—they have riflemen scouting out ahead of them."

"Binds Two—their army stretches back farther than my eyes can see."

From behind the barricade, Joseph watched the blue army form up into order on the plain.

A dozen sprigs of gray-white smoke blossomed up from the far end of the meadow, joining together into a pretty, cottony cloud. There was a boom as of a big ceremonial drum thumped by a circle of mallets, then the barricade erupted with flying metal and pieces of wood and of human beings. As the splinters pattered down, a colorful object moving laterally caught the corner of Joseph's eye. It was the war-painted body of the mighty Red Jacket, running back toward where the baggage horses were tethered, leading a stream of other warriors inspired to follow him.

Joseph wiped Red Jacket out of his mind and turned his attention to the lines of bluecoated or buckskinned infantry advancing. They stopped just short of musket range, fired a useless volley, and fell back to reload, then repeated the procedure. Joseph and those of his Volunteers with long rifles managed to pick a few off, but the attacking infantry seemed content just to keep the defenders occupied while the artillery lobbed in shells. It seemed odd.

Joseph climbed one of the trees that hadn't been chopped down for the barricade and looked around. The muddy green arc at the foot of the hill to his left had sprouted blue and white and dun-colored flowers, as a wing of the American army waded through the marsh.

He scrabbled down out of the tree and ran along behind the

barricade, trying to ignore the stabbing sensation whenever his right foot hit the ground. "Colonel Butler!"

"Yes, Captain Brant?"

"The rebels are making for the hill!"

"I know that, but the damned Delawares won't—"

"Let me take a third of the men from the right flank to stop them!"

"Very well. But only a third!"

Old Smoke shouted over the gunfire: "I'm going, too!"

Joseph shouted back: "You'll never make it up the hill!"

"Hah! I'll be waiting for you at the top!"

Joseph's party got to the base of the hill while most of the rebel party were still wading the marsh. Old Smoke had already planted himself behind a tree and was dropping blue-coats as they came within range. Joseph found himself a handy boulder to crouch behind and joined in. Cornplanter was there as well, and a few Delawares, among them a delicately boned woman who could shoot like a frog tonguing flies.

Soon there were hundreds of rebel soldiers working their way up the hill, and waves more wading through the marsh. All that Joseph and the others could do was try to slow them down, firing at every patch of blue or of sun-bleached home-spun that showed itself, until the numbers got too many, and then slipping back to another rock or tree or deadfall farther up the slope. The only hope of stopping the advance was to make it so costly that the American commander might decide the game wasn't worth the candle.

Joseph threw himself down behind a jagged pine stump with musket balls spraying splinters from its roots. He looked back over his shoulder and saw that he was almost at the summit. He turned his head forward again and stuck it out to risk a peek downhill, immediately snatching it back as the stump shuddered with another barrage of bullets.

He thought back over the picture that had presented itself to his eyes in that glimpse. Below the smoke puffs of the front line of rebels advancing from tree to tree, blue and white lines were forming up on the side of the hill to fire down at the backs of the men behind the barricade. He hoped John Butler would have the sense to realize that the barricade was now a death trap. He had no doubt that those of his own Volunteers still down there would realize it, with or without orders.

Old Smoke was reloading in a hollow that could barely hide a rabbit. Joseph called to him: "I think we're finished."

Old Smoke nodded, threw back his head and pealed out, *"Oonah,"* which in these circumstances could be roughly translated as "Let's get the hell out of here."

The Delaware woman with the deadly eye chose that moment to spin around and roll helter-skelter down the hill. She came to rest against a ragged jackpine. A skunk-hatted rifleman leaped out and straddled her, raising a scalping knife. Joseph put a bullet through the skunk's side stripe and then turned and ran.

He gauged they'd have about a minute's grace before the rebels realized they weren't going to get shot at anymore and started running after them. It should give just enough of a lead to stay beyond rifle range.

By the time Joseph got down the back side of the hill, his lungs felt like they'd been breathing acid fumes. Old Smoke was grunting along just ahead of him. As Joseph caught up to him, Cornplanter swerved over from the other side and yelled into Old Smoke's ear: "Where's your horse?"

Old Smoke just shook his head. It did seem unlikely that those who'd joined Red Jacket to flee would've paused to consider which horse might've been Old Smoke's.

Joseph took hold of Old Smoke's left arm and Cornplanter the right and they jogged along together. Every now and then came the sound of a gunshot from behind, but no musket balls caught up with them.

By the time they reached the town of Chuknut, Joseph's right foot felt like a live coal had been implanted in the heel. The town was deserted, except for the pigs and chickens, which had no premonition that the houses they were roaming through were about to become their roasting pyres. Once he and Cornplanter had dragged Old Smoke through the town and beyond the farthest-flung orchards and cornfields, Joseph gauged their pursuers wouldn't be able to resist stopping to loot and burn. They slowed to a walk, all three of them gasping and Old Smoke spitting blood.

At the next Delaware town upstream, the remnants of Brant's Volunteers waited with other contingents of John Butler's army. There was no more talk of standing battles. All they could do now was split off into separate bands and try to harass and impede the invading army enough that the approach of winter would eventually force it to turn back.

The American commander, a General Sullivan, proved too smart by half. Even though Joseph and his war band followed so close they often cooked their venison on the invaders' campfires, there were no straggling parties to pounce on. From Chuknut the rebel force cut across country to the Lake of the Senecas and marched along its eastern shore, burning everything that had been built or planted by human hands. Joseph finally gave up hoping for stragglers and circled ahead of the American army to warn the towns in its path.

One night, Cornplanter crouched by Joseph's campfire and said in a voice no louder than the tiny bell that hung above his mouth: "Red Jacket has been talking. . . ."

"And the sun has been rising in the east and setting in the west."

"He and the Royaners he's been talking to are sending a messenger to the enemy camp tomorrow, begging the American general not to burn any more towns, promising to quit fighting for the king—and even to join up with the rebels—if their towns are spared."

Joseph looked away from the fire into the dark, and could feel his *onikonhra* sinking into it. He asked the darkness what to do. One night wasn't long enough to convert everyone who might've been persuaded that it was safe to sell himself to the Town Destroyer. Joseph had no doubt that those who planned to send the message would regret it once the congress held Niagara and no longer needed to pretend to respect the Stanwix Line. But by then it would be far too late.

There was no one left to tell him what he should do. Gets Business Done, King Hendrick, his wise grandmother and mother, even Carrying News, had all followed his father down the strawberry road. Little Abraham and the Reverend Wheelock were still alive, but their voices were no longer any help to him. As for the generals and colonels in the chain of command, Joseph was coming to the terrifying notion that they couldn't tell him how to win this war.

There was his sister, though, and he could hear her voice no matter how far away she was. He said to Cornplanter: "Who will be the messenger to General Sullivan?"

"Your wife's nephew, the one that wears the red porcupine crest roached to his hair."

That made Joseph hear Trembling Earth's voice as well, trying not to sound too prideful when she talked of her nephew the baggataway hero. He looked up at the stars, but the night was clouded over.

He pushed off from the ground, left Cornplanter squatted by his campfire and walked over to the campfire where Brant's Volunteers' Big Knives were settling in for the night. He sprinkled a bit of tobacco into the fire, packed his pipe and offered his tobacco pouch to Ezra Hawkins. Once their pipes were going, he murmured: "Ezra, you must know by now that you and those friends of yours who were with us from the start have become as good at scouting through the woods as any Mohawk."

"Why thankee, Cap'n Brant. I wouldn't go so far as to say I'm *that* good at it yet, but it's nice of you to say so."

"We Hodenosaune—we Iroquois—have strict laws against committing any act that would deprive the *orenda* of our confederacy of any portion of its strength. Although I've come to think of all Brant's Volunteers as Mohawks, you are not under that law.

"Tomorrow, an Iroquois will leave here bearing a message to the rebel army. He is a young man who wears a stiff mane of red-dyed moose hair and porcupine quills on his head. I would be very grateful if you and a friend or two would place yourselves along the trail and stop him."

"What shall we do with him, Cap'n?"

"Bury him where no one will find him. But leave him his scalp."

CHAPTER 51

As the last songbirds abandoned the rose garden behind Molly's rented house in Montreal, news began to trickle in of the summer's campaign in the west. The rebel army had retired to winter quarters before reaching anywhere near Niagara, but they'd burned every town and cornfield between Onondaga and the Genesee. Sir John Johnson's Royal New York Regiment and the garrison of regulars at Oswego had whiled away the summer without seeing one rebel soldier.

News had a habit of trickling its way to Someone Lends Her a Flower and the Brown Lady Johnson, from everywhere except the one place she was hungriest to hear of. A messenger arrived at her house with a letter, and she leaped on it and tore it open without looking at the outside. But it wasn't from Peter Warren, it was from Trembling Earth at Niagara.

My dearest Molly,

I am now your sister by English law as well as in my heart. One of the girls taken prisoner at Cherry Valley became friendly with one of the officers of the garrison here. They asked John Butler to marry them. Joseph was surprised Butler could do that, since he is not a Minister, and interrupted the ceremony to ask. When Colonel Butler explained that he is also a Justice of the Peace, Joseph said "Don't put your book away" and came to fetch me. I suspicion you already had some inkling your brother has a string of romance in him.

He and Isaac have quarreled again and Isaac has left his father's house, we don't know where, some say across the river to Butler's Barracks, which would be like him, to spite his father for saying he was too young to go to war by enlisting with Walter Butler. Sometimes I think your brother and his son would like each other more if they loved each other less. No doubt when Isaac is grown to be a man and out from under his father's shadow they will make their peace.

I must tell you that I fear for the Hodenosaune around Fort Niagara this winter. There are so many more here than last year, and more homeless ones coming in every day, but John Butler says he has no more provisions than he had last autumn. Now that I have a voice among the Clan Mothers, I do what I can to help my uncle Tekarihoga keep our people from losing hope, but our *orenda* limps without Someone Lends Her a Flower to lean upon.

Binds Two does what he can, but he must use so much of his strength to fight the war, he has little left to fight the Indian Department. He is fierce with anger over what happened this summer, and talks of leading his Volunteers out on snowshoes to punish the Oneidas who showed the white men the Forbidden Path. That will mean we will be without his voice in the Indian Department for much of the winter. Will you be coming to Niagara soon?

I yearn for this war to end.

> Your sister,
> The Trembling Earth

Molly lowered the letter and looked out at the petal-strewn rose garden. But what she saw outside the window was snowed-in, makeshift huts in the woods around Niagara, and shivering children who were far too old to still be wearing moccasins with holes in them. She said to herself, "Well, Molly m'gel, did ye think to loll about here all war long?" then called Abraham to hitch up the carriage.

At the Department of Northern Indian Affairs, she informed Daniel Claus that John Butler would need several times more supplies this winter than last, and asked him to arrange passage for her and the children to Niagara, "Except George and Martha and Peggy, of course—they'll stay in school."

"I'm afraid that won't be possible, Molly."

"What won't be possible?"

"Arranging passage. Every available foot of boat space has

to be used for transporting troops and provisions before freeze-up."

"I'm not planning some bleedin' pleasure cruise! Do you think I *want* to spend the winter shivering in a stone barracks at Fort Niagara instead of snug and warm in my house here? The king has a few thousand new allies waiting at Niagara: provided they aren't allowed to starve to death before the next campaign, or begin to believe they'd be better off suing the rebels for peace."

"I don't have the authority to countermand military orders. Only the governor could—"

"Well write to the governor, then, and explain the situation."

"Very well. But I don't expect it will do much good."

A week later Daniel Claus came to her house somewhat sheepishly. He said: "I've received a reply from the governor."

"What did he say?"

"Ahem. 'Miss Molly is to act as she sees best.' "

The first available transport was a small fleet of deckless bateaux ferrying supplies to Carleton Island. Molly gambled that once at Carleton Island, she'd be able to get onto one of the last ships of the season carrying provisions from the depot there to Fort Niagara.

From Montreal the boats were poled and lined up the rapids, with the oarsmen plodding along the shore and shallows, and white foam spraying over the gunwales. At the little village of Lachine, the boatmen climbed back onto their rowing benches and carried on up the broad St. Lawrence, running up their sails when the wind blew fair. Molly sat watching the last bright leaves spinning off the trees on the riverbanks, wondering how long she had before the ice set in.

At Carleton Island there was a lake ship already anchored in the harbor, with soldiers lined up waiting to be rowed on board, so she went straight from the wharf to the captain in command of the fort and requested room on the ship for herself and her household. He said: "I can't do that. There is not to be any transporting of civilians until all essential supply shipments and troop movements have been accomplished."

"The governor himself said I was to act as I see best! He put his signature to it."

"That letter is directed to Guy Johnson as head of the Indian

Department. It says nothing of military matters. I will arrange for you and your children and servants to be quartered in the officers' barracks."

"We can't stay here!"

"With all due respect, Miss Molly, I have other matters on my plate than worrying about where you and your children would prefer to stay. The Officer of the Day will see to quartering your family. Now if you'll excuse me, I have a small matter of a dispatch from the commanding general to attend to."

She fumed out, looking for the building housing Indian Affairs. It wasn't hard to spot. There was a ragged flock of Caniengas and Cayugas slouched in front of it. Her path toward it passed by the fort gates, where two young Hodenosaune women were playing the leg-wrestling game for the benefit of the sentries. She called out to them in Canienga: "Why don't you simply tie your skirts over your heads and tattoo a price on your asses? Your mothers must have work they need help with."

"Yes, Oyander."

As she approached the ragged-looking crowd in front of the Indian Office, some of them straightened their spines and called out to her. She touched hands with a few of them and said softly: "Have the dwellers under the Tree of Peace become a race of beggars?"

"The Tree of Peace has been cut down, Oyander."

"It has *not*. A few of its roots have been burned, but they will grow back."

A woman whined: "Guy Johnson promised he would have blankets for us today, but now he says there are none."

"I will speak to him. Oh—and is John Deseronto on the island?"

"Yes, Oyander. He brought his warriors from the east some days ago."

"It should be made known to him that I am here now."

Inside, Guy Johnson was standing at one end of a long room yelling in English at an old Cayuga Royaner standing at the other end staring at the floorboards: "I'm not the horn of fucking plenty! Do you think I just snap my fingers and blankets magically rise up out of the— Good God, Molly . . ."

"Hello, Guy." She reminded herself that Guy had suffered

troubles of his own. When the Indian Department made its escape from the Mohawk Valley, the long, rough trail to Oswego had ended with Mary Johnson screaming her life out bearing a dead baby in a sodden tent.

"When did you get here?" he asked.

"Barely a moment ago. What's this I hear about blankets?"

"You keep your damned nose out of this! *I'm* the one that has to deal with all the endless demands, and damned Claus not paying heed to a word I write him, and John Butler whining from Niagara."

"I am aware yours isn't an easy job, Guy. But *you* should be aware that we of the League of the Hodenosaune don't take promises lightly—even when they're made by a man so pissdrunk he can't remember if he promised blankets or baskets. And if you ever raise your voice to me again, I'll see to it that the governor puts you on a front line with a red coat on your back and a bayonet in your hand."

She found "Captain John"—as the English called Deseronto—in a smoky hut outside the fort, councilling with those war chiefs and Royaners who'd washed up on Carleton Island. John Deseronto had had as hard a war as anyone. He'd almost lost an arm in a skirmish with rebel scouts. He'd developed a habit now, when sitting in council, of casually cradling that supposedly healed arm in the other, as though he were only adopting a posture of relaxation. But the permanent pain lines etched under his eyes belied the pose.

Molly threw down a few strands of wampum in front of their council fire and said: "Brothers—I have it in my mind that it would be a mistake for you to go out in scattered parties to punish the Oneidas. Wolves know they are stronger in a pack. Wait until Binds Two comes."

Deseronto said: "Binds Two is not the war chief of all the Hodenosaune, despite what his white friends may think."

She and Deseronto and the others sawed it back and forth for a while—although the conversation was inhibited somewhat by the hut being too low-roofed to stand and gesture—until one of the Royaners picked up her wampum strings and said: "We men will speak of this among ourselves, Someone Lends Her a Flower, and return your wampum tomorrow."

"Tomorrow" turned out to be three days later. Deseronto said graciously: "It has been decided we will wait for your brother."

"I think this is a wise decision you have made. And while the warriors are waiting for Binds Two, there is something very useful they can do here."

"What is that?"

"Build a longhouse."

"What? Why?"

"The Hodenosaune here on Carleton Island are growing lost. They need a place to live."

"Of course they do. We are fighting this war so that the places where we live will be ours again forever. But in the meanwhile, no longhouse ever built could be big enough to house all the people here."

"Forgive me, Deseronto, I did not speak clearly. I meant a place for the people to *live*. A ceremonial longhouse. Most of the people here have always lived in the valley of the Caniengas, or by Cayuga Lake, or within sight of the three hills of the Onondagas—where the ceremonies and festivals of the turnings of the year are woven into the landscape. To those people, to be Hodenosaune is to be in those places, so they are cast adrift now.

"But when I was a Mingo girl on the Ohio, my mother and father always made sure there was a Dream Speaking at the Midwinter Moon, a Green Corn Festival at harvest— even if the Green Corn Dance was only two women carrying the eldest of the Three Sisters around a fire. So I grew up knowing I was a Keeper of the Dawn, even though I had never set foot east of the Sunset Gate. In the same way, we can remind our people here that they are not broken, homeless wanderers, they are still the Six Nations of the Great League of Peace."

"Someone Lends Her a Flower, we have enough to do trying to build shelter and find food in the forest and lake to eke out what little the Indian Department gives us, without building ceremonial longhouses."

The other war chiefs and Royaners turned out to be of the same opinion, so Molly called a council of those Clan Mothers who were on Carleton Island. The morning after the council, she and her daughters and the Clan Mothers and a few other women and girls carried a motley collection of axes, hatchets, and saws to a meadow Molly had scouted out. The meadow was half grown over with young poplar trees. Poplar wasn't the best wood for longhouse poles, but Molly didn't expect it would have to stand for longer than a few years.

She selected a likely looking tree, put her hand on it and whispered, "I ask thee to give thy life that we may have life," then drew back her ax and swung. It was an awkward swing—she'd rarely used an ax except vertically to chop up firewood—but she expected she'd get better as she went along. She tried to keep an eye on Susanna and Nancy felling poplar shoots with a penknife. The chunking of other axes and hatchets and the rasping of saws rose up around her.

Deseronto and a few other warriors approached uncomfortably, looking abashed at seeing women and girls doing the men's work of clearing land. Deseronto said: "What are you doing?"

Molly pulled her ax loose, panted, "Building a ceremonial longhouse," and swung again.

"Damnit, Molly!" English was better than Canienga for expressing exasperation. "Even if you did manage to get up a framework before winter, there's no way in hell you'll get enough elm bark together to cover it."

"I know how to solve that problem," she said, and raised her ax again.

Deseronto let out a sound that wasn't quite a sigh or a snarl, spat, "Give that to me," took the ax from her hands and waved her back. He said to the tree, "I thank thee," and cocked the ax. Deseronto's swing was a practiced, long, clean arc. But there was a hitch in it, and when the ax head bit into the wood, his face tensed with pain as the shock traveled up his crippled arm. Nonetheless, he tugged the blade free and swung again. The wood chip that flew out was bigger than all of Molly's little chips combined.

The warriors who'd approached with Deseronto came forward to take charge of axes and saws. Soon there were other men coming out of the woods carrying axes of their own. One of them raised his ax toward a particularly straight, young tree. Molly called out: "No! Only trim that one. And . . ." She pointed to another one about ten paces away. ". . . that one, as well."

The warrior looked confused. She arced her arms over her head. He got a dawning look and shinnied up the tree to start slicing off its branches, even though it swayed with his weight. When both trees were trimmed, they tied ropes to their tops, bent them toward each other, and lashed them together to form the first hoop of the longhouse frame, firmly rooted in the earth of Turtle Island.

As the skeleton of the longhouse took shape, Molly went to see the fort commander again. "Captain, in the depot here— what with all the ships that come and go—there must be at least a few patched, worn-out old sails that are no longer strong enough for anything but making tents."

"Your people want to make tents now?"

"Just one very big tent. It only seems fair that the sails of the king's ships should become the sails of our *orenda*." The captain looked as though he hadn't the vaguest notion what that was supposed to mean, but she hadn't expected him to.

As the wind hurled snow around outside, Juba bustled about setting out the tea service, with Miss Elizabeth and Miss Magdalen lending a hand. There were always guests for tea in their set of rooms in the married officers' quarters—usually Iroquois from the heart-twisting camps outside the fort. Mistress Molly had given strict orders that the girls weren't to take more than one slice of bread or one biscuit at tea, so the guests could eat the rest.

But the orders had been suspended for today. Several junior officers had been invited to tea with Mistress Molly's daughters. Juba looked at the table and said: "Let's see, now . . . I s'pose, Miz Elizabeth, you'll want your place set next to that young Dr. Kerr. . . ."

Juba could feel the heat of Miss Elizabeth's blush without having to look at her. Miss Magdalen giggled. Miss Elizabeth protested: "He isn't so young—that is—"

"Oh well, if he ain't so young, you won't want to be sitting anywheres near him. I'll set you at the far end of the table."

"Juba!"

"I'ze just trying to follow your inclinations, Miz Elizabeth. You can be set anywheres you want, just have to tell me. Ain't nobody ever going to know what you want less'n you tell 'em."

The officers arrived, with their boots and buttons polished and their hats under their arms, and sat down at the table with the girls they'd come to flirt with, and their mother to chaperone. Actually, it looked to Juba like Mistress Molly was doing more flirting of her own than chaperoning. Juba could see her holding herself back a little bit to let her daughters shine, but also enjoying showing her daughters there was no need to fear creatures who were so easily beguiled. And if anyone could beguile ... Maybe some parts of Mistress Molly had dropped a little lower since she'd passed her fortieth year, but so had her voice, growing throatier and fuller, so that wise young men thought twice before replying to her latest bit of banter, and unwise ones ended up stammering.

Juba had no doubt, though, that banter was all there was to it. No dozen living men put together could ever take the place of the one lying underneath the church at Johnstown.

Juba was just starting to smile to herself at the sight of Molly thinking of nothing but frivolity for a change, when a specter appeared in the doorway: a frost-rimed winter wolf with the eyes of a hunted doe. After the first startled instant, Juba saw that it was Captain Joseph, wearing a mantle made from the mask and forequarters of a gray wolf's pelt. But it wasn't just the mask cowl that made him look wolfish. His face had grown even leaner, with hard lines scoured around the eyes and mouth, and there was a gray tinge in his skin. Juba could feel his cheek burn her lips when Mistress Molly kissed him hello.

Young Dr. Kerr said: "I believe you have a touch of frostbite there."

Captain Joseph said, "I know," and flopped down beside the fire. Juba brought him a cup of tea, and he surprised her by asking if there was a bit of rum or brandy to put in it. She'd never thought of him as much of a drinking man. As she went to fetch the decanter, she heard him ask behind her: "Have you had any news of Peter Warren?"

"*Have you?*" leaped out of Mistress Molly.

"No."

Juba turned around with the decanter to see Molly looking down at her slack hands in her lap and shaking her head.

The officers who'd come to tea attempted to make conversation with Captain Joseph about the war. He replied civilly enough, but Juba could see he was as impatient with these dewy soldier boys as she would be with a green kitchen maid who had opinions on the dinner menu.

When the officers left, eager to brag to their messmates that they'd had tea with Captain Brant, Mistress Molly squatted down on the hearth rug beside her brother and the two of them began to talk in Mohawk. They were still talking when a bell rang in the courtyard. They didn't appear to hear it. Juba said: " 'Scuze me, Mizt'ess Molly, but that was the bell for us to go down to supper in the officers' mess."

Captain Joseph sighed: "I don't particularly fancy spending the evening trading campaign tales with Lieutenant This and Major That."

Mistress Molly said: "Would you fetch us up two plates, please, Juba."

"Yes'm."

As Miss Elizabeth and her sisters crossed the courtyard toward their table in the officers' mess, Juba headed for the cookhouse and found the big-mustached cook sergeant who ruled the roost. " 'Scuze me, Sergeant, sir, but could you please load me up two plates to take back?"

"For Miss Molly and her brother?"

"Yes, sir."

"Consider it done. There'll be disappointment in the officers' mess—everyone's eager to get a look at Captain Brant. Is it true he carries a sackful of scalps with him wherever he goes?"

"Not so far as I ever seed. I 'spect it'd weigh him down some."

The sergeant laughed as though she'd made a joke. "I expect you're right, with all the men they say he's killed."

"Well, that's what a man's s'posed to do in a war, ain't it?"

"True enough, but not all men enjoys it."

"Who says he enjoys it?"

"Everybody."

" '*Everybody* say. *They* say.' What'd you know about it? You never come no closer to a war'n I have—just cooking briskets and walloping skillets."

"I don't take that kind of talk from nigger wenches."

"Oh please forgive me, Massa Sergeant, sir, for telling the truth. Now, you going to finish filling them plates or do I has to go tell Captain Joseph you said he has to come fetch 'em himself?" She looked down at the two plates piled with boiled-gray beef, boiled-gray cabbage, and boiled-gray potatoes. "Anyone ever tell you about pepper?"

She carried the plates back to their quarters and then went to the servants' mess for her own supper. Gone were the days of Fort Johnson, when servants and masters all sat down at the same table.

When she came back from supper, the plates she'd brought had been licked clean and Mistress Molly and Captain Joseph were still talking. They were still talking long after all the girls had gone to their beds. Juba's bed was on the floor of the room that served as sitting room and parlor, but she didn't mind being kept awake by the two voices rising and falling, with a chuckle in them one moment and a sigh the next. She could follow parts of what they were saying, as their conversation moved from stories of their children to stories of a warrior who'd been killed to stories of the Indian Department and back again.

The voices stopped. A moment later Mistress Molly whispered: "Juba . . . ?" Juba got up and went to her. Captain Joseph had fallen asleep on the hearth rug, and Molly was trying to drag it and him out of reach of flying sparks without waking him. Juba took hold of the other edge of the rug and helped her, then fetched one of her own blankets and draped it over him.

Juba stood looking down at the firelight playing across the sleeping wolf. Most faces softened in sleep, but without the sweetening effect of those velvet eyes, his looked even harder. She wondered how much more sharp-honed and hard-forged a man could get without breaking.

Mistress Molly whispered from beside her: "All those men I keep pushing out onto the war road . . ."

Juba whispered back: "Ain't you that made this war, Mizt'ess Molly. And if you'd been raised up to be a warrior, 'stead'n a Clan Mother, you'd've been the first to go."

"Yes, so I can *say*, Juba."

* * *

Molly only had her brother at Carleton Island for two days before he set off across the frozen channel between the island and the south shore, breaking trail for a line of snowshoed warriors. A month later Deseronto and most of the others came straggling back and the garrison was treated to a scalp dance. Deseronto told her: "Binds Two parted with us at Oswego, to lose no time getting back to Thundergate. He said to tell you we did not make the same mistake as the rebel invaders made last summer: that of creating more vengeful warriors than widows and orphans. He is one hard-driving war chief, your brother. Perhaps too hard."

"Do you think the Oneidas will ever again guide invaders along the Forbidden Path?"

"Were I them, I wouldn't."

"Then my brother drove you as hard as he should."

Deseronto murmured: "Someday he would be well off to count up Brant's Volunteers and notice they do not include the whole of the Six Nations."

At the Midwinter Moon, Molly stood in the ceremonial longhouse with a belt of white wampum in her hands. The ribs of the longhouse stood out like claw marks against its sun-glowed, canvas skin: a cold white dome with a border of blue around the bottom where the snow banked up against its walls. Looking out at the hunger-pinched faces and the sprung-ribbed bodies clothed in tattered blankets and scraps of worn-out army uniforms, she wondered how she could have the temerity to say anything to them. But she had to.

"Brothers and sisters . . . grandmothers and grandfathers . . . daughters and sons . . . as the new year dawns, we confess to each other the bad thoughts and deeds of the old year, and give thanks that we still have breath to do so.

"Out of all the bad thoughts I had in the old year—and those who know me will tell you I have more than a few bad thoughts—the worst was to think we had little to give thanks for. I was wrong. There is our *orenda*.

"Despite all our enemies have done to us, are we not still Hodenosaune? Are we not still the people who heard the words of Hiawatha and the Peacemaker, and do not those words still live? The Fire That Never Dies still burns— although not at Onondaga, it will there again.

"Because the day is coming soon when our warriors and the

king's soldiers break the Town Destroyer. And then we will go back. Back to the Three Hills of the Onondagas. Back to the Lake of the Senecas. Back to Canajoharie—"

Something caught in her throat and she couldn't go on. But someone else said in a whisper that echoed through the longhouse: "To Oquaga."

Someone else said: "To the Genesee."

"To Unadilla."

"To the Chemung."

"To Chittenango Falls."

"To Taughannock."

"To the River of the Caniengas . . ."

CHAPTER 52

Joseph would always remember 1781 as the year the Hodenosaune won the king's war for him. The new year had barely begun when an urgent summons came to his quarters from the Indian Department. He found John Butler practically capering around the office, with a dispatch in one hand and a splashing tumbler in the other.

Colonel Butler brandished the dispatch at him and crowed: "Joseph! The rebel army in Pennsylvania has mutinied! They killed some of their officers and are laying siege to their damned Continental Congress in Philadelphia! Their New Jersey regiments are following suit!"

"What? Why . . . ?"

"*Why?* You overmodest great dolt, because of *you*! Because of *us*—the military wing of the Department of Indian Affairs. Because for the last three years the Mohawk Valley and Wyoming and all the rest have been growing nothing but fireweed and widows. No flour or beef to feed the rebel troops, no wool to clothe them, no cowhide to shoe them. They're starving and freezing to death, that's why!"

Not much later in the year, Cornplanter and Old Smoke burst into his quarters shouting, "Fort Stanwix!" and then doubled over with laughter.

The two Senecas managed to regain their composure, and Old Smoke said solemnly: "Yes, Fort Stanwix . . ."

"There was a fire there. . . ." Cornplanter intoned gravely.

"Yes," Old Smoke nodded, "a big fire. Nothing left of Fort Stanwix but ashes."

"Funny thing," Cornplanter mused, "it had been raining hard for three days and nights and the river had flooded, but still the place burned to the ground."

"And in the middle of the day, too . . ." Old Smoke tugged thoughtfully at his pendulous lower lip. ". . . with all the bluecoat garrison there to fight the fire. . . . But luckily, not one of them was even scorched. They all lived to shoulder their muskets and march back to Schenectady."

"And the oddest thing of all . . ." Cornplanter wrinkled his forehead and toyed abstractedly with a gold-weighted, ragged flap of earlobe. "   is that all winter long they've been sending messages back to Schenectady, crying they were starving and miserable and couldn't they please come home?" Then he and Old Smoke both fell about the room laughing again.

Cornplanter caught his breath, clapped Joseph on the shoulders and grinned: "What do you think of that, Binds Two? The British army with all its cannons couldn't take Fort Stanwix, but we did—just by burning a few cornfields."

As each further dab of news came in to paint a picture of the enemy chewing its own limbs off, Joseph would've thought his *onikonhra* should grow wings. Instead, he sat drinking rum and brooding on his Teacher, Little Abraham, and on Old Isaac. When he'd set off on a winter raid a year ago, he'd met them coming toward Niagara, along with two other Royaners—four old men traveling hundreds of miles on snowshoes to bring an offer of a truce between the Continental Congress and the League of Peace.

Joseph had sent them on to the fort with an escort bearing a sealed message to Guy Johnson, who had made his escape from Molly on Carleton Island by declaring that John Butler couldn't carry the Indian Office at Niagara and Butler's Rangers at the same time. The message had read: "All I would say to you concerning them is, to pretend to be friendly with them at first before these Indians who are going with me to war; I think after we are all gone from Niagara then you may do what you think proper."

What Guy Johnson had thought proper was to clap them into the dungeon of Fort Niagara. After six months Joseph had managed to convince Old Isaac and one of the other Royaners to go along with him on a raid and at least put up a show of trying to convince more Oneidas and Tuscaroras to come and fight for the king. They'd put up a good enough show that Old Isaac and his partner were now allowed to roam free about Niagara, if they didn't stray too far. But Little Abraham and the fourth Royaner hadn't seen the sun for more than a year now.

Joseph mixed enough rum with his brooding to begin to think that maybe Little Abraham had changed his mind by now, and to convince himself that he could stomach a visit to the dungeon. He pursued an erratically dignified course down the moonlit corridors and staircases to the offices of the Niagara Indian Department. An ensign seconded to Indian Affairs was on duty while the mighty colonels, Johnson and Butler, snored in their beds. Joseph said to the ensign: "Come with me. I want an officer of the Indian Department to bear witness."

"Begging your pardon, Captain Brant, but you're in no condition to—"

"Drunk as a lord I'm still in a better condition than any of your lords and masters. Come with me."

The dungeon was a windowless, heartless room just down the hall from the council chamber where Brant's Joseph used to translate for Gets Business Done in his dealings with the western tribes. The Corporal of the Guard lighted the way along the corridor, saying: "Watch your steps, sirs. What with the ground thaw and all, this floor's slipperier'n the Queen of France's drawers."

As the corporal shot back the bolt on the slab of a door, a ghost of a voice called from beyond: "Is it morning yet?"

"Not yet, me old darlin'. You've got visitors. Back off the

door, now—Sergeant'd have me guts for garters if I mangled you in throwin' it back."

The corporal's lantern showed a stone-ceilinged cow byre whose straw should've been changed some weeks ago. The puff of cold air through the doorway tasted like a wine cellar for a vintage of mushrooms, urine, and stale sweat.

In the farthest corner, a blanket-wrapped bundle of dry sticks sat bobbing back and forth in time to a chant that had no vowels left in it. In front of the doorway stood a shriveled little owl shading its eyes against the light. The owl squinted hard, then hooted: "Binds Two? Binds Two . . . ?"

Joseph said softly to his old Teacher: "I greet thee, Royaner."

"Is the war over?"

"Not yet." Joseph had to pause to swallow a couple of times. "I came to ask you, Grandfather, to come out on the war road with me. If Old Smoke can take the war road on a horse, so can you. You need not sharpen up your hatchet, only speak to those of the Longhouse who still think they can tread a middle road, and tell them that the Town Destroyer will turn on them if the king does not destroy him."

"It is kind of you to come to see me, grandson. But you should understand that an old man's *onikonhra* does not bend easily, nor has it much reason to. I said from the beginning that we should let the white men fight their war around the Tree of Peace while we stay under it. I am too old to lie."

"King Hendrick always said that it was his little brother who was the strong one in the family."

"Hendrick always talks as much out of his back hole as his front. Do you have any messages you would like me to give to him?"

Joseph turned and stumbled back out into the corridor. As the cell door shuddered back into place, he turned on the ensign attached to the Indian Department, butting his hands against the red-coated chest. "You call *us* savages? If we torture a man at the stake, it's finished in a few hours!"

The ensign pushed back, saying, "Don't you go manhandling *me*, you—" and Joseph slammed him against the wall.

The ensign shot a fist up that caught him on the point of the chin and rattled his teeth. Joseph rocked back on his heels and then grappled, banging the white man's head against the stone wall, ignoring the fists thudding into his ribs and the boots kicking at his legs. The ensign got hold of his scalp lock and began to pull his head back, so Joseph put a knee in his groin to loosen his grip and then tripped him up, throwing him sideways to the floor. But before Joseph could spring, the Corporal of the Guard took hold of him from behind, saying: "Now now, sir—gentlemen shouldn't be brawling like common soldiers."

Joseph hadn't spent all those years wrestling with Big William without learning how to deal with a bigger man who had him wrapped up from behind. He reached his right hand over his shoulder to cup the back of the corporal's neck, and then jackknifed forward as he pulled with all the strength he could put into his right arm. The corporal sailed over his back with a surprised squawk, turning over in the air and coming down on top of the ensign. Neither one of them showed any signs of getting up again soon, so Joseph went home.

He woke up the next morning feeling terrible in more ways than one. It took him till midday to summon up the courage to poke his head out his door and go apologize. The ensign merely heard him out, purse-mouthed, and then turned his back. The Corporal of the Guard, who was propped up in an infirmary bed with his right arm in splints, said: "Oh, that's all right, sir. I'd been tryin' to think me up a way to get a bit of bed rest—the damp plays hell with a man's bellows. Do you think, sir, once me wing's set to rights again, you might show me how you done that?"

Niagara was a small community, and word got around quickly, especially such entertaining word as Captain Brant drunkenly attacking a fellow officer. Joseph spent the next few weeks finding it difficult to meet people's eyes, particularly Trembling Earth's. Isaac didn't have to say a word to remind him of all the pious fatherly lectures against getting drunk and belligerent. As the snow melted slowly off the battlements, Joseph wished the spring would hurry along so he could escape to the war road, but wondered how he would presume to command warriors when he couldn't even keep command of himself.

South of Detroit, where the Sandusky River flowed into Lake Erie, was the rendezvous Joseph had appointed with his

Big Knives last autumn. Ezra Hawkins saluted: "How do, Cap'n Brant. All present and accounted for."

"*All?*" Joseph looked around at the total of seventeen ragged men, where he'd expected to find a force strong enough to serve as a magnet for all the scattered western tribes. "Where are the rest?"

"Well, Cap'n . . . there *has* been a few gone down over the years. . . ."

"Not *that* many."

"Well, and some's got their local Safety Committees breathin' down their necks. And some says four years of war's a tech more'n they'd bargained on. And some just plumb figure there ain't much sense in dyin' for the sake of a few more Injun huts when it's just a question of time now before George Washington admits he's had his wooden teeth kicked out. But you and me and the old boys, Cap'n, we can do the needful."

Joseph muttered grimly: "Not alone we can't."

They started up the Sandusky in canoes. There wasn't much of a current to paddle against. In its lower reaches the river was more of an overgrown mud puddle seeping its way through a flat, featureless country of beaver bogs and scrubby meadows.

At the Wyandot town of Upper Sandusky 160 warriors from various tribes were waiting, and a smattering of white Tories, all under the nominal command of an Indian Department translator named Simon Girty. Joseph had never met him before, but had heard of him. When children, Simon Girty and his brothers had been captured and adopted by the Senecas.

Simon Girty turned out to be a monstrously tall, handsome fellow with a nose ring, who liked to brag that he'd taken more rebel scalps than any man alive. The one he said he most yearned to hang from his belt, though, was that of the only one of the four Girty brothers who hadn't declared himself a loyalist. The fact that Simon had switched sides once or twice himself didn't seem to be a consideration.

All the Tsklelelis flitting from the south said the rebel expedition to pillage the Sandusky country and push for Detroit numbered five hundred to a thousand, but hadn't started up the Ohio yet. Joseph set off south with his Vol-

unteers and Simon Girty's younger brother and a Cayuga
war chief with a personal following of a couple of dozen
warriors—barely a hundred men all told. Simon Girty was
to hurry after them with the main body as soon as reinforcements arrived from Detroit.

Joseph's war band left their canoes behind and took to
the woods. When they reached the Ohio, Joseph drank from
the river of his childhood, the river the Muskingum flowed
into.

A scout brought word that the rebel army was just ahead,
rowing upriver under a big striped flag. Joseph said: "How
many?"

"Maybe fifty."

"Fifty? That's not an army."

"But there's a lot of men in each boat."

Joseph faded back into the forest and watched the river
through the leaves. The flag appeared around a bend, with a
ragged flotilla stretched out behind it. The invaders were traveling in everything from canoes to skiffs to flatboats. Most of
the rowers and paddlers and lounging officers appeared to be
militia, who'd been known to desert the instant rations got
short, or to run at the sound of the first enemy gunshot. They
weren't singing any jaunty boating songs.

But even if they were all green militia, they were far too
many for a hundred men to take on. Joseph led his hundred
sneaking along behind them, and sent a runner to circle
ahead and inform Simon Girty that they had the invaders in
a vise.

Long before sundown Joseph halted to make camp, so
they'd be far enough behind that their cooking fires couldn't
be seen from where the rebels pulled into shore for the night.
Not that there was much to cook, but hot cornmeal soup tasted
better than cold, and wasn't quite so apt to coagulate in the
stomach.

One of Ezra's Big Knives, who'd dropped off by the side of
the trail to deal with the effects of the last of their beans, came
running. "Cap'n Brant! There's another camp of 'em behind
us!"

Joseph got a chilling feeling that he'd been the one caught
between the jaws of a vise. "How many?"

"Only one campfire, so there can't be that many."

Joseph took twenty of his Volunteers and went to look. There was a sentry who never heard a thing except the sound of his throat being cut. Beyond the sentry was a foolish bonfire shooting sparks at the stars. Joseph counted only six silhouettes moving back and forth against the flames. But there could be a good deal more of them already bedded down, and the two boats drawn up on the shore were loaded down with a lot of supplies for only half a dozen men.

Joseph circled his hand through the air and pointed to his left, to signal his twenty to slip through the shadows and make an arc around the camp. When he heard an owl hoot that wasn't an owl, he howled out his war yell and all the others did the same.

The men around the bonfire flung themselves to the ground or scrambled to cock their muskets or broke for the river. As the echoes of the wolf pack faded up toward the moon, Joseph called out: "I am a British officer. If you surrender, you will be treated as prisoners of war."

There was a pause, and then a voice called back: "Will you personally guarantee our safety?"

"I can guarantee that if you don't surrender, the next breath you take shall be your last. Throw down your weapons and stand up."

They did. As Joseph came out of the woods into the fire-light, the one uniformed man among the new prisoners took one look at his scalp lock, and the painted chest between the lapels of his red coat, and said: "You ain't no British officer!"

"I most certainly am. I am Captain Brant."

"Thank Christ! They say you don't torture prisoners."

"Not as a general rule. Provided they're not reluctant to give me information."

"The general sent us to lag behind with supplies for another company of a hundred or so that's trying to catch up with him. They was supposed to link up with the main army some while ago, but the general's moving too fast—so as to get deep enough into Indian country no one else'll dare desert."

"How much farther behind is this other party?"

"Maybe a day or so."

The two boatfuls of supplies were more than welcome in Joseph's camp. As his Volunteers and Cayugas chortled over the divvying up of ammunition and provisions, he sat contemplating where best to surprise the "company of a hundred or so."

There was a place his war band had passed and repassed in their secret dance with the invading army up and down the Ohio. On first sight Joseph had been willing to swear he remembered the place from the days when his father would take the family traveling in his canoe. On one side of the river was a creek mouth with a hill beside it. On the opposite shore was a tangled canebrake. With Ezra's long rifles at the top of the hill, the Cayugas hidden in the undergrowth along the creek mouth, and the bulk of Brant's Volunteers in the canebrake, they would have the rebel boats in a cross fire.

But when they came to the place the next day, the Cayuga war chief looked at the landscape, wrinkled his nose, squinted at the sun and shook his head: "No—I don't think this is a good place to fight. A little farther upriver would be better."

Joseph stepped in close to the Cayuga chief and said as patiently as possible: "While we stand here chewing feathers, or looking for a better place upriver, the enemy will pass us by safely and make their main force outnumber ours even more than it does now. This is where we'll fight."

"Not me. And not any of the warriors who have chosen to follow me."

"This is not a baggataway game."

The Cayuga chief just snorted.

Joseph didn't even think about it. His right hand tugged one of the king's brace of pistols out of his waist sash and his left hand wrenched back the cock. There wasn't enough room between his torso and the Cayuga chief's to point the pistol, so he just held it upright.

The Cayuga chief laughed in his face: "Don't think you can threaten me! If you pull that trigger on me, your life belongs to my brothers."

"I don't make threats." The Cayuga chief went up on his toes as the pistol ball drove up through the tender flesh behind his chin and into his brain. Blinking against the smoke, Joseph replaced the spent pistol, drew and cocked its mate, and said: "Which of you still choose to follow him?" The Cayugas headed for the thickets at the creek mouth to lie in wait.

They didn't have to wait long. The rebel reinforcements came singing at their oars, something about Jimmy cracking corn. Like the supply squad with their bonfire, the choristers had made the mistake of assuming that the main body of their army would have cleared the river of any Indians ahead of them. Two volleys killed a third of them, leaving the rest screaming for quarter.

Joseph's war band carried on marching upriver, slowed and almost doubled by its prisoners. Two days after the ambush, they had to scuttle farther into the woods to avoid the main body of the invaders rowing back downriver, looking for their reinforcements.

Joseph turned his force around to tag along behind them, laughing outwardly at the jokes about how well they were all getting to know this stretch of the Ohio. Inwardly he was wondering where the hell Simon Girty was, and all the men supposedly coming from Upper Sandusky.

Finally, an advance scout from Simon Girty brought word that the Delawares, Wyandots, and Girty's Tories were only a day's march back. Joseph sat down to wait for them. Their combined force made almost seven hundred men. Now it was their turn to chase the invaders who'd come to chase them.

They'd almost caught up to the rebel army when a couple of Joseph's Caniengas captured two stragglers who said their general had decided to disband and send everyone home after accomplishing nothing. Simon Girty and the Sandusky chiefs decided to do the same, just when they had a disorganized and unsuspecting enemy floundering within their grasp.

Ezra Hawkins said: "I know it rankles, Cap'n, but it looks as we ain't got much choice."

Joseph laughed: "Rankles?" The word was comically inadequate. "The Continental Congress is already teetering on the edge. If we had wiped this army out ... How many times, Ezra, must we see this war prolonged by people who claim to be on our side?"

At Fort Detroit, Joseph was vaguely aware of being carried along the dock and settled into a private room. He had stabbed himself in the thigh trying to sheath his own sword after using it to end a difference of opinion with Simon Girty. The wound had become poisoned.

Some while later, Trembling Earth was bending over his bed. She'd been there before, as had a lot of other visitors—the wolf with his father's voice, Big William. . . . But this time her face looked haggard and worried, instead of set in her usual serene expression. And this time, when he raised his hand to her cheek, it didn't pass right through, but bumped against it.

He said: "How did I get here?"

"By canoe, and they carried you. Or so they tell me."

"I don't even recall leaving Detroit."

"You didn't. When the news came to Niagara, I came here."

From then on, whenever he woke up, she was there with a cup of water or a spoonful of soup. She bathed his leg with poultices that at least made it smell better. He fought to make himself awake so he could see her, but coming back from the dreamworld meant coming back to the pain.

At one of those times, she said: "Did you know Walter Butler is eating strawberries?" He shook his head. "I told you before, but I thought you might not have heard me. The Mohawk Valley militia were waiting for them—"

"Isaac?"

"He came back safe."

"Ah. Are you certain about Walter Butler? He's been said to be dead before."

"The stories are all too much alike to be Tskleleli's. The Rangers had retreated across the river and stopped to keep the militia from following them. An Oneida shot Walter and then ran across the ford to finish him while the rest of the Rangers fled.

"The only place the stories differ is the end. Some say Walter begged for quarter and the Oneida said, 'Cherry Valley quarter!' and chopped him with his hatchet. And some say Walter said, 'Do you know who I am?' and the Oneida said, 'Yes,' and put a bullet through his eye."

Joseph couldn't quite bring himself to say, Hai, Walter, but he did say: "Poor John."

"You never much cared for either of the Butlers."

"I know, but it was still his son."

There was a doctor who came and went and murmured in distant corners with Trembling Earth. Joseph didn't have to hear them to know what they were murmuring; his leg told him. Once, when Trembling Earth was peeling off the latest fouled mass of slippery elm bark and elderberry ointment, he said as banteringly as he could: "Could you make love to a man with one leg?"

"If the man were Binds Two."

He tried to imagine life with one leg. Old Smoke's legs were both next to useless, and he still managed to go out on the war road. But there was no need to worry about hopping along the war road. The rebel invasion of the Sandusky had just been the kicking of a frog's legs after its head was crushed in. By the time he was back on his feet—or foot—the war would probably be over, and he'd be back rebuilding his farm at German Flats. A man could farm on a peg leg.

One evening the doctor kindly brought around a bottle of French brandy, which was certainly not very patriotic these days, but tasted good. The good doctor seemed far more eager for Joseph to enjoy it than to sample it himself.

About halfway down the bottle, the doctor turned his back for a moment and Joseph's blurred eyes saw a flash of a saw blade emerging from a satchel. Strangely, he also saw General Herkimer puffing his pipe at Oriskany. Nicholas Herkimer had come out alive from Oriskany Ravine, only to die of a botched amputation of his wounded leg.

Joseph bellowed: "No! Better to die of the disease than the cure!"

The doctor looked hurt, but Trembling Earth said: "If my husband says no, then it's no." The saw went back into the satchel.

When the doctor had gone, Joseph held up his hand for Trembling Earth to come and take hold of it, and said: "The war will be over soon, and the colonies back under British law. Under British law, even if I leave nothing in writing, the farm at German Flats will be yours, and my land at Oquaga—"

"No! Don't even speak of it."

"I must. Do you think I *want* to? I would've let the doctor take my leg if I was certain I'd survive it. But if I die—"

"You *won't!*"

He didn't. By the new year he was up hobbling about on both legs, using Trembling Earth's ample shoulders for a crutch. It was then the news came of the surrender.

Joseph had been fully expecting to hear of the surrender any day, as another starving, shivering winter forced the Town Destroyer to give in to the inevitable. The news that came was of the surrender of General Lord Cornwallis and all of His British Majesty's forces south of New York.

CHAPTER 53

The crows came back to Carleton Island from the south, bearing the raucous first news of spring, and news came. from the east that the negotiators for the king and the Continental Congress had signed a preliminary peace treaty in Paris.

There were no details as yet, but that didn't prevent Molly from floating about with a grin like a drooling idiot. Despite Cornwallis's surrender, the king's armies still controlled New York Town and almost everything north of it. So the best the congress could hope for was some sort of compromise republic south of Philadelphia, which wouldn't affect the League of Peace or the Stanwix Line in the least.

The only thing that kept her from soaring off the ground was that she'd still had no word of Peter Warren. But that was bound to come soon, now that the only warring going on was in a council room in Paris, just as the day was bound to come soon now when she and her children and all the other Hodenosaune could go home.

The last patches of snow melted away and sweeter-voiced birds joined the crows, but still not even Tskleleli came singing any songs about the terms of the preliminary treaty. It seemed odd to Molly that something so important to so many people shouldn't have a few rumors leaking out around its edges. So she went to see the major now in command of Carleton Island.

The major said: "I find it just as annoying as you do, Miss Molly. One would think that those of us who've been fighting this war all these years would be allowed at least a scrap of information on how it's ending."

But he didn't seem to her to be all that annoyed. He seemed nervous. And he smelled of fear. She said: "Oh, by the by, Major, might you arrange passage for me to Montreal as soon as possible? It's high time I reminded those of my children still in school that they have a mother."

"It's still early in the year for traveling," he said. "If you wait until the summer, you'd have a much more pleasant journey. For that matter, come the summer, young George and his sisters will be back between school terms anyway, and you would save yourself the journey."

"You're not a mother, Major, you don't know how these whims of intuition can worry at us."

"Well, if you're set on it, Miss Molly, of course I'll have my adjutant see to it. Ha ha, I'm only being selfish—you know how much easier my life is when you're here to explain things to your people." It seemed to her, though, he had other reasons to try to talk her out of going closer to the sources of news.

In Montreal she broached the subject of the preliminary treaty to Daniel Claus and then to Sir John Johnson. They both claimed to be utterly ignorant of even rumors about its contents, but both seemed as nervous as the major had been. She was quite sure they were both pretending ignorance, but couldn't inveigle her way around the pretense.

So she arranged matters so that she and Ann Johnson Claus would be alone one afternoon for tea. After Ann had poured, Molly sipped her Darjeeling daintily and said: "I always love to visit here and see you and Daniel so happy. Oh, I know every marriage has its rough and smooth, but you do seem happy."

"We are. Or I am. Daniel would be if they stopped appointing people over him who care nothing for the Indian Department except the salary."

"I wish your father could see you now—so I could plague him with 'I told you so.' He was so dead set against you marrying such an older man—and a non-Irishman to boot. I still have the letters Daniel sent me, begging me to put a word in."

"He told me of those."

"I expect he tells you a lot of things. That is the difference between a happy marriage and one that isn't: if you talk to each other, in rough or smooth. I expect you know as much about his work as he does."

Ann giggled. "Maybe more. But don't tell him I said so."

"I expect he's even talked to you of this preliminary treaty signed in Paris."

Ann's mouth and eyes flared open as though the pond ice just gave way beneath her skates. She clammed her mouth shut again and her eyes looked betrayed.

"Ann, I know it might seem ridiculous, given so few years between our ages, but I always thought of you and poor, dead Mary as my daughters as much as any of the ones I carried and bore. There is something evil in the wind about this treaty. What is Daniel afraid to tell me?"

Ann twined her fingers into her skirt and kept her mouth sealed.

"I am not asking you to betray your husband. Whatever he and John are trying to hide must come out eventually. After all that the Hodenosaune have suffered and lost fighting for the English, why are the English lying to us now?"

Ann's eyes were wet, and her vestigial excuse for a chin was trembling, but her lips didn't part. Her distress was so palpable that Molly felt like someone torturing a child. Ann had never been strong, and it seemed unfair to take advantage of all her soft spots learned from years of being family. Anyone with a heart would stop.

Molly thought of all the other daughters and sons of Clan Mothers and tightened the screws: "All right, Ann, I will only ask this one more question of you: If your father were still alive, would he lie about this to me?"

Ann wiped her nose and snuffled: "There are only rumors so far. . . ."

"That's better than nothing."

"They say . . . They say the king has agreed to draw a

boundary line down the middle of the St. Lawrence River and the Great Lakes. Everything north of it will be British North America. Everything south of it will be the American Republic."

" 'South of . . .'? But that's . . . that's the Mohawk Valley. . . . That's the whole Six Nations! What do they say about the Stanwix Line?"

"They say the diplomats had more than enough to sort out without worrying about Indians."

"If there is any truth to this, they had better start worrying about Indians."

Molly hurried back to Carleton Island and opened Tskleleli's cage. The little birds flew quickly: in not very long at all, an urgent message traveled west from the governor in Quebec, inviting Captain Brant to come have words with him at his earliest convenience.

Juba was plucking a chicken behind the new house when she saw Captain Joseph coming up the path he'd gone down a month ago on his way east. He looked sickly. It wasn't because of the limp in his left leg. He'd had that when she saw him last, and it hadn't made him look sickly. If anything, the trace of a limp had given him an extra kind of jauntiness, something like old King Hendrick's grinning tomahawk scar. Alongside him walked an old Mohawk man that Juba thought maybe she recognized from the days at Fort Johnson and Johnson Hall. But she couldn't be sure; they all looked alike.

They stopped in front of her and Captain Joseph said: "I greet thee, Juba. Are the family all inside?"

"I b'lieve Miz Nancy's out to the front of the house. And then, Miz Martha and Mistah George and—"

"Forgive me, Juba, I should've made clear that I didn't mean those of the family at school in Montreal. Would you be good enough to fetch Nancy in and make sure the family are all assembled together? Then we shall come in."

Juba sloshed the chicken back into the plucking tub, slapped the feathers off her hands and went around to the front of the house. Miss Nancy was playing her favorite game: getting Abraham to hold his arm straight out from his shoulder so she could jump up, wrap her arms around it and swing from it like it was a tree limb. Pretty soon Abraham would have to stand on a stump if she was going to have much of a jump at all.

"Miz Nancy, your uncle Joseph's here—"

"Uncle Joseph!"

"Yes, but he says the family's all got to be 'sembled together 'fore he'll come in the house."

Miss Nancy ran for the front door. Juba started after her and then looked back to see Abraham shifting his weight uncertainly from foot to foot. "Well come along, Abraham. After Fort Johnson and all the rest, if you and me and Jemmy ain't family, I don't know who the Jesus is."

"Don't you be taking the Name in vain, Juba," he replied, but he fell in behind her toward the house.

She found Molly in the parlor sorting through a pile of clothes to see what might still be fit to be handed down to younger sisters. "Mizt'ess Molly—Captain Joseph's outside, but he says he and his friend won't come in till all the family's together."

"His friend?"

"A white-haired old man I think maybe I remember from the valley. I think maybe he's one of the ones you calls a Keeper of the Faith, but I ain't certain."

"And they won't come in until . . . ?" Mistress Molly's hand fluttered up to her throat as she said it.

There was a clattering and chattering as Miss Nancy's sisters followed her back down from upstairs. The noise hushed as the girls hit the foot of the stairs and saw their mother. Juba backed into a corner, watching Molly sit down and smooth her skirts—with her eyes on the backs of her hands—like a proud soul about to be whipped. The slanted black eyes came up to find Abraham, and Mistress Molly nodded.

Abraham lumbered to the back door and came back trailing after Captain Joseph and the old man. Captain Joseph looked around the room and said: "At a place called Mud Island, outside Philadelphia, in the campaign of 'seventy-eight, Peter Warren died."

Juba's fist flew up to her mouth and she bit the back of it, keeping her eyes fixed on her mistress. Molly was sitting stiff-backed in her chair with her head up and her jaws trembling and her hands gripping the chair arms so hard that her arms were vibrating. Her son had been dead for five years.

Captain Joseph said: "He died of a fever that killed more soldiers than the rebels did. The doctors could do nothing to help him."

Mistress Molly whispered: "I could have."

The old man who'd come with Captain Joseph held up a string of black wampum and began to sing:

"Hai,
Peter Warren Johnson,
Hai hai,
You were a young man of great promise,
Hai,
Quick-minded and brave,
Hai hai . . ."

Captain Joseph moved to stand behind Molly's chair. She raised one hand off the chair arm, and he took hold of it over her shoulder. The young misses were still sobbing and holding onto each other, but Juba could see the older ones drawing strength from their mother fiercely occupying her throne, with the tears pouring down her face and her voice cracking out strongly: "Hai!"

The old man finished his song, put the string of dark beads in Mistress Molly's hands and said: "Now, be thou condoled."

There was a silence, with Mistress Molly looking down at the beads and everyone else looking down at the floor. Then Miss Magdalen pushed her red Irish hair out of her black Mohawk eyes and said in a quavery voice: "Do you remember the time Peter came home for Christmas from Albany, and Father had bought him a new pony, and he said . . . ?"

Molly sat staring dully at the string of purple-black beads that were all she had left of her beautiful son, listening to her daughters talk out their grief. After a while the stories ran down, as everyone grew exhausted with emotion. Joseph said: "I beg you all to forgive me, but I must talk with my sister alone for a little time."

The girls each came to touch and kiss her before leaving the room. Juba took the Keeper of the Faith into the kitchen to get him something to eat. Joseph closed the parlor door, poured out two glasses of sherry from the decanter on the side table, gave her one and pulled a chair up close to hers.

He said: "I know it's cruel to ask you to think of other matters now . . . but I know you will want to know what the governor had to say, and I can't stay here long. I'm supposed to be traveling with the surveyor general and Deseronto, but I took ill in Montreal and fell behind."

" 'Took ill'?"

He waved it away. "Just a twinge in my heart. Too many years spent running along the war road and sleeping in the rain. But those days are numbered, not mine.

"All that you heard about the preliminary treaty and the boundary line is true. But the governor believes it can still be changed. He urged me that if I have any influence among the great, now is the time to use it. So I'll write to the Duke of Northumberland and Lord Percy and others I met in England. But the governor pointed out that the men negotiating for the king in Paris are men who have spent their lives playing a game of chess on a chessboard that is all the world. They have been known to sacrifice a pawn or a rook for an advantage in position elsewhere."

"It is not they who make the sacrifices."

"They might yet be swayed to listen. The governor is sending them dispatches that were sent to him from commanders of frontier forts who are terrified of what the Indians might do if this treaty is signed."

"They have good reason to be. Pontiac's war would seem like a tea party."

"Well . . . there is another possibility, which is why I was traveling with the surveyor general. The governor may not have the power to change the treaty, but he does have the power to do something else. He held out an offer to buy a new home for the Hodenosaune north of the boundary line."

"And you *took* it? We already *have* homes—in the Valley of the Caniengas and the other five nations! My son *died* for that!"

"I have not accepted the offer. It is only in case the peace terms can't be changed."

"*We* have lost no war! We were destroying the Town Destroyer's armies when the English surrendered!"

"If the worst comes to pass, the king will pay compensation for any lands or property lost in—"

"*Compensation?*" She was hammering on her chair arms with both her fists, splattering sherry in all directions. "How can they *compensate* us for giving away what was not theirs to give?"

Through the blur across her eyes, she saw her war-ravaged brother folding into himself and away from her, like husk-covered Si-isha when all her straining at impossible tasks earned only mockery and insults. Molly took hold of herself, applied her sodden handkerchief to her eyes and nose and said: "Forgive me, Binds Two—you are only being careful to prepare for that which might not come to pass."

"If it *does* come to pass, Someone Lends Her a Flower, what else are we to do? Launch a new war whose only purpose is to kill as many Englishmen as possible before the remnants of the League of Peace are wiped off the earth? Go back to our valley and see what mercy we get from the congress? If the king *has* betrayed us, are we to spend the rest of our lives mourning what we have lost, or building something new for our children?

"And," he actually managed a smile, "there will be more children to build for. Now that I'm not spending all my nights out on the war road, or resting up between campaigns . . . Trembling Earth has declared that our first son will be named Joseph." He added, shaking his head, "As a son of Trembling Earth's, someday he might be Tekarihoga."

"He will already be something more than Tekarihoga."

"What's that?"

"Joseph Brant."

He puttered his lips and looked at the ceiling, but she could see she'd accomplished her intention, which was to wipe away the moment when she'd screamed her rage at him. Now that the moment was gone, she knew that everything he'd said about the choices facing the Hodenosaune was true. But the echoes of his words weren't as loud as the echoes of the whispers in the sail-skinned longhouse: "Canajoharie . . . Ononda-ga . . ."

* * *

When the crows next came back from the south, every human being on Carleton Island was packing to move north. The new border drawn down the middle of the St. Lawrence and the Great Lakes left it unclear whether the island was in British or American territory, so the British were building a new fort on the ruins of the old French one where the Cataraqui River flowed into Lake Ontario. Two new houses were being erected beside the new fort, for Miss Molly and Captain Brant. The rest of the Canienga exiles would settle just west of there along the Bay of Quinte, on the land the king's money had bought from the Mississaugas for his loyal Mohawk allies.

Molly dutifully went about doing what was necessary to pack up her household one more time, and to convince her fellow refugees that the Fire That Never Dies would burn just as brightly on the Bay of Quinte, but something had snuffed out the fire inside her. Perhaps it was Peter Warren. Perhaps it was that the signing of the Treaty of Paris, with no more mention of the True People of Turtle Island than of trees or rabbits, had proven that the Covenant Chain she and Gets Business Done had spent so many years polishing had always been hollow. Perhaps it was George, who'd gone out on his first campaign and his uncle Joseph's last—a futile attempt to draw the diplomats' attention to the fact that the Continental Congress had no control over the Mohawk Valley—and had come back with his left hand a two-fingered claw.

Not that she had any regrets about choosing the king over Congress or neutrality. As choices go, Gets Business Done had been right that the king at least had to appear to live by the letter of his laws. While the king's governor had been buying the Bay of Quinte for the Caniengas, Congress had already been making inroads into Oneida land and making it clear that they didn't give a damn about the Stanwix Line. And the king had granted Miss Molly Brant an annuity equal to her brother's captain's pay. The annuity and the compensation for the property she'd lost made her a wealthy woman again, but all that meant to her was that she'd be able to take care of her children until they could take care of themselves.

She still hadn't finished packing when her brother appeared on her doorstep on his way from Niagara to Quebec. He said: "I passed through Cataraqui. They have the grist mill and the sawmill built, and my house is half finished. I expect yours should be up soon. However," his eyes glinted with a secret, "I don't expect we'll occupy them long."

She had an impossible flare of hope. "You've heard something about going home!"

"No . . . nothing more than the old story of the king promising to make the Americans return all confiscated property. If the king promised today that the sun would rise tomorrow, I would spend a fitful night beside my window.

"But the Senecas, you see, have been begging the Caniengas not to settle so far away from them . . ."

"I know."

"What the Senecas say makes sense—that the farther the Six Nations are scattered, the weaker our *orenda*. The Grand River flows south to the Lake of the Eries not far from the Sunset Gate. I mean to ask the governor to buy us the valley of the Grand River."

"Suffering Judas, Joseph—he's already bought the Bay of Quinte for us!"

"Oh, I don't think it will be impossible to convince him they should buy us the Grand as well. They owe us at least that much."

"What they owe us, Joseph," she said wearily, "and what they'll pay are sadly not the same."

But she sparked to life again when she and her children arrived at Cataraqui to discover that not only was there no house there for them to live in, the chief of engineers had never heard of an order to build one. She saw to it that he heard of it soon enough. The house went up in jig time and Molly settled into it and settled back into her numbness.

The two Brant houses at Cataraqui stood on the base of the hook of land the new fort was built on, looking out over the inner harbor and sheltered from the storms on the lake. The forest behind them had more birch trees than elms, and there wasn't a tulip tree to be seen.

The house beside Molly's stood empty until the last ship of the season from Niagara. The longboat slicing through the red and yellow leaves calicoing Cataraqui harbor bore her brother and his family—except for Isaac, whose decision to winter at Niagara disappointed no one but his father. As the boat neared the wharf, Molly smiled to see that baby Joseph and his mother looked to have come through their ordeal none the worse for wear.

The two houses became a kind of extended longhouse, constantly filled with visitors from next door or from the Bay of Quinte. As Molly got the chance to get better acquainted with the woman Trembling Earth had grown into, she became increasingly convinced that Joseph's wife was not only going to make a good mother to his children, but also to the Turtle Clan. Trembling Earth had a stately calm that Molly could never aspire to. When that tall, majestic figure with the beautiful, placid features entered a room, everyone tended to talk a little softer and listen a little harder. And what perhaps boded the best of all was that the one subject Trembling Earth had a fierce opinion on was that, half white or no, she was Canienga. She didn't seem to mind the notion of her children getting a white education, but other than that, they were to grow up Hodenosaune and proud of it.

Molly was aware that there were other people at Cataraqui besides her and Trembling Earth getting better acquainted over the winter. A township had been laid out for white loyalists who didn't care to take their chances south of the line. Among them was a certain John Ferguson, who seemed to have a particular interest in Magdalen. A Captain Farley from the garrison was at least as interested in Peggy. And Dr. Robert Kerr's new posting was only a few steps away from Elizabeth's new home.

The only jarring element to Molly's snowed-in longhouse was her brother's periodic announcements of each new hurdle cleared in his plan to get the government to buy the Grand River for the Caniengas. As it became clear that Joseph's plan was going to happen, Deseronto announced that he would stay on the Bay of Quinte regardless. Molly strongly suspected that Deseronto's attachment to the Bay of Quinte would've applied to any place where Joseph's shadow didn't fall across him. Some two hundred others who were tired of being scratched around Turtle Island like fleas said they would stay with Deseronto, but all the rest of the Caniengas at Cataraqui would melt away with the snow.

A few days after the Midwinter Moon, Joseph came running across from his house, brandishing wampum strings and trumpeting: "Look at these! They come from Oneidas and Cayugas, asking if they can join us at Grand River! It won't just be a home for us Caniengas, but for all Six Nations!"

"I'm not going."

"What?" He looked like she'd just shot him in the stomach. "Why?"

It was a good question, since she hadn't known she'd made the decision until it came out of her mouth. She said: "This place is close enough to Montreal that I can still visit the girls in school from time to time, and George at his job in the Indian Office. Magdalen and Peggy and Elizabeth would be heartbroken if I took them away from their young men—they might even refuse to go with me. And Deseronto will need an Elder Sister to keep him reminded what it is to be Hodenosaune."

"So do I."

She shook her head and wiped her eyes. "You will have plenty of other Oyanders at Grand River. And with Trembling Earth, you don't need me to take care of you."

"You and I can't have gone through all that we have just to end up apart from each other."

"You won't be on the other side of the world, just the other side of the lake."

He screwed his face up like Muskingum and said. "It's a damned big lake."

Throughout the remainder of the winter, he kept trying to change her mind, and she kept wavering without admitting she was wavering. As the ice melted off the lake, the Keepers of the Dawn packed up once more to follow the sun. The moment inevitably came when Molly found herself standing in front of her brother at the end of the dock as the last boat waited to carry him out to the transport ship.

He said: "You could still change your mind. The captain would grumble if I told him he had to wait another day or two while you packed your household together, but he would do it nonetheless."

She found it difficult to speak, but managed: "I think I have only one move left in me, and you know where I'm saving that up for."

He put his hand up to cup her ear, making a roaring seashell padded with her hair. She took hold of his wrist and turned her head to kiss his cupped palm, not sure whether the salt taste came from his hand or her eyes. He said: "Thy *onikonhra* shall always live in mine, my sister."

"And thine in mine. And where the two twine together . . ."
He said with her: "There grows the Tree of Peace."

END

AUTHOR'S NOTE

*If this book had contained all the documented convolutions and upheavals in the lives of Molly and Joseph Brant and Sir William Johnson, you couldn't pick it up without a forklift. If you're curious about the events that didn't fit into this story—or that my editor decided didn't fit into this story— there are more than a few biographies of Joseph and Sir William, although only one I know of of Molly, and that one is the frustrating kind that lists no sources to tell you what was research and what was guesswork. There are also many books on the Iroquois in general and on their part in the American Revolution.

If you do dip into any of those biographies or histories, you will probably come across details large and small that disagree with this book, and you may get the disappointing feeling that I've played fast and loose with historical facts. Allow me to head that disappointment off at the pass.

The detail that looms the largest is that most books referring to Molly will tell you that after Sir William died, she moved back to Canajoharie. The tradition in Canada, where loyalist stories were hoarded like Patriots' south of the border, is that she moved back into Fort Johnson. But I found more reasons than loyalist oral tradition to believe that was true.

It's undisputed that after Sir William died, Sir John moved into Johnson Hall, and that Guy and Mary Johnson were living at Guy Park, and Daniel and Ann Claus had a house of their own. *Someone* moved into Fort Johnson, and the Johnsons did like to keep things in the family. Although Fort Johnson was willed to John, it's not unheard of even today for a father to will a house to his son, with the understanding that

457

the widow will have the use of it for her lifetime. Records are very scanty for the early years of the rebellion (pardon me, War of Independence), but it is recorded that the Tryon Committee of Sequestration confiscated Fort Johnson in 1777, the same year that Oriskany made the Mohawk Valley too hot for Molly Brant.

Someone out there may yet prove me wrong, but the source that most people use to prove Molly was at Canajoharie is the memoirs of Daniel Claus, who wrote that she moved back among her own people and opened a store where she sold mostly rum. It's amazing the number of sordid little details that only Daniel Claus knew about a number of people. For instance, he is the only source for the story that King Hendrick met his end ignominiously, by being beaten to death and inexpertly scalped by the women and children of the Canadian Iroquois' camp. What women and children would be doing on the war road in the first place is beyond me. It's true that women and children accompanied the Senecas to the siege of Fort Stanwix, but the Senecas had been told it was a holiday expedition to eat the king's beef and watch the king's men trounce the rebels (pardon me, Patriots).

Claus is also the only source for the idea that Molly was disfigured by smallpox not long after she grew to be a woman. I was working myself up to putting Molly through a horrible bout of smallpox when I came across a reference to her "clear complexion" by a guest at Johnson Hall.

Another area where other books might give you the disappointing notion that this one is untrameled fiction has to do with Molly and Joseph's early life. I've followed the handed-down tradition that they were both born on the Ohio, but some say they were born in Canajoharie (Daniel Claus again), and Joseph's most recent biographer has patiently sifted through old parish records to come out with a plausible theory that their mother was a certain missionary-cowed Margaret Brant. It might be true, but since the theory depends upon yet a third marriage in between A Man Tying on His Snowshoes and Mr. Brant, I didn't feel bound by it. As for the coincidence of the name, the hills were filled with Brants in those days. Big William even had a brother named Brant Johnson, but I figured my editor would tear her hair out—or mine—if I tossed that name into a pot overflowing with Brants and Johnsons.

Margaret Brant's recorded submissiveness to missionary tyranny also doesn't jibe with the fact that virtually all the scraps of evidence attached to Molly and Joseph's father refer specifically to his unregenerate fierceness as a warrior. The only one that doesn't is the vague oral tradition about his death: "He got sick and everybody ran away." After a couple of centuries of being passed from mouth to ear and language to language, it could easily have started out as: "He went crazy and everybody ran away."

The whole area of who married whom when has been a playground for everyone who's written about the Brants and William Johnson. Various historians have dated the beginning of Molly's cohabitation with William Johnson as anywhere from 1753 to 1759, when Johnson's first written reference to her appears, when she was pregnant with Peter Warren. Joseph's first marriage was solemnized some years after I have him and his Margaret living together, but the ceremony was a mass marriage of several Mohawk couples—including Big William and his wife—performed by a missionary newly arrived in the valley. No one knows how long Joseph and Trembling Earth had been living together when Joseph called out to John Butler at Niagara not to put his book away.

If you go looking into other accounts than the one you are holding in your hands—and have, I trust, paid retail for—you will undoubtedly find some very different interpretations of the characters. Various historical personages who passed through this narrative—Red Jacket, Nicholas Herkimer, Joseph's first wife, etc.—are portrayed here only as they would have been perceived by our hero(in)es, as far as written evidence, oral tradition, and guesswork can determine.

But some of the people in this book aren't portrayed differently in other books, because I had to make them up. Horace was invented out of the tradition that Molly left the valley after her overseer was killed, but I don't think he would have been out of place in a Johnson Hall known to include the two Bartholomews, blind Mr. Kain the harpist, the obscene parrot, etc. It's possible that Juba was also invented. Sir William's will refers to "*young* Juba, the sister of Jemmy," but he may have been having his little joke.

There are a great many differing opinions in print on the three people at the center of this story. Whether my opinions are correct or not, I did take all the recorded evidence I could get my hands on and try to stay true to it. Of the three, Joseph was the easiest (easi*est*) because he was the subject of much curiosity and study during his life. Several portraits were painted of him, but the two that were done on his two trips to England told me his story—even allowing for the difference in the two artists' styles. The first portrait, done on the eve of the Revolution, shows a sleek-looking, almost arrogant young man. The one done just after the war shows a scoured face that is mostly large, dark eyes that have seen things you don't want to know about.

Most of the incidents I've placed the adult Joseph in are documented, although some only sketchily, but little is known about his childhood and adolescence. Who knows whether or not he saved Sir William's life at Lake George, but the fact remains that Sir William took an interest in Joseph's life far above and beyond the call of brother-in-lawhood.

When it came to writing about Sir William Johnson, an odd thing happened—one of a series of odd things I'll get to later on. For various reasons, I had to start sketching out the first draft of this story before I had all the research materials I'd like (as if there is such a thing). The only information I had on William Johnson was of the Great Man school of history that doesn't indulge in physical details or senses of humor or any naughty bits that might tarnish the subject's example to future Boy Scouts. Despite that, it seemed to me that he wouldn't have been a stoic product of the Age of Reason, but a product of the riotous earlier days of *The Beggar's Opera* and Tom Jones's squire. And for some reason, it also seemed to me that he must've been a large man with large appetites. So I started writing him that way, expecting I'd have to go back and change it all when I found out I was wrong. But the more information I accumulated, the more it became clear that William Johnson—for all his getting done of business—was indeed a big, booming bruiser of a hedonist who was known to banish interfering missionaries with bellows of: "Any man less mild than me would've clapped you in irons!" Makes you wonder sometimes who's in charge here, me or them.

As to the question of just how crooked his dealings with the Indians were (Joseph waxed rather bitter about that in later years), the fact that kept coming back to me was that it was

Johnson's own decision that it wouldn't be proper to stay in the fur business when he became Superintendent of Northern Indian Affairs—no one in the government thought there was anything improper in a man making as much money as he could any way that he could.

You may be niggled by a feeling that I've exaggerated William Johnson's military reputation for the sake of effect. Allow me to assure you that that would be impossible to do. When the Austrian General Daun was kicking England's allies all across Europe, Horace Walpole wrote: "I believe that the future of the world will come to be fought for somewhere between the north of Germany and the back of Canada between Count Daun and Sir William Johnson."

Of the three principals in this story, Molly was by far the least recorded during her lifetime—partly because she was a woman, partly because most of her political activities were conducted in the shadowy world of the longhouse, partly because she seems to've wanted it that way. If you're niggled by a feeling that I've exaggerated *her* effect on larger events, here's a quote from J. T. Flexner's much-awarded biography of Sir William: "[Molly Brant] was undoubtedly the most powerful member of her sex during the Revolutionary period . . . She far overtops the currently accepted heroine Abigail Adams, who has become a cult figure because she occasionally and ineffectually expostulated to her important husband about women's rights." I have nothing against Abigail Adams, but the difference is that Sir William Johnson occasionally expostulated to his important *wife*.

The two magnetic poles I tried to keep hold of to try to be true to the real Molly Brant—much like the two portraits of Joseph—were two of the few firsthand accounts of her. One was John Butler's story of Colonel "Stacey's" head (there is no evidence whether Colonel Staccia was or wasn't one of the ransackers of her house, but *something* made her demand his head three times). The other comes from an English diarist who visited Johnson Hall: "[Molly Brant's] features are fine and beautiful; her complexion clear and olive-tinted . . . She was quiet in demeanour, on occasion, and possessed of a calm dignity that bespoke a native pride and consciousness of power. She seldom imposed herself into the picture, but no one was in her presence without being aware of her." I did try to keep in mind that both accounts were of the same woman.

Fortunately, a few witnesses did recount some of her doings around the council fire—such as the time she reduced Old Smoke to tears in convincing him to take the war road—so at least there is enough evidence to get a general flavor. But much of Molly's activities can only be inferred. The very fuzzy eyewitness account of General Herkimer's abortive peace conference at Unadilla says that the Iroquois delegation consisted of Joseph, Cornplanter, Big William, and "an Indian woman." I don't know which other "Indian woman" it could've been.

If any portraits of Molly were ever done, they've disappeared. So I based her physical description on photographs of another self-willed, mischievous Mohawk girl who mesmerized a much older white man—Grey Owl's Anahareo.

I suppose there is actually a fourth major character in this story—the League of Peace—and as much of it had to be pieced together by semieducated guesswork as any of the other characters. When I said the inner workings of the Six Nations in Molly's day were shadowy, I meant not only to eighteenth-century white men, but also to today's Six Nations. Part of the reason is a change in the spiritual practices that were woven into all aspects of Hodenosaune life.

At the beginning of the nineteenth century, Cornplanter's half brother, Handsome Lake, had a series of revelations that resulted in what's known as the Longhouse Religion. By the mid-nineteenth century, no Iroquois could be found who wasn't either a Christian or a follower of Handsome Lake. The Code of Handsome Lake was intended partly to enshrine the old ways, partly to alter them. It's hard to say exactly which of the old ways were enshrined, which altered, and which eliminated. It remains a matter of debate among today's Iroquois whether there were fifty Royaners or several fewer.

As for the Oyanders, it's not even known whether or not they had ceremonial names to be passed on from one generation to the next. My guess that they did was based on the fact that Molly was apparently known as both Someone Lends Her a Flower and One Against Two (or One Against Several, depending on the translator). But even that "fact" is dubious, since the only source for all the assertions that she was named

Degonwadonti is a passing mention in an eighteenth-century letter that's *assumed* to refer to Molly Brant.

Many of the places this story took place in have been preserved. The Daughters of the American Revolution bought Oriskany Ravine as a historic battlefield. What struck me most about the place was that fifteen hundred men could have fought on such a narrow piece of ground. They must have had to stand on corpses to get at each other. If you do go, I hope you can ignore the plaques declaring Oriskany the first great American victory because Herkimer's militia were left in possession of the battlefield. I suppose the plaques are no more obscene than English and Canadian historians' deliberations on whether Oriskany was a stalemate or a British victory. What it was was a slaughterhouse.

Fort Johnson and Johnson Hall still stand, restored and maintained by painstaking professionals and humblingly dedicated volunteers. If you go to Fort Johnson, the guides may tell you, as they told me, that the kitchen was in a separate building. Perhaps that's true, but a pamphlet among the others available there makes a very convincing case for the kitchen having been in the cellar, as I have it and as it is at Johnson Hall. If you go to Johnson Hall, I'm afraid you won't see the bordello wallpaper I mentioned. But one of the restorers told me of finding a mouse nest lined with the most garish, red-flocked wallpaper he'd ever seen. Perhaps it came from a later occupant, but given Sir William's taste in retainers and menagerie ... Actually, drawing a line between his household staff and menagerie would've been difficult.

I had a great deal of help in the writing of this book. Donald B. Smith of the University of Calgary generously sent me material he had on hand and pointed me to several wellsprings of information. Barbara Graymont, in well-deserved retirement from decades of teaching and writing about the Iroquois, kindly responded to a couple of questions whose answers aren't published anywhere. W. G. Spittal of Iroqrafts was not only a source for many useful Iroquois Reprints, but also answered a couple of extracurricular queries. Wanda Burch and the restorers at Johnson Hall saved me a lot of travel inconvenience by showing me around on a day when the place wasn't officially open to the public, and provided pleasant inside tips along the way. (Hey, they were on their lunch break, no slacking off involved.) Both Wanda Burch and Mae Andreae of Fort Johnson kindly replied to mailed queries about details I hadn't known I needed to know when I was there.

But it seems at times I also had another kind of help—the "odd things" I referred to above. In the interests of my still being allowed to walk about the streets with minimal supervision, let's just call it coincidence.

When King Hendrick first appeared in this story, I hadn't yet got my hands on a physical description of the historic original, but for some reason, I decided he should have a large scar on his face. It was only much later that I came across the descriptions and portraits of Hendrick with his grinning tomahawk scar. I gave William of Canajoharie green eyes long before I learned that his father's eyes went green in certain lights. I started referring to William Johnson as Big Billy long before I knew that Blind John Kain the harpist was eventually replaced at Johnson Hall (Mr. Kain wandered off to Philadelphia and committed a murder) by a fiddler known as Little Billy. "Little Billy" suggests there was a "Big Billy" to distinguish him from.

I'd always had trouble understanding how a battle as fierce as Oriskany could've been interrupted by a mere rainstorm. On the one day in my crowded research trip when I could get to Oriskany, the sky opened up with such a torrent that even semi trailers just pulled over to the side of the interstate to wait it out.

There was another odd thing that had to do with that fourth principal character I mentioned. When I was first trying to piece this book together, pushing the story line ahead while frantically tearing through catalogues for research material I knew would take months to track down, it suddenly struck me that I had a book with "Iroquois" on the cover tucked away in a box somewhere. Some years earlier, my wife, the everpatient (ha!) Jane Buss, had brought me home some old books she'd come across while mucking out the basement of a theater she was running (the job description was Producer/Janitor). The one with "Iroquois" on the cover turned out to be Horatio Hale's *The Iroquois Book of Rites*, written in the nineteenth century in collaboration with his friend Chief George Johnson. Hale can be disputed on minor details, but when it comes to trying to grasp some understanding of pre-Christian, pre–

Handsome Lake Hodenosaune, Hale's book is the mother lode. How that book ever found its way into the basement of that theater, and why I didn't just ship it off to the used book store along with all the others that had nothing to do with the subject I was working on at the time, I'll never know.

And then there was the matter of the twins, the Creator and Destroyer. It seemed to me that the image of Good and Evil figures struggling over the world was just a bit too handy for Christian missionaries. It seemed to me, for no justifiable reason, that the precontact story of the Twins must have been much more fluid, much more a matter of forces of nature than of good and evil. So I wrote it that way, and used it as a key to the way people in Canajoharie Castle saw things differently from the people in Schenectady. But as I collected more and more versions of the legend, all of them referring to the Good Twin and the Evil Twin, I had to give in to the evidence that I'd just been projecting my own predilections onto the Iroquois. I was just about to start the second draft and change it all back again, when up popped this obscure old reminiscence: "The Indians did not call these [the Twins] the right and the wrong. They called them . . . the right and the left."

Other odd things happened, but I'd best not strain your patience and my already strained reputation for levelheadedness. And there are a few more things to say about the people this book was about.

Molly lived out the last years of her life in the home of her daughter Magdalen, who had married John Ferguson, in the town of Kingston, as Cataraqui had been rechristened. All of Molly's daughters married influential white men—doctors, military officers, legislators—except Mary, whose name I changed to Martha when my copy editor grew flustered at trying to tell the difference between Molly's daughter Mary Johnson and Catty Weisenberg's daughter Mary Johnson. Molly's Mary never married, so I likely don't have to worry about her descendants coming after me for messing with her name. George settled down with a Cayuga girl on the Grand River and became generally known as Big George, despite his crippled hand. Anecdotes of "old Molly Brant" suggest she remained lively despite debilitating bouts of what seems to have been arthritis. She died at the age of sixty or sixty-one, but it had been some sixty years.

The year before Molly died, Joseph suffered the greatest crisis of his crisis-filled life. His beloved son Isaac went for him with a knife in a tavern. Joseph defended himself by slashing Isaac across the forehead—the same blow he'd used to put Simon Girty temporarily out of commission. Unlike Simon Girty, Isaac refused treatment and kept tearing off his bandage. Isaac died.

No one blamed Joseph except Joseph. The general consensus was that it had been an accident and that the only reason Isaac had lived as long as he had was that everyone was too afraid of his father to kill the nasty little son of a bitch. But Joseph declared that a man who had murdered his own son soiled everything he touched. He resigned his military commissions, removed himself from the council and locked himself in his house, where he sat staring at the dirk that had slashed Isaac.

The Oyanders and Royaners went into a panic at losing Joseph's voice—although there were always jealousies, no one could deny that the Hodenosaune who'd stayed south of the border were seeing their lands whittled down to nothing, while Joseph Brant had been doing a remarkable job of making the British authorities keep their promises. A campaign ensued to bring Joseph back to life: the commander-in-chief refused to accept the resignation of so estimable an officer as Captain Brant; the council sat in solemn judgment of Isaac's death and declared that Joseph must pay a blood-price of supporting Isaac's wife and children (which he'd already been doing since the day Isaac married); letters of support poured in to Joseph from Sir John Johnson, Deseronto, the Reverend Doctor John Stuart (now the minister at Kingston). . . . The campaign worked. Perhaps the campaign happened spontaneously, but it seems unlikely to me that Molly wouldn't have had some hand in pulling her little brother out of the fire one last time.

In his later years, Joseph moved away from Grand River and built an estate on land granted him by the Crown as a loyalist officer. When I was reading accounts of "Old Chief Brant," I felt an odd sense of déjà vu: a large man with a limp, a bumptious sense of humor and a taste for good whiskey, living on a manor-house estate carved out of the wilderness, serving as the middleman who spoke for the Six Nations to the

British authorities and vice versa. . . . He had become Gets Business Done.

Joseph died eleven years after Molly. His last words are reputed to have been: "Have pity on the poor Indians; if you can get any influence with the great, endeavor to do them all the good you can." Although he was buried on his lakefront estate, the bells of the Mohawk church at Brant's Ford on the Grand River rang for twenty-four hours.

The intertanglement of Molly and Joseph's lives didn't end with their deaths. Molly's eldest grandson, William Johnson Kerr, married Joseph's youngest daughter, Elizabeth, and by all accounts they lived as happily together as any two people can. No one thought twice about their blood relationship; they were of different clans.

A few years after Joseph's death, his name came to be reviled throughout the English-speaking world. A Scottish poet named Thomas Campbell penned an astoundingly popular epic titled "Gertrude of Wyoming," describing how "the monster Brant" slaughtered the innocents of the Wyoming Valley. Joseph's son, John—who did become Tekarihoga—traveled to Britain on other business and made a point of confronting the poet with the fact that "the monster Brant" was nowhere near Wyoming when the Rangers and Senecas descended. Campbell politely declined to take John's word for it, until John produced a letter that Joseph had written from Oquaga to Niagara to tell the Niagara storekeepers that his wife and sister were to have unlimited credit on his account. The letter bore the same date as the Wyoming "massacre," and Oquaga was and still is a hell of a long way from the Wyoming Valley.

Thomas Campbell agreed to preface all future editions of his epic with an explanation that Joseph Brant bore no part in the events portrayed, but Campbell refused to change the name within the poem—he'd invested too much of his genius in coming up with clever rhymes for "Brant." But Campbell's retraction started to bring a lot of other old stories out of the woodwork. Today, in the volunteer-maintained museum at Cherry Valley—where memories could be expected to be the bitterest—the diorama of that terrible day in 1778 asserts that Joseph Brant was forced to be there by forged orders and tried to save as many lives as possible.

Molly and Joseph continue to be figures of some controversy two centuries after their deaths. There will probably never be an end to the debate on whether they weren't more interested in their own welfare than that of the longhouse. (How can there be an end to a debate on whether two particular human beings were perfectly selfish or perfectly selfless?) Nonetheless, in 1850 Joseph's coffin was unearthed and carried by relays of Hodenosaune all the way from Burlington Bay to Grand River to be reinterred beside the Mohawk church, and a heroic monument and statue of him now stands in the city of Brantford.

As for Molly, the headstone she was buried under in Kingston was so unspectacular that many people—including yours truly—have been known to make the erroneous assumption that she was buried in an unmarked grave. Given that she was a major donor to that church, and that Magdalen and John Ferguson—a man of considerable political influence—would certainly have been at the funeral to see that things were done right, I can only assume that the reason Molly's grave was so matter-of-fact was because that's how she wanted it. I hope she doesn't mind me erecting this rather rough-edged, paper monument. In fact, sometimes I get the eerie feeling she gave me a hand.

ALFRED SILVER

Published by Ballantine Books.
Available at bookstores everywhere.